The characters and events portrayed in this book are fictitious. Any similarity to real persons, living or dead, is coincidental and not intended by the author.

ISBN: 9780645467505

Cover design and illustrations by: Lexie McMillan

For Duckie

THE FUGITIVE

Phoenix Page raced down the ancient steps, bare feet pounding against concrete as he hurtled past old vending machines and derelict apartment buildings, icy wind biting his face and whipping through his tangle of red hair. He hadn't even spent an hour in the Middle Ring of Veracity, yet already Phoenix had concluded that everything in the miserable dump of metropolis was as bleak and grey as the threadbare prison uniform he was wearing. Had he stopped to check though, Phoenix would have realised that his grey prison clothes were not as grey as he would have liked, a deep, damp crimson spreading across the fabric at alarming speed.

Early morning sun crept over the mighty wall that encircled the mountain's peak behind him as he chased his long, distorted shadow further and further down the concrete slope, praying to gods he didn't believe in that the adrenalin would keep him moving until he found a place to hide. At least the energy surge he had created moments earlier had fried the power network of the entire city and frazzled communication with all the surveillance drones that roamed the dreary streets.

If only the effort of such an impressive feat hadn't damn-near killed him.

He skidded around a corner at the base of the stairs, tripped over a pile of empty bottles and cans, stumbled onwards through a maze of dank alleyways, then staggered to a stop before a towering residential building, at least thirty floors high, the bricks stained with decades of grime.

Phoenix leant against a dead tree at the front of the building, his hand pressed against the wound under his shirt. His forearm was also bleeding, but that was of less concern so he ignored it. Dizzy with fatigue, he watched people shuffle about their day, draping wet washing from windows, complaining to neighbours about the power outage, or trudging off to work dangerous, poorly paid jobs.

No one spared him a second glance. Clearly, assisting a bleeding, shaggy-haired nineteen-year-old dressed in grey rags was not worth the risk.

Phoenix couldn't blame them. You didn't survive in Veracity by sticking your neck out for other people.

Which is why he was surprised to see a girl of roughly seventeen striding towards him, hands buried in the pockets of her faded denim jacket, the buckles of her boots glinting in the sun. She stopped a safe distance away and folded her arms.

"You're having a bad day," she said by way of greeting.

Phoenix glanced at the blood seeping through his shirt then smiled back at her. "Nice of you to notice."

The girl pushed her short hair to the side. It was warm brunette, a shade lighter than her skin, and it fell with a refined elegance that Phoenix's curly tangle of red could never hope to compete with.

She eyed the crimson bloodstain like a seasoned sailor eyeing the sea. "Stabbed?"

"Shot," Phoenix replied. "Barely."

"Barely?"

"The bullet grazed my side." Phoenix offered another smile. "I've lived through worse. I don't suppose you have a first aid kit though? Or even just somewhere I could nap?" He grimaced as a wave of nausea swept over him. "I'm not picky. I'll sleep anywhere. I once slept through an entire armed robbery in a tavern full of drunk ogres and mountain trolls. Mountain trolls are loud, by the way. They win arguments based on volume alone."

The stranger considered him in silence for a moment then slipped a hand into the back pocket of her jeans. "I'll call the hospital."

"No!" Phoenix lunged for the slim, handheld device and it clattered across the pavement as he swayed on his feet. Stepping away from the tree had been a mistake.

The girl swung a knife at him so quickly he didn't even see where she'd drawn it from.

"Sorry." He backed up until he was pressed against the dead tree trunk.

"Touch me again and I'll make your day so much worse." The girl didn't lower her blade.

"Understood."

They sized each other up a while longer before the girl seemed to decide that a haemorrhaging idiot wasn't much of a threat. She tucked her knife into the sheath at her side then glanced at her discarded phone.

Phoenix swallowed. "If you call that hospital, you might as well sentence me to death."

"I'm trying to help you."

Phoenix shook his head. "They'll find me. I can't go back. Please." He sank down the tree, his weary legs folding beneath him. "I can't..."

"You're losing blood," the girl said.

Phoenix closed his eyes. "Blood? Who needs it? I'm fine. I'll just... sit here for a bit..."

The girl clicked her tongue. "I've watched too many people die." She retrieved the little communication device and frowned at the screen. "The network is down."

"Still?" Phoenix said with a nervous laugh. "I caused quite a fuss, didn't I?"

The girl narrowed her eyes. "Who shot you?"

"Nobody friendly."

"Was it Flamegate?"

Phoenix shifted uncomfortably under her gaze.

"I thought so," the girl said. "Your rebel tattoo needs adjusting, by the way." She pointed at the five black dots inked over Phoenix's collarbone, arranged like the five on six-sided dice. "Flamegate owns everything and everyone on Earth. You really think anybody stands a chance against that?"

"Yes, actually," Phoenix mumbled, pulling his shirt higher to hide the mark. "But this tattoo isn't what you think." Distant sirens pierced through the background buzz of city life—a pack of hungry wolves closing in on wounded prey. Phoenix pushed himself to his feet. "Sorry to bother you. I'll go."

"You need somewhere to hide, right?"

Phoenix paused. "Well... if you're offering," he said, one hand fighting to keep blood inside his body, the other supporting his weight against the tree. "I'd hate to seem desperate."

The girl chewed her lip for a second then nodded at the building behind her. "Follow me." She walked off without waiting.

Phoenix clutched his side, trying not to collapse as he followed her into the dark foyer.

"The elevators aren't working," the girl said, passing the sealed metal doors and heading for the stairs.

Although grateful he didn't have to endure the confined space of an elevator, Phoenix slowed at the foot of the stairwell. "You're not at the very top, are you?"

"Fifteenth," the girl replied, already a flight ahead.

Phoenix nodded. "I can make that."

He couldn't.

He reached the third floor and slumped against the wall.

The girl cast him a wary look. "You don't have the plague, do you?"

Phoenix laughed, then stopped because it was excruciating. "If I had the plague, I wouldn't be able to talk. Or move, for that matter. Which would be... inconvenient... since I intend to save the world from its fast-approaching collapse." He hesitated. "Tricky business though, world saving. Especially when the worlds have a habit... of changing on you." He tipped his head back against the wall, his eyes squeezed shut. "Realistically speaking, the whole universe is a lost cause. But where's the fun in being realistic?"

"You sure use a lot of words to answer simple questions," the girl said, hitching his good arm over her shoulder. "Come on."

"If I don't make it," Phoenix began, but the girl didn't let him finish.

"You'll make it."

They took the next few flights in silence, Phoenix concentrating on his breathing, trying to ignore the strange glances the girl kept giving him as they climbed step by careful step towards the fifteenth floor.

"Your eyes..." the girl said, squinting at Phoenix's face.

Phoenix cringed. "I'm aware the gold flecks make people uncomfortable."

"I didn't notice outside," the girl said. "They're..."

"Glowing," Phoenix finished. "I know."

"They're pretty creepy."

"A more mawkish individual might describe them as ancient galaxies glimmering in the far reaches of space."

"I'm rarely mawkish."

"I'm starting to sense that."

"I wouldn't call them galaxies," the girl added, as they neared her floor. "More like sad fireflies at the end of a long night."

Phoenix gave a weak laugh. "You caught me at a bad time."

"I'd noticed."

They stepped out into a narrow corridor lined with old-fashioned wall-lamps and fake timber flooring. The lamps flickered into life as they approached.

"Power's back," the girl noted, before stopping at an ugly metal door. She tapped a card over a sensor and the door swung open with a click. Phoenix staggered inside then stretched out on the carpet beside an old couch. The girl edged to the window behind him and peeked through the blinds.

"Flamegate's on the move," she remarked, as Phoenix studied the curious black scorch marks that stained the stranger's otherwise beige ceiling. "They've got trucks and tanks and everything patrolling the streets. All the billboards are flashing red."

Phoenix responded with a drowsy nod. "I'd expect nothing less. They'll want to make a big show of it. Sirens, soldiers, those swanky podcars with flashing lights... I should be flattered." He rolled onto his side. "I like your place. Nice carpet. If I die, at least I die on nice carpet... I always thought I'd go on cement. Did a fire burn through here? What happened to the ceiling?"

"Do you always talk this much?"

"Only when I'm awake." Phoenix closed his eyes. "Phoenix, by the way. Phoenix Page."

"Belinda Loft," his rescuer muttered. "My friends call me Bee."

Phoenix smiled. "Thank you, Bee."

"They're imposing a city-wide lockdown."

"Are you suggesting," Phoenix said, "that my cowering

behind the safety of your couch is in some way connected to the biggest manhunt this city has ever seen?"

"Am I wrong?" Belinda asked.

Phoenix kept his eyes shut. "The twisted maniacs at the research facility just lost a beloved pet."

He heard the frown in Belinda's voice. "Research facility?"

"Inside Flamegate Tower," Phoenix said, pointing half-heartedly towards the window, beyond which stood the colossal mountain that the expansive city of Veracity was built upon. "Big stone building at the top of the summit. Electrified wire along all the walls. Guards with guns at every corner... I escaped this morning, and now here I am, bleeding all over your floor."

Belinda crouched beside him with a bundle of bandages and a bottle of spirits. "You were a prisoner inside Flamegate Tower itself?"

"Yeah." Phoenix winced as she pulled back the sodden fabric of his shirt. "Since I was five."

Belinda raised her eyebrows, no doubt surprised by the array of older scars crisscrossing Phoenix's body.

"You weren't kidding," she said. "You really have lived through worse."

"I can't go back," Phoenix mumbled, a dense fog enveloping his brain. "Please..." His hand slipped from his side and fell to the floor.

"Don't worry," Belinda said, unscrewing the spirits bottle. "An enemy of Flamegate is a friend of mine."

"If I die here, I'll die in both worlds."

Belinda paused. "*Both* worlds?"

"Earth is your world," Phoenix said. "But Yonder... Yonder is mine." He gasped as she poured the clear, potent-smelling liquid over his side. "I've got family, you know," he said through clenched teeth. "Back there... in my world. The world where I started... It's better than this place."

Bee chuckled. "Most places are."

"There's never enough time," Phoenix murmured, before the darkness closed in and he left Earth behind.

~

Phoenix woke on his back to the comforting sound of violin music, stretched out under a lonely tree in a lush, gloriously green field. Sun glinted through the leaves above him, warming his face as a soft breeze whispered conspiracy theories through the tall grass.

He blinked in the sudden glare then grinned at a surly, heavily tattooed young man sitting against the tree, staring at nothing as he played a gentle tune upon a battered old fiddle. He was older than Phoenix, already twenty-five, but his dark eyes and intense demeanour made him seem even older than his years. Enhancing his menacing appearance was his long black hair and bulky frame, which gave the unnerving impression of a pirate mixed with a bear.

"The ever-vigilant Simon Wolfe," Phoenix said as he sat up. "Good afternoon. Is it afternoon? It feels like it is."

The man frowned at him, cutting the melody short.

"Light help us," Phoenix said. "How long have I been gone? You're starting to get a beard."

Simon rubbed his bristly chin, his eyes creased in concern. "You've been out for three days."

"It felt longer," Phoenix said, bundling his hideous, multihued overcoat tighter around his shoulders. It was patched in so many places it was hard to tell which was original fabric and which had been stitched over the top.

"What happened?" Simon asked.

Phoenix shrugged and took Simon's fiddle. "I've been busy," he said, plucking absently at the strings. "Escaping prison... stopping Flamegate from permanently destroying the balance of the worlds..."

Simon's jaw dropped. "You escaped?"

"Well, more delayed than stopped, really," Phoenix said,

strangling the poor instrument in his attempt to pluck a tune. "They've lost *me*, at least. And I stole their only void-stone. That should annoy—"

"Phoenix," Simon interrupted. "You *escaped*?"

Phoenix lowered the fiddle. "Yeah. Why do you sound so surprised?"

"You're free?"

"As a bird."

"But?"

"*But*," Phoenix said, handing Simon his instrument again, "they shot me. And I think I'm dying."

Simon closed his eyes.

"Relax." Phoenix leant against the tree, taking a moment to appreciate that this body, at least, wasn't leaking copious amounts of blood. "If I drop dead without warning, convey my condolences to the grieving masses, and apologise on my behalf to all the people I've been meaning to apologise to." He folded his arms, watching the wind ripple over the surrounding hills of long grass. "And while we're on this morbid topic... thanks for saving my skin more times than I care to count. Life wouldn't have been the same without you." Phoenix smiled and elbowed his friend in the ribs. "I suspect it would've been significantly shorter, and not nearly as appealing."

Simon rolled his eyes. "Can I keep your trumpet then?"

Phoenix laughed. "Fine. Rob me of my belongings. They're no use to a corpse."

"Great," Simon said. "Thanks."

Phoenix gazed at the sky, silent as a breeze rustled the leaves and tugged his ginger hair. For a moment, he was completely distracted by the flight of clouds overhead.

"Red," Simon said. "You'll be okay."

"Yeah..." Phoenix tapped his fingers with all the composure of an over-caffeinated squirrel.

"You survive that Light Festival every year," Simon added. "A little puncture wound isn't going to slow you down."

Phoenix grimaced. "Hmm..."

"Well, I know you didn't *completely* survive last year..." Simon continued, with the air of someone trying to take back hurtful remarks, "but temporarily dead is definitely better than permanently dead, and if you can bounce back from something like that, I'm sure you can pull through whatever is happening to you now."

"I'm sure you're right," Phoenix said, then sprang abruptly to his feet. "At least I'm not bleeding profusely on anyone's carpet here."

"Are you with someone you can trust?" Simon asked, standing as well. He was even more intimidating at full height, easily dwarfing Phoenix, whose head didn't come close to the shoulder of his enormous friend.

Phoenix thought of Bee, standing over him with her steady, calculating eyes and her knife.

"I hope so," he said, dusting dirt from his ugly coat. Simon often complained that the tatty, rainbow garment made Phoenix look like a child playing make-believe, as it hung past the ground and had sleeves far too long since it had been tailored for a much taller man.

Phoenix was content, however, to ignore the fashion advice of a hairy, magically impaired warlock whose attire mimicked that of a gothic motorbike gang, complete with buckles, intricate chains, and two full sleeves of elaborate tattoos that extended all the way to the knuckles on his hands.

"What about that stolen void-stone?" the warlock asked, returning his fiddle to its case.

"Destroyed it," Phoenix replied. "As promised."

Simon's thick eyebrows knitted together, the doubt evident upon his often-unreadable face.

Phoenix heaved a sigh. "Relax. I'm spontaneous, not suicidal. Flamegate won't use that stone, and neither will I."

Simon shook his head, unconvinced, as a gust of wind swept over the hills, bringing with it the faint smells of a faraway farm.

"New plan." Phoenix clapped his hands together. "Make your own way to Karvil."

"Why?" Simon asked, tightening the clasps of his jacket. "I thought you wanted to speak with the inventors. We're only a day's ride from the city."

Usually the thought of visiting the quirky band of inventors living in the capital of Yonder would bring Phoenix great joy, but today, he had more pressing concerns.

"You go," he said, while Simon began collecting their luggage from under the tree. "I think I'll go home."

Simon dropped the satchel he had meant to swing over his shoulder. "What?" He narrowed his dark eyes. "To Bloodwood?"

"It's been ten years," Phoenix said, waving vaguely at the distant hills towards the infamous town where he'd been born. "I should let my so-called family know I'm alive. I wonder if Nan still bakes that bread I like."

He strolled away from the tree, uncomfortable that it was the *only* tree amongst the eerily forsaken slopes. Although the grasslands seemed harmless during the day, savage monsters emerged from beneath the ground at night. Monsters, he was sure, that he had conveniently slept through while Simon was left to guard Phoenix's unconscious body.

"You won't make it," Simon said.

"Huh?" Phoenix looked back, preoccupied with thoughts of claws, spines and teeth.

"Alone," Simon said. "You'll need help."

"My old life..." Phoenix paused, preferring not to be bogged down in resentment or guilt. "Bloodwood has a dark past. Warlocks with zero respect for privacy don't need to see it." He put two fingers to his mouth and released a loud whistle. In answer to his call, a dark, shaggy mountain-horse came cantering over the nearest hill, skipping to a stop perilously close to Phoenix's feet before exhaling a belligerent snort.

Phoenix scratched the gloomy-eyed animal behind the ear. "Hello Gulliver."

"You're serious?" Simon said, passing Phoenix his single, raggedy rucksack in which he stored all his worldly things. "If you die, nice knowing you? If not, see you later in Karvil?"

Phoenix swung the tattered bag over his shoulder and gave a dry laugh. "Essentially, yes. I'll meet you at the Inventors' Guild." He climbed lithely onto the horse's back, no reins and saddle-free, then tensed and rubbed his side. The pain from Earth was troubling him here too – an ominous sign. "I won't stay in Bloodwood long." He turned Gulliver toward the horizon, the swaying grass continuing as far as the eye could see.

"How long should I wait before collecting your trumpet?" Simon asked. "Is an hour a respectable-enough mourning period?"

"Funny," Phoenix said. Then he toppled from the horse. Gulliver bolted forward before cautiously circling back to check his rider.

The burly young warlock crouched beside Phoenix, listening for his breath.

"Alive," he muttered. "Barely." He looked up at the horse. "He might be dying."

Gulliver flattened his white-tipped ears. "Well…" he said, projecting his dull, monotonous voice directly into Simon's head, "I'm not exactly surprised."

COMPLICATED

Phoenix opened his eyes to discover himself shirtless upon a tiled floor, a pale, fashionably dressed young man leaning over him wearing glasses and a bloodied pair of rubber gloves. Tall cupboard doors stretched upwards around him while a rusty fridge purred like an asthmatic tiger beside his head.

"Hold still," the stranger said. "Just stitching you up."

"What?" Phoenix tried to pull away but pain shot through his body and he groaned.

The man tutted. "Hold *still*."

"Who are you? Where am I? Where's Bee? Did she call the

hospital? If I'm in hospital, someone's going to get hurt. I have things to do. Hell! Stop *prodding* me!"

The gloved man sighed and withdrew his hands. "Damn, Bee. He does like to talk."

"I'm not a huge fan of silence," Phoenix said, lifting his head a little and trying to look around. Bee's kitchen was cramped but tidy, filled with antique cooking appliances and the smell of tea and toast. "Bee's here? What's going on?"

Bee smiled pleasantly from a chair in the corner, gripping a cup of steaming tea. "Phoenix, meet Jayden, the man saving your life. Jayden, meet Phoenix, the bleeding, barefoot stranger who nearly died behind my couch." She spoke warmly, but her gaze remained guarded behind wisps of dark hair. "Believe me when I say we despise Flamegate more than anybody, and I need you to trust us. Tell us what you know."

Phoenix glanced at the man beside him, noting the crisp button-down shirt and the vexingly symmetrical face, then turned back to Bee. "Where's this guy from?"

"This guy," Bee said, "is my boyfriend. He's also a vet. In training."

Phoenix blinked. "A *vet*?"

Bee offered a guiltless smile. "In training."

Jayden grinned. "I work with rodents, mostly."

Phoenix reassessed the flawless smile and blond, perfectly shaped waves of hair. He couldn't help but feel suspicious of anyone who spent more than three seconds on hair maintenance.

"Well," he said, "I appreciate the help."

"As you should," Jayden said, preparing a piece of gauze to stick onto Phoenix's side. "The whole city's in lockdown. What the hell did you do?"

"I upset some very powerful people," Phoenix replied as he sat up.

Bee leant forward in her chair. "Why does Flamegate want you so much?"

"I'm a link between worlds," Phoenix said. "A portal to the void itself."

Bee pulled a face. "What drugs did you give him?"

"Nothing," Jayden replied, pressing the bandage a little too forcefully against Phoenix's aching ribcage. "He's as delusional as you think."

"Flamegate wants access to Yonder," Phoenix said. "Though it's less about land and more about wanting Yonder's seemingly endless energy supply. Twenty-third Century Earth isn't exactly bursting with void vitality, you know what I mean?"

Jayden frowned. "We have zero idea what you mean."

"Let's say we believe you." Bee set her teacup upon the tiles at her feet. "Flamegate isn't happy stealing everything from this world? They're trying to steal from others too?"

Phoenix thrust his finger at her. "Exactly! Cross-dimensional supremacy. And unlimited access to the greatest power source ever discovered. It's why they established the Night Order in the first place."

Bee stiffened. Outside, a chorus of sirens wailed as a fleet of military podcars roared through the steep, narrow streets.

"The Night Order?" she asked faintly.

"Yeah," Phoenix said, scratching at a bandage around his arm. "They're the elite of Flamegate's inner circle. I don't suppose you can spare some food? I haven't eaten in days."

Bee rose from her chair, rummaged through a cupboard, then wordlessly passed Phoenix a bag of dried fruit. She didn't return to her seat. Instead, she leant against the fridge, arms crossed tightly over her chest.

"Magicians," Phoenix said through a mouthful of apricot. "In Yonder. That's how it started. They stumbled upon a way to access the void."

"*Magicians.*" Jayden shook his head.

"What exactly *is* the void?" Bee asked.

Phoenix stopped chewing as he tried to process how ignorant they were. "The empty space between worlds," he said. "Inconceivable source of energy... capable of altering Time... home of the Shadows? They don't teach you this stuff at school?"

Bee gazed at him in silence while Jayden sent her a look of exasperated bewilderment.

"This is worse than I thought." Phoenix waved a slice of dry apple at Jayden's face. "You don't think Flamegate stepped in to take care of your plague-ridden, war-ravaged planet because they actually *cared*, do you?"

Jayden didn't reply.

"The void divides our worlds," Phoenix explained, "but it also connects us. If Flamegate doesn't stop upsetting that balance, the void will split open and Shadows will descend upon Earth. Our worlds will collide. The universe will swallow itself. It's happening already. This infatuation with power needs to end. Flamegate has to be stopped. I—" Phoenix paused. "Do you own a horse? I smell horse."

Jayden scowled. "We can't trust this guy, Bee. Look at his freaky eyes, for god's sake. Our families made the mistake of opposing Flamegate," he lowered his voice, "and look where it got them. Everything this kid says is insane."

"Listen," Phoenix said, addressing Bee. He had decided already that she was in charge. "I get it. Why trust a guy with no shoes, a bullet hole, and what many assume is an illegal activist tattoo?"

Jayden pointed at the five dots upon Phoenix's chest. "You're telling me that's not a rebel ranking? Bee has one practically the same."

Phoenix cast Bee a look and she rolled up her sleeve to reveal an almost identical tattoo over her bicep, though the five dots were encircled in a simple ring of flames.

Phoenix sighed. "Although I agree with their general sentiments, I'm not a rebel. At least, that isn't why I have this mark." He frowned into the depths of the dried fruit bag. "There were five of us," he said eventually. "Able to enhance the void's power or pass freely through the divide."

He picked out another apricot and took a bite. "Our captors, wishing to distance themselves from the fact that we were complicated individuals with hopes and dreams and sparkling personalities, assigned each of us a number. A number is easier to abuse."

"So, what?" Jayden said, his tone loaded with mocking disbelief. "You're *Prisoner Number Five*?"

Phoenix tossed a raisin into the air and caught it in his mouth. "I prefer Phoenix, if it's all the same to you."

"And the other four?"

The smile slipped from Phoenix's face. "Dead."

"You have an impressive imagination," Jayden remarked.

"You have an impressive ability to annoy me."

"I just saved your life."

"I just saved the world."

"Did you?" Bee asked, interrupting the exchange from her position by the fridge.

"In a way," Phoenix replied. "I broke into a high-security lab, stole a void-stone, damaged an expensive Flamegate facility, then cut a microchip from my own arm and got shot. All so I could deprive a corrupt organisation of a lethal weapon, thus doing the universe a great deal of good. I think I deserve a little credit."

Jayden groaned. "Today is not going as I expected it to go."

"You and me both." Phoenix took a deep breath then stood up, amused to see Bee's hand move swiftly to the knife at her belt.

Phoenix chuckled and handed her the bag of dried fruit. "What do you expect me to do? Bleed in your eye?"

"You need rest," Bee said, watching suspiciously as Phoenix moved towards the other side of the kitchen, using the countertop to take some of his weight.

"No," Phoenix said. "I need a bulletproof vest, a long-range camera-drone, and more time." He stopped and squeezed his eyes shut, a deep rumble filling his brain. "I might've forced too much void-energy through my body over the past few days." He lowered himself to sit on the tiles again.

"Take it easy," Bee insisted.

"Those magicians," Phoenix said, his palms flat against his ears. "The Shadow Masters of Yonder. They came to Earth after an experiment went wrong."

"We've rescued a lunatic," Jayden mumbled, while Bee removed her denim jacket and tucked it behind Phoenix's back.

"But the void damaged their magic abilities," Phoenix continued as Bee eased him down, "so the Shadow Masters were trapped."

"Uh-huh." Bee nodded patiently. "Take a nap before you hurt yourself."

"Eventually..." Phoenix said, having sunk completely to the tiles, "after sabotaging the planet and pretending to save it, they formed the Flamegate we know and love today."

Jayden looked pointedly at Bee. "This nut needs to leave."

"This nut is telling the truth," Phoenix said. "Flamegate developed a global network of influential people and spies. They control everything. But at the heart of it all there's still the Night Order, a group of magic-wielding fanatics dedicated to harnessing the energy between worlds..." Phoenix wrapped his hand around the bandage on his arm. "That's why they're so interested in freaks like me."

"Flamegate are ruthless, power-hungry overlords, sure," Jayden said. "But magic aliens investigating mystic space energy? Come on, Bee. This is cracked."

Bee was leaning against the fridge again, a small frown creasing her brows.

"It's the truth," Phoenix insisted, still clutching his bandaged arm. "You believe me, right?"

Bee considered him in silence, and Phoenix was painfully aware of how unhinged he looked, with dishevelled hair and glowing eyes. He suddenly wished he was wearing a shirt.

"Maybe," Bee said at last.

Phoenix smiled. "That's a start."

"Rest." Bee signalled for Jayden to follow her out.

Phoenix watched them leave. The abrupt end to conversation left him uneasy, as though the rustic little kitchen might swallow him whole. Eventually he fell asleep to the sound of a far-off helicopter, distant sirens, and Belinda's fridge whirring in much the same way as Flamegate's excruciating void-capturing-device. That terrifying contraption was known as the Crush, and Phoenix had no doubt it would've haunted his nightmares had he been capable of sleep.

Sometimes he was grateful that he couldn't dream.

~

Simon Wolfe shifted in the saddle of his horse, which he had borrowed off an imperial soldier several years ago and curiously forgotten to give back.

Afternoon sun shone pleasantly upon the Yonderian countryside. Birds were singing sweet and merry tunes. And a group of tiny, three-horned goblins were playing violent war games in the long grass. It was a beautiful day, but Simon didn't care. He was worried.

Lately, it seemed, there was no shortage of things to be worried about. The frustratingly limited nature of his own magic seemed almost negligible compared to the growing fragility of balance in the universe. Yonder was experiencing an era of strange, unprecedented change. Shadows were spreading like a disease across the land, and reports of objects, people, even entire towns, simply vanishing from existence had become so commonplace that many people had chosen to stop questioning it. Resigned tolerance was easier.

Simon, however, refused to accept that sometimes, with no warning at all, tangible parts of reality would simply disappear.

Above all these worries though, the unconscious, shaggy-haired nitwit slouched on the sullen horse plodding ahead continued to be Simon's biggest concern.

"Gulliver," Simon said, "do you think he'll mind?"

The horse ignored him, as he usually did. Despite his rare linguistic capabilities, Gulliver preferred to remain annoyingly mysterious and aloof.

Simon rolled his eyes. "Moody old mule."

Phoenix started to stir.

"Horse," he said as he sat up, his red hair as scruffy and unkempt as the mane of the horse he was travelling upon. "I'm on a horse."

"Yep." Simon rode forward so he and Phoenix were side by side, the hills stretching into the distance behind them and plumes of chimney smoke visible beyond the horizon ahead.

Phoenix frowned at him. "*Why* am I on a horse?"

"I wasn't going to carry you," Simon said, as a purple goblin darted past, triumphantly waving another goblin's head. An angry, clamouring horde of orange goblins charged after it, brandishing tiny fists and spears.

"Anyhow," Simon said, "I'm glad you're awake. We're almost there."

Phoenix's frown deepened. "Almost where?"

"Bloodwood," Simon answered.

Phoenix wrenched Gulliver to a stop. "Sweet holy *Light*, Simon! *Bloodwood*? Why the hell are we going to Bloodwood?"

"You wanted to?" Simon said, un-surprised by the reaction. After nearly ten tumultuous years of travelling, he had grown accustomed to Phoenix's rapidly changeable moods.

"Yeah," Phoenix said, "when I thought I was *dying*!"

"You're not dying then?"

"I found a vet," Phoenix replied. "That's not the point. I'm not going to Bloodwood. And I'll be damned if I let you near the place."

"Shame," Simon said. "I'm going anyway."

"Dammit, Wolfe." Phoenix raked his hands through his hair. "The last thing I need is you and your creepy magic digging up that town's miserable past."

"But I've always wanted to see this home of yours." Simon rode ahead, and after a moment of staring numbly into thin air, Phoenix reluctantly followed behind.

"What are you scared of?" Simon asked, as they reached the crest of the final hill.

Phoenix cringed. Below them, sprawled on the edge of a forest that bordered the gulley and vanished into the distance, was a town so battered and rundown it might've been dismissed as the ruins of an ancient civilisation—a civilisation long since annihilated by famine, plague, or a stampede of migrating trolls. Crowded with ramshackle stone homes and countless farms with spiked walls to keep wild beasts away, Bloodwood could only be described as grim.

The only industrial-looking feature amongst the otherwise unsophisticated, shambolic mess was the maze of thick, metal pipes that crisscrossed around buildings and over streets, eventually converging at a large, factory-type building in the centre of town.

A darkness settled behind Phoenix's eyes.

"My favourite kind of Shadow will always be a dead one," Simon said, "but you can't deny that Bloodwood's an historical treasure."

"Historical death-trap, more like," Phoenix said, unable to take his eyes from the sleepy mess of houses nestled in the shallow gulley below.

"It can't be that bad," Simon reasoned.

"Can't be that..." Phoenix shook his head. "Bloodwood has been passing down secret energy-harnessing techniques for generations. See that factory down there, where all the pipes lead?"

Simon frowned. "Yeah?"

"That's where void-energy is processed, to make it safe for public use."

Simon nodded. "An impressive feat."

"Sure," Phoenix said. "But refining void-energy and storing it within convenient, family-friendly disks is no easy task. Anyone not killed from mishandling it dies from over-exposure to the extreme energy levels radiating around here. Failing that, they're slaughtered by one of the Shadows that live nearby." Phoenix hugged his coat around his shoulders. "No one in Bloodwood dies of old age."

"Are we going or not?" Gulliver asked, his voice echoing dully inside both Phoenix and Simon's heads.

Phoenix scowled. "Why keep a town in a countryside filled with monsters, *right* beside a forest with the largest surviving Shadow population? All for a bit of power? They're out of their minds."

"Red," Simon said, adopting the firm, no-nonsense voice he reserved exclusively for his erratic, universe-hopping companion. "They're your family."

Phoenix didn't say anything, which unsettled Simon, because usually Phoenix never shut up.

"Just let 'em know you're alright," Simon added.

"I'd hate to lie to them," Phoenix said. Then he swore under his breath before charging full-speed down the hill.

BLOOD MATTERS

Phoenix slowed Gulliver to a trot and waited for the warlock to catch up. Once he did, they moved slowly through the maze of crumbling homes, following the dusty streets towards the far end of town by the woods.

"Where is everyone?" Simon asked as they passed through the deserted town centre, most shopfronts boarded up or uninviting, with curtains tightly drawn. His horse snickered nervously while Gulliver lumbered indifferently on.

"They're either hiding in their homes..." Phoenix replied, "hunting Shadows... or dead."

"This place used to be much more... vibrant," Simon

observed, his gaze roving around the town square.

"Your retrospective hocus-pocus is exactly the reason you shouldn't be here," Phoenix muttered. "What's the point in watching a bunch of ghosts bumble about with their boring, non-existent lives? Especially here. It'll only depress you."

"They're not ghosts," Simon said, watching the entrance to what appeared to be a long-abandoned butcher shop, hooks and chains hanging eerily from the walls. "They're echoes of the past. Actual events seen through time-frames invisible to everyone else. You know this."

"Whatever," Phoenix said wearily. "You see dead people. It's disturbing."

Simon dismissed him with a shrug. "I can't help it." His grave eyes followed the network of pipes that traversed from one tumbledown building to the next. "The Shadows..." he began.

"Don't." Phoenix grimaced, trying not to imagine the horrific scenes that Simon could see from Bloodwood's past. "I don't want to know."

They rode to a weather-beaten house near the very edge of the woods, its thatched roof weighed down with age and star-shaped leaves from the surrounding bloodwood trees. Scorch marks blackened the stone walls, as they did all the surrounding dwellings. The home's only redeeming feature was a thick row of purple flowers that grew like weeds along the rickety front fence, but even they appeared bedraggled and bleak.

Phoenix examined the house with the same apprehension he might view a boulder teetering above him on the edge of a cliff.

"This is unwise."

"Says the idiot who challenged a giant to an arm-wrestling match," Simon said under his breath.

"Giants are sweethearts compared to Nan," Phoenix said, then he jumped from Gulliver's back and Simon followed his lead. Leaving the horses by the gate they walked to the front porch, but instead of knocking, Phoenix stopped and stared miserably at the door. The town was poisoning him, like he'd known that it would.

"I'd rather be on Earth." He rapped his knuckles against the door and waited, arms folded and fingers tapping in an attempt to distract himself from his thoughts.

"Interesting trees," Simon said, nodding at the forest in what Phoenix presumed was an attempt at non-panic-inducing conversation.

Phoenix half-smiled. Bloodwood trees filled most people with dread, but he liked their vast, snarly canopies and red, twisted limbs. Despite the forest's sinister reputation and haunting sense of impending doom, it had always been the safest place for him to hide. Not even void-collectors ventured past the outer edge of the woods, regardless of the incredible energy that existed beyond.

Phoenix scratched nervously at his left arm, a habit he'd developed on Earth soon after the first microchip had been planted beneath his skin.

"These grandparents of yours really that frightening?" Simon asked.

"You've no idea." Phoenix hammered on the door again. "You need more friends," he added abruptly. "You live an embarrassingly solitary lifestyle. I'll die first, that's guaranteed. But what if I'm killed and Jess is kidnapped by pirates? Who will you talk to? Gulliver, I suppose, but he thinks you're a twit."

"If Jess were kidnapped by pirates, she'd conquer their ship and sail home herself. Secondly, Red..." Simon allowed himself a small smile. "*Relax.*"

"Relax?" Phoenix tapped his foot distractedly. "Golden advice, Simon. Quality council. Thanks."

A chair scraped from inside and Phoenix clenched his fists beneath his sleeves.

"With any luck," he said, eyeing a red gem hanging from the roof, "a Shadow will storm out of nowhere and we can take that as a socially acceptable sign to run away." He edged sideways so the decorative gem no longer dangled directly above his head. "Let's just—"

The door creaked open and an old lady with fierce green eyes stared out, her vivid red hair streaked with grey and her animal-hide clothes as weathered and crinkled as her skin.

Her wintery stare fell upon Phoenix and his breath caught in his throat.

"*Nan*," he said. "Hi."

In one sweeping gaze, the woman evaluated him from the top of his tangled hair to his battered brown boots, and she didn't say a word.

Phoenix cracked a well-practised smile. "Nan, this is Simon Wolfe... Simon, this is my grandmother, Matilda Elway. We were just passing through, so..." With a sharp snap, Matilda closed the door on his face.

"Well," Phoenix said, "that was less painful than I thought it would be." He started walking away, but Simon grasped his shoulder and spun him around.

"You'll regret it if you leave now."

"Debatable," Phoenix said, but he took a small breath then pounded on the door. The old woman opened it again, her eyes no less fierce.

"Why are you here?" she asked.

"I'm well, thanks," Phoenix said. "How are you?"

"Ten years," Matilda said, holding up each of her spindly fingers, as though Phoenix needed a visual aid to remember just how long a decade was. "We thought you were dead."

"Did you miss me?" Phoenix asked, genuinely curious.

His grandmother scowled. "Ten years. Light forgive me; I can hardly look at you."

"Nothing's changed," Phoenix said. "That's comforting I suppose."

Matilda's eyes blazed. "You don't belong here," she said, dropping her voice to an angry hiss. Simon raised his bushy eyebrows.

Phoenix chuckled. "No one belongs here. And yet here you all are. *Fighting Shadows.*" He slouched against the doorframe. "I was dying, by the way. But fear not. Circumstances changed and now I might live a little longer. Should we hug? We can hug, if you like. To demonstrate our shared affection and relief."

Matilda glared at him, unimpressed beyond the need for words.

"You're right." Phoenix maintained his easy smile. "Foolish idea. Best not to act related."

Matilda swallowed, and for a second a flicker of what might've been sadness passed behind her eyes. It was, however, swiftly replaced by the same cold edge that had been present before.

"Leave," she said. "Bloodwood is not a town for fragile flowers like yourself."

"Now hold on," Simon started to say, but Phoenix spoke over him.

"After everything, you still think I'm *fragile*?"

Matilda held his gaze. "You're too weak to survive this town."

Phoenix's stomach twisted in on itself. Simon, meanwhile, looked away with a quietly uncomfortable noise as though regretting his involvement in what was clearly a longstanding family feud.

"This was a mistake." Phoenix turned away, and this time Simon didn't stop him. Instead, the warlock gave Matilda a curt bow before following Phoenix across the yard.

"Don't let the wards get you on the way out," Matilda grumbled.

"For Light's sake, Nan..." Phoenix marched back towards the gem hanging over the porch. "I can live with the wards. I ran from *you*." He ripped the ornament free then held it before him, clenching it tightly in his fist. His skin burned under invisible flames, searing pain roaring through his body until he collapsed, an impenetrable gloom falling over his eyes. The darkness squeezed at him so tightly that it drove the very air from his lungs.

Like whipping off a blindfold, his vision cleared and he was on his knees, Simon looming over him, one hand gripping Phoenix's shoulder while the other held the gem.

"Haven't missed that." Phoenix managed to speak despite the tightness in his throat. "I'm an idiot," he added with a feeble laugh. "I shouldn't be here."

"Most sensible thing you've said yet." Matilda stood by the door, arms folded over her chest.

Phoenix gazed out at the gloomy town, annoyed with himself. He wasn't sure what he'd been trying to prove. Whatever it was, it had backfired spectacularly.

A group of robed ladies glared at him from across the street, murmuring urgently in what Phoenix imagined to be a heated debate about whether to confront him with words or just skip ahead to what they *really* wanted to do, which was shoot him through the chest with poison arrows before lashing him to a stake and setting him on fire.

"Listen," Phoenix said, looking away from the gathering crowd. "I was trouble from the beginning. I don't blame you for holding a grudge."

Matilda raised her sharp chin, a chin that greatly resembled Phoenix's own. "The day you entered this world was the day we lost everything," she said softly. "Yet I cared for you like a mother would." Then, after a painfully long pause, "I think you should leave."

"Nan..." With an effort, Phoenix stood and took a step toward his grandmother, extending his hand, compelled by some absurd instinct to embrace her or touch her arm. She recoiled further into the entranceway, as though fearing a single touch would turn her to stone.

Phoenix left his hand hanging for a moment then turned away. "Have a good life."

"Wait."

Phoenix glanced over his shoulder to see a stout old man

beside the house, shaky and small beneath slack trousers and a baggy shirt. His clouded grey eyes held a profoundly regretful expression that Phoenix had long tried to forget.

"*Teddy*?"

"Welcome home." The man smiled with misshapen lips, eaten away by years of void exposure. Soft tissue was always first to go.

Phoenix backed away. "I'm not staying."

"We have sandwiches," Teddy said, and Phoenix stopped in his tracks.

Simon rolled his eyes.

"Come inside," Teddy said gently. "Before anyone tries to repay you for what you did."

Phoenix glanced uneasily at the scowling group of women across the road, then tugged the hood of his coat up to conceal his frustratingly recognisable hair.

"Free food," he said resignedly. "Can't say no to that."

The silence in the living-room was louder than Phoenix cared to endure. Heavy, dust-filled curtains prevented most outside sounds from entering the house, leaving him acutely aware of the soft wheeze in his grandfather's breath, and the large pendulum clock that ticked stridently in the corner of the room. His grandparents sat opposite him on shabby couches he remembered climbing when he was young, while Simon leant against a window inspecting the red gem, holding it up behind the curtain so it captured the fading afternoon light.

Phoenix tapped his fingers against his knees while his grandparents fixed him with expectant stares. After what felt like enough time to recite all thirteen verses of Bloodwood's traditional ballad of honour, pride, and glory (sung only on very solemn occasions or at the very, *very* worst of parties), Phoenix finally cracked.

"Family." He spread his arms wide. "What did I miss?"

Matilda's eyebrows shot skywards. "You left this town in ruins, without waiting to see who'd survive. *Now* you want to know what you missed?"

"I was nine," Phoenix said. "Nine-year-olds aren't exactly known for great coping techniques."

"You can't outrun this town." Teddy leant across the low table and placed a twisted, three-fingered hand on Phoenix's knee. "It's in your blood."

Phoenix laughed. "Teddy, I can't outrun Death or the inevitable progression of Time. But this town? *This* is a matter of geography. One foot after the other towards any location that isn't here."

"Cowardice." Matilda spoke as though Phoenix's mere existence insulted her. His existence, Phoenix conceded, was probably insulting to everyone in Bloodwood.

"You betrayed us," Matilda added. "You betrayed everyone. This town grieved, *for years*. That's what you missed."

"So... nothing good." Phoenix took a sandwich from the tray between them, choosing to focus on food rather than the fury emanating from the woman who long ago had taught him how to read—a kindness for which he was still grateful, despite everything else.

"Is this a Shadow-deterrent?" Simon asked, brandishing the red gem that had brought Phoenix down with such ease.

Matilda nodded. "Bloodwood specialty," she said, before facing Phoenix again. "Your condition's grown worse."

"Don't start," Phoenix muttered.

Simon frowned at the stone. Phoenix didn't care to imagine the connections he might've been making. At least the gem was interesting enough to keep Simon in the present. The dark shadow of Phoenix's family history was not something he wanted to cast upon anyone else, especially the warlock, who had already been forced to deal with the more confronting aspects of Phoenix's unconventional life.

"So," his grandfather said. "You've been travelling?"

Phoenix grinned. "Like a feather in the wind."

"With him?" Matilda asked, nodding at the window.

"Unfortunately," Simon said, still captivated by the gem.

Phoenix chuckled. "And Jess, too, but she's busy. Off on a secret mission we're not allowed to be part of. Well, *I'm* not allowed to be part of. She says I'm too dangerously impulsive."

"You *are* dangerously impulsive," Simon said, strolling over from the window and helping himself to the sandwich tray.

Phoenix smiled as Simon made himself comfortable, the timber chair squeaking loudly under the weight.

"And you're travelling in search of what?" Teddy asked.

"Trouble, mostly." Phoenix sank his teeth into a second sandwich. "Our latest ill-advised hobby is attempting to end rampant misuse of the void. It's difficult though… since no one believes how much danger we're in. That's greed for you, right? Obviously you two are familiar with that."

Matilda dug her nails into the arms of her chair—like a disgruntled bird, digging into its perch. Phoenix had often thought his Nan resembled a grouchy bird. All sharp and mean and uncomfortable with hugs.

"Just wait until the universe implodes from reckless exploitation of void-energy, causing endless Shadows to flood in from beyond the void," Phoenix said. "*Then* people will listen. If they're alive. Which they won't be." He took another bite of his sandwich. "Ignorance is bliss I suppose. You two, for instance—"

"You still believe you live in two separate worlds," his grandfather interjected.

Phoenix stopped chewing. Matilda narrowed her eyes and a stifling tension settled upon the room.

"You're sick," Matilda said flatly. "You always were."

Phoenix swallowed. "And yet… despite everyone's best efforts… here I am. Not dead."

"*How* sick?" Simon inquired.

Phoenix shot the warlock a look. "Stay out of this."

"That goes against my better nature," Simon argued. "What was wrong with you?"

Matilda lowered her voice. "Death has stalked Phoenix since birth."

"*Stalked* me?" Phoenix laughed unconvincingly. "A little melodramatic, don't you think? Why does Death need to stalk?"

"We wanted him to be normal," Teddy said, his words wavering with emotion that Phoenix had no wish to hear. "Phoenix wasn't like other children. Some days he barely had energy to breathe."

"I summoned a healer," Matilda said, and Phoenix cringed at the memory. A mountain of a man with beefy hands and a volcanic voice, in heavy boots and a sweeping cloak of fur that rustled with secrets at the slightest touch.

"Maulbrak." Teddy nodded slowly. "A Shadow Master who didn't vanish after the war."

"Maybe Death skips," Phoenix mumbled, tearing the crust off his bread. "Prances about with streamers and balloons. Giggling, probably."

"Maulbrak arrived on Phoenix's fifth birthday…" Teddy rubbed his eyes with work-worn hands, a catch in his voice. "He said blasting our boy with raw void-energy might ease the illness within."

Phoenix slumped back in the chair.

"And did it?" Simon asked.

"I hate you," Phoenix mumbled. Glumly, but not with a great deal of conviction.

"Maulbrak suppressed the worst symptoms," Matilda said. "Restored Phoenix's strength. Built his resistance to the wards that surround our town."

Teddy bowed his head. "But the treatment caused something worse."

Phoenix groaned and buried his face in his sandwich.

"The dreams started," Matilda said.

The ensuing silence grew heavier by the second. Eventually Phoenix stood up. "Dreams," he said, wiping crumbs off his face. "Happy now, Wolfe?"

"Please." Simon smiled at Matilda. "Continue."

Phoenix sighed then looked about the cluttered room. Disk-powered lamps shed gentle light upon aging furniture and an assortment of other disk-powered contraptions. A creepy, miniature merry-go-round rotated silently upon a paper-laden desk while a lump of bread baked within an oven. A rusty heater glowed warmly beside a glass cabinet burdened with decades of accumulated junk.

"You redecorated," Phoenix said, gesturing meekly at the flaking walls.

Matilda dismissed him with a wave. "He'd talk such nonsense," she said, while Phoenix walked away from the table, the floorboards creaking beneath his feet. "Strange technologies. Human experiments. Brutal guards to imaginary prisons."

"Look," Phoenix said. "The curtains are new."

"We hoped it was a phase," Teddy said. "But then people in his dreams started dying."

"*That lamp*," Phoenix said, raising his voice and pointing towards the corner of the room. "I definitely don't remember that lamp."

"One," Teddy said. "He always spoke of a friend called One."

Phoenix stood motionless before a tall bookshelf loaded with parchment and packages and suspicious glass jars, his hand hovering shakily above an ornate paperweight that had sparked his curiosity a second earlier but now held no interest at all. All at once, he felt as though he were six years old.

"Please," he said softly. "Stop."

His grandfather turned to peer at him. "They're dreams, Phoenix. Not a second life."

"It's *one* life," Phoenix said. "Constantly passing through the void."

Simon leant back in his chair, contemplative as he continued to listen and eat.

"You never even left Bloodwood," Teddy added.

Phoenix threw his arms up in frustration, his ratty, multicoloured sleeves hanging past his hands. "Ever since that brainless *healer* came, there've been *two* of me!"

Matilda scoffed. "Very convenient."

Phoenix grabbed one of the jars from the shelf then slammed it onto the low table for everyone to see. The crimson substance within splashed against the lid then dripped slowly back down the sides.

"You want to talk about convenience?" Phoenix growled. "Your blood supplies are running low."

Discomfort crept over Matilda's features and Teddy lowered his head.

"Thanks for lunch," Phoenix muttered, before seizing the entire sandwich-tray and leaving the room with a flourish of his ugly coat.

"He's tetchy today," Simon remarked as he shrugged out of his leather jacket and bundled it in his lap, revealing the dark, intricate patterns displayed along his arms. He carried on eating, unconcerned by the family drama around him, immersed in his thoughts.

Matilda and Teddy eyed him uncertainly, no doubt assessing his striking tattoos and considerable size.

"Wolfe..." Matilda said. "You're a warlock?"

"Of sorts," Simon replied. He reached out to take the jar of blood then swirled it before him like a connoisseur of fine wine.

"*Of sorts*?"

"My powers are limited." Simon removed the lid of the jar then pulled the gem from his pocket and dropped it inside. The blood bubbled and hissed in response before bursting into flames.

Simon frowned. "*Fascinating*."

He looked up and scanned the room, his eyes locking upon an empty space beside the display cabinet as he focused on a scene that no one else could see. A single glimpse of Phoenix's past was all Simon needed to rise to his feet.

"Phoenix isn't sick," he said, shoving the jar into Matilda's hands. "You are."

"You're friends?" Matilda asked.

"Our lives collided when I was fifteen," Simon said, "living on the streets. Red was nine. I practically raised him."

Matilda pursed her lips. "Be careful, young warlock. He's much more dangerous than he looks."

RUNNING AGAIN

Phoenix was outside ranting to Gulliver, who was lying in the garden showing no sign of wanting to move.

"Complete waste of time," Phoenix said, ramming sandwiches into his bag as suspicious eyes watched from darkened windows of nearby homes. "It's not like I expected them to suddenly believe the same line I've fed them since I became whatever it is that I became. The impossible dimension-skipping nutcase. Still, a little understanding would've been nice. Get up, would you? We're leaving."

Gulliver flicked his ears then wilfully rolled over in the dirt, flattening an unfortunate three-horned goblin that happened to be passing by in the process.

"Can't you be like Tugger?" Phoenix asked, thrusting his hand towards Simon's horse, which was standing obediently by the gate where Simon had left him by a post, idly munching flowers and grass.

"*Tugger*," Gulliver said, his voice echoing in Phoenix's mind, "is an idiot."

Phoenix rolled his eyes. "Let's go to Karvil," he said. "We'll save people from their own stupidity and the growing hordes of restless Shadows, focus our energy on not dying, and forget this sweaty armpit of a town even exists. Where's Simon?"

"Just listening to you ramble," Simon said, standing in the doorway of the old house, florescent bees humming around him. Another goblin scurried out to tug vainly at her comrade, still trapped beneath Gulliver's rump.

"I can't be here," Phoenix said. "I'll save the universe from someplace else. Karvil sounds good. The inventors are always happy to see us."

"You're running away?" Simon asked as he followed the path to the front fence.

"Executing a tactful retreat," Phoenix said, meeting the warlock by the gate. "I thought this place might have answers, but it doesn't."

"Perhaps it does have answers and you're merely too scared to ask the right questions."

Phoenix narrowed his eyes. "Listen, warlock. Just because you have a beard now doesn't mean you're allowed to spout clichéd words of superficial wisdom." He slung his bag over his shoulder. "I'm leaving. Effective immediately."

Simon folded his formidable arms. "I'm staying."

"All the best to you then." Phoenix started walking, his patched clothes trailing the road and the gravel crunching beneath his feet.

"Red," Simon said. "The void grows more unstable every day. You've said so yourself. The world is running out of time."

Phoenix slowed to a reluctant stop, gazing sadly down the street of humble stone homes. Crowds watched from afar, reaching cautiously for weapons or whispering to other townspeople nearby. The misdemeanours of Phoenix's past had clearly not been forgotten by the victims he'd left behind.

"You can't avoid this place forever," Simon insisted. "Whatever happened here... it can't be worse than the end of the world."

"Interesting theory," Phoenix said. "I'll meet you in Karvil." He started walking again then leapt backwards as a sizzling jet of vivid blue lightning slammed into the ground before him, scorching a patch of gravel inches in front of his feet.

He spun to look at Simon, who appeared entirely unapologetic about blasting electricity behind Phoenix's back. The last crackling forks of energy snapped from the warlock's body and fizzled away as he leant against the gate.

"Would it kill you?" Simon asked. "Staying here?"

Phoenix smiled. "If I say yes, will you let me leave?"

"You'll survive a few days," Simon said, more to himself it seemed than to Phoenix. "This town is connected to everything. I can feel it."

"Simon," Phoenix said, "I'm not welcome here. My own family—"

Simon leapt over the fence, agile for a man of his immense size. He grabbed Phoenix by the arm and frogmarched him away from the watchful gaze of onlookers to the very edge of town, where the houses stopped and the swaying grass met the woods, the sun sinking gradually behind the trees.

"Do you feel it?" Simon asked, gazing into the depths of the forest, still gripping Phoenix by the arm.

Phoenix gave up trying to squirm free and instead looked apprehensively at the dense wall of trees. The darkness called him, beckoning him into the shadows like a long-lost friend.

"The wave of childhood memories I tried hard to repress?" he asked mildly. "Yeah, I feel it. Can we go now?"

"Bloodwood was built here for a reason," Simon said. "Founded by Shadow Masters at the very start of the Shadow Invasion. To this day, it remains Yonder's first defence."

"Words simply cannot describe the extent to which I do not care."

"That war ended fifty years ago," Simon continued, still staring into the woods. "The Shadow Masters vanished within a year of declaring victory, but their methods of harnessing void-energy remain with this town. As do Yonder's most resilient Shadows."

"The Shadows of Bloodwood Forest," Phoenix said, and a sudden whisper of wind quivered through the bloodwood trees. "What's your point?"

"Shadows didn't exist in Yonder before the war," Simon said, looking away from the forest at last. He released Phoenix's arm. "So where do they come from?"

It finally dawned on Phoenix why Simon had brought him to the edge of the woods.

He repressed a shudder. "They come from the void."

"And how do they get here?" Simon pressed.

Phoenix gulped. "Through the Gate."

"Exactly." Simon turned his gaze upon the trees again. "The biggest, most powerful void-tunnel in existence. Hidden in Bloodwood Forest."

An embarrassing, nervous burble of a laugh escaped Phoenix's mouth before he could prevent it.

"I'm not taking you to the Gate, Simon. Not in a million years."

Simon blinked in surprise. "You know where it is?"

"What? No," Phoenix said. "Its location is secret, known only to a very exclusive group of professionals. There are legends… theories… Nothing of substance."

"Interesting." Simon leant down so his eyes were level with Phoenix's face. "You've *seen* it."

"This new beard of yours," Phoenix said, leaning away from Simon's intense stare. "Will it be staying with us long?"

"That Gate is important," Simon said, ignoring Phoenix's question. "Maybe my brother passed through here. And if Yonder and Earth really are destined for some kind of multidimensional collision, investigating Bloodwood may be our only chance at securing a future for everyone."

Phoenix squinted at Simon's chin. "Deranged hermit," he said. "That's the vibe. Someone who disappears into the woods to take up birdwatching or poetry, then marries a tree."

Simon sighed and turned away. "Your grandparents," he said, trudging towards a dense patch of purple flowers by the edge of the forest. "They said you have a condition."

"*Had*," Phoenix corrected. "They cured me, remember?" He placed a hand over his heart and grinned. "Blasted me with the divine blessedness of pure void-energy, all at the tender age of five. I'm now a bottomless well of tappable vitality. A sacred vessel of Light. An impossible wonder of—"

"Your nan said it was getting worse."

Phoenix's face fell. "I'm just tired."

"Perhaps." Simon crouched to rip a bunch of flowers from the ground. The same flowers, Phoenix realised, as those that had been growing along the front fence of his old home.

"These are vigilantiums," Simon said, somewhat paradoxical with his wild hair and dark, thuggish attire as he brandished the bouquet.

Phoenix raised an eyebrow. "Why the lesson in horticulture?"

"They're a protective plant," Simon said, stepping closer to Phoenix. "They ward off Shadows." He crushed the flowers between his fingers, zapped them with a gentle flare of green lightning, then held his hand out near Phoenix's face, the crumpled petals quivering upon his large palm in the afternoon breeze.

"Smell them."

Phoenix smiled stiffly and took a step back. "I'd rather

not." But he caught a whiff of their potent perfume and immediately felt the spores burning down his throat.

"Crap."

"I knew it," Simon said, his voice reaching Phoenix from afar. "Shade."

Phoenix's knees buckled beneath him and he was ejected from Yonder before his face even hit the grass.

~

"Vanquished by flowers," Phoenix mumbled, his eyes still shut. "That's embarrassing."

He could hear Bee's fridge buzzing against the wall, and the sharp smell of cleaning products stung his nose. Everything ached.

"We should take him to the Lower Ring." Jayden's voice drifted over from beyond the kitchen. "Leave him with people who can afford the risk. People with nothing to lose."

Bee's response was short and cold. "He wouldn't survive ten seconds in the Lower Ring."

Phoenix sat up, careful not to disturb the bandages covering his wounds. A low, pounding hum pulsed inside his brain, but he tuned it out, concentrating instead on the conversation unfolding on the other side of the kitchen bench.

"He's important to Flamegate," Jayden said. "I'm sure he's immunised against the plague."

"How can you be so callous?" Bee asked.

"That's rich, coming from you."

Phoenix couldn't see Bee's face, but he could imagine the glare that met Jayden's remark.

"Sorry," Jayden said. "I'm just worried. We're in well over our heads."

"Phoenix stays."

Phoenix crouched low and peered over the counter. Bee was recumbent on the couch, staring up at the scorched ceiling with her hands behind her head while her boyfriend sat upon the armrest.

"This will come back to bite us, Bee." Jayden gestured towards the kitchen, not noticing the mop of red hair or attentive pair of eyes visible above the countertop. "That kid sent all three rings into lockdown. Whatever he's involved in runs deeper than anything our families dabbled with, before Flamegate started punishing them one by one."

Bee sat up and scowled.

"He stays," she said, and Phoenix frowned, wondering why the knife-wielding stranger was so keen to keep him around.

Jayden leant forward and clasped Bee's hands. "He's going to destroy everything we've built for ourselves."

"Which is what?" Bee asked. "Our freedom is a lie."

There was no kindness in Jayden's laugh. "Believe me," he said, standing from the couch. "We have more freedom now than if we're found assisting that criminal."

Phoenix straightened up and walked into the living-room, taking the pair by surprise as he plonked himself beside Bee.

"Flamegate won't rest until they find me," he said. "I agree with the grumpy one. It's time for me to leave."

"Glad to hear it," Jayden said. "I'll fetch your shirt." He left the room without another word.

"Where will you go?" Bee asked, as gunfire sounded in the distance outside. Phoenix gazed at the patch of blood staining the living-room floor then looked up with a half-hearted smile. Despite the frequency with which he saw it, the sight of his own blood unsettled him in ways he couldn't comfortably explain.

He wove his fingers together and tried to look relaxed. "I should make the most of my newfound freedom," he said lightly. "Travel. Explore Veracity. I've always wanted to see the Lower Ring. I hear its infested with mutant cats."

Bee studied him in excruciating silence, her expression an impassive mask. Sirens wailed outside as surveillance drones moved like industrious bees through the endless sprawl of the Middle Ring.

"Here." Jayden tossed Phoenix's prison-shirt across the room. "We washed it."

"Appreciated." Phoenix pulled the shirt over his head. It was a bleak, bullet-holed reminder of his haphazard escape, but at least the thin layer of fabric made him feel less naked before Bee's penetrating stare. "I'll be on my way then. Thanks for everything."

He stood to leave but Bee grabbed his wrist. Phoenix tensed and resisted the sudden urge to fling her across the room and start smashing things.

"Wait," Bee said. "The Lower Ring..."

"Is a deadly, miserable region of wretchedness reserved entirely for the defiant, desperate and dying," Phoenix finished, carefully prying her fingers away from his arm and taking a step back. "Just because I've spent fifteen years incarcerated within the Upper Ring does not mean I know nothing of the dangers that lay beyond it. You'd be surprised how much knowledge one acquires growing up in a high-security prison."

Bee chewed her lip then turned to face Jayden.

"I need him," she said quietly. "He knows things."

Phoenix raised his eyebrows.

"Reconsider," Bee said. "Don't go to the Lower Ring. Stay with us."

"What?" Phoenix and Jayden responded in unison.

"You mentioned the Night Order," Bee said. "They killed my parents. You being here exactly two years after they were killed is no coincidence. You have inside knowledge of Flamegate. You wear a tattoo like the heroes of rebellion stories that my parents told me when I was young. You can change things. Free people. End the suffering. I'm sure of it."

It was the first time Phoenix had seen Bee so animated.

"Your expectations of me are worryingly high," he warned. Then he frowned and tilted his head in uneasy bemusement. "The Night Order was here?"

"We helped you," Bee said. "Now help us."

Phoenix shook his head, preoccupied with why the Night Order, the lethal, twisted heart of Flamegate's insidious organisation, would bother themselves with Bee. They usually only involved themselves in matters of extreme universal importance.

"Look," he said distractedly. "The best I can do to repay you is put as much distance between us as possible. I need to get away. From you. From Flamegate. From everything."

"If he's so keen to vanish into the Lower Ring, let him," Jayden said. "It's no field of daisies, but even Flamegate will struggle to find him there. It's for the best."

"Absolutely," Phoenix said. "For the best." The deep, throbbing hum pulsing in his ears was growing increasingly difficult to shut out. "So, if you'll excuse me, I have a meeting with some mutant cats." He turned to leave again and Bee stood resolutely from the couch.

"I'll come with you."

"Light help us." Phoenix covered his eyes with his hand.

"Wait." Jayden's voice fluttered with trepidation. "Are you serious?"

"Are you coming?" Bee asked.

Phoenix looked between them. Jayden stood speechless, his arms hanging limply by his sides.

"I'll grab supplies." Bee set to work gathering items from around the house while Phoenix and Jayden watched in mute bewilderment.

Eventually Jayden shook his head. "Screw this," he muttered. "I'm out." He headed for the door and Bee made no move to stop him.

"He'll be back," she said after the door slammed shut, leaving her and Phoenix alone. "And stop frowning. I'm helping because I expect your help in return." She moved to the window and beckoned him to follow. "Look. The minefield we need to navigate our escape through."

Phoenix peered past the blinds at the filthy city sprawled beneath the afternoon smog. Veracity stretched for miles around the great mountain it had been built upon, divided into three enormous rings that spread out from the impressive, castle-like tower at the mountain's peak. Phoenix had never viewed Flamegate Tower from an outsider's perspective, and seeing the fortress in its entirety, lording over everything below as a firm reminder of Flamegate's strength, sent a chill down his spine.

He tore his gaze away.

"Have you always lived in the Middle Ring?" he asked, watching as menacing, four-legged robots scanned the streets below.

Bee scoffed. "Yeah. Middle Ring peasant through and through. The closest I get to the slimeballs in the Upper Ring is during the big three-day Light Festival they hold every year."

Phoenix scratched anxiously at the bandage around his arm, trying not to think about last year's festival and his brush with Death.

"You know how to get out of here then?"

"There's an old subway system," Bee said. "Governed by Veracity's strongest gangs."

"Sounds fun."

"I have connections with people inside," Bee said. "Once we hit the south tunnel we'll have guaranteed rite of passage. All the way to the Lower Ring."

"Out of the frypan..." Phoenix said, and Bee nodded.

"Into the fire."

A deep thrumming filled the air and they gazed up to see a Flamegate helicopter roaring towards the apartment building, its red lights glaring straight at them like wicked eyes.

Bee closed the blinds. Phoenix studied her as though she were a confusing piece of abstract art.

"Listen," he said. "Don't you have family or friends or something you should be thinking about?"

"My boyfriend just bailed and my family is dead." Bee pulled a backpack over her shoulder. "What weapons are you good with?"

"Anything imbued with raw void-energy tends to suit me well," Phoenix replied, following her toward the kitchen again.

Bee opened a drawer. "Well, I have breadknives. Or a rolling-pin."

Phoenix leant over the countertop and took a plain silver spoon. "I'll be fine. Can I ask a question?"

Bee shrugged and started rummaging through the pantry for food.

"What did the Night Order want with your parents?"

"Nothing," Bee said darkly. "They were killed in cold blood by three ladies in cloaks."

"Sisters of the Night Order rarely do anything without reason..."

"There is *no* reason my parents shouldn't be alive!" Bee glared at him. "I just want change. The world wasn't always like this, Phoenix. Before Flamegate..." She trailed off, and Phoenix understood. Flamegate had a knack for inciting an empty, immeasurable sense of helplessness and despair.

He wanted to say something uplifting, but he was too distracted by the low buzzing in his ears and the blinking red light on the microwave. Blinking red lights set him extremely on edge.

The front door swung open and Jayden returned, his expression grim.

"I've called Flamegate," he said. "Collectors are on their way."

A rush of terror surged through Phoenix and the spoon he was holding clattered to the floor.

Bee rounded on Jayden, eyes wide in disbelief. "You didn't."

"I had to," Jayden said, standing a wary distance away near the exit. "You can't ruin your life for some prison-rat you just met."

Bee grabbed the rolling-pin from the drawer and marched towards him. "You *idiot*."

Phoenix stood frozen behind her, his mind racing with increasingly improbable theories and ideas.

"Flamegate were desperate to find him," Jayden said, eyeing Bee's rolling pin with unease. "They said they'll give us a reward!"

"Of *course* they're desperate to find him." Bee jabbed the rolling-pin into his ribs. "He's a risk. The chink in their armour. Our biggest shot at making things right again."

Jayden backed against the wall.

"Holy Light..." Phoenix murmured. "The Night Order."

Bee and Jayden looked back at him as the helicopter roared past the window, its rotors pounding a rhythmic rumble throughout the sky.

"Time," Phoenix said vacantly.

"Time?"

"There were rumours..." Phoenix retrieved the spoon, his head spinning, "that one of the Sisters can jump through Time." He looked around, tapping the spoon nervously against his knee. "Something went wrong. They'll be back. We need to leave."

Jayden frowned. "What?"

"*We*," Phoenix said, "as in us, the collective. *Need to*, meaning it's imperative to our survival. And *leave*, as in, relocate immediately to someplace less perilous."

Jayden laughed incredulously. "All of us?"

"Flamegate will not reward you for my capture. They'll have you killed."

"If you say so," Jayden said, shouldering past Phoenix to wait on the couch for Collectors to arrive.

Phoenix felt ready to explode. The loud drone in his brain was growing unbearable. All he wanted was to disappear, preferably to a secluded tropical beach, with no-one around to hear him yell angry obscenities into the void.

"Saving you was not worth the drama," Jayden added glumly as he ran a hand through his golden waves of hair.

Phoenix cracked.

"Holy Light-crushing bleeding *Mother of Shadows*." He pointed the spoon at Jayden as though challenging him with a sword. "*Listen*," he said, with more authority than he thought himself capable of. "Scary ladies in cloaks will appear right here after leaping ahead from the past and they're going to finish what they set out to do today before they mistakenly landed two years ago in the wrong time. Do you *want* to be electrocuted to death?"

Jayden cast a sideways look at Bee, who was standing by the door, watching Phoenix warily.

"Time-travel," Jayden said, the frustration evident in his voice. "He's talking about time-travel."

Phoenix's own frustration rocketed to new heights.

"I'm talking about keeping you alive," he said.

"Why trust you?" Jayden demanded from the couch.

"How does *not dying* sound?!" Phoenix snapped. The rest of his anger was cut short by a faint boom in the distance, and a sudden, tingling sensation that made him feel ill.

"What was that?" Bee asked, her gaze flicking to the window. Everything seemed disturbingly quiet.

Phoenix crouched and waited for his aching head to clear. "Activity from the void," he said, before adding uneasily, "The helicopter's gone."

"Where?" Bee wondered.

"Good question." Phoenix drummed the spoon rapidly against the floor then sprang to his feet like a startled cat. "I'm on a tight schedule," he said, rushing for the exit. "You two do what you like." He yanked open the door then instantly slammed it shut and leapt backwards, his stomach plummeting to his toes.

"*Damn*."

The door flung open and three ethereal figures, hooded and cloaked in long crimson robes, swept like darkness into the room. Phoenix stiffened, momentarily paralysed by the three expressionless red masks that gazed down at him.

Bee charged past, snapping him back to reality as she pushed by him with her knife raised over her head. Phoenix lunged forward and seized her arm.

"*Not now*," he said, propelling her back towards her infuriating boyfriend, who had already scampered out of the living-room into the kitchen.

"Please wait here," Phoenix begged, ushering Bee behind the kitchen counter before darting back into the living-room to confront the three faceless strangers in red.

A soft chuckle arose from behind the mask of the tallest Sister as she glided to a stop before him, her two companions standing silent on either side.

"Apologies for our tardiness," she said, lowering her thin, silk-veiled body into a deep, deliberate bow. "How long since our last encounter?"

"Two years," Bee said, joining Phoenix beside the couch.

Phoenix closed his eyes in the vain hope that the situation would improve by the time he opened them.

"I don't believe we've met, child," the tall woman said, her voice as frighteningly unreadable as the lacquer red mask concealing her face. "Are you important?"

"*You...*" Bee snarled, as Phoenix carefully stepped in front of her.

"She's the girl," murmured another Sister. "From today."

"Extraordinary." The tall woman removed her mask, revealing wrinkled pink skin, thin lips, and heavy bags beneath aging eyes. She squinted at Bee.

"What a remarkable change in character," she said. "I see you've grown tougher these past few years... Good for you."

"Why did you kill my parents?" Bee demanded, her voice shaking with rage. "They'd signed a contract! They weren't a threat anymore!"

Phoenix swayed slightly on his feet, his head throbbing with the low, insufferable droning that only he could hear.

"Oh, you precious thing," said the tall woman, stepping closer, backing them further against the couch. "Do you think we cared about your parents? Sister Azalea here," she gestured serenely at the Sister who hadn't spoken yet, "made a mistake today. I did not handle the disappointment well. I have, I fear, quite a temper." The woman raised her palm and aimed it directly at Phoenix's chest. "So come along, Five. You are, after all, the only reason we were ever here."

Phoenix felt Bee's gaze boring into his back.

"Oh," Bee said faintly. "They came for you."

Phoenix nodded, his eyes fixed on the three women before him. The maskless Sister smirked, trapping him in the maliciousness of her stare.

A prickly memory scratched at the back of Phoenix's mind. He had seen that smile during the last Light Festival, moments before being strapped into the void-collecting Crush and enduring no small amount of indescribable pain.

"You're the reason my parents are dead..." Bee sounded as though she were talking to herself more than accusing him, but Phoenix had difficulty detaching himself from the guilt.

"I'm the reason lots of people are dead," he murmured, clenching the spoon he was still holding in his fist. Then he took a deep breath and stepped forward. He doubted he'd have more than one chance at digging everyone out of this mess.

"Nerine," he said, dredging the Sister's name up from some bleak, murky corner of his past. "The fact that you've not attacked me yet suggests you're being cautious. Very wise, considering I just stole a void-stone and escaped Flamegate, a prison no-one else has escaped in the history of forever. I'm a terrifying anomaly amongst anomalies. A frightening force that outwitted Flamegate's finest and demolished an entire laboratory of expensive, heavily guarded research. I am, to put it mildly, the most formidable foe you're ever likely to face."

Sister Nerine smiled, her palm still pointed at his chest. "Do you think Flamegate is afraid of you?"

Phoenix grinned. "I think Flamegate would be stupid

not to consider the very real risk of me blasting us all into obscurity." A sharp pain shot like a blade across his arm and he frowned uneasily at his unscathed skin. "That's concerning."

At that moment a portly, bearded man sauntered along the corridor outside.

"Just thought I'd check in, Belinda," he said, poking his head through the front door. "You're late on rent again." He paused, appraising the situation he'd stumbled upon.

"Seem to be interrupting..." he said, and Phoenix's heart sank as a flash of recognition passed over the man's face. "Wait a sec. That's the kid everyone's looking for."

Without taking her eyes off Phoenix, Nerine flicked her aim to the new arrival and an orange cloud of energy twisted down her arm, sparking and crackling like a storm. Before the man could even vocalise his disbelief, Nerine released all the lightning at once and it shot from her palm, slamming into the unfortunate man's chest.

Jayden yelped from the kitchen and Bee tensed by Phoenix's side. Phoenix watched grimly as the man crashed to the floor, a dark, fern-like pattern emblazoned across every inch of his now lifeless skin. The stench of burning meat overpowered the air, and Phoenix tightened his vicelike grip on the silver spoon.

"Well," he said. "I've had enough." With impressive speed, he threw the spoon at Nerine's face then clapped his hands together with a fierce slap. By the time Nerine had swatted the crude projectile out of the air, Phoenix had already pulled his hands apart and a dark green stone with delicate gold streaks interwoven across it was hovering between his palms. He snatched the stone into his fist then tossed it into the air where it floated freely above his head, emitting a soft but powerful hum.

"I have a bad habit of collecting these," Phoenix said, enjoying the look of dread that had crept into Nerine's narrowed eyes. "They're dangerous. I should quit. I know. I have a problem. That's not the point. The *point*... is that I'm not to be trifled with right now." Bee and Jayden gaped while the three Sisters tensed, waiting for Phoenix's next move.

"You wouldn't dare," Nerine said.

"Wouldn't I?" Phoenix asked, with as much galling facetiousness as he could deliver. "The stones are connected to the void, and the void is connected to me." He slung an arm around Bee's shoulder as though inviting her in on a joke, losing strength by the second but trying not to let it show. To his relief, Bee wrapped her arm around his waist and quietly held him steady.

"You need me alive," Phoenix added. "But, if I *have* to release the power of the void and destroy us all, I will."

He clung tighter to Bee, painfully aware that he might, in fact, have overestimated himself.

"On the other hand," he continued confidently, "if you let me go, we all leave this building with our lives. Hooray. Three cheers for option two. You have thirty seconds. Make up your mind."

Nerine scoffed. "You're bluffing."

"Twenty seconds," Phoenix said, while the green stone hummed weightlessly above his head.

Nerine's thin smile stretched even wider across her deceptively calm face.

"Right," Phoenix said. "Ten seconds… and I'll do it."

"He's fading," Nerine said. "Contain him."

The two Sisters behind her raised their hands to point at Phoenix and Bee, red lightning building rapidly around their outstretched arms.

"Three," Phoenix said weakly. "Two… One."

With a deafening bang, the apartment was flooded by white light. Ceiling lamps exploded in bursts of sparks and shattered glass. Jayden ducked behind the kitchen counter and Phoenix slipped exhausted to the floor, Bee awkwardly easing his fall as the green stone continued spinning overhead.

"Phoenix…" Bee said. "Was that you?"

Phoenix looked up. Shards of glass hung immobile in

the air, frozen as though trapped in time. The three Sisters stood motionless, the lightning from their hands stationary before them, reaching for Phoenix and Bee. The streaks of red lightning stretched unnaturally still, casting stark shadows around the room.

"I didn't do anything," Phoenix said. He opened his hand and the green stone glided into his palm and disappeared, returning the relentless droning to the shadowy confines of his own head. "That bang... the light... it wasn't me..." He closed his eyes. "Someone interfered. But this time-catch won't last. You and Jayden have to run."

"Then let's run." Bee reached down to help him up, but Phoenix slumped into the couch, his head on his knees.

"Far too early to mess with void-stones again," he mumbled. Then he giggled at himself. "Oops."

One of the Sisters broke free from her stiff pose and stalked forward, stepping easily through the shattered glass and jagged lightning that sat inactive in the air. Bee gripped her knife.

"The time-catch was me," the woman said, in a voice Phoenix had spent years working diligently to forget, rich with warmth and passion and strength. "You must leave. All of you."

Phoenix sat up like a scruffy ragdoll. "*Alice*?"

The Sister knelt before him and took off her mask, exposing deep, intelligent eyes and thick, dark hair that bounced lightly around her youthful face.

"They call me Sister Azalea now," she said, gently tilting up his chin. Only then did Phoenix realise that a trickle of blood had dripped from his nose to his lips.

"You joined the Night Order?" He looked searchingly at her face. "Why? Did they break you?"

"I've been working against Flamegate," Alice said, dabbing him clean with the sleeve of her robes. "Sabotaging them from within. The balance must be restored, Phoenix. Our time has come."

Phoenix stared as though she were a ghost, vaguely aware of Jayden tiptoeing out of the kitchen and Bee standing on guard with her knife.

"All these years?" Phoenix asked.

Alice smiled. "I'm glad you're free," she said, then leant in close and clasped his hands tightly in her own. "Now, about these stones..."

Phoenix barked a strained laugh. "Our reunion shouldn't be about some mysterious quirk of geology. I thought you were dead." His eyes drifted out of focus as he tried to hold onto Earth. "I guess you want me to stop using them too?"

"Not exactly," Alice said. "They're the best hope we've got." She placed her hands on either side of his face and he swallowed the unexpected bubble that caught in his throat.

"Flamegate will pay for what they did to us," Alice said. "I promise. But I need you to stop running from what you are."

"A fearless, inspirational visionary?"

"What you *truly* are."

"And what might that be?" Phoenix whispered.

Alice glanced up at Bee and Jayden before leaning forward and planting a light kiss upon Phoenix's forehead. "A means to an end," she said.

Phoenix wanted to question her further, but he had, infuriatingly, lost his treasured ability to talk.

"Freedom comes at a price," Alice added. "Sacrifices have to be made. By all of us." She stood abruptly. Phoenix tried to catch her sleeve, but his limbs had given up on him too. The most he could do was watch Alice turn away.

"I'm sorry about your parents," Alice said, handing Bee a scrap of paper. "Find this address. You'll be safe there." She inspected the Sisters locked in place behind the rigid jets of red light. "I'll make it look like Phoenix overpowered us," she said. "Please. Take care of him."

Bee looked down and Phoenix quietly held her gaze, unable to apologise or explain.

"I don't understand," Bee said, breaking away from

Phoenix's helpless stare.

"It will make sense in time," Alice replied as she placed the eerie mask upon her face once more. "I'm not afraid," she added softly. "I've lived well. I've made a difference. It's his turn now."

Phoenix's eyes drooped shut.

"This time-catch is weakening," Alice said. "Do be swift."

Phoenix felt himself being lifted from the ground, his arm pulled tight over Bee's shoulder.

"Here." To his surprise, Jayden's voice interrupted the low humming within Phoenix's brain. His other arm was stretched across Jayden's neck, and then they were moving, his feet dragging uselessly along the ground.

This was the start of something bigger than Phoenix had anticipated. He needed to speak with Alice. He needed to reconsider his options. He needed to not be the epicentre of chaos for a change, constantly drawing people into the inescapable whirlwind of calamity that he brought with him always.

The void washed over him and he let himself sink.

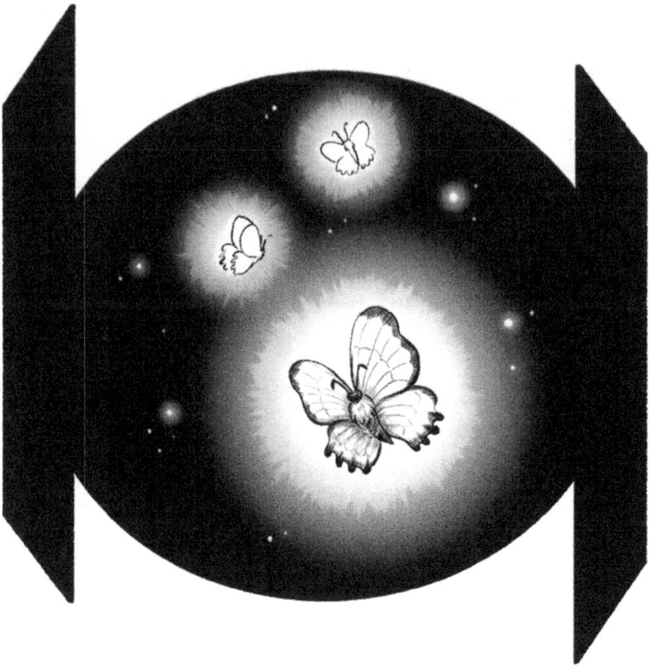

THE WARLOCK WAITS

"Drowning," Phoenix had said, only a month or so after Simon had first met the scrawny nine-year-old. They were camping in an abandoned farmhouse not far from Karvil City, escaping a freak rainstorm that was sweeping the land outside. "It feels like drowning."

"What does?" Simon asked, trying to light some kindling in an old fireplace that hadn't been used for years. He was sixteen, already tall and broad-shouldered and covered in complex tattoos.

"You asked what happens," Phoenix said from the improvised fort he had assembled in the corner of the room, an architectural masterpiece constructed from damp clothes and rotting furniture left by the previous residents of the neglected stone house. "If I try to stop switching bodies and just stay in one place. Holding onto the world. It's like drowning."

"You ever drowned before?" Simon asked, prodding impatiently at the smouldering twigs as water droplets leaked from the ceiling.

"Uh-huh. Hundreds of times."

"That's a lie."

Phoenix poked his head out from under a sheet-covered chair. "Well maybe not hundreds. But once. In a bath."

Simon shook his head. "You should not be allowed near water," he muttered.

Phoenix frowned. "But I like swimming." He crawled out from the fort and climbed on top of the broken bed it had been erected around. "Swimming is like flying," he said, balancing precariously on the bedhead. "Underwater. Flying through water. Like being a bird. Or a fish, maybe. I guess swimming is more like being a fish. Are we having fish for dinner again?"

Simon took a deep breath then leant into the fireplace, gently blowing onto the flames. Phoenix leapt from the bed and wandered over to watch the warlock's efforts.

"Can't you just use magic?"

Simon scowled. "It's not that easy."

"What's the point in being a warlock if you can't use magic?" Phoenix asked, leaning his bony elbows against Simon's back and peering over his shoulder at the struggling flames.

Simon swept him away with his arm.

"It's complicated," he said. "And Edgar told me not to push myself."

"Edgar?"

"My teacher."

Phoenix sat with a huff, tucking his knees under his chin. "Are you even a real magician?"

Simon rolled his eyes. "Yes."

"Are you broken?"

Simon cast a wary look at the innocent-eyed kid, wondering how seriously to respond. Phoenix waited patiently for an answer.

"Am I broken...?" Simon said, after he'd let the bitter idea bury itself in his mind. "I guess so."

Phoenix nodded solemnly. "Like me."

Simon turned his attention to the fireplace again. "No one's like you," he said grimly, thinking of the massive, inconceivable energy stored within the young boy.

"Hungry," Phoenix said, springing up without any warning at all. "I'll find food. Not fish, though. I'm sick of fish." Before Simon could stop him, Phoenix had scampered barefoot out into the rain.

"Pocket-sized gremlin," Simon growled. He gave up on the fire and pushed himself to his feet, stiff and sore from weeks of travelling with an unpredictable little twerp for company.

He paused by the door, an immense shift in void-energy causing his hairs to stand on end. It was like experiencing a sudden drop in temperature, or a strange, tickling change in the direction of an icy wind. He knew what to expect next, but the knowledge did little to quell the unease that rose within him.

He strode out into the downpour and found Phoenix in an overgrown field a short distance from the house, facedown in the mud, water drenching his ratty clothes and flattening his dishevelled mop of red hair.

Simon knelt beside him, content to do nothing but observe for a moment, unconcerned by the heavy rain.

"You're a freak," Simon said.

Phoenix showed no indication of having heard him.

Simon rolled Phoenix onto his side, uncomfortable with how defenceless the boy was. There was something deeply unsettling about this sleeping state. It was unnatural. Like being both dead and alive.

"I could ditch you," Simon said. "Leave you here in the mud."

Phoenix remained oblivious.

"It might be better for both of us," Simon added. "In the end."

A soft rumble of thunder rolled over the pastures and Simon bowed his head. The cold seeped under his clothes, chilling him to the bone, but still he remained on his knees.

Eventually he shook his head then tossed the bedraggled kid over his shoulder.

"Sorry, Red," he muttered, trudging back to the shelter of the farmhouse. "You're worth too much."

The deep, solemn clang of a distant gong pulled Simon from his reverie and he found himself sitting on a lichen-covered rock by the edge of Bloodwood Forest, the last of the evening sun peering over the trees. The twisted shadows of branches stretched into town, falling across Phoenix, who was still sprawled in the grass where the vigilantium flowers had knocked him out cold.

A group of young, uniformed children were darting from streetlamp to streetlamp throughout town, inserting energy-disks into slots at the base of each post. One by one, lights flickered into life, bathing the streets of Bloodwood in an amber glow.

Simon frowned and scratched his rough beard, wondering how long Phoenix would remain unconscious with the day already creeping towards night. Soon the Shadows would be at their strongest, and it seemed unwise to remain so close to the darkening woods.

The gong tolled gravely from within town again, and Simon wondered if it might be the signal for something important.

As the thought crossed his mind, Phoenix's grandmother came trudging around the corner of a nearby house. Her worried expression faded the moment she saw Simon, replaced immediately with a tight-lipped scowl.

Simon was equally displeased to see her. He stood almost without realising and planted himself squarely between Phoenix and the woman, like a protective dog guarding a bone.

Matilda frowned at the inert figure sprawled behind Simon's back. "I see our mighty warrior has collapsed again."

Simon felt the heat rising at the ends of his fingers, and he willed himself not to blast deadly lightning at the woman who had provided free lunch, despite how acutely repulsed he was by her character.

He folded his arms across his chest. "There's only one reason Red would be born weak against anti-Shadow defences."

"You think he's a Shadow?" Matilda asked, raising her eyebrows in the same mocking way Phoenix was often inclined to do.

Simon glowered. "I may not be a great magician," he said. "But I'm not an idiot."

"It's not impossible." Matilda shrugged. "Shadows can take human form." She stepped towards Phoenix again but Simon blocked her.

"Through possession," he said. "And not for long. Not without destroying the human's body beyond repair."

"Does he look well to you?" Matilda asked.

"He's not being possessed by a Shadow," Simon said. "Admit it. Someone did this to him."

Matilda scoffed. "He did this to himself."

The deep gong sounded again. Simon glanced at the town, which somehow appeared even bleaker than it had in the afternoon, shrouded in sombre shadows and heavy silence aside for the clanging gong.

"What is that?"

"A warning," Matilda said, sidestepping the magician then crouching by Phoenix's side. "Shadows have been sighted." She ran her fingers through Phoenix's hair, gently brushing it away from his eyes. "He shouldn't be here," she said softly. "It's not safe."

Simon watched her, suspicious of the sudden change in demeanour.

"He's a Shade," he said flatly. "I don't know how, but he is."

The wind settled as the final toll of the gong faded into the evening.

"Please wait here," Phoenix mumbled.

Simon frowned. Phoenix rarely spoke in his sleep. It usually only occurred when he was overly stressed, or trying to hold onto his body, resisting the change between worlds.

"Phoenix entered this life in the midst of a fire that destroyed half the town," Matilda said, uninterested in the sleep-talking. "A mere taste of the misfortunes that followed in his wake." She retrieved an empty jar from a leather bag at her waist and unscrewed the lid.

"He's not a Shade," she added, placing the jar in the grass.

"Look," Simon grumbled, as Matilda gently took Phoenix's hand. "Deny it all you want."

"My daughter," Matilda said, pushing Phoenix's sleeve down to his shoulder. "Our only child. *She* was a Shade. A near-perfect human-Shadow hybrid."

"Phoenix's mother?"

"She partnered with a human."

Simon's brows creased together. "What's that make Phoenix?"

"A mistake." In one effortless movement, Matilda pulled a knife from her belt then slit a deep cut across Phoenix's arm.

"*Hey*!"

Matilda waved Simon away. "Relax," she said, raising the jar beneath Phoenix's arm to catch the blood. "He owes us this much."

Phoenix grimaced in his sleep. "That's concerning."

"*Owes* you?" Simon said as a breeze whistled through the forest behind them. "His mother was a weapon. Her contaminated blood is the reason he's so weak against magic that's designed to *protect* people."

Matilda gazed at him as though she pitied his ignorance. "My daughter's blood keeps him alive," she said. "A mere human couldn't survive what Phoenix has become. But a human with a dash of Shadow blood? That's a different story."

The gong echoed from within town, signalling the sighting of yet another life-sucking monster. Matilda lowered Phoenix's arm then sealed the jar.

"The Shadows are particularly bold this evening," she said, pushing herself to her feet. "Go, before the situation intensifies." She turned to leave.

Phoenix sat bolt-upright and drew a long, ragged breath as though emerging from too long underwater.

"*Alice*."

"Alice?" Simon repeated. The name sounded familiar.

Phoenix gazed at Matilda's back as she walked into town, vanishing into the maze of dusty streets and tumbledown homes scattered beneath the dusky-red sky.

"Bloodwood," Phoenix muttered. "Wonderful." He stared groggily at his sliced forearm for a moment. "That's new."

"Your nan," Simon said, crouching beside him.

Phoenix nodded, unsurprised.

"Just blood?" he asked mildly. "Or did she sneak away with an entire kidney?"

"Blood." Simon delved into his rucksack and pulled out a long strip of cloth. "Do you know why?"

Phoenix just gazed at the clouds, transfixed by the rolling swells of orange and red.

"Your blood," Simon said. "Why does she want it?"

Phoenix said nothing.

"Oi." Simon waved the fabric in front of Phoenix's face.

"Blood?" Phoenix said vaguely. "What? Oh... Nan." He took the cloth and pressed it absently against his bleeding arm. "Dunno. I've long suspected she's a vampire. She probably adds it to her tea. How many void-stones do you think I could activate at once?"

"Huh?"

"Alice said they're our best hope," Phoenix said. "Someone in Flamegate mentioned that fifteen could be enough to close the Gate. The most I've used at once is four, but I could probably manage another ten or so. Briefly. In the right circumstances."

Simon groaned and passed a hand over his face. "You said you destroyed them!"

"I also said I could outrun a lightning hog," Phoenix said as he tied the strip of cloth around his arm, pulling one end tight with his teeth. "That was a lie. Though I haven't actually tried. It's on my to-do list." He stood and buried his hands in his pockets, looking thoughtfully towards the evening sky. "Why do I put everyone in danger?"

Simon sensed that Phoenix was on the verge of making one of his more drastic decisions, one that would undoubtedly lead to horrendous trouble for everyone involved.

"Did something happen?" he asked.

"You and Jess, Belinda Loft, Alice and One, the twins..." Phoenix paused. "I think she sells it."

Simon frowned.

"Nan," Phoenix said, plucking a bunch of leaves from a nearby shrub and shredding them compulsively in his hands. "My blood. Sometimes she sells it."

"Because it's powerful?"

"I guess." Phoenix stared at him intently for a moment. "You're making me uncomfortable," he said at last. "I think it's the escalating beard situation going on."

Simon rolled his eyes and stood up.

"It freaks me out," Phoenix said, tossing the mutilated leaves into the grass. "Your usual stubble's fine, but this excessive face-fur is giving me the creeps." He started to walk away but then stopped and spun around.

"More importantly, Wolfe..." He seized Simon's beard, yanking him down so they could see eye-to-eye. "Kicking me out of Yonder like that... How *dare* you?"

Simon blinked in surprise at the sincerity of Phoenix's gaze. The golden flecks swirled slowly around the dark green of Phoenix's eyes, a phenomenon Simon had seen before, and never in correlation with anything good.

"I've spent my entire life being poked and prodded and experimented on by people wanting to test their wild theories and selfish ideas," Phoenix said, lazily keeping Simon still by the wiry hairs of his chin. "I expect as much from Flamegate. I expect as much from my own family. But I had hoped for more from my friends."

Simon swallowed, struggling to think of an appropriate apology for forcing Phoenix back to Earth. A crowd of bickering goblins crashed through some fernery and scrambled towards a dense patch of weeds, biting and screeching and pulling at each other's ears in what appeared to be a brutal battle for a half-eaten toadstool, but neither Simon nor Phoenix spared the creatures a second glance.

"*Next* time you'd like information about me, just ask," Phoenix said. "I'm no stranger to casual acts of exploitation, but a word to the wise, warlock. It takes a lot of effort to keep all this restless energy inside. You never know when I might just..." Phoenix raised his other fist in the air then mimed an epic explosion.

Simon said nothing. The distant chatter of goblins faded into the forest, muffled by the whispers of trees.

Phoenix grinned and released Simon's beard.

"I'm joking," he said, slapping Simon lightly on the face. "Don't look so nervous." He turned and wandered aimlessly in the direction of the woods. "Mother of Shadows, I need a nap."

Simon rubbed absently at his bristly cheek. "I wanted to confirm it with my own eyes."

Phoenix nodded. "Quite understandable," he said, planting himself on the large, lichen-covered rock Simon had been resting upon earlier. He leant forward and massaged his temples for a while before stopping abruptly to look up. "Confirm what exactly?"

"Your Shadow heritage."

"Oh." Phoenix looked away. "Boring."

"Red, you're practically a Shade."

"How are you even surprised?" Phoenix asked. Then he leapt from the rock and stared into the dense wall of trees, Simon moving cautiously to his side.

"Shadow," Simon said, peering into the woods. The final rays of sun dipped unnoticed below the horizon, night falling like a veil across the land.

"Bloodwood has a shield," Phoenix said softly. "It's one of Yonder's strongest magic domes. *Supposed* to deter Shadows."

"I felt it when we arrived," Simon said, straining his ears.

"Shadows don't often stray close to town," Phoenix added, not looking away from Bloodwood Forest. "Even being near the barrier is painful. Sends them mad."

Something smashed through the trees not far ahead, and Simon tensed, squinting into the gloom.

"The Shadows are misbehaving," Phoenix murmured.

Simon raised his hands, bracing himself to release all the magic he could control as deep, guttural snarls filled the darkness, something heavy dragging through the undergrowth at shocking speed.

Phoenix turned to Simon, a manic grin stretched across his freckled face. "This is interesting."

"Don't even think—" Simon started to say, but Phoenix had already bolted into the forest, flinging himself over rocks and logs and darting beneath low-hanging branches as though the gathering darkness was no hindrance at all.

"If a Shadow doesn't kill him, I will," Simon grumbled as he barrelled through the trees after Phoenix's retreating figure, chasing the sounds of growls and crushing vegetation, but he soon lost track of the most impulsive person he'd ever known.

He slowed to a stop and looked around, his eyes adjusting slowly to the limited light. Gnarled, arthritic trees twisted upwards into the mottled canopy far above his head, strips of bark hanging like rags from their knotted branches, empty seedpods rattling like bones in the gentle breeze.

Simon closed his eyes and tried to sense Phoenix's presence. Usually, he was easy to locate with the high level of void-energy pumping through his blood. Here in Bloodwood, however, it was difficult to differentiate between Phoenix and the actual void, which seemed to emanate from all parts of the forest at once.

He caught a vague trace of Phoenix's usual, distinctive force and began in that direction, picking sullenly through undergrowth and vines until a rush of void-energy surged over him like a wave, accompanied by a deep drone that filled him with dread.

Void-stones were the rarest, most sought-after gems in existence, formed over centuries in areas with strong connections to the void. Very few people could activate one and call upon its power without being killed. Even fewer could wield that power for longer than a few seconds and with as much exuberant ease as Phoenix did.

But Simon knew that all power came at a cost.

Fearing the worst, he raced through the woods, both relieved and concerned when the throbbing hum fell silent but the faint trace of Phoenix's presence lingered weakly behind.

He found Phoenix crouched in a small, moonlit clearing before something hairy and round.

"You are the bane of my existence," Simon said, manoeuvring his large body between the trunks of trees. "Those stones won't keep you safe every time, Red. You can't just—" He paused, finally realising that Phoenix was sitting before a battered human head.

Phoenix gestured at the lifeless object. "I made a friend," he said, and Simon huffed with the weary exasperation of a man who had long ago given up trying to change people.

"Where's the Shadow that murdered him?" he asked.

"Scampered with the body." Phoenix rose to his feet and stared down at the grisly artefact. "A shame, really. I wanted a chat."

"With a *Shadow*? They can't talk."

"Why would it leave the head...?" Phoenix wondered, not paying attention to Simon at all. "Is this some kind of message?"

"I don't think Shadows are that sophisticated," Simon said, strolling cautiously across the grass.

Phoenix began pacing the clearing as Simon knelt before the head. It had belonged to a young man with straggly hair and deep-set eyes.

"If they're getting through Bloodwood's shield, it means they're getting stronger," Phoenix said, twigs crackling underfoot. "Or at the very least, more ambitious." He paused beside a tree and sagged against it, staring up at the forest ceiling where large, luminescent butterflies were flittering amongst the star-shaped leaves.

It dawned on Simon that Phoenix rarely ever allowed himself to look this utterly tired, despite the fact that he hadn't technically slept for fifteen years.

"Can I tell you the truth, Wolfe?" Phoenix asked, not looking away from the fluorescent insects overhead. "If I can't do what Alice seems to think I should do, all of us are doomed. Flamegate knows it. The people of Bloodwood know it. Yet they continue to interfere with the void." He pulled his rainbow coat tighter around his shoulders, even though the night was tranquil and warm.

"Void-energy forms the very foundation of both societies," Phoenix said, hugging himself against the non-existent cold. "But those greedy idiots running Flamegate... And the archaic, glory-obsessed traditionalists who call Bloodwood home... They'd all rather die with power than live without it."

Simon started rummaging through his bag in search of something to transport the head.

"The Shadows must realise too," Phoenix added sleepily, his wavering gaze directed at the twinkling circle of night sky above the clearing. "Shadows exist in that unfathomable space between the here-and-there and the then-and-now..." He closed his eyes. "And they know that things are seeping through the cracks... Disappearing. Reappearing. Collapsing." He pressed his palms against his eyelids. "They're using the confusion to expand territory. It's like the Shadow Invasion all over again. We do *not* need another Shadow Invasion." He paused, his hands still against his face. "We should return that head to Bloodwood."

"One step ahead of you," Simon replied, gently lifting the head onto a square of fabric that had been floating around amongst his supplies. He straightened up and studied Phoenix uneasily. "Red, are you alright?"

Phoenix laughed unexpectedly, fell silent, then bubbled into laughter again. He sank down the trunk of the tree then squatted defeatedly in the grass.

"I'm no different from them."

Simon frowned uncertainly.

"Like moths," Phoenix said. "We're drawn to things that destroy us." He cracked a sudden grin. "How do you feel about camping in the woods?"

"Not thrilled..." Simon said, his brows furrowed in mounting concern. "Why?"

"I might have overestimated myself a little in the last few days," Phoenix confessed. "I need rest."

"In a Shadow-infested forest?"

"I should keep away from Bloodwood for a while."

Simon wanted to stay in town and learn more about its history and the void and the mysterious Gate hidden deep in the woods. But Phoenix was hiding something, and anything Phoenix Page refused to talk about was generally more important than any passing interests Simon might have.

The warlock scratched thoughtfully at his beard. "We could leave now," he said. "Ride to Karvil City like we planned. See the inventors. Meet up with Jess."

Phoenix shook his head and stood up. "Tomorrow. There's something I still have to do."

“Meaning?” Simon watched as Phoenix grabbed his bag from beside the head.

“Surprise an old friend,” Phoenix said with a smile. “Though I doubt she’ll want to see me. Aha!” With a triumphant flourish, he pulled half a sandwich from his bag then took a bite. “Get comfortable,” he said, pointing the fluff-covered bread crust in Simon’s direction. “I’ll take first watch.”

“Red,” Simon said, not even sure where to begin with the questions he wanted to ask, but Phoenix spoke over him.

“I spent two days in Yonder crippled by void-stones. Then three days sleeping under a tree while I escaped a supposedly inescapable prison on another planet.”

Simon wasn’t sure of the point Phoenix was hoping to make.

“You’ve been watching out for me that whole time,” Phoenix said, wandering away to the edge of the clearing again. “Get some rest.”

Simon opened his mouth to argue but then gave up before saying anything.

Arguing with Phoenix was a lot like arguing with the weather.

“Fine,” he said gruffly. “Wake me if you feel like passing out.”

THE PRISONER

Phoenix sat at the very top of an old bloodwood tree, crouched upon a branch like a stone gargoyle surveying the forest below, his shoulders hunched and his arms wrapped around his knees. The sun was rising in the distance as a breeze played with his multicoloured coat, fluttering it beneath him like a sheet.

He felt refreshed, buzzing with an energy that made everything around him seem impossibly slow. Even the birds darting about catching insects in the early morning light seemed to do so at a pace that only confirmed their blissfully limited comprehension of the passing, finite nature of Time.

Phoenix envied their ignorance.

'Lucky fools,' he thought, drumming his fingers impatiently against his arms. He stood sharply then spiralled his way down the deep-red trunk of the tree, hopping from branch to branch before dropping painlessly onto the grass below.

Simon lay in the middle of the clearing, snoring like a giant in an echoing cave.

"He never sleeps beyond daybreak," Phoenix said. "I told you he was tired." He glanced expectantly at the disembodied head, perched on the square of fabric that Simon had found. The head stared back, its pale features set in a stiff expression of pain and surprise. The night had done nothing to improve its appearance.

"We should wake him," Phoenix added. "Not that I don't appreciate your company. You've been perfectly affable."

The head said nothing as Phoenix rummaged through his bag, eventually pulling out a small trumpet that had seen better days. Rust nibbled at the keys, and the silver plating was covered in countless scratches and dents.

"You have to admit though," Phoenix said as he polished the trumpet with the end of his sleeve, "our conversations have been somewhat one-sided."

He strolled to where Simon was dozing then leant forward, pressing the mouthpiece to his lips. He took one long, deep breath then blasted the loudest, highest, most brazen note he could master, sending a flock of startled birds erupting from the trees in a cacophony of squawks and shrieks.

Simon's eyes snapped open in alarm and Phoenix played a brief, shrill tune before pocketing the trumpet, grinning from ear to ear.

"I trust you had a pleasant sleep?"

Simon glowered.

Phoenix laughed then tossed Simon's bag against the warlock's chest. "Sorry to wake you, but Roger and I were getting impatient."

Simon sat up and rubbed his eyes. "Who?" he asked groggily.

Phoenix gestured calmly at the head.

"You named it?"

Phoenix nodded as he slung his own bag over his shoulder. "Come on. Things to do. People to see." He lifted the head by the cloth it was resting upon then carried it out of the clearing, confident that Simon would follow begrudgingly behind.

"No incidents overnight then?" Simon asked as they traipsed through the forest.

"Couple of low-level Shadows," Phoenix said offhandedly, knowing the news would bother Simon immensely.

"*What*? You didn't wake me?"

"No need," Phoenix said. "I dealt with them. Mind your step. These mushrooms are explosive. Blast your head clean off your shoulders."

"How did you deal with the Shadows?" Simon demanded, his cumbersome boots tiptoeing around the mushrooms barely visible beneath the moss and fallen leaves. "You could hardly support your own weight yesterday."

Phoenix turned to face him. "Didn't I say?" he said as he walked backwards, the bodiless head staring blindly out from where it rested in the cloth. "I just needed some time. It's been a rough few days, what with escaping prison and being shot and my increasingly unstable relationship with the increasingly unstable void. On top of all that, staying in Bloodwood was harder than I expected it to be." Phoenix stiffened suddenly as his heel came down upon one of the mushrooms. He locked eyes with Simon and they stared at each other, Simon's expression even more horrified than the time he'd found Phoenix about to plunge his tiny, twelve-year-old hand into a deadly hornet's nest.

Phoenix cracked a grin then spun around to walk forwards again. "I was joking about the mushrooms."

Simon growled in frustration. "Well, you seem better at least."

"The great outdoors," Phoenix said. "It does wonders."

A spider the size of a cat scuttled across the path in front of them, but Phoenix ignored it. The woods were much less sinister during the day, alive with small creatures and brightly coloured plants, beams of sunlight streaming through gaps in the trees.

Phoenix would've been content to remain in the woods forever, but Alice had left him with responsibilities, and he'd let too many people down already to allow himself to disappoint her.

"What's the plan?" Simon asked from behind.

"Nothing you'd approve of," Phoenix replied as they neared the edge of the forest. "In short though, stop the universe from destroying itself by eliminating that which destroys it."

"How?" Simon asked. "Shadow numbers increasing... things vanishing into thin air like they'd never even existed... Squabbles over energy... It all traces back to the void. You can't eliminate the void, Red."

"No," Phoenix said as he pushed past a massive branch. "But I can contain it. Maybe." The branch swung behind him and smacked Simon in the face. Simon scrabbled with the scratchy leaves before grabbing the entire branch and snapping it cleanly in half.

"Contain the void?" he asked, refusing to let Phoenix distract him from the conversation.

Phoenix nodded. "Contain it. Control it. Lock it away somewhere safe. I need to get to Karvil. The Guild has—" He paused, Bloodwood's protective shield buzzing ahead.

"They heightened security," Simon noted, apparently sensing that the energised dome enveloping Bloodwood was running at near maximum strength.

"At least the barrier isn't glowing red," Phoenix said. "When they amplify it enough to glow red, *then* you know there's trouble."

They exited the line of trees and found themselves in the rear garden of Phoenix's old house. Phoenix made a beeline for the back door, the anti-Shadow wards already gnawing away at the extra energy he had gained in the woods.

"We'll deliver Roger," he said, stopping by the door. "Visit my friend Fay. Then high-tail it out of here to the city." He glanced behind him, expecting to find Simon by his side, but the warlock was standing in the middle of the yard, his dark eyes fixed upon a small garden-shed that Phoenix had deliberately chosen not to see.

It was nothing extraordinary. A tall, stone structure that could squeeze perhaps six people inside if everyone agreed not to move their arms. A couple of rusty metal barrels sat outside by the decaying wooden door, empty canisters for raw void-energy, an outdated storage system that hadn't been used by void-collectors for many years.

Phoenix swallowed uneasily, wondering what snippets of the past Simon had inadvertently stumbled upon. Judging by the deep frown on the warlock's whiskered face, it was unlikely to involve anything pleasant.

"Listen," Phoenix said, tucking the head securely under his arm. "Whatever you're seeing now is not our concern."

"You never told me," Simon said, still gazing towards the vine-covered little shed, lost in his visions of the past.

Phoenix just knocked on the door and waited.

"I'm really starting to hate this town," Simon said, joining Phoenix by the back of the house.

"They're only doing what they think is right," Phoenix mumbled, resisting the anti-Shadow wards still urging him out of Yonder.

The door opened and Matilda greeted them with her usual unwelcoming frown. Phoenix opened his mouth to make some sarcastic quip about how pleased he was to see her, but exhaustion swept through his body and he lost his grip on the head. He fumbled to catch it but Roger rolled innocently inside like a pumpkin dropped from a cart.

Matilda pursed her lips.

"Delivery," Phoenix said feebly, pointing at the head as he leant against the house. "He was taken near the edge of the woods."

"The shield is unstable..." Matilda murmured, gazing sadly at the sightless face by her feet. "You need to get away from here, Phoenix. This is because of you."

"Because of *me*?!" Phoenix laughed in disbelief, still trying to maintain his hold on Yonder. "How can a Shadow attack be because of—" He stopped and shook his head. "Forget it. Where can I find Fay?"

"Faydelia Leon?" Matilda almost laughed. "You are the last person in the universe that girl wants to see."

"Well the fate of the universe might depend on me seeing her," Phoenix said. "Does she still live by the bookstore?"

Matilda clicked her tongue. "Her family died, Phoenix. Or did you forget?"

Phoenix scratched at his left arm, even though the microchip had only ever existed in his body on Earth, then turned and started walking away.

"Take care of Roger," he muttered, before he fell face-first into the weed-riddled garden, instantly leaving Yonder behind.

~

The first thing Phoenix noticed upon his return to Earth was that he was lying on his side upon a comfortable bed. He was facing a simple, timber set of drawers, upon which rested a glass of water, a digital clock, and the silver spoon that Phoenix had taken to protect himself with in Bee's apartment. It seemed odd that the spoon was there. He was sure that he had thrown it.

Beyond the drawers was an open window and a tantalising patch of clear blue sky. The kind of sky that Phoenix had stared wistfully at from Flamegate Tower. The kind of sky that always seemed just a little too far out of reach.

The second thing Phoenix noticed, which in hindsight perhaps ought to have been the first, was that he couldn't move.

He couldn't blink.

He couldn't breathe.

A string of panicked swearwords rushed through his head, but after a moment of confused terror, he pushed the fear down, forcing himself to think rationally.

This had happened before.

Although the window was open, the lace curtain blowing into the room was eerily still, like a photograph. And although he couldn't move his eyes, he could see that the clock read 2:13. He slowly counted a minute in his head. Then another. Then a third, just to be sure.

The clock hadn't changed.

Phoenix wanted to yell, but there was nothing he could do. He was trapped, gazing out the small window of his mind at that single moment in Time, an involuntary observer of the utterly mundane.

'This will pass,' he tried convincing himself. His connection to the void had exposed him to all sorts of abnormal experiences throughout his life, but there was usually some degree of equilibrium amongst the madness. This little hiccup would be over soon enough.

All Phoenix had to do was wait.

'This will pass.'

Minutes stretched into hours and Phoenix worked desperately to distract himself from the creeping darkness that lurked always, dutifully ignored, at the back of his mind, the insufferable silence threatening to swallow him whole. He thought purposely about nothing of importance, counting down from large numbers, reciting crass poems that he remembered from childhood, imagining alternate versions of reality where he was free to live his own life.

But as the hours dragged on his resolve faded, and

the solitude began playing tricks with his mind. Old fears blossomed into voracious monsters with agendas of their own, and Phoenix crumbled before them, unable to suppress the dark uncertainties that had plagued him as far back as he could remember.

What if nothing he did made a difference? What if he died inside a cage? What if the darkness consumed him?

…

What if he deserved it?

Phoenix panicked alone and Time stood still, indifferent.

STICKS AND STONES

Simon and Matilda gazed quietly at Phoenix for several uninterrupted seconds, neither of them happy about having to engage in one-on-one conversation with the other.

"Well, bye then," Simon said dully, before heaving Phoenix into an undignified fireman's-carry.

"What's your objective in all this?" Matilda asked, still standing by the back door, shaded from the morning sun rising steadily over the town.

Simon gazed back at her from the centre of the overgrown yard, Phoenix draped limply over his shoulder.

"What do you gain for your trouble?" Matilda pressed.

"I know more than anyone that caring for Phoenix is a commitment no one would accept without considerable reward."

"Caring for Phoenix?" Simon repeated with a cynical laugh. "Is that what you call it?" He turned his back on her and started trudging off towards the side of the house.

"He's far from innocent, you know?" Matilda called. Simon stopped then slowly turned around, facing Matilda with the same fierce determinedness that had kept him alive for so long.

"My daughter was a Shade," Matilda said. "I expected her to be an outcast, but this whole town adored her. She was useful. Phoenix just couldn't live up to her name."

"Well, you sure took advantage of his little quirks," Simon said coolly. "You treated him like a farm animal."

Matilda clicked her tongue. "It's not what you think."

"No?" Simon marched back to stand before her. "Because here's what I think." He glared into Matilda's eyes. "I think you defiled the sanctity of life and created a powerful, very unstable being custom designed to cater to your twisted ideals and insatiable greed. I think you've been exploiting Phoenix since the day he was born. And most importantly..." He pointed accusingly at the woman's face. "I think you're more of a monster than Phoenix could ever be, and one day, your sins will come back to haunt you."

Matilda tilted her head, her greying red hair falling over her tightly folded arms. It bothered Simon how similar the old lady was to the boy hanging over his shoulder. Matilda even had the same intensely green eyes, though they lacked the golden flecks that made Phoenix stand out as something so undeniably *other.*

"Quite a speech," Matilda said wryly. "He's rubbed off on you, hasn't he?"

Simon rolled his eyes, shifted Phoenix's weight with a shrug, then left the scowling woman behind.

He paused out the front of Phoenix's old home to stare

thoughtfully up and down the street. People were already slinking out of their houses, refreshing the protective wards around their crumbling properties and preparing to gather energy from around the perilous town.

The two horses were nowhere to be seen, but they'd likely left to eat grass beyond Bloodwood's borders while the nocturnal grassland monsters slept safely underground.

Less than pleased at having to communicate with Phoenix's antisocial horse, Simon attempted to contact the snarky equine anomaly with his mind.

"Gulliver?" he tried. "You nearby?"

"Hills," the horse replied in Simon's head, after a deliberately long pause. "Doing horse things. You wouldn't understand."

"Can you meet me in Bloodwood?" Simon asked, starting to walk towards the town centre where the factory stood, Phoenix still slumped over his shoulder like a sack of potatoes.

"We are frolicking," Gulliver said after another long pause, his voice heavy with unappeasable boredom. "Rolling in the grass. Running in circles for no reason at all. Neighing. I love being a horse."

Simon closed his eyes. "Light grant me patience," he muttered, then he added in his mind, "Is Tugger with you?"

"Tugger is an idiot."

"Listen," Simon said. "I need you both here. We're leaving town. Phoenix is unconscious again."

"That is nothing new."

"Did you know about the void-chamber?" Simon asked, recalling the rundown shed at the back of Phoenix's house.

"He never mentioned one..." Gulliver said. "But I'd guessed."

Simon sighed. "Ten years, and he's still hiding things."

"We all have secrets."

"Gulliver, he's planning something big."

For a long while, the horse remained silent. A young couple with crossbows and spears slung across their backs stared openly at Simon as he strode by, suspicious of the lifeless body draped over his shoulder, concealed by Phoenix's crudely patched hood. Simon offered a curt nod, but they offered no such courtesy in return.

"Fine," Gulliver said. "We'll meet by the west gate."

Simon thanked him then continued on, ambling past flame-blackened homes and the winding labyrinth of metal pipes that transferred void-energy across the land. Eventually, he reached the town centre with its battered buildings all leaning against one another, like weary soldiers in need of sleep.

Occasionally the translucent, near-colourless figures of people from years gone by would flicker before him, enacting silent scenes that had long since faded into the realms of history. A dog chasing its tail. A travelling actor dancing to an unknown song. The pale silhouettes of merchants gesticulating theatrically from behind now-forgotten stalls.

Scattered amongst the scenes of life, however, were fleeting flashes of the dead. Stiff, lifeless bodies strewn in towering mounds along the sides of the road while children wailed, unnoticed, in the middle of the street. Ghostly people dashed by, running from invisible foes, clutching at wounds or screaming soundlessly for help. Despite Phoenix's remarks about the barrier keeping Shadows away, Simon knew that on at least one occasion, Shadows had nearly decimated this town.

Simon ignored the broken glimpses of the past with a patience that had taken a lifetime to develop, concentrating instead on what was present and real.

He stopped outside the factory where raw void-energy was collected and processed for public use. It was the tallest building in town, and the only one not made from timber or stone, its shimmering metal walls forming an enormous, unembellished cube, devoid of windows and as far as Simon could see, doors.

The hundreds of pipes that crisscrossed around

Bloodwood plunged into all exposed sides of the monumental cube, as though it were a mighty beast that had been pierced with arrows or ensnared in thorny vines.

"Beautiful, isn't it?" someone said, sidling alongside Simon to gaze upon the silver monstrosity.

"Grotesque," Simon said, "is more what I thought." He glanced at the stranger by his side, an enormous old man with a scruffy beard not unlike Simon's own, though age had turned it completely grey. He wore boots the size of extravagant cheese platters, and a fur-lined jacket capable of serving as a tent.

A smile crinkled the massive man's eyes. "You're not from around here, are you?"

"Born in a pine-tree forest by the sea, actually," Simon replied.

"I too am but a humble traveller through this town," the man said, leaning heavily against an ornate walking-stick so thick in diameter that it was barely distinguishable from the trunk of a young tree.

"This here is the pride of Bloodwood," the man added, pointing ahead with the finely detailed cane. "The reason they risk their lives every day."

"Their dedication is admirable," Simon said, frowning at the factory again.

"And what might your life be dedicated to?" the old man asked, a hint of sly amusement in his voice. "Traversing the countryside with a tragic runaway like Phoenix Page."

Simon stiffened.

A deep chuckle rumbled from the man's chest.

"He sure must be in trouble if he chose to return to this place," he mused, peeking under Phoenix's hood.

Simon stepped out of reach.

"Don't mean to discomfort you," the old man said with a playful smile. "Only I know that trouble for Phoenix means trouble for everyone... He's the epicentre of the storm."

"*That* we can agree on," Simon said, eyeing the man

suspiciously. "What do you want?"

"To offer my help."

"Why?"

"He's an asset. Besides, I have a soft spot for the little guy." The man indicated toward Phoenix with a large open hand. "May I?"

Simon said nothing.

"Trust me. I'm a professional." The man lunged forward and slammed his hand against Phoenix's back. Simon staggered backwards under the sudden pressure at the exact same moment that Phoenix started yelling, roaring with a wide-eyed intensity that quickly drew the attention of townspeople walking by. Phoenix rolled swiftly from Simon's shoulder, plummeting to the cobblestoned ground before springing up with his hands raised in front of him, ready to defend himself against whatever calamitous situation he had woken to.

"Red?" Simon said cautiously, noticing that Phoenix was well beyond even his usual levels of highly-strung restlessness. His gold-flecked eyes darted furtively around at the gathering crowd before resting at last upon the massive stranger that had struck him across the back.

Phoenix's eyes narrowed. "*You,*" he snarled, walking towards the old man.

"My dear boy," the man said, leaning casually upon his hefty walking-stick. "It's wonderful to see you."

Phoenix kicked the stick out from the man's grip then seized it from the ground before pointing it menacingly at the man's chest.

The man smiled behind his silver beard, unconcerned by the hostility. "Now, before you hurt yourself, allow me to say..."

Phoenix thrust the stick forward and a crackling swirl of golden light twisted down the wooden staff before crashing into the man's chest, blasting him across the road and into the startled crowd. Simon watched in bewilderment as Phoenix whipped the walking-stick up and pointed to where the stranger had skidded on his back to an earth-shuddering stop.

The man erupted into booming laughter and began pushing himself up, but Phoenix thrust the stick forwards and a fresh jet of light surged out and knocked him off his feet.

"A fine display of gratitude!" the man hooted from the ground as Phoenix marched towards him. Simon glanced uneasily at the jittery, rapidly growing crowd, realising that several people had drawn weapons and were looking increasingly impatient to use them.

"Phoenix," Simon said, stepping delicately into the conflict just as Phoenix raised the staff over his head, presumably to bring it plunging into the prone man's chest. "Do you want to rethink the need to steal walking-sticks and assault the elderly? You have an audience."

Phoenix hesitated, his glare fixed upon the man smiling up at him from the pavement. The crowd muttered amongst themselves, Phoenix's name uttered with animosity, passed about like dirty money from one person to the next.

"It does seem childish," the man said. "After everything I've done for y—"

Phoenix roared and brought the stick swinging down, but Simon leapt forward and caught it before it could slam the air out of the old man's lungs.

"Red," Simon hissed under his breath, carefully twisting the staff out from Phoenix's hands, amazed at the amount of energy stored within it. "Seriously, take it easy."

Phoenix blinked as though in a daze.

"Simon," he said after a pause. "I'm running out of time."

Before Simon could respond, a stone came soaring from the direction of the onlooking crowd and smashed into Phoenix's shoulder. Phoenix turned in surprise as a second stone came hurtling towards his head, not quite ducking aside in time to prevent the rocky edges from grazing his cheek in a spray of blood. He glared defiantly at the crowd.

The old man on the ground started chuckling again.

"Time for me to go," he said, easily pushing himself to

his feet.

Phoenix grabbed the enormous stranger by the jacket. "Why are you here?"

The man smiled benignly back. "My dear boy," he said, calmly taking his walking-stick from Simon, who was now well and truly confused as to what was going on, "this was merely a social call."

The man presented Phoenix with a simple business card. "I work in Karvil now," he said. "Come see me if you're ever in need of a real magician."

Something in the way he said 'real' sent a rush of bitterness flooding into Simon's brain, distracting him from the shower of rocks that had been launched anew from the crowd. A bulky stone bounced harmlessly off Simon's back while a smaller cracked audibly against the side of Phoenix's skull.

"*Lay off!*" Simon bellowed at the mass of people, and a fork of blue lightning sputtered involuntarily from his hand.

"Get out of Bloodwood!" a woman yelled, flinging another stone.

More people started shouting.

"Coward!"

"Traitor!"

"We should've killed you, Shade!"

Phoenix took the insults in silence, his hand pressed against the cut on his head while his face grew more and more flushed.

The old man chortled, still offering the business card for Phoenix to take. "Don't waste your time with these idiots."

Phoenix quietly took the card, his bloodied hand staining the fine white paper the moment he touched it.

The man beamed in approval. "Good boy." Then he grabbed both Phoenix and Simon by the shoulder and silence engulfed them, the clamorous crowd vanishing from sight. For a second Simon couldn't breathe, whisked through absolute darkness before finding himself standing in a lush paddock, accompanied by Phoenix, the colossal old man, and several bemused-looking cows.

They had arrived in the rural outskirts of Bloodwood, still within its protective dome, the occasional, lonely farmhouse standing staunchly upon the tops of nearby hills. The more urban area of town remained visible at the end of a long dusty road which wound its way past Bloodwood Forest, meandering through fields of crops, cattle and grass.

"Well, after that generous act of kindness, I shall be taking my leave." The enormous man lowered himself into a bow.

Phoenix scowled. "We don't need your help, Maulbrak."

"Maulbrak?" Simon repeated. "*The* Maulbrak?"

Phoenix just scrunched up the business card and jammed it into the pocket of his coat.

"The magician your grandparents hired to make you stronger?" Simon added.

"The very same," Maulbrak said with a smile. "The greatest magician you'll ever meet."

"I doubt that," Simon said, and the old man smirked.

"Yes, I knew your teacher. Edgar was a good friend."

"You knew him?" Simon asked, distracted by the fact that Phoenix had turned his back on the both of them and was walking determinedly across the paddock towards a distant gate.

"I was sad to hear he vanished," Maulbrak continued. "I had great respect for his work in void-mapping. He was a true innovator."

"He was many things," Simon said, watching Phoenix get further and further away. "Not all of them good."

"He had great plans for you, you know," Maulbrak said. "He'd be disappointed, I think, to see how little you've progressed."

Simon felt the heat travel swiftly to his fingers again. He turned his incredulous gaze upon the old man. "Excuse me?"

"You could be so much more, Simon Wolfe." Maulbrak's

eyes twinkled with a spirit that enjoyed cruelty. “I’ll see you in Karvil.” With that, the old magician disappeared into thin air, leaving Simon bristling with an anger that threatened to manifest into physical energy if he didn’t settle his thoughts quickly enough.

He took a steadying breath then scanned the paddock to see where Phoenix had stalked off to. The idyllic countryside extended beyond the edge of Bloodwood, further than Simon could see. Cows stood dolefully in the sunshine, swishing their tails as tiny birds hopped about in search of worms. In the shade of a nearby tree, a suspiciously peaceful group of goblins stood in a sombre circle, surrounding a large speckled egg, chanting softly in what might have been considered prayer.

Phoenix, however, was nowhere to be seen.

CONFRONTATIONS

Phoenix was having a heart attack.

At least, he thought he was having a heart attack. He wasn't sure whether it was the prolonged exposure to Bloodwood's barrier, the explosive rage at being confronted with Maulbrak, the clash with resentful townspeople, or the overwhelming relief at being able to move his body again... but something had sent his heart into overdrive.

He sat gasping in the long grass upon the top of a hill, leaning against a rotting fencepost with his hand clutching at his chest, as though clawing his heart from his body would somehow make the situation more bearable.

"You need anything?"

Phoenix squinted upwards to find Simon towering above him, blocking out the sun.

He didn't answer, too busy trying to force his frantic breathing under control. Simon stood quietly for a moment then folded his immense body into a sitting position by Phoenix's side.

Phoenix knotted his fingers through his hair. "Talk about something," he muttered.

"Like what?" Simon asked, gazing out at the sea of grass.

Phoenix shook his head. "Anything."

The silence grew heavier, closing in like thick evening fog.

"Are you dying?" Simon asked after a while.

"*Seriously*?" Phoenix laughed, dispelling much of the panic. "Talk about the weather. The turbulent political climate of last century. The absurd mating rituals of endangered mountain trolls. I don't care. Just leave my mortality aside for the moment, alright?"

Simon folded his arms. "You've been different. This past month, especially... but ever since last year—"

"Last year." Phoenix cast the warlock a sideways glance, his heart still kicking sporadically against his ribs. "I died, Wolfe. I was dead. Now I'm not. I'm very lucky. Let's move on."

"I've known you ten years," Simon continued. "We've spent most of that investigating void-tunnels... making money from playing music... helping people understand energy..."

"So?" Phoenix asked, a little more aggressively than intended.

"*I* was the one obsessed with the void," Simon said. "You were only ever interested in enjoying yourself. Suddenly you want to play hero?"

Phoenix held his tongue, barely conscious of his thumb rubbing fierce circles against his forearm in an attempt to soothe the recurring, imaginary itch created by his life outside

Yonder.

"What's going on, Red?"

Phoenix stayed silent, wondering where to begin. Simon deserved the truth. He'd find out soon enough anyway.

"Look," Simon said, leaning back against the fence. "Whatever the problem is... Jess and I will support you. You know that."

Phoenix closed his eyes, raking his arm with relentless nails.

"We're worried about you," Simon said.

"You and Jess are always worried about me," Phoenix mumbled. "You treat me like I'm a fire-breathing kitten allergic to sunlight and plants."

The warlock's laugh was brief. "We want what's best for you."

Phoenix stopped scratching, reluctant to put his fear into words.

"What if that's not possible?" he asked carefully. "What if I'm supposed to suffer for other people to be safe?"

Simon frowned. "Sounds like a load of horse crap to me."

"Truly," Phoenix said, nodding with overzealous approval as he reached out to clasp Simon's hand, "your input is invaluable. Thank you, Simon. Such wisdom." Phoenix stretched out on his stomach. "This conversation no longer interests me." He log-rolled down the gentle slope, slowing to a stop as the ground levelled out not too far below, grass seeds clinging to his coat and shaggy hair.

"Another smoothly executed avoidance manoeuvre," Simon drawled from the crest of the hill.

Phoenix shook his head like a dog fresh from a pond then propped himself up on one elbow. "How long was I unconscious?"

"Today?" Simon said wearily. "Maybe an hour?"

Phoenix's eyebrows shot to the top of his head. "An *hour*? I was trapped for days."

Simon waited for Phoenix to elaborate.

"Stuck in Time. On a bed," Phoenix said. "Present but not present. Staring at a spoon. Why was the spoon there? What happened to Bee? Is Alice alive? *Light*, I'm hungry. Can you toss down my bag?"

Simon gazed at him for a moment then reached unhurriedly for Phoenix's bag against the fence. He slid it down the hill and Phoenix grabbed it, tipping all the contents out onto the grass.

"Has this happened before?" Simon asked, as Phoenix dug through the eclectic assortment of articles in search of food, pushing aside crumpled papers, his trumpet, pocket-sized books, and a rusty keychain holding over a dozen ancient keys.

"Once," Phoenix said. "During one of Flamegate's experiments last year. Spent hours staring into the unkempt nose hairs of Brother Aphelion, the ugly egghead who happened to be checking my vitals at the time."

"You were separate from your body?"

"More like separate from *Time*," Phoenix said, fishing out one of his nan's lint-covered sandwiches from the day before. "Probably a side-effect of the Crush."

"That Earth machine the Shadow Masters built?"

Phoenix nodded. "It acts like a magnet, drawing in huge amounts of energy at a time." He took a bite of the now exceedingly stale bread. "It was the pull of the Crush that drew me into Flamegate in the first place," he added. "The day that hack of a healer, Maulbrak, tried to make me into less of a freak. Unfortunately, I ended up stark naked in a glass cage on a foreign planet, surrounded by surly scientists in cloaks, and I've been awake ever since..." Phoenix chuckled dryly. "It was the start of a very long day. Want some bread? It'll crack your teeth."

Simon declined.

"Originally," Phoenix said, tearing off a chunk of solid crust, "the Crush was designed as a means of collecting raw void-energy from across the universe. It was indiscriminate.

Like tossing a net into the heart of the void and hauling in whatever energy it could retrieve." Phoenix paused, side-tracked by a parade of goblins trudging by, the goblin in front cradling an egg. They disappeared into the long grass, humming a sombre tune that floated away on the breeze.

"*Unfortunately*," Phoenix said, as he popped the last of the bread into his mouth, "Flamegate has fine-tuned the Crush's capabilities."

"It's targeting you specifically?" Simon guessed.

Phoenix hesitated, his cheeks bulging with food. He had always been impressed with how quickly Simon could grasp concepts that would have flummoxed almost anyone else in Yonder.

Phoenix swallowed. "I've been hooked up to that machine so many times, it's no wonder it can lock on to my energy signature."

"You'll go back to that prison?"

"Possibly," Phoenix said. "Probably. Eventually." He started gathering his belongings and returning them to his bag. "But the Crush is unreliable. I can resist it for a while. That's why I was stuck. Different parts of the void pulling me in different directions at the same time, and I froze in the middle somewhere I suppose."

"That Maulbrak..." Simon began.

Phoenix grunted. "He's a slimy, scheming, self-aggrandising, manipulative manifestation of pure evil."

"He helped you," Simon said. "Jolted you back into the regular flow of Time."

"Maulbrak doesn't help people," Phoenix said darkly. "He helps himself." He tensed suddenly and narrowed his eyes, peering above the horizon.

"He took us away from those mad townspeople," Simon added.

"They have every right to be mad," Phoenix mumbled. He pushed himself to his feet, his gaze locked on the distant skyline.

The wind had changed.

"If you're serious about stabilising the void," Simon said, watching Phoenix from atop the low hill, "I'll help. But I need more information. What happened in Bloodwood?"

Phoenix turned from the sweeping view to face Simon as the wind intensified, pushing against him, sucked out towards the horizon like the sea thirstily drawing in a tide.

"I was stupid," Phoenix said, the wind pulling his coat, whistling past his ears. "No one was supposed to die."

An ear-splitting boom cracked behind him. The powerful gust of air blasted against his back, slamming him into the side of the hill and launching him up the slope. Simon crashed backwards into the fence, somehow managing to seize Phoenix by the ankle and pluck him from the air as he went flying overhead. Startled cows stumbled against each other, goblins hurtled through the sky like colourful, unrestrained kites, and an old barn nearby was ripped from its foundations, the wind roaring through with unnatural strength and speed. Simon swung Phoenix into the ground, where he rolled several feet through the grass.

Phoenix clamped his hands against his ears, deafened by the familiar, throbbing hum that accompanied extreme activity from the void as vertigo swept over him, tilting the world forwards, endeavouring to tip him from the ground so he'd tumble into the sky.

The wind settled as quickly as it had intensified, calming into a gentle breeze as though nothing had happened at all. Phoenix lay still, his face pressed against the dirt, his head spinning, vaguely aware that the anti-Shadow barrier surrounding Bloodwood had weakened so dramatically that it was barely even there.

The droning sound rattling Phoenix's skull eventually faded enough for him to realise that a different sound was reverberating through the sky.

A sound that didn't belong in Yonder at all.

His eyes snapped open and he scrambled to his feet,

dashing along the ridgeline to collect Simon, who was furiously trying to disentangle himself from the damaged fence.

"Well," Phoenix said, flipping a fencepost out of the way, "that's one mystery solved."

Simon remained sprawled on his back, gaping wide-eyed at the sky behind Phoenix's head. "What in the name of Light is that?!"

"Just a helicopter." Phoenix glanced behind him, where the monstrous Flamegate machine was racing towards them, its red lights piercing through the clouds. "Nothing to worry about. I *had* wondered where it went..."

"It's coming straight for us."

"They were circling Bee's apartment just a second ago," Phoenix said, grabbing Simon's arm and attempting to heave the heavy warlock off the ground. "They're probably just as surprised as you."

Simon stood uncertainly, but Phoenix grabbed his jacket and pulled him down the hill before he could start asking more questions.

"Best keep out of its way."

"That thing," Simon huffed as they bolted across the fields in the direction of town. "It's from Earth?"

"It's about to crash." Phoenix slowed to a jog and turned around. The helicopter was veering sideways, rushing for the ground. The switch between worlds was a death sentence, helicopter collision or no helicopter collision.

Very few people could pass through the void and survive.

Phoenix sprinted back in the direction he had just come, his eyes locked on the helicopter as it spiralled out of the sky.

"Oi!" Simon called, but Phoenix paid no attention, picking up speed as he ran to where he expected the helicopter to fall, not far from the dirt lane that wound its way past the woods.

The helicopter smashed into the road, its rotors

spraying up gravel and dust and its tail cracking cleanly in half as the whole ill-fated contraption flipped onto its side. The wreck only began to settle as Phoenix approached, stepping cautiously around the debris, his focus on the two people trapped inside.

Phoenix recognised the thin, silver-haired co-pilot as Brother Magma, a member of Flamegate known for his temper and creative torture techniques. The pilot, however, was a stocky young girl Phoenix had never seen before, barely old enough to have completed her training.

Phoenix clambered over the wreck and leant through the shattered front window to assess the damage. Magma was unconscious, bleeding heavily from the side of his head, but the girl looked up with dark, unfocused eyes.

"You're the one... we're looking for." Her muscles twitched from all the void-energy coursing through her veins, ripping apart her cells.

"Yeah," Phoenix muttered, squatting precariously on what was left of the main console. "Phoenix Page. Nice to meet you. What happened? Did you mean to pass through the Gate?"

"Is this Yonder?" the girl asked. "My father... used to tell me stories... about Yonder. I've always dreamt... of seeing it..."

"That's lovely," Phoenix said. "But the void. How did you get through? Did you force open a tunnel?"

"I'm cold..." the girl whispered.

Phoenix gazed at her a moment, his jaw clenched. The helicopter creaked around him, uncomfortable with its final resting place. Eventually he breathed a small sigh, slipped off his coat, then wrapped it around the pilot's shoulders.

"What's your name?"

"Constance..."

"Can you move, Constance?"

The girl didn't answer. Phoenix leant further into the helicopter and unbuckled the pilot's safety belt before pulling her out through the window.

"Who's your dad?" he asked as he slid down the nose of

the helicopter onto the grass.

"Brother Astros," the girl mumbled through the curtain of bushy hair that had fallen across her face.

"One of the less evil ones," Phoenix said gently before Simon arrived, breathing heavily with both bags of luggage on his back and sweat beading across his brows.

"Show her the sky." Phoenix pressed the wounded pilot into Simon's arms. "The trees. Something nicer than this. I'll stay with this one." He jabbed his thumb at Magma, still strapped limply into the co-pilot's seat.

"Uh..." Clearly, Simon had not yet come to terms with the extra-terrestrial machine.

Constance reached up to touch his face. "Dad?"

Simon frowned at her. "Sorry... no."

"Hurry," Phoenix said. "She wants to see Yonder."

Simon hesitated, conflicted between his desire to ask questions and the need to assist the wounded girl. Phoenix raised his eyebrows at him and he nodded.

"Sky," the warlock said gruffly. "Trees. Understood." He took the young pilot and carried her easily up a hill towards the shade of a distant bloodwood tree. A crowd of heavily armed townspeople was assembling along the road, observing from afar as the strange debacle unfolded. Phoenix turned his back to them and clambered over the front of the helicopter once more. The Brother's breathing was shallow and his eyes remained closed, blood leaking down the side of his swollen face.

"You're back."

Phoenix jumped in surprise, cracking his head against the folded metal above him before looking around to see a young woman standing before the cockpit, her ears adorned with gold and her freckled nose pierced with a plain silver ring. Dirty blond hair tumbled to her waist in a knotted nest of dreadlocks and curls, and her clothes were dusty and torn. Despite the decade that had passed, Phoenix recognised her immediately.

"*Fay?*"

"You're the talk of the town again, Phoenix."

"Can't say I'm surprised," Phoenix said, watching her with a strange mixture of fear and nostalgic fascination. "You're not alarmed by this alien air-vehicle that just plummeted from the sky?"

Fay gave a small shrug. "It's not the first time some foreign oddity has burst through the void into this town. The fact that it coincides with your arrival doesn't shock me."

Phoenix cringed. "Fair enough," he mumbled, before ploughing on. "Listen. I'm happy to see you. But now isn't a great time."

"I went to your house."

Phoenix cracked a smile. "As did I. Terrible idea."

"Your nan said you were looking for me."

"I was." Phoenix glanced uneasily behind him, aware that Magma was slipping rapidly closer to nonexistence. A dead Brother would be no use at all. "Fay, can this wait?"

Fay scowled at him with level-eyed concentration; a lion preparing to swipe him from where he sat.

"Why were you looking for me?"

Phoenix sighed in defeat. "I need help."

"*Help*?" Fay's yellow eyes widened. "I lost everything because of you, and you want my *help*? I thought you'd come to apologise!"

"I'm not asking you to forgive me," Phoenix said. "But I *am* trying to make up for what I did. I have a plan. And right now, that plan involves making polite conversation with this gentleman behind me." He turned and leant into the helicopter, pinching Magma sharply on the ear. "Wake up, loser."

"Who is he?" Fay asked stiffly.

"Someone who won't be missed." Phoenix slapped Magma a few times on the cheek, but the Brother didn't open his eyes. Fay moved closer, peering over the battered door for a better look.

"This man is dangerous," she said. "I can feel it."

"You should've met him when he *wasn't* dying." Phoenix flicked the man on the nose.

"Is he here because of you?"

"Partly," Phoenix said, grasping the lean, unconscious Brother by the shoulders. "But he's also a by-product of destructive societal norms born from the greed of two insatiable civilisations. So I can't be entirely to blame." He started shaking Magma back and forth, flicking blood in every direction. "I'm trying to fix things, Fay."

The dying Brother opened his eyes and glared at him. "Five."

Phoenix tensed, his grip tightening upon Magma's shoulders. "Welcome to Yonder," he growled.

Fay shook her head. "This will not end well."

Phoenix ignored her, his focus on the bruised, arrogant face leering up at him from the co-pilot's seat. He wanted to remain calm, but there was a hatred boiling under his skin that was impossible to fully suppress.

"You've brought nothing but trouble, Phoenix." Fay stepped away from the wreckage, her voice heavy. "Just go back to the Shadows where you belong."

Phoenix turned but Fay had already vanished like smoke, her dusty garments left abandoned in the grass below.

"Your girlfriend is gorgeous."

"Shut your trap." Phoenix tapped his fingers restlessly against the cracked display panels, his eyes scanning the grass for movement, but Fay was gone.

"You stole Flamegate's only void-stone."

Phoenix glared at Magma. "Safer with me than with you lot."

"Really?" The Brother chuckled, blood dribbling into the corner of his mouth. "Your body's degrading. You can't change your fate."

"No," Phoenix said wearily. "But maybe I can change the world."

"I doubt that."

"Last year," Phoenix said, "you pulled me back from the dead."

"So?" Magma asked with a crooked grin. "Planning another trip?"

"If I were, could Flamegate pull me back again?"

Magma just smirked.

"Answer me!" Phoenix yelled.

Magma ran his tongue over his swollen lips then spat a mouthful of blood at Phoenix's face.

"Answer my questions," Phoenix said, grasping Magma's arm, "and I'll drag you out to see Yonder one last time."

Magma smiled and closed his eyes. "You think I'm interested in the nostalgia of our primitive home? I won't die here. I'm part of something sacred... Something eternal." He leant back and laughed—the growing, hysterical laughter of a man who no longer cared how unhinged he looked.

A dry, prickling heat descended upon the mangled helicopter and its surroundings as Magma lost himself to his own euphoria. Paint peeled from metal panelling and moisture fizzled from the air. Phoenix slipped hastily from the broken window and backed away, dry grass snapping beneath his feet. The manic laughter stopped abruptly as Magma looked Phoenix in the eyes.

"In Flamegate, we are immortal."

The Brother clicked his red, blistering fingers and everything within the immediate vicinity, including Phoenix and the twisted helicopter, was engulfed by a gigantic ball of fire and smoke.

NOT WITHOUT A FIGHT

Simon had been kneeling by the young pilot with his back to the extraordinary sky-machine when the explosion blasted through the quiet serenity of farmland, followed by the startled shouts of townspeople who had been watching from nearby.

"Red..." The warlock looked over his shoulder at the cloud of smoke billowing from the blazing wreck below the hill. "*Red*!" He started to stand but the pilot clutched his fingers.

"Dad," she whispered, stretched out beneath the lone bloodwood tree.

Simon stared at her in desperation. "The Light will keep you warm." He pulled gently from her feeble grip and turned toward the devastated helicopter again, only to find he needn't have worried.

Phoenix had emerged from the smoke, practically naked and covered in ash. He spotted Simon beneath the tree and limped purposefully up the hill, his arms held protectively over his head as soot and strips of metal rained down from the sky.

Simon glanced back at the girl, dismayed to find she had breathed her last breath. He knelt beside her and delicately eased her out of Phoenix's coat. By the time the coat was free, Phoenix had arrived and was standing, visibly shaken, in the shade.

"Good thing I'm somewhat heat resistant," he said, inspecting his ragged, now-blackened boots, the only clothing to have remained on his person.

"Somewhat?" Simon repeated. "You're only *part*-Shade. How are you unscathed after that?"

"Clothes didn't fare so well," Phoenix said, gesturing unnecessarily at his exposed body. "And a few chunks of metal hit me in the back, so I suspect that'll bruise."

Simon passed Phoenix his coat. "What the hell are you?"

"Enigmatic," Phoenix replied, slipping his arms through the patched, overly long sleeves. "Extraordinary. Sleep-deprived, mostly." He nodded at the pilot, suddenly serious. "Is she still...?"

"No." Simon frowned morosely at the dark-haired girl. "What should we do with her?"

"She'll crumble into dust soon. There's nothing more to be done." Phoenix knotted the belt of his coat around his waist and pulled tight. "Now... where did Fay scamper off to?" He turned to walk away but froze as the urgent rhythm of drums began pounding from the direction of town, echoing off the hills.

As if responding to some divine order that could not be

ignored, the armed townspeople who had been watching the fire fanned out along the road to face the woods, drawing their crossbows and slingshots and an impressive array of other weapons that Simon had never seen. People began streaming out of nearby homesteads—entire, solemn-faced families with heavy, complicated backpacks slung across their shoulders. Further masses of people came filing down the streets from the centre of Bloodwood, many bearing elaborate packs equipped with toggles and canisters and long, silver hoses with spears at the end.

The whole town was its very own powerful, frighteningly efficient army.

"Light forgive me," Phoenix murmured. "It's happening again."

"What is?" Simon asked, watching the scores of newly gathered townspeople position themselves in small groups across the fields, every set of eyes fixed upon the stretch of dark forest.

"Bloodwood's shield was damaged when the helicopter arrived." Phoenix wilted against the tree. "We're about to be attacked."

"By Shadows?"

Phoenix pointed glumly at the woods as the first of the terrible, two-legged creatures slunk out from behind the trees, charcoal-grey skin wrapped tight around its long, skeletal limbs, its golden eyes staring out from a flat, disturbingly humanlike face.

Although Shadows had rarely been seen beyond Bloodwood Forest since the war fifty years ago, the fearsome creatures still sent dread throughout all of Yonder. They could wield pure void-energy as though it were as harmless as water, and slice through limbs with their claws alone.

Simon's Shadow experience was limited, but he knew to avoid injury at all cost. For if your body was broken enough and your mind too feeble to resist, the Shadows could crawl inside. Their lanky solid forms would shift into vaporous, swirling masses of dark grey before plunging down the throats of their victims to seize control.

And just like that, the human would bow to the monster's every command. For a few excruciating moments they'd be a puppet, until the energy tore the body apart from within and the human collapsed in an exhausted heap.

Nobody survived longer than an hour once a Shadow took control.

The Shadow paused in the shade of the tree-line, taller than a house, silent and shrewd as it surveyed the scene with wide, glowing eyes.

Simon clenched his fists as more of the slender, hairless creatures joined the first Shadow by the edge of the woods. "There are hundreds of them."

Phoenix slipped further down the tree, and only then did Simon guess how drained he'd become after the helicopter ordeal.

"Aim!" someone yelled from the crowd nearest to the woods. The command was passed across the expanse of farmland faster than wildfire catching in dry grass.

"Looks like Amelia Kurt climbed her way up the ranks to general," Phoenix said, watching the woman who had issued the first command. "She used to teach Shadow-trapping to all the local kids. Truly terrifying."

"Hold!" the woman bellowed, and Bloodwood stood in wait.

"We're going to have to fight," Simon realised.

Phoenix pressed his hands together. "Yep."

"No void-stones," Simon warned.

Phoenix laughed. "What else am I supposed to do? Sweettalk the life-sucking monsters into surrendering?"

Before Simon could respond, the Shadows charged forward as one, tearing across the stretch of grass with long, bounding strides, their lipless mouths gaping open in hungry snarls.

"Fire!" Amelia roared, and spears soared across the sky,

slamming into the first wave of monsters. Some of the smaller Shadows crumpled to the ground, but most merely wrenched the spears from their bodies and tossed them aside without stopping.

Phoenix threw his hand up and a green, golden-veined void-stone shot into the air and hovered above his head, emitting a deep, monotonous hum.

"Phoenix," Simon began, but an ominous glint of exhilaration danced behind Phoenix's eyes and he bolted off down the hill toward the incoming Shadows, the stone following behind like a faithful pet.

"Look alive, Wolfe!" he called over his shoulder. "Bloodwood needs us!"

Simon grimaced as the towering creatures tore through the small army of townspeople closest to the woods, deadly claws slashing deftly through the human barricade, ripping through bodies and pinning people to the ground. Already, several monsters had poured into injured townspeople that then stumbled to their feet and turned upon their own side. The possessed humans fought without fear, eyes blazing with golden light until the energy consumed them from within and they crumpled, no more than empty husks left to die as the Shadows returned to their physical forms and continued rampaging.

Simon had encountered Shadows before, but never like this. He had seen small Shadows. Weak Shadows. Lonely and confused Shadows who had been spat out by sudden void-tunnels and were still trying to make sense of the world. But this... this endless, unified stampede of horrifying, willowy creatures that could invade your beaten body before throwing you away like a useless rag... this was the nightmare that haunted children and adults alike.

Phoenix threw himself into the fray, a surge of golden energy blasting from his hands and knocking a Shadow off its feet before it could seep into the limp frame of a girl it had been trying to possess.

Simon took one final look at the pilot stretched beneath the tree behind him then raced after Phoenix into the chaos below the hill, his limited magic already crackling along the tattoos of his arms, shifting through the colour spectrum from low-energy-blue to a more destructive red.

It was all a scuffling mess after that—a frantic confusion of dodging and ducking and blistering blasts of red and gold light. Amongst the madness, two wiry Shadows slammed Simon to the ground, their claws hooking into his back while he struggled to gather enough magic to defend himself.

"Hey," Phoenix said from nearby, with far more enjoyment than Simon thought really appropriate under the circumstances. "My warlock. Get your own."

A wave of golden light washed over Simon and both Shadows tumbled off his back and rolled into some townspeople nearby, who promptly thrust spears into the creatures' sides. The Shadows writhed as crackling energy spiralled from their bodies, coiling swiftly around the spears like gold thread spinning itself onto a reel.

Simon looked up to find Phoenix standing beside him, his red hair as wild as the grin on his face, golden flecks swirling around the green of his eyes as two glimmering void-stones circled like vultures above his head.

"*Two*?" Simon said, scrambling to his feet. "You're using *two*?"

"Lecture me later," Phoenix said, smacking a Shadow on the back and launching it several dozen feet toward the forest in a burst of gold light. "For now, let's focus on the problem at hand." He flicked his fingertips against another golden-eyed creature and it soared skywards in a flailing display of long bony limbs, crashing into two Shadows further down the hill.

"They're heading for town," Phoenix said, oblivious to the blood leaking from his nose. "The Shadows, I mean. I *think* they're planning to take out the factory."

"Shadows don't make plans," Simon said, channelling all his unreliable magic into his palms and launching a sputtering ball of red light at a passing Shadow. It tripped but swiftly picked itself up and continued charging for Bloodwood, knocking townspeople aside with blasts of gold identical to those that Phoenix could produce.

"Well, intentional or otherwise," Phoenix said, "they're heading for the centre of town."

He was right. Most Shadows weren't even bothering with the army of townspeople. Instead, they were storming across the grassy slopes toward Bloodwood, and the best the outnumbered townspeople could do was chase after them and hurl attacks from behind.

"They're relentless," Simon said, watching the Shadows storm closer to Bloodwood while still more poured from the woods, indifferent to the barrage of arrows and explosions of light the people were discharging. The fight moved on like a swarm of bees, leaving Simon and Phoenix surrounded by wounded and dead as the boundless horde of Shadows streamed past. "How in the name of Light did we end up in this mess?"

Phoenix shrugged. "You made the mistake of being my friend. Can't do that and not end up, at least once, in a largescale Shadow attack triggered by unstable energy levels and the slow collapse of an overexploited void." Phoenix chuckled to himself. "Remember the good old days when you were supposed to kill me?"

"Simpler times," Simon grumbled, scanning the countryside for some kind of inspiration, anything to suggest that the most legendary town in Yonder was not about to be obliterated by the monsters it had dominated for so many years. "How are we supposed to defend Bloodwood now?"

Phoenix brought his hands together with a smile and before Simon could protest, a third void-stone hovered above Phoenix's head, spinning in slow circles and adding to the low, aggravating hum.

The nearest Shadows slowed in their charge for town, their huge, unblinking eyes turning upon Phoenix. Like curious cats, they circled back, forming a wide ring around Phoenix, Simon, and the three weightless stones.

Simon reached cautiously for a shadow-spear abandoned in the grass, the long bar of sharpened metal pulsing with energy stolen from the Shadows it had impaled. "Phoenix. Stop."

"I have to fix things," Phoenix said, his palms open before him.

"They want those stones," Simon said, watching as the crowd of Shadows grew, the towering creatures jostling against each other as they fought to stand at the front of the shrinking ring.

"Good," Phoenix said.

There were at least fifty of the creatures now, all wide-eyed and silent. Not a single one attacked, although further away, more Shadows continued their assault upon town.

"What are you waiting for?" Phoenix demanded, the golden flecks swirling furiously behind his bloodshot eyes. "You want void-stones? Fight me for them!" He flicked his hand and sent a dozen Shadows flying backwards, not even needing to touch them for the force to propel them away.

The remaining Shadows bared their jagged grey teeth and pounced, showing no interest in Simon at all, who was all but trampled into the ground as they clawed at Phoenix and the spinning stones. Phoenix countered with wave upon wave of blazing light, knocking Shadows back as easily as someone swats away flies, but streaks of white crept steadily to the ends of his hair, the red hues fading as swiftly as Simon's hopes of getting Phoenix out of Bloodwood alive.

He shoved his way through the throng and grabbed Phoenix by the hood of his coat, wrenching him back as claws swiped through the air inches from Phoenix's face. "Let me deal with this."

"Please," Phoenix said. "We both know who's stronger in a fight."

Simon thrust his spear into the ribcage of the closest

Shadow. "They'll tear you apart," he said, as the unlucky creature collapsed at his feet.

"Shadows don't scare me."

"I'm talking about the stones," Simon growled.

"I know what I'm doing." Phoenix threw both hands out to the side and a surge of golden light blasted every Shadow within a twenty-foot radius toppling backwards, limbs cracking as they hit the ground and smashed against each other in a tangle of skeletal arms and legs.

Simon took a deep breath in the relative calm as the gangly grey creatures struggled to their feet. "I know you think they help," he said, his voice deliberately steady as he tightened his grip on the spear. The distant shouts of townspeople merged with the humming void-stones in a disturbing, headache-producing cocktail of menacing sound.

"They anchor you to the world," Simon continued. "They make you feel strong. But, Red..." He searched gropingly for the right words. "You need to listen to me for once. Those stones will kill you."

"Not today." Phoenix drew another stone from between his palms and tossed it into the air, where it joined the low, throbbing drone.

"*Four*?" Simon hissed.

Phoenix raised his hands, ready to blast every Shadow so far into the forest they'd never even find Bloodwood again, but Simon had had enough. He stretched into the furthest depths of his magic, drawing it out to his fingers, bracing himself for the backlash that was sure to follow the recklessness of releasing all his power at once.

"The entire void is on my side," Phoenix said, addressing the Shadows at large. "Leave Bloodwood alone."

The Shadows swarmed forward and Simon let go. A jagged stream of red lightning surged from his palm, burning a chasm through the torso of the nearest Shadow. The energy whipped around, the fiery river of light coursing through each monster until all of them crumpled to the ground, smoke issuing from their tattered chests.

Simon fell heavily to his knees.

Phoenix slowly lowered his hands, frowning at the smouldering grey bodies slumped in the grass.

"Bit excessive, wasn't it?" he said, the four void-stones circling overhead, their deep drone so intense it felt as though the sound was within Simon's own brain. "I wasn't planning to actually kill them... Though I suppose it sends a message... We need to hold them back until Bloodwood can recharge the shield. Can you move?"

Simon raised the spear and pointed it wearily at Phoenix. "Release the stones."

Phoenix didn't budge.

"I'm not going to stand by," Simon said, "simply watching as another person I care about is ruined by powers that should never have been tampered with in the first place."

Phoenix smiled, wind whipping through his now-snowy hair.

"I'm not your brother, Simon." There was a touch of pity in his voice. "I can handle this."

"Release them," Simon said, "before I *make* you."

Phoenix launched a blast of energy at the forest behind him. A tree exploded with a deafening crack, leaving nothing but scattered splinters and shredded foliage. Simon flinched but remained on his knees.

"I need to fix things," Phoenix insisted, embers whirling about his eyes like autumn leaves in a storm. "Any attempt to stop me would be a waste of both our time." He paused and wiped his nose with the back of his sleeve, frowning uncertainly at the blood.

Simon seized his chance and flicked the spear upwards, slashing a thin cut under Phoenix's chin. Before Phoenix could react, Simon grabbed him by the shoulder and slammed him backwards into the ground.

Phoenix barely had time to catch his breath before Simon pushed the spear against the cut. As soon as it touched

Phoenix's blood, a stream of golden light began spiralling from Phoenix's neck along the spear and Phoenix snarled, struggling to twist himself free.

Simon held him down, watching grimly as the light drained from behind Phoenix's bulging eyes.

"Stop!" Phoenix gasped, and Simon sat back, dropping the glowing spear into the grass.

Phoenix coughed and wheezed as he rolled onto his side.

"You're welcome," Simon muttered. "Now recall the damn stones."

Phoenix took a shaky breath then slowly unfurled one of his fists. The stones glided into the palm of his hand, silencing the persistent hum as they disappeared. A fog lifted from Simon's brain in the hush that followed, but Phoenix was still trembling, air hissing through his clenched teeth.

"Humans shouldn't touch those stones, Red."

Phoenix closed his eyes, his muscles finally becoming heavy and limp. "I'm not human."

Simon felt the shift in void-energy as Phoenix slipped away. The red returned to the tangle of hair, and before long Phoenix looked much as he had ten years ago after he'd dashed out of the abandoned farmhouse into the pouring rain, defenceless and small.

Simon gazed out at the mayhem closer to town, bodies of both Shadows and townspeople littered far and wide across the rolling green fields as pockets of fighting raged on.

"You're human enough."

HELP

Phoenix kept his eyes shut, rain battering against a window and pounding the roof. The noise drummed against his brain and made him want to reach up and pull the pillow over his face, but he didn't have energy to move. He just lay on his back with his eyes closed, feeling lost.

The mattress sank gently as someone sat beside him on the bed.

"Idiot." Their voice was deep and warm, and Phoenix knew without looking that it was Alice. "I work hard to keep you alive... Why must you insist on making that task so much more challenging than it needs to be?"

Phoenix opened his eyes and stared at her. She looked as she had in Bee's apartment, cloaked in crimson robes, her dark curls falling past her shoulders and the eerie red mask held loosely in her hand. Morning sun bled through the dreary rain beyond the window, causing long, early-hour shadows to shroud half her face in gloom.

"Alice," Phoenix said, struggling to articulate anything more intelligent than her name. She smiled at him and brushed the hair out of his eyes. His hair was longer than he remembered, but he thought little of it, more interested in making sense of what had been happening on Earth.

"I can't stay," Alice said. "I just wanted to say goodbye before making that time-catch. Someone has to help you all escape from that snake, Sister Nerine."

"Haven't you already done that?"

"No, but I'm sure I'll succeed, because here you are, safe and sound. Despite your stupidity. It's a good thing Simon's around, otherwise who knows what state you'd be in? Are you *trying* to get yourself killed?"

Phoenix started to sit up. "You know Simon?"

Alice pushed against his chest, pinning him down with just a finger. "I know a lot of things, Phoenix. More than you will ever comprehend." She released him then rose from the bed, gliding away to gaze sombrely out the window into the rain.

"What about Bee?" Phoenix asked. "And the grumpy one. Are they safe?"

"Bee and Jayden are sleeping in the room next door," Alice replied. "This is a safehouse set up by an old friend of mine in the Lower Ring."

"The Lower Ring..." Phoenix gazed drowsily at the dusty cobwebs hanging from the ceiling. "A long way from my humble cell."

"Yes, but Flamegate still hunts you. You must keep your head down."

"I'm a veritable agent of chaos, Alice." Phoenix smiled

and closed his eyes again. "Trouble will find me even if I bury my head in the sand."

Alice's wry laugh was barely audible over the rain. "I don't doubt that."

"You'll stay with the Night Order then?" Phoenix winced as he sat, slowly and laboriously, as though struggling to lift an enormous weight. "They'll kill you if they find out you betrayed them. Helping me escape..."

"They won't kill me." Alice shook her head. "I'm too valuable. But they certainly won't trust me at first."

"Then run." Phoenix swung his legs over the side of the bed, planting his feet on a round, vibrantly colourful rug beneath him. The sheer effort made his head spin and he closed his eyes for a minute. "Go to Yonder. Start a new life."

"My role is not over," Alice said. "I belong with Flamegate for now."

"Alice, please." Phoenix scratched anxiously at his arm, the bandage Jayden had provided mysteriously absent. "They'll lock you up again. Torture you. Turn you into a number. A tool. A *thing*. You don't deserve that life."

"And you do?"

"Maybe." Phoenix stood and nearly tipped backwards before catching himself on the side of the bed, feeling as though he hadn't used his muscles in months.

Alice watched silently as he lifted his shirt. The bullet wound had become nothing more than a barely visible blemish amongst a vast collection of earlier scars, etched permanently into his skin like the five dots inked upon his chest. He pulled tentatively at his cyclonic hair and discovered that if he straightened it out, it extended well past the end of his nose.

"How...?" He looked searchingly at Alice, his pulse quickening despite his efforts to remain calm. "How long have I been unconscious?"

Alice breathed a small sigh. "Two whole months."

Phoenix opened his mouth then closed it again upon realising that nothing he said could convey how utterly beyond his control the world felt. He sat on the edge of the mattress and clasped his hands together, his foot tapping restlessly against the rug.

"How long do I have?"

"That depends," Alice said, returning to sit beside him on the bed. "Both your bodies are being pulled toward Flamegate. But the Crush will take longer to claim you if you keep your strength up, so for Light's *sake*, Phoenix, be smart. If you stay away from anti-Shadow wards, and only use void-stones when there is absolute need, you can stay alive long enough to prepare for the alignment of the Gates. By my predictions, that should happen in one month's time."

Phoenix rushed through some calculations in his head, soon confirming the event Alice was referring to.

"I was right," he said, his throat tightening in fear. "You want me to close the Gate during the Light Festival."

"Yes."

"I have to go back."

Alice held his gaze. "I must play my part, and you must play yours."

"I suppose hurling myself into the Gate in Yonder whenever the impulse takes me won't be enough to fix this mess?"

"I'm afraid the only way to ensure the Gates are aligned is to enter from this side. Otherwise we risk the void reopening, and all our efforts would be for nought."

"Any chance I'll survive?" Phoenix asked mildly.

"You should always make an effort to try." Alice gave him a strange look, as though debating whether to say something else. She smiled ruefully instead as the rain continued to beat against the roof.

"Truly overthrowing Flamegate will require some planning," Phoenix said after a pause, reaching for the glass of water and the silver spoon upon the bedside cabinet, desperate for something to fidget with. "I'm only one person. Well, essentially one person. For practical purposes, I'm only one person."

Alice smiled. "You have allies, Phoenix. I've explained what I can to Belinda and Jayden, and they've worked admirably without you. They'll speak to you once you're stable again."

"Stable?" Phoenix dipped the spoon into the glass and started swirling the water.

"Your timelines are unbalanced," Alice said, as Phoenix stared at the whirlpool he was creating. "Partly because the Crush is throwing you off... Partly because you've been weakened by Bloodwood... Mostly because you've been messing around with void-stones so much."

Phoenix put the glass down. "I thought you wanted me to use them?"

"Within *reason*," Alice said, taking his hand. "You need to make the most of your limited time, not squander it on a few Shadows. Flamegate should be your priority. Close the Gate, and you reduce Flamegate to a powerless flock of sheep without their shepherd. Balance will return. Peace will prevail. You'll save the world."

Phoenix smiled. "No pressure, of course."

Alice leant forward and pulled him into a hug, enveloping him in the soft, silken fabric of her cloak. She smelt, strangely, of sea salt and campfires.

"I know you'll do the right thing," she whispered.

The rain hammered furiously against the window as though demanding to be let inside.

"I have to go." Alice squeezed his hand then stepped away from the bed, her fingers still entwined in his as though she were planning to pull him to his feet. "Time may be something akin to infinite, but we have very little of it to waste."

Phoenix frowned, resisting the pull of Yonder trying to sweep him away. "Will I see you again?"

"It's complicated." Alice reluctantly let go of his hand. "You will see me. Many times, actually. Though the next time I see you myself..." She chewed her lip. "You'll see. Time-travel is both a marvel and a curse."

"You're too selfless for your own good."

"Says you." Alice gazed at him, her expression caught somewhere between sadness and tender admiration. "I know you could have escaped Flamegate years ago if you'd just bothered to try."

Phoenix stilled, staring unblinkingly at the colourful rug under his feet. The bright, kaleidoscopic patterns swum before him like reflections on a pond.

"You only stayed because you couldn't bear leaving the twins." Alice crouched in front of him, forcing him to look her in the eyes. "You're not nearly as deplorable as you think you are, Phoenix."

Phoenix swallowed. "The twins are dead."

Alice nodded. "You wouldn't be here otherwise."

"You and I..." Phoenix trailed off as though trying to recall a distant memory. "We're all that's left. One is gone. The twins are gone. For years, I thought you were gone. How many more people have to lose their lives because of these power-obsessed pricks?"

"No one lives forever." Alice stood and smiled the saddest smile in the universe, loaded with secrets too heavy to share. "Use the stones," she said gently. "Fifteen should suffice. Activate them when the Gates align. We can't win this fight with mere optimism, so be prepared. Be careful. Be brave." She placed the red mask over her face then gazed down at him, her expression conveyed only through the intensity of her eyes. "More than anything, you'll have to be brave."

And with that she was gone, vanishing in a flash of light that warmed the room. Phoenix withdrew further onto the bed, leaning his back against the wall. He pressed the pillow up to his face and growled into it until his lungs were empty, then he sank quietly into the blankets and left Earth behind.

~

Phoenix woke to the familiar smell of horse and the bristle of Gulliver's mane against his face.

"Afternoon." Simon's rough voice reached Phoenix from somewhere further back. The warlock had a knack for knowing when Phoenix returned, explaining that immense energy disappeared whenever Phoenix left and returned once he was awake again, leaving Phoenix to wonder what occupied his unconscious body while he was in another world. It was the sort of existential question that would have prevented him from sleeping had sleep actually been possible.

"I'm sorry for treating you like a Shadow earlier, but you had to be stopped."

Phoenix said nothing, allowing himself to be carried along by Gulliver while a cool breeze tickled his skin. He wondered what had happened in Bloodwood and whether the Shadows had been banished yet.

"Exactly how many stones do you possess?" Simon asked.

"Secret," Phoenix mumbled, not opening his eyes.

"*Phoenix*." Phoenix heard the threat in Simon's voice and gave a small sigh.

"Twelve."

A cold silence followed and Phoenix reluctantly opened his eyes. He was facing a rolling stretch of grassy hills, and guessed they were travelling along the old highway out of Bloodwood toward Karvil City. He couldn't see Simon, but he could hear gravel crunching beneath hooves not far behind.

"Unbelievable..." Simon said. "Do you have *any* idea how many times Jess and I have had to save your life?"

Phoenix closed his eyes again, half-hoping Earth would pull him back.

"We've seen you at your worst, Red," Simon continued. "Helped you through problems we couldn't even pretend to understand. And this is the thanks we get?" He drew a weary sigh. "If you can't care about your own life, at least have the decency to care about ours."

The comments hurt.

"Listen!" Phoenix snapped as he sat up. "I never asked—" He stopped midsentence. Simon was teetering forward on his horse, cradling his arm against his chest, his face pallid and his jacket ripped and soaked in blood.

Phoenix's sudden anger melted into guilt. "Well. You look horrendous."

"That's what I get for having to drag an unconscious, senselessly reckless idiot through a battlefield on my own because your wretched horse is too much of a coward to come pick us up," Simon said irritably.

"I fight my battles with measured words and strategically employed silences." Gulliver's voice was as monotonous as ever. "The squabbles between human and Shadow do not appeal to me at all."

"We could have been killed," Simon said.

Gulliver swished his tail, calmly leading the way along the dusty road as the troubles of Bloodwood fell further behind. "Take my refusal to collect you as a compliment. I had complete faith that you would reach my location of safety unharmed."

"I broke my arm, shredded my back, and probably cracked every single one of my ribs," Simon hissed.

"Yes," Gulliver said. "You are an extraordinary disappointment."

Phoenix shook his head. "Simon, I'm sorry."

"Good," Simon muttered. "You should be. Just stop using void-stones."

Phoenix grimaced. "I can't agree to that, Wolfe. I need them."

"Where'd you even find so many?"

"Maulbrak," Phoenix said. "He gives me any void-stone he comes across."

"Since when?"

"Since always."

"First time I heard about it," Simon said, and Phoenix shifted uncomfortably.

"Maulbrak has ways of going unnoticed. Masking his presence… Stopping time… He's a powerful warlock."

"What's his deal with you?" Simon pressed.

Phoenix sighed dramatically. "We have a complicated relationship."

"Meaning?"

"Meaning I do pretty much anything he asks," Phoenix said with a shrug. "Because he offers me void-stones. And I accept them. Because I'm pathetic."

They plodded along without speaking, the road winding leisurely through meadows that would have been charming were it not for the occasional animal carcass or sleepy pair of eyes peering out from hollows in the ground. Phoenix distracted himself by picking grass seeds out of Gulliver's fur until the tense atmosphere became unbearable.

"I'm sensing some anger." He glanced back at the sullen magician, and Simon rolled his eyes.

"You promised you'd destroy those infernal rocks."

"Deadly, multidimensional orbs of densely concentrated raw void-energy capable of modifying the very structure of Time and space? You seriously think I could destroy something like that? I'm flattered."

Simon glared at the deserted road ahead, scowling into his beard.

"Bloodwood," Phoenix said at last, fumbling for some way to break the prickly silence. "What happened?"

"No idea," Simon replied dully. "But seeing as so many Shadows were interested in you and those gems, I figured we should leave Bloodwood to take care of itself." He glanced sharply to the side of the road. Phoenix, too, caught a glimpse of dark fur as a small, indistinguishable animal darted through the grass.

They eased the horses to a standstill and scanned the silent slopes. Sandwiched between two low ridges, the road was an ideal location for ambush by humans and monsters alike.

Phoenix hopped nimbly to his feet, standing on Gulliver's rump for a better view, the wind buffeting his coat in a gentle reminder that he still wasn't wearing any undergarments to replace those that had burnt to ash.

Simon pointed into the swaying grass. "We have company."

They squinted at the hill, watching the grass shift and twitch as something approached the road. Phoenix grinned as the scruffy, yellow-eyed creature came into view.

"That's no cat," Simon said, shrouding his good arm in a crackling cloak of blue lightning. "What do you want, charlatan? Speak, or I will fry you."

"Wait!" Phoenix leapt from Gulliver's back and sprang upon the cat as it tried to dash away. It yowled and scratched at anything it could reach.

"Well, hello," Phoenix said, lifting the cat by the scruff of its neck.

"Who are you?" Simon demanded, lightning arcing into the air. "Why are you—" The lightning fizzled away like a disappointing firecracker and Simon swayed upon his horse, his ashen face twisting in pain.

Phoenix cast a wary look at the magician, contemplating the worrying truth that despite his resilient nature, Simon did not possess an unlimited supply of either magic nor blood.

Phoenix turned his attention to the yowling, spitting little animal again.

"Listen," he said quietly, kneeling by the side of the road. "Hate me all you like. Curse me. Condemn me. That's fine. I get it. But please help my friend."

The cat glared at him, its crooked whiskers twitching in the breeze.

"Fay," Phoenix said. "Please."

The cat twisted out of his grip then transformed smoothly into a naked young woman with freckles and knotted blonde hair that fell as a tangled curtain over her breasts.

"Leon Clan," Simon mumbled. "Great."

Fay gave him a frosty look then faced Phoenix again. "I didn't come to help you. I followed out of curiosity."

Phoenix smiled as he stood up, dusting the gravel from his knees. "There's a saying about that, I think. Curiosity and cats..."

"What you said earlier," Fay said, hands upon hips. "Is it true? Are you really trying to fix things?"

"I can't bring your family back," Phoenix said uncomfortably, and Fay shook her head, her mismatched earrings glinting in the sun.

"The void is unstable. *Can you fix it*?"

"I'm going to try," Phoenix said. "But I need help."

Fay pulled thoughtfully at a long dreadlock falling alongside her face. "And you have a plan?"

"Uh... Kind of."

Fay studied him a moment, twirling her finger through her hair. "Follow me."

"You can't heal him now?" Phoenix asked, as Fay started walking away.

"I've been fighting Shadows all morning," Fay said, making no effort to hide the accusations directed at Phoenix on the matter. "I need my energy for myself."

Phoenix glanced at Simon, wondering how long the warlock could last without medical attention. Karvil City remained hours away.

Fay huffed impatiently. "I live in the marshlands with Gloria and Jack. They'll have everything we need."

"The ward-makers?" Phoenix raised an eyebrow. "They're still alive?"

Fay just leapt forward and transformed gracefully into the long-haired cat before disappearing into the grass.

"Best keep her in sight, Gulliver," Phoenix said, then he took Simon's horse and led it off the road, following the bouncing brush of the cat-tail as it wound through the grass up the hill.

"Is she the one you were looking for?" Simon asked.

"Yeah." Phoenix stepped cautiously around a burrow in the side of the hill, likely home to a creature with lethal claws and too many teeth. "*Hopefully*, she can help me lock away the void."

"Is that actually possible?"

"Let's hope so."

Simon shook his head, too tired to understand. "Can we trust her?"

"That depends," Phoenix replied, "on whether she can trust me."

"Can anyone?"

Phoenix gave a soft laugh. "Apparently not."

They walked on, the cat leading the way, Gulliver trailing after it, and Phoenix guiding Simon's horse while Simon sat stony-faced with his broken arm pressed against his chest. The dusty highway could no longer be seen, and they were soon surrounded by nothing but whispering hills dotted with the occasional, spindly tree.

"I do care," Phoenix said eventually, steering Simon's horse around a ditch. "You and Jess... you're not irrelevant. I wish you could be, sometimes. But you're not."

He paused, wondering whether Simon would say anything.

"Whatever I am," Phoenix added, "it's not by choice. I hate being dependent on people. I don't *want* help." He leapt over a small stream then encouraged Simon's horse to follow. "But I'm not stupid. I realise I need fulltime babysitters just to survive."

He paused again, but Simon merely stared ahead at Gulliver and the cat.

Phoenix scratched at his unruly hair. "Anyway," he said, wishing the silence could be broken by something other than his own desperately upbeat voice. "You should know that I'm grateful, and I'm going to make it up to everyone. And once I've finished closing off the void, you won't have to worry about me again."

He glanced up at the warlock. "Did you want to participate in this conversation, or should I just keep talking until you forget how annoyed with me you are?"

Simon twitched an eyebrow but said nothing.

"Cats," Phoenix said.

Then he spent the next fifteen minutes voicing his thoughts on the feline species and Simon listened with the slightest, begrudging hint of a smile.

OPEN BOOKS

"We make an odd party," Phoenix observed, still talking for the sake of talking because Simon hadn't said anything yet. "A telepathic horse, a human parading as a cat, a sulky magician, and a space-travelling runaway. Perhaps I should compose a song about us."

"Please don't," Simon murmured, wearily massaging his brow. The sun was sinking closer to the horizon, stretching everyone's shadows and cloaking the hills in golden light. If they didn't reach their destination soon, they'd have to contend with grassland monsters emerging from their underground network of dens.

"We're here." Fay leapt from the grass as a young woman with no care at all for the usual social conventions regarding clothes. "Don't touch the water-plants."

"Oh," Phoenix said, forgetting where exactly they had been walking to all this time. Then he remembered that Simon was behind him with severe Shadow injuries and he snapped to his senses again. "Thanks."

Fay smirked before morphing easily into the scruffy cat and stalking away around the base of a large hill. Phoenix slowed as the wetlands came into view. The marsh extended almost as far as the eye could see before eventually meeting a distant backdrop of tall, leafless trees that made eerie silhouettes in the fading light.

A humble cottage was situated, some might argue unwisely, on a small mound of land in the middle of the marsh, built at the end of a long, timber walkway raised like a jetty above the watery ground. The quaint, chaotically assembled home looked in genuine danger of tumbling down, covered in vines that clung to the walls and blanketed the roof, crawling to the top of a tall, crooked chimney that overlooked the sweeping plains of rustling reeds, flowers and mud.

"This place hasn't changed at all." Phoenix grinned as they stepped onto the elevated path, leading Simon's increasingly reluctant horse while Gulliver dawdled behind, the planks bending beneath everyone's weight.

They soon reached the small island in the centre of the marsh and stepped through the rotting picket fence that surrounded it. Phoenix shuddered as they passed the Shadow-wards around the perimeter—weaker than the shield around Bloodwood, but still strong enough to make him want to spend as little time there as necessary.

"You look uncomfortable," Simon said as he climbed gingerly from his horse, apparently in too much pain to notice the energy in the air.

"I'm in the disturbing presence of your beard," Phoenix mumbled, then he smiled and nodded at the front porch of the house where dream-catchers, wind-chimes and talismans rattled and clanged in the breeze. "Shall we?"

Fay trotted ahead and slipped effortlessly through a cat-flap installed in the door while Phoenix helped Simon up the steps, leaving the horses to trample the soggy yard.

"Wow," Simon said, once he and Phoenix stepped inside.

Phoenix looked around at the dark, disorganised room and immediately felt himself relax, despite the menacing sign over the fireplace reading, 'Defend Until Death', written in what appeared to be blood.

Cluttered shelves packed with curious items and aging books lined every inch of available space upon the walls, while the floor was occupied by even more stacks of dusty texts and a variety of intricate, metallic contraptions that ticked and tocked and occasionally made dinging sounds or spat out colourful puffs of fire and smoke.

"Impressive," Simon remarked, bending down to inspect one of the spindly metal machines. "The processes involved in this are adapted from ancient systems of magic that haven't been seen since before the age of the Shadow Masters. And these *books*," he added, staring almost reverently at a mound of books beside the nearest machine. "These are priceless. Works of the great First Magicians, the founders of magic theory as it exists today. This one here—"

Fay coughed from the doorway into a narrow corridor that twisted out of sight. She had wrapped a motheaten blanket around her shoulders and clipped it together with a broach fashioned from the gold-plated skull of a rat.

"Sorry to interrupt," she said, "but I believe we came here for a reason."

Phoenix chuckled and pushed Simon towards the door. "Come on, Grandpa."

Fay led them into a small, high-ceilinged room, empty aside from a large cushioned chair behind a desk which was draped with silken cloth and loaded with crystals, stones and beads. Phoenix wrinkled his nose against the assault of potent perfumes that mingled with the smell of mildew and dust.

"So tell me," Fay said, waving her hand and bidding two new seats from thin air, summoned from the storage room that Phoenix knew was under the house. "How do you plan to fix the void?"

"Uh-uh." Phoenix shook his head. "Warlock first, questions later."

"I don't see why he can't heal himself," Fay complained, spinning one of the chairs around to face Simon. "A warlock who can't heal himself is a disgrace to the vocation. Sit."

Simon wearily did as he was told.

Phoenix grinned and sat down in the opposite chair. "The delicate art of healing isn't really his thing."

"I suppose his magic's better suited to unrestricted expulsions of destructive force," Fay guessed coldly, extending Simon's tattooed arm and deftly pulling his jacket off, peeling it away from the cuts covering his shoulders and back. "You're from the Wolfe Clan, no? The Wolves are all the same. Rough. Hot-headed. Crude."

Simon winced as Fay began tapping her fingers along the visibly bent bone in his forearm. "And you?" he said through a clenched jaw. "Leon Clan, obviously."

"Did my cat form give it away?" Fay purred, inspecting the wounds on his back. "You know... For a Wolfe, you have less magic than I would expect."

"The problem," Simon said, "is that I have too much."

Phoenix stood again and went to look out the window behind the desk, already uncomfortable with sitting still.

"A cage?" Fay asked softly. "Fascinating. Who constructed it?"

"Edgar." Simon gazed blankly at the untidy, charm-laden desk. "My teacher."

"Edgar's an excellent name," Phoenix said, watching the horses through the window as they uprooted all the edible-looking plants. "You don't meet enough Edgars these days."

"Edgar Wolfe?" Fay said. "He's a legend."

"I was too young to control the magic given to me," Simon said. "He just wanted me to be safe."

Fay took a glass bottle from the desk and dripped some of its foul-smelling contents onto Simon's back. His skin sizzled audibly and he sucked air through his teeth, the wounds mending themselves with incredible speed.

"How much of your power can you use?" Fay asked, while Phoenix paced restlessly around the tiny room, occasionally stopping by the desk to inspect one of the unusual items scattered there.

"Edgar gave me more access each year," Simon replied, "but he disappeared before he could open the cage completely." He shrugged a shoulder. "It's like trying to move water using only my hands..."

"Interesting." Fay pressed a sickly-scented cloth over his arm. "Think about something pleasant."

Simon frowned apprehensively. "Huh?"

There was a flash of light followed by a spine-tingling crunch. Simon roared and doubled forward onto his knees.

"Gentle with him, Fay," Phoenix said. "Low pain tolerance, that one. Not nearly as tough as he looks."

"This predicament of yours," Fay said, not even acknowledging that Phoenix had spoken. "Nobody from the Wolfe Clan will help?"

Simon straightened his back, eyes watering. "No."

"You Wolves really are as hard-hearted as the stories claim." Fay patted his head. "You're healed, by the way."

"My gratitude," Simon mumbled. He folded his jacket in his lap then looked at the young, tangle-haired magician with a frown. "I'm the only Wolfe left."

Phoenix paused at the back of the room where he'd been tracing cracks in the timber doorframe. The warlock rarely spoke about this.

"I heard rumours," Fay said after a moment's thought. "A rogue Shadow attacked all the clan members. Drained the magic from their bodies."

Simon gazed out the window where Gulliver was making churlish faces behind the glass, poking his tongue out and showing all his ugly teeth.

"I know the clans have their differences," Fay said, "but I never wanted to believe that one of the three great magic institutions had gone extinct."

"Maybe it was for the best," Simon said. He scratched pensively at his beard. "Are there many Leons around here?"

Fay looked darkly at Phoenix and he promptly bowed his head.

"Not anymore," she said, while Phoenix stared purposely at his toes. "The Shadow attack ten years ago took a heavy toll. The Leon Clan is scattered, but we persevere."

Simon nodded slowly. "Good."

"I'm the only Leon in these parts," Fay added. "I became an apprentice of the ward-makers when Bloodwood was rebuilding itself, since I had nowhere else to go. They're Bear Clan, but they accept me as their own."

"Where *are* Gloria and Jack?" Phoenix asked, poking his head out the door to peer down the corridor.

"Probably in town," Fay replied waspishly, "dealing with the latest wave of destruction you caused."

"I had a lot less to do with it this time," Phoenix said. "Though I don't suppose that's much comfort."

Fay scoffed. "If you truly have a way to stabilise the void, explain. In as *few* words as possible, how will you fix this?"

"Gate," Phoenix said.

Simon rested his head in his hand and closed his eyes.

"What?" Annoyance flashed across Fay's face, and Phoenix laughed.

"The Gate," he said. "The original Flamegate from which my least favourite organisation draws its name. The Gate where the greatest volume of energy passes every day. The Gate that connects Earth and Yonder and provides direct access to the void. I'm going to close it. Permanently. So it can never be opened again."

Fay bristled at the proposal. "You want to prevent access to the void? Have you lost your mind?"

"Ah." Phoenix smiled and waved a finger at her. "Now *that* is a debate for another day." He dropped into the remaining seat and reclined back with one leg crossed comfortably across the other while his foot bobbed rapidly up and down against the floor.

Fay scowled and grabbed hold of his knee, forcing it down so he would stop tapping his foot. "You said you would *fix* the void, not eliminate it!"

"*Fay*, my fine feline friend." Phoenix took her hand in both his own. "The void is dangerous. That machine that fell from the sky? That's just the beginning. Reality will dissolve. *Everything* will disappear. Every city. Every town. Every infinitesimal particle of everything that ever existed will vanish like it never even was."

"You can't just *lock away* the void," Fay snapped, withdrawing her hand. "Yes, things are a little unpredictable now. But that only means we have more reason to collect energy and sell it to all of Yonder. People need protection. Demand for void-energy has never been this high."

Exasperated, Phoenix sprang to his feet and started pacing again. "What happened to you?" he asked desperately. "You've turned into one of them."

"Them?"

"*Them!*" Phoenix waved at the door in the general direction of Bloodwood. "Selfish, short-sighted, *stupid* people, so caught up in their pursuit of void-energy that they become oblivious to everything else. Completely incorrigible idiots. That blind arrogance is exactly what will get us all killed."

"I hope you're listening to yourself," Simon muttered, his head still cradled in one hand.

Phoenix folded his arms. "Look, I get that you're angry at me. But using void-stones for the purpose of helping humanity and exploiting void-energy for personal gain are two incredibly different things." He turned to Fay again. "We're facing total obliteration from the very thing we thought would protect us. It's not worth—"

"The void's power saved *you*, didn't it?" Fay cut in. "You'd still be sick and weak if it weren't for that magician who filled you with the grace of the void." The rest of Phoenix's rant caught in his throat and he froze.

"You think I was *saved*?" he asked eventually. Then he sank into the spare chair again, the Shadow-wards surrounding the cottage giving him a headache.

"Fine," Fay said, while Phoenix pressed his fingers against his eyelids. "Let's say sealing the void really is the only solution to all this... Do you honestly imagine you can lock away something as immense as that?"

"Would I risk something this outrageous if I didn't believe it might work?"

Fay gave a humourless laugh. "Your assessment of risk has always been questionable." She started rummaging through a drawer under the desk, eventually retrieving a large jar of green liquid and three polished timber cups. She filled each cup then passed one to Phoenix, one to Simon, and kept the last for herself. "A speciality from the Forest of Lost Things. Drink." She raised her cup in a silent toast then took a sip while Simon sniffed cautiously at the contents of his beverage. Phoenix lifted his cup to his mouth.

"*Red,* wait."

Phoenix paused to look at Simon, who was watching Fay with narrowed eyes. She smiled back without a word.

"Nothing," Simon muttered at last. "My mistake. It's safe." He held his cup to his mouth but then put it down once Phoenix had taken several gulps of his own.

Phoenix couldn't help but feel the two magicians were watching him a little too keenly.

"Now then," Fay said, leaning forward with a guileful smile. "The Shadow attack on Bloodwood today. Was that your idea?"

"Nope." Phoenix took another swig of his drink. It was

surprisingly refreshing for something that had been kept in a dark drawer within a dusty jar. "I've spent ten years regretting what I did to that town. Why would I want to do it again?"

"Well why did you do it in the first place?" Fay asked softly. "Ten years ago."

"Come on, Fay. You know as well as I do." Phoenix leant back in the seat. "Bloodwood was out of control. I was nine, and I already knew people were going too far. We had more energy than we needed, but still we took from the void. We slaughtered Shadow after Shadow after Shadow. Tortured them for the void-energy they contained. Poisoned them with anti-Shadow wards... And folks wonder why they keep attacking us." Phoenix took another sip then giggled. "I just remembered I'm not wearing any pants." He leant forward, grinning from ear to ear. "Fay, I was caught in a fire but I'm perfectly fine. That's strange, right? Do you think I'm strange? Simon thinks I'm strange. And rightly so, I suppose... I've been awake for fifteen years. The day just goes on and on and on and..."

Fay scowled. "Ten years ago."

The smile slid from Phoenix's face. "You could justify anything for the sake of Bloodwood's prosperity. People kept dying and killing and ignoring their humanity in this ongoing, senseless quest for power." Phoenix gulped down more of his drink. "What are your thoughts on Simon's beard?"

"Hundreds died," Fay said, ignoring his question. "Because of you."

Phoenix held her gaze. "I was young and stupid. I thought I could make it all stop."

"So you betrayed Bloodwood on the basis of morality?" Scepticism played across Fay's face. "You thought working with *Shadows* was a morally sound thing to do?"

Phoenix laughed a little louder than intended. "I was a kid. I wasn't making honourable decisions about the ethics of energy consumption. I did what I did because I was afraid."

"Afraid?" Fay's eyes widened incredulously. "We're all

afraid, Phoenix. Everyone in Bloodwood has to grow up cold and fierce. We're taught that dying for our town is an honour. I've been fighting Shadows since the day I could walk. Do you think I *enjoy* it? What gave you the right to be so... so..."

"Weak?" Phoenix offered.

Fay gave a stiff nod.

A creeping unease lurked at the back of Phoenix's mind, but it was strangely easy to ignore.

He drained the last of his cup.

"You never saw it," he said, reaching across the table and taking the jar of emerald-coloured drink. "You never saw what the adults made me do. And I was too scared to tell you." He poured himself another. "Scared that you'd be afraid. Scared that you'd look at me the same way Nan did. Scared that you'd tell everyone."

"Tell everyone what?" Fay squinted at him suspiciously.

"My role in securing Bloodwood's claim to the void." Phoenix took a sip, a pleasant haze supressing the worry behind his thoughts. "If more people knew, maybe I'd be forced to do more things. This body tolerates an awful lot, but I'm not sure I could've survived much more."

"I don't follow," Fay said, while Simon remained broodingly quiet, his hands clenched in his lap.

"Nan said I was special," Phoenix said, stretching out on the chair. He hadn't felt this relaxed in as long as he could remember, and wondered why Simon was frowning so gravely, or why Fay's eyes were so tense. "I did things no one else would do."

Simon glared at the floor as though it offended him.

"Things?" Fay pressed.

Phoenix gulped down the rest of his drink then stood and looked distractedly around the room.

"I can withstand dangerous levels of raw void-energy," he said, placing his empty mug upon the cluttered desk. "So I was given tasks." He rested one knee on the desk then glanced at Fay. She made no move to stop him, so he crawled onto the desk and stood upon the centre of it.

"Sometimes I'd go into the woods and ambush Shadows on my own," he said, eyeing the rafters supporting the roof. "Or I'd enter contaminated Shadow-traps to retrieve dead Shadows and humans alike." He folded his arms, staring up at the timber beams. "If I jump, do you think I can pull myself up there? I suddenly feel the need to experience this room from a loftier vantage point."

"Let me catch up," Fay said. "You were given dangerous tasks because you were special?"

"Nan said it was my duty to live for Bloodwood's sake," Phoenix replied, reaching for the jar of green drink. "She said I was helping people. And for a long time… I believed her." He drank straight from the jar. "My blood's more adaptable than a Shadow's. Contains the same energy, but it's easier to use. Nan was always taking my blood." He paused, eyes fixed on the rafters above. "To be honest, that wasn't so bad. It was the void-chamber behind my house that I felt least comfortable about."

"Void-chamber," Fay repeated, shooting Simon a bewildered look.

"They rip energy away from anything trapped inside," Simon muttered.

"I know what a void-chamber is," Fay snapped. "I'm just surprised. They're illegal now, after fears they might be used to create more Shades."

"Illegal or not," Phoenix said, "Teddy and Nan have one. I stayed there for hours on end whenever Bloodwood wanted an energy boost." He set the jar down. "I don't suppose either of you have had void-energy extracted from your bodies before, but it's not exactly a pleasant experience. If you can imagine being twisted inside out, though, chained to a rock at the bottom of the sea, you're close enough." Phoenix launched himself into the air and managed to snatch one of the beams above the desk. He clambered onto it then sat with his tatty coat wrapped around him and his feet hanging far above the floor. “Why am I telling you this? This feels like something I didn’t want to discuss.”

“You wanted a way out…” Fay said carefully. “But did you really have to go so far as to side with Shadows?”

Phoenix gazed despondently at the ends of his long sleeves. “Bloodwood planned to send me into the heart of the void. They wanted me to go through the Gate, *in person*, and plant a collection of wires that would channel energy back into town.” He gave half a smile. “I’m just the son of a Shade. Nobody cared that I might lose my mind or my skin would melt off. Nan told everyone I could survive. But I was nine. And I panicked.”

“What happened?” Fay asked softly.

Phoenix swallowed. “I ran away into the woods. I let the Shadows in. I surrendered my body. And… well…” He faltered, the comforting haze no longer shrouding him in a blissful daze of disengagement. “You know the rest.”

“Yeah,” Fay said. “Five-hundred Shadows swarmed upon our little town in the single greatest tragedy since the Shadow War. Hundreds of innocent people—” She stopped midsentence. “Are you crying?”

Phoenix wiped his hand over his eyes then inspected his fingers as though he’d never seen them before.

Simon sighed and stood up. “He was a messed-up kid who made a mistake. Now are you going to help us close the void, or not?”

“I’m not myself today,” Phoenix said to his knees.

Fay chewed her lip, sizing Simon up. “What do you want from me?”

“Red seems to think you have something of value.”

Phoenix brushed his tears away and straightened up.

“A charming personality and superior knowledge on void behaviour.” He leapt from the beam. “Also… another void-stone.”

Simon exhaled slowly. “Of course.”

“Why the void-stone?” Fay asked.

"I'll do exactly what I refused to do ten years ago," Phoenix answered, dusting down his coat. "But this time it'll be on my terms. And I won't run away."

"You *should* run away," Simon said. "You can't endure the heart of the void. Not again."

"Again?" Fay repeated.

"Last year," Phoenix said with a wry smile. "It was quite a journey."

"It killed you!" Simon said, his already imposing voice rising in frustration.

"Briefly," Phoenix mumbled. "I came back."

Fay stared at him in thoughtful silence, her eyes impossible to read.

Simon massaged his brow. "What's your plan, Red? Waltz through the Gate into the heart of the void, somehow activate those gems... then what?"

"Fifteen stones could reverse the pull of energy away from the worlds," Phoenix explained with a shrug. "Instead of spilling outwards, the energy should concentrate around the stones, and all the holes would close."

Simon scowled. "*That's* your bright idea?"

"Do you have any brighter ones?"

"You'll be trapped inside."

Phoenix grimaced. "Potentially."

"What am I supposed to tell Jess?" Simon demanded. "Sorry, dear, I know you wanted me to keep an eye on our friend, but he's decided to throw himself into the depths of empty space again. You won't survive."

Phoenix smiled. "Don't be so dramatic. Maybe that spare body of mine will be useful for a change. In any case, let's be real, Wolfe. My little life weighed against the safety of the entire universe? Bit of a no-brainer, isn't it?"

A sharp snap interrupted and they turned to see Fay closing the latch of a small, ornate box.

"Faydelia Leon," she said, extending her hand to Phoenix, "at your service."

Phoenix gazed at the green, gold-streaked gem offered in her palm.

"I'll help," Fay said. "Just... do whatever's necessary to stabilise the void."

Phoenix reached out then cautiously took the stone. It hummed briefly before vanishing from sight.

"You'll want to sit down," Fay added. "That drink I gave you will put you to sleep soon."

"A truth tonic?" Phoenix guessed, but Fay shook her head.

"You can still lie. It just reduces your inhibitions so you're less likely to hide the truth."

"Not a particularly nice thing to offer guests," Phoenix said as he lowered himself into a chair. "I'll admit it was refreshing, but there's a bitter aftertaste of personal violation that I could probably do without. Have you ever tried an ice-fruit smoothie from that market in Central Karvil? Those drinks are like a slap in the face on a cold winter's day. I bought one two years ago and—" Phoenix's head fell forward onto his chest and within a second he was breathing peacefully with his eyes closed.

Fay settled back in her chair. "I like him better when he's sleeping, don't you?"

OUT OF PLACE

Phoenix woke with the young, bespectacled veterinarian looming over him, his hand under Phoenix's shirt as he pressed a cold stethoscope against his chest.

"This is intimate," Phoenix said.

Jayden pulled his hand away in surprise. "You're awake."

"As a rule, yes," Phoenix said, sitting up against the wall at the end of the bed.

"Welcome back," Bee said from the doorway, looking cheery and relaxed despite the dark circles under her eyes. "We knew you'd wake up today."

Jayden nodded. "Alice told us your timelines would

settle."

"You've been napping since we fled the Middle Ring," Bee said, burying her hands in the pockets of the scrappy denim jacket she'd been wearing when she and Phoenix first met. "We haven't spoken in two months."

"Yeah..." Phoenix said. "One month until—*OW, man!*" Jayden jabbed Phoenix's arm with a needle probably designed for elephants and injected him with something excruciatingly cold. "What was that for?"

"Now that your timelines have stabilised," Jayden said, putting the syringe into a plastic container, "this'll give your body strength."

"And help you fight the pull of the Crush," Bee said as she walked across the large, rainbow rug into the sunny bedroom to sit at the end of the bed. "We can't have you zapping off to prison yet. We have work to do."

"A *lot* of work," Jayden said, slinking his arm around Bee's shoulder as he sat by her side. "We need to get organised before the Light Festival begins."

"We need everything ready before the Gates align," Bee added.

"Apparently," Jayden said, "that'll be your best shot at locking away all this energy that's throwing the universe out of whack."

"And Flamegate will be powerless against the uprising against them," Bee said with a smug smile.

Phoenix studied them in quiet befuddlement.

"You seem very well informed," he said at last.

Bee nodded. "Alice sat down with us not long after we brought you here. She told us everything."

"I doubt it," Phoenix said. "Alice never tells anyone everything."

"If we're being honest," Jayden said, pushing golden locks behind his ears with annoyingly casual nonchalance, "I'm not happy about any of this. But your time-travelling friend is very persuasive."

Bee pulled a chocolate cookie from her pocket and Phoenix suddenly realised how hungry he was.

"Did she mention the risks?" he asked, addressing the cookie rather than Bee, hoping the snack might levitate magically towards him, helpless against the gravity of his gaze.

"Resisting Flamegate has never been a safe decision," Bee said, unwrapping the delicacy from its packaging. "But this world is our home. And we're going to fight for it." She took a bite, hesitated, then passed him the rest. "How do you feel?"

"Overwhelmed, most days," Phoenix said, gladly taking the food. "Thanks." He wolfed it down then rolled from the bed and bounced to the window, wrenching the lace curtains to the side.

"The Lower Ring! Are the rumours true? Is everyone riddled with the plague? Is the pollution unbearable? Are there mutant cats?" Phoenix pushed the window open and stretched the whole top half of his body outside. A shabby garden grew two floors below, overgrown with old, knotted trees and flourishing weeds. Teetering, once-impressive brick terraces stretched along both sides of a silent, potholed street, beyond which loomed a crumbling, multilevel shopping complex besieged by dirt, vines, and the ravaging effects of time.

"Well, it's a wasteland," he said, watching a clunky, three-wheeled robot poking through a pile of scrap metal by the side of the street. "But not nearly as horrifying as I expected it to be."

"The location isn't that bad," Jayden said. "It's the locals you need to be worried about. Thieves and murderers. Ruthless drug-lords. Almost every second person has some horrible disease. And don't even get me started on the wildlife. Even the herbivores are eating each other."

Phoenix continued to gaze outside, his eyes drawn at last to the great wall in the distance that encircled the mountain beyond, the mountain's peak crowned with the monumental nightmare of Flamegate Tower, home to the miserable prison.

"You two are immunised against the plague, I hope?"

"Yeah," Bee said from the bed. "Our parents helped repair the wall around the Upper Ring in return for healthcare when we were kids."

"Our families met during construction," Jayden added. "It was the start of something beautiful."

"They formed their own rebel group," Bee said.

"I was talking more about our relationship," Jayden muttered. "We met as kids at one of the meetings."

Phoenix turned away from the window. "A rebel group?"

"They met every week to discuss Flamegate's slow takeover of the world," Bee explained. "It started out harmlessly enough. Just a few concerned families, worried about future generations."

"But it grew into something a little more organised," Jayden said. "Much more of a threat."

"They were forced to disband," Bee said, as Phoenix hopped up to sit on the windowsill. "Members started vanishing one by one. Killed or thrown into prison. Made examples of. Forced to sign contracts in return for their lives, or the safety of people they loved."

"My parents were tortured when I was eight," Jayden said. "They were never the same after that."

"Where are they now?" Phoenix asked.

Jayden frowned, as though deciding whether Phoenix was worthy of an honest response. Eventually he shrugged slightly and shook his head. "They've moved on."

"Phoenix," Bee said. "Alice told us about that prison. She told us about the things you both went through."

Phoenix swallowed uneasily and started scratching at the pale scars on his forearm. "Your point?"

"All of us want to see Flamegate brought to its knees," Bee said. "All of us have reasons to fight. But none of us can do it on our own."

"And I suppose with a little courage, determination, and good old-fashioned teamwork, the three of us united can defeat a global network of evil?" Phoenix asked with forced optimism, still scratching his arm.

Bee smiled. "More than just three of us." She stood from the bed and Jayden followed her lead. "Come on. We'll show you around."

The safehouse, it transpired, was huge. The small bedroom where Phoenix had been sleeping neighboured a much more commodious room shared by both Jayden and Bee, and a bathroom, more luxurious than anything Phoenix had ever seen, was located at the end of the thickly carpeted hall.

Following the industrious hum of busy conversation and bustling movement, they descended an elegant staircase into an enormous living/kitchen/dining area, the open-floor space adorned with countless lamps and a chaotic mess of antique furniture.

The chatter died the instant Phoenix came into view as dozens of people stopped what they were doing to stare. A group huddled on couches around a small coffee table peered curiously at him over a mix of sleek, high-tech tablet-screens and bulky, outdated computers. Another team gathered around a large dining-table looked up from the messy collection of charts they had been browsing, while a band of silent, military-type individuals lurking by a cluttered workbench in the far corner of the room took a break from cleaning their assorted weapons to watch Phoenix with narrowed eyes.

"Phoenix is awake," Bee announced to the crowd.

"About time," someone muttered.

"Welcome to the Alliance, kid." A man wearing a bright pink apron tossed a bread-roll from the kitchen and Phoenix snatched it from the air.

"Thanks," he said, shooting a questioning look at Jayden and Bee.

Bee seemed to be enjoying herself. "There's more," she said. "Let's start downstairs."

Phoenix and Jayden followed her down the staircase into a spacious, dimly lit basement that made Phoenix uncomfortable even before his feet reached the cold concrete floor.

"The infirmary," Bee said, gesturing at the rows of narrow, old-fashioned army bunks lining the windowless walls. All twenty or so beds were occupied with resting figures, most covered in bandages, many with broken limbs suspended from frames built overhead.

"Who are they all?" Phoenix asked, trying not to compare the hushed, suffocating basement to anything he'd encountered within Flamegate.

"At least half are fulltime rebels," Bee said, lowering her voice as a nurse changed the bandages of a patient at the far end of the dark room. "They were injured stealing information from the Upper Ring two days ago. Narrow escape from an ancient sentinel robot just inside the wall. If it were any of the newer models they mightn't have been so lucky."

"And the others?"

"Mixed bag," Bee said. "We help whoever we can."

"You Phoenix?" The girl having her bandages changed spoke from the other end of the room. She had fluffy dark hair and acne scars all across her narrow face. She couldn't have been older than fifteen.

"Depends who's asking," Phoenix said, strolling over with Bee and Jayden in tow. "But you seem friendly enough."

The girl grinned as the nurse taped fresh bandages around her arm. "People say you're destined for great things."

"I'm destined for several things, I imagine," Phoenix said. "Not sure how great any of it will be. Hungry?"

The girl's smile grew as she took the bread-roll Phoenix was offering. Phoenix noticed five small dots tattooed upon the back of her hand, like the five on dice, encircled in a dark ring of flame.

"It's a ranking method, right?" Phoenix asked, pointing at the tattoo. Behind him, Bee and Jayden had struck up a conversation with the nurse about securing medical supplies from someone named 'Little Mick'.

"A reward, really," said the girl, flexing her hand and admiring the mark. "Adapted from a Flamegate branding system. Everyone starts with a five. But there are four other achievements to earn." She pulled her sleeve up, revealing a square of four dots inked upon her upper arm, again surrounded by a dark ring of flame. "Only other badge I have is the four. You get this if you dedicate over a year to the rebellion."

Phoenix ran his hand over the back of his neck.

"Numbers given as a reward," he said, pretending not to notice the masked, silent figures appearing along all the walls, afraid that looking at them might make them real. Afraid they'd come to life just to watch as he was forced into a rigid chair, strapped into position, plugged into the Crush as the sound of music and festival crowds played through speakers in the ceiling.

All at once, reality dropped away, Phoenix's heart pounding in his ears as the basement walls blurred around him, moving closer, swallowing the clueless patients resting in their beds. Phoenix knew what would happen next. The music would stop and the countdown would begin, the crowd outside chanting in unison, their voices blasting through the speakers as they shouted down from ten to one while Phoenix cursed and struggled until zero arrived. Then someone would flick the damn switch and Phoenix would disappear into the darkness, his broken howls lost amid the cheers of the oblivious crowd.

Phoenix closed his eyes.

One last time.

"You going to black out again?" The girl's question interrupted Phoenix's terror, loosening its spell.

He blinked, reluctant to check whether the masked watchmen were still prowling around the edges of the room.

"Not sure." He folded his arms and stared at the ceiling. "How long have you been rebelling against Flamegate?"

"All my life." The girl seemed unaware of the faceless

figures bleeding through the shadows in the walls, so Phoenix forced himself to look and the visions melted into the gloom, the infirmary returning to the peaceful space it was designed to be.

He breathed a small sigh.

"Dangerous business," he noted, and the fluffy-haired girl laughed.

"Just being alive is dangerous business these days." She took a bite of the bread-roll then pointed at Phoenix's chest. "Ink a fire-ring around that and you could be one of us, you know. A proper rebel."

Phoenix shifted his shirt a little to hide the dots over his collarbone.

"Maybe." He needed fresh air. "What's your name?"

"Bailey." The girl beamed. "Remember me. I'll be making history."

"Take care of yourself, Bailey." Phoenix clapped the girl on the shoulder. "Best be on my way. Overslept by two months this morning. Lots to catch up on." He left the girl to recover from her injuries then stepped casually into the conversation taking place behind him, entering what appeared to be a debate about bananas.

"Those fruit hampers were meant for Ms Tippet." The nurse was a small, angry-looking man with a spectacular handlebar-moustache. "There were well-wishes from her students written on handmade cards *clearly* visible beside the oranges. Ms Tippet is very ill, and her students are very concerned. He can't just take gifts intended for someone else."

"Well, it is his house," Jayden said with half a shrug. "I guess he feels entitled."

"He's unbearable." The nurse scowled, pulling irritably at his brittle moustache. "Sulking about. Never saying anything unless it's condescending or rude."

"He's been pretty generous," Bee reasoned. "And he's patient with all the kids."

The nurse scoffed. "His bad attitude will bring down

morale, and in times like these, Belinda, that's almost as dangerous as the plague."

"He's as miserable as the plague," Jayden said.

"I'll have a word with him," Bee promised.

"These are not my clothes," Phoenix announced, feeling an intense need to interrupt.

Bee, Jayden, and the moustached nurse all turned to face him.

"No," Jayden said after a pause. "They're mine. Well, they were."

Bee folded her arms and frowned at the simple blue shirt Phoenix was wearing over striped pyjama trousers. "Your prison uniform wasn't worth keeping."

"Besides," Jayden said, with the hint of a smirk, "you wet the bed the first day we arrived."'

Phoenix groaned and pulled a fistful of hair over his eyes.

"Probably a survival tactic," Bee said. "Your body's way of preparing to sleep for such a long time."

"What *are* you, exactly?" Jayden asked.

"I'm..." Phoenix trailed off, annoyed with himself for not knowing how to answer.

"You were basically hibernating for two months," Jayden added, the smirk now less of a hint and more a blatant display of superiority. "Definitely the strangest person I've met. And I've met a lot of freaks lately."

Phoenix flashed a grin at the grouchy nurse.

"Phoenix the Incontinent," he said. "Lovely to meet you." He turned sharply back to Bee. "Can we go?" he asked. "Upstairs. Outside. Anywhere, really, with a higher window-to-wall ratio."

Bee glanced at the arm Phoenix was raking his fingers over, then nodded. "Yeah. Sure."

The ground floor was bustling with activity when they returned. Eyes tracked Phoenix's every move as he followed Jayden and Bee past the packed couches and crowded tables into the kitchen near the front of the house.

"I'd love to make you kids a meal, but I'm a little strapped for time." The man in the pink apron busied himself loading large plastic containers onto a trolley. "Soup Kitchen Day at the Campus Ruins. Help yourself to anything in the fridge, though."

"Thanks, Vince." Bee helped lift the heavy containers from the counter onto the trolley. "Stay safe."

"Will do." The smiling cook backed the trolley out of the kitchen then wheeled the food away, through the front door and out of the house.

"This place..." Phoenix began, and a smile stretched across Bee's face.

"Impressive, right?"

"Everyone here is working against Flamegate?" Phoenix jumped up to sit on the kitchen counter by the sink then grabbed an empty mug from a drying-rack.

Jayden sighed. "You mean is everyone here mad? Yeah."

"Didn't I say you'd make a difference, Phoenix?" Bee said, as Phoenix filled his mug from the tap. "Alice promised everyone that with your help, Flamegate can be beaten. You brought all these people together. Spurred them to act."

Phoenix paused and cast her a wary look, water gushing from the faucet and overflowing from his mug down the drain. "Did Alice tell *everyone* I would close the Gate? That seems presumptuous. What if I fail?"

"A time-travelling superhero believes you'll succeed," Bee said. "What could go wrong?"

Phoenix grimaced as he stopped the tap. "Time-travel requires you to navigate a complex web of possible outcomes and potential opportunities," he said. "It can take a whole lifetime just to figure out the path of a single tree, and people are infinitely more complicated than plants." He took a sip of water, his heels tapping idly against the cupboard beneath him. "Alice has dedicated her life to understanding future events so that she can destroy Flamegate," he continued. "*All* of us are pieces in that ambitious plan. And yes, Alice may have set us on the right path and removed a few obstacles, but things can still go wrong. Nothing is guaranteed."

"You're already making excuses and you haven't even done anything yet," Jayden muttered.

Bee rolled her eyes. "Give it a rest, Jay."

"Someone's got to hold him accountable," Jayden said. "Seeing as we've all invested so much into this."

Before Bee could respond, a pale, middle-aged man with spikey white hair and shockingly blue eyes swept into the kitchen and began rummaging through one of the drawers. He seized a knife then spun around to face them.

"Flamegate," he said hoarsely, waving the blade in their direction to accentuate his point, "have laser-cannons now."

He trudged out to the dining-room and collected a wad of papers from the table by stabbing the knife through the entire pile and taking it away on a skewer.

"Who's that?" Phoenix asked as the man stomped out of the house, the front door slamming behind him.

"Ghost," Jayden replied dully. "He basically controls the entire underground tunnel system running beneath Veracity."

"He's very anti-Flamegate," Bee said, watching through the kitchen window as Ghost slouched across the messy yard and out onto the rundown suburban street.

"Bee loves him," Jayden said. "Sometimes we don't see him for weeks. But he drifts in every now and then, to make suggestions or kill someone."

Bee tsk-ed. "He's not that barbaric... Though I recommend not getting on his nerves."

Phoenix nodded slowly, trying to take it all in. "Duly noted." He glanced across the room beyond the kitchen. A group of muscular individuals were staring at him as they cleaned their hoard of weapons, having moved on from their stash of pistols to a seemingly endless rifle-supply.

Phoenix offered the group a friendly toast with his mug of water, having no desire to be shot at again. A man and woman with equally severe crewcuts waved him over with excited, childish enthusiasm that seemed excessive for anybody with access to guns.

Phoenix slipped from the counter and strolled over to join the pair at the long table. Their smiles widened as he approached with Jayden and Bee.

"Nice to have you with us," the woman grinned with a punch to Phoenix's arm. Her practical haircut was accompanied by a black bandanna covered in cartoonish smiley-faces, while several bright, plastic studs decorated her ears.

"Heard all about you, of course," the man added. "Glad to have you onboard." Both he and the woman were standing with their feet shoulder-width apart, as though ready to drop into squat exercises at any given moment. Their dark-clothed companions stood a few paces away, tending to the weapons strewn across the workbench without a word.

"Ruby," the woman said, hand upon her chest.

"Rex," the man said, mirroring the woman's gesture. "Like the dinosaur."

"Phoenix," Phoenix said, with another tip of his mug. "Like the bird. Though I get the feeling everyone in Veracity already knows who I am."

"Alice says you can take out Flamegate's power." Ruby raised her eyebrows at him. "Quite a claim."

Phoenix laughed before he could stop himself. "I agree." He passed his mug to Jayden, who took it unquestioningly and then frowned as though unsure how annoyed he was supposed to be.

Phoenix picked up one of the rifles and started turning it over in his hands, surprised by how light it was.

"You mean to say it's a lie?" Rex folded his arms, his massive biceps bulging through his sleeves.

Phoenix paused, one eyeball pressed against the metal as he peered down the barrel into the dark. Bee reached over and cautiously pointed the rifle toward the ceiling while Jayden and the two gun-slinging fitness fanatics watched Phoenix expectantly.

"Listen," Phoenix said. "Once I access the Gate, I'll be able to close it." He placed the weapon on the table again. "Probably." He retrieved his mug from Jayden, took a sip, then nodded down the long table. "Where'd all these firearms come from, anyway?"

"Ruby and I work for VIRP," Rex said, a touch of pride in his voice as he gazed at the half-a-dozen or so people busying themselves at the bench.

Phoenix frowned. "Virp?"

"The Veracity Inter-Ring Police Force," Ruby explained.

"So... Virpf."

"The F is silent." Rex placed a hand on Ruby's shoulder. "The point is... anyone true to the Force is ready to make a stand. We've been corrupted by Flamegate for far too long."

Phoenix rubbed his eyes. "This all escalated more than I thought it would while I was asleep..." He finished his drink then strolled back into the kitchen with Bee, Jayden, Ruby and Rex following behind like ducklings trailing after their mother.

"Usurping Flamegate once their precious power is removed won't be a problem," Ruby said, while Phoenix refilled his mug at the sink. "Not with all these resources on our side."

"The Alliance has connections in surprisingly high places," Rex said.

"And predictably low ones," Jayden added under his breath as Phoenix hopped up to sit on the counter again.

"It's an interesting fusion, really." Ruby slipped her arm into the nook of Rex's elbow.

"Rubes and I are getting married after the Light Festival." Rex nudged the woman with his shoulder. "If everything goes to plan, that is. The entire Alliance will be invited."

"Thieves, spies, police-officers, time-travellers..." Ruby listed people off on her fingers. "Cyber-criminals, professors, assassins, experts in all kinds of weird fields..."

"Gonna be one epic party," Rex said with a grin.

"Parties aside," Phoenix said, tapping his fingers along the rim of his mug, "Flamegate is a global empire with not only advanced technology, but also advanced magic. What we really need are a couple of decent magicians."

"This may come as a surprise to you," Jayden said, "but magic is hard to come by around here."

"This may come as a surprise to you," Phoenix countered, "but magic has existed on Earth since the dawn of Time. You just don't understand how it works yet."

Jayden opened his mouth to argue but Bee slipped her hand into his and he fell quiet, glaring sullenly at the floor.

"Well, even without magic, Phoenix," Ruby said, "we'll support you closing that Gate."

"The Gate itself is your responsibility, and yours alone." A thin, elderly man garbed in a long, black dressing-robe walked slowly past the crowded tables into the kitchen, his wispy white hair falling past his waist. "Failure would be catastrophic. Try keep that in mind. It would be such a shame for you to let us down."

A hush fell across the house. Even the people huddled on couches with laptops and tablets resting upon their knees stopped tapping at their keyboards to look up at the prowling figure.

"The Great Awakening," the old man said, slouching against the fridge, his pale, grey eyes scrutinising Phoenix as though he were a science experiment that could explode at any second. "I hope you're feeling adequately refreshed. We're all expecting such wonderful things from you. Have you secured the necessary number of void-stones required for your ever-so-heroic task?"

Phoenix placed his mug carefully on the bench, suddenly on guard. A strange, invisible energy flickered through the air, unnoticed by anyone else.

"I need two more stones." Phoenix frowned. "Nice to meet you, by the way. Phoenix Page." He leant forward, offering his hand for the stranger to shake.

The old man remained where he was. "I know who you are. Your reputation precedes you."

"And you would be...?" Phoenix asked, withdrawing his rejected hand.

"I'm something of an evil mastermind," the man said. "An instigator of progress. A facilitator of deadly deeds." He gestured serenely at the people scattered about the house. "This entire organisation exists because of me. Even this home, where you have slept peacefully for two months contributing nothing of value, belongs to me."

"This safehouse is yours?" Phoenix frowned, ignoring the slight against his character. "You're the friend Alice was talking about?"

The man gave a humourless smile. "My name is Edgar."

"Edgar?" Phoenix couldn't prevent the grin that grew instantly upon his face. "You don't meet enough Edgars these days. Simon's teacher was called Edgar."

The old man swallowed, a muscle twitching above his brow. "Teacher," he said, stepping away from the fridge, "is not a title I will ever be deserving of." He turned to leave. "Consider the niceties out of the way. Don't talk to me unless you absolutely must."

"What a ray of sunshine," Phoenix muttered, as the old man shuffled off towards a closed door, presumably leading to his private bedroom where he could sit in haughty silence away from everyone else.

It was then that a large figure appeared from nowhere with a brief, near-deafening *whoosh*, like an airlock being opened on a plane. The visitor paused, crouching on the tiles in the middle of the kitchen, his face hidden behind a tangled curtain of dark hair.

Bee leapt into action and grabbed a meat-knife from the drying-rack. Jayden threw is hands above his head. Someone by the paper-laden table seized a stapler to defend themselves with while half-a-dozen guns clicked into place and aimed at the new arrival crouching on the floor.

Phoenix, however, had frozen upon the counter. He recognised those broad shoulders and black leather clothes, and as the young man drew himself up to his full and impressive height, Phoenix also recognised the dark eyes, bushy eyebrows, and the rugged beard that had grown even fuller than when Phoenix had seen it last.

"I'm late," Simon said, pulling his hair back into a messy ponytail. "I can feel it. The time-markers are off." His jacket wriggled on its own and he pulled down the zipper, allowing a large, brightly coloured parrot to pop its head out and peer curiously about the room.

"This used to be easy," Simon continued, tickling the parrot under its beak. "Bee, I might have to leave Phoenix to you for a while. Don't let him—" He looked up and saw Phoenix staring at him in confused shock.

"Red!" Simon said in surprise. "You're okay."

Phoenix pulled himself together. "*I'm* okay? Of course I'm okay. Why wouldn't I be okay? More importantly, what... on Earth... How... *What*?"

"Phoenix..." Bee said warily, still pointing the knife at their unexpected guest. "Who is this guy?"

The warlock frowned uncertainly, his eyes roving from one guarded face to the next, eventually meeting the near-mortified stare of Edgar standing by the door at the back of the room.

The parrot gave a loud squawk and Simon tickled it under its beak again. "We seem to have made a mistake, Mittens," he murmured.

"Simon," Phoenix began, but the warlock cut him off.

"Until next time," he said, and with that he and the parrot vanished before everyone's eyes, accompanied once more by a loud *whoosh*. His departure shifted the void-energy Phoenix was connected to, and before he could even think about moving someplace more comfortable, he had slipped to the side, his head crashing into the kitchen sink as a deep, thunderous rumble filled his ears.

He was vaguely aware of Ruby and Rex moving forward to catch him, Bee frowning, and Edgar standing motionless by the bedroom door before the entire scene went black and the pull of Yonder swept him away.

HISTORY REPEATS

Phoenix woke with a start, feeling oddly as though he had been shot from a cannon, the fierce rumble in his ears fading gradually into a less unbearable hum. Simon sat in the chair opposite while Fay stood to the side, gazing uncertainly at Phoenix as she leant against the cluttered desk.

They were still in the sickly perfumed room, night having fallen completely upon the marshland outside, disk-powered lamps illuminating the cosy space indoors.

"Simon," Phoenix said, his fingers clenched tightly around the armrests of the chair he had been slumped upon. He straightened up and fixed the warlock with an incredulous stare. "You're here."

Simon raised his eyebrows. "I might not agree with your idiotic plan to throw yourself into the heart of the void, but I'm not about to walk off and leave you to make more stupid decisions on your own."

"There were only five of us," Phoenix added, leaning forward with panicked urgency. "You can't be in that world. You can't."

"What are you talking about?"

"Hardly any of us could control it," Phoenix said, as Fay twisted a dreadlock around her finger, watching Phoenix with yellow, unblinking eyes. "Alice had the most skill in void-manipulation, and they abused her until there was nothing more they could take. They forced her to join them. If you can manipulate the void at will, you're even more valuable to Flamegate than I am. If they realise you can switch worlds..."

"Phoenix, I can't switch worlds."

"*Yet*," Phoenix said, gripping Simon by the shoulders. "You can't switch worlds *yet*." Filled with restless energy, Phoenix stood, searching desperately for something to do. "This is bad, Wolfe. I don't know how to stop this."

Gulliver's lacklustre voice broke through Phoenix's feverish mind. "Visitor," the horse said. "Possibly hostile."

Phoenix, Simon and Fay shared a cautionary look as three solid knocks thumped upon the front door of the cottage.

"We should be careful," Simon said, but before he'd even finished the sentence, Phoenix had dashed out of the room. Whoever was behind the door began knocking again, each blow sending shudders to the floor. Phoenix threw the door open and stepped nimbly out of the way as a massive grey fist came swinging down from above his head.

The massive grey fist belonged to a beefy arm, which in turn was attached to an enormous torso, upon which wobbled the bald, beady-eyed head of a troll.

Phoenix grinned as the stony face glared down at him.

"We're a long way from any troll settlement," he said, "so

I assume you serve the smarmy High Chief of Yonder. To what do we owe the pleasant surprise?"

"Pack your bags." The troll, clothed in what appeared to be a sack covered in wormholes, twigs, and living moss, shouldered her way inside then stood hunched in the entrance, the back of her hairless grey head pressed against the ceiling. "This is an evacuation. Who else lives here?"

"I do." Fay stalked out from behind the corridor where she'd been observing with Simon, who remained watching cagily from the dark.

Her ears had grown pointed and furred, pulled back like those of an angry cat.

"What's going on?" she asked.

The troll's surly expression remained unchanged as she peered down at Fay. "This is the home of the ward-makers. You must accompany me to Karvil. The High Chief has ordered all citizens seek shelter in the capital and prepare for war."

One of Fay's ears twitched, but she showed no other indication of being concerned.

"War?"

"Yes, war." The troll rolled her small eyes impatiently. "With Shadows. They can no longer be held within the confines of their usual territory. Bloodwood has fallen. The land is unsafe. You have been ordered to leave."

Phoenix raised his hand. "Sorry. Can we just go back a little? Bloodwood has *fallen*?"

The troll scowled at him. "Your questions can wait. Pack your bags. We must leave."

"And what if we choose to stay?" Fay asked.

The troll's nostrils flared. "I am Fidelity Ethel Thunderstone, leader of the Grey Guard, personally appointed by the High Chief as head of the Tracking Division, Master of Rocks, and unparalleled winner of the International Skull-Crushing Championship in Helburfort five years in a row. Not *once* have I failed the High Chief." She pointed a large, stubby finger at Fay's face. "This house is marked as belonging to powerful, war-capable wielders of magic. I insist that you accompany me to Karvil. If you do not come willingly, I shall take you by force."

"Unlikely," Phoenix said, side-stepping between Fay and the troll's finger. "I have direct access to pure void-energy, *this* young lady could steal your eyeballs long before you even realised you were blind, my friend lurking in the corridor could blast you off your feet without any effort at all, and my horse doesn't look like much, but he truly is an obstinate jerk. You are outrageously outnumbered. When you say *fallen*... Are there survivors? What happened?"

The troll took a step towards him and lowered her face to his, so close that Phoenix could see the thin scars running over her nose and along her cheeks. "Are you refusing a command from the High Chief?"

"I might show more interest if you weren't refusing to answer my questions," Phoenix said.

They sized each other up for a moment, the troll eventually seeming to decide, as many others had done before her, that arguing with Phoenix was a tedious waste of energy.

"The power factory," she said, straightening her back again, "has been destroyed. Shadows have swarmed upon what is left of the town. The only survivors are the few that were smart enough to retreat."

"Oh." Phoenix was silent for a short while. "I see." He walked away to one of the bookshelves then stared at the lines of dusty books, trying to get his thoughts in order while the spindly magic-machines cluttering the room hummed and clicked around him.

"The Bloodwood power factory supports all of Yonder..." Fay said. "It generates the anti-Shadow defences of every city and town. If there's to be another Shadow War and Bloodwood is already out of action..."

"Yes," the troll snapped. "Yonder is in danger. But there's enough reserve energy in Karvil to protect it longer than anywhere else, *which is why you must join the war preparations*. I will not ask nicely again."

"*How*?" Phoenix said, turning from the books to stare imploringly at the troll. "How could Bloodwood have fallen? They have the strongest warriors. The best anti-Shadow weapons available. They're too experienced. There must be some mistake."

"Bloodwood was betrayed." The troll reached into her moss-covered tunic then pulled out a large parchment scroll. "We are looking for this human."

She unfurled the paper and Phoenix frowned at the red-haired, green-eyed, freckled young man in the illustration staring back at him beneath the WANTED title. His own name was written across the bottom-right quadrant of the page above a brief list of features, including his height, approximate age of nineteen, and even a mention of his tendency to fidget with his hands and scratch his arm.

"How hard are you looking exactly?" Phoenix asked.

"More importantly," Fay said, "how big is the reward?"

Phoenix shot her a look and she flashed her pointed teeth in a playful smile.

"The palace has been searching for this felon for many months," the troll said. "His capture is of utmost importance to the High Chief's plans. Anyone who hands him over would receive a very generous reward."

"Fidelity Ethel Thunderstone." Phoenix folded his arms and grinned at her. "Are you *honestly* head of the Tracking Division?"

"Wait." Simon strolled into the light and whipped the parchment from the troll's hand. "I recognise this mop-head."

Phoenix raised an eyebrow. "Really?"

"Why's the High Chief want him?" Simon asked, tapping the poster. He'd left his jacket in the corridor, exposing the elaborate tattoos covering his arms. "What's his crime?"

The troll frowned at Simon indecisively, her beady eyes squinting at the lines of dark ink. "Cavorting with Shadows," she said after a pause. "Sabotage of Bloodwood's defence systems. Terrorism against Yonder. It's believed he has several void-stones, and lured Shadows to Bloodwood."

"Is there evidence?" Simon asked.

The troll shrugged. "Endless witness-reports."

"Fidelity." Phoenix spoke from beside the bookshelf where he was inspecting the spines of every book. "How good is a troll's eyesight? Never mind, I found the encyclopaedia. Carry on."

"You said the High Chief has been looking for this guy for months though," Simon said, and the troll sighed.

"He has a long history of anarchist behaviour," she explained. "He's the illegal cross between a pure human and a Shade, capable of interacting with raw void-energy, and able to house Shadows within his body without being killed."

"That so?" Simon glanced at Phoenix to find him sitting in the far corner with his nose buried in a book.

The troll nodded her bald head. "Ten years ago, he let himself be possessed by three Shadows at once. He used that power and turned upon his own town." She snatched the parchment from Simon and rolled it into a scroll again. "He slaughtered countless Bloodwood citizens," she added darkly, "then took down the shield, allowing other Shadows to enter and do the same. I witnessed the aftermath. The carnage was unspeakable. Even by troll standards."

Phoenix gulped and peered over the top of an encyclopaedia article about troll physiology. Simon was staring at him in thoughtful silence while Fay glared at the floor, her fists clenched by her sides.

"Apparently," Phoenix muttered, "a troll's eyesight is terribly poor. Though they have an excellent sense of smell."

"So... this guy allowed three Shadows to possess him and betrayed Bloodwood a decade ago..." Simon said slowly. "Then what?"

"He disappeared," Fay said, raising her head and fixing Phoenix with a steady gaze, her ears pressed flat against her ratty hair. "Like a coward."

"And *now*," the troll said, pointing the rolled-up scroll at Simon's face, "he's wanted by the High Chief."

Simon shook his head. "That was ten years ago. And the fall of Bloodwood only happened today... There's something else. Something more."

"Do you recognise this criminal, or not?" The troll narrowed her eyes. "If you withhold information from the High Chief—"

"Fidelity." Phoenix closed the heavy book and stood up. "The High Chief would want to see this traitor personally I suppose..."

The troll frowned. "Indeed."

"That is convenient," Phoenix said, returning the book to its shelf.

"Convenient?"

"And the power factory," Phoenix added. "We could repair it in a day or so, surely."

The troll stared at him in disbelief. "A *day*? Are you daft? The Shadows... the logistics... the materials... It could take years. Yonder is facing a critical power shortage at a time when we need power most."

Phoenix leant against a display cabinet. "That's a fine bargaining chip, I suppose."

"Bargaining chip?"

"And the shields," Phoenix said, taking a small gold machine from the cabinet beside him, a tangled mess of tiny levers, toggles and gears. "Around Karvil City. There'd be enough reserve energy to last a good... what? Six weeks? Seven?"

"Four."

"Four..." Phoenix murmured, turning the curious little device over in his hands. "Seems *both* worlds are destined to face their demons within a month."

"What?"

"The Light Festival on Earth with the alignment of the Gates," Phoenix said. "The uprising against Flamegate. The potential collapse of civilisation in Yonder with the dawn of a second Shadow War, once the shield around Karvil inevitably fails." Phoenix twiddled with the tiny apparatus, turning knobs and flicking switches that he simply could not fathom the use for.

"Events have a funny way of coinciding," he added, holding the inexplicable device up to the light. "Each world is just a distorted reflection of the next. We're going not so much in circles but in spirals it seems. Everything charging towards one critical point. A cataclysmic event to unite all the species of all the worlds... Humans. Shadows. Trolls. Jellyfish. Those tiny, spotted frogs you find under rocks sometimes." He lowered the instrument to his eyes and turned a small wheel. "Nobody is immune. Not even the greedy scumbags that got us here in the first place." He jumped in surprise as a minuscule gold bear clicked out from a hidden compartment tucked underneath. "What *is* this delightful little contraption?"

"Is he sick in the head?" the troll asked, looking blankly at Fay.

"Yeah." Fay gazed at Phoenix as though she couldn't quite make her mind up about him, wavering somewhere between fascination, frustration, and ten long years of resentment. "He probably is."

Phoenix placed the instrument back on the shelf then strolled towards the troll. "Thank you for your concern. You've been incredibly helpful. But we can manage on our own."

Fidelity began to object. "But the High—"

"Yes, yes," Phoenix said, gently ushering her outside, pushing against her enormous back. "The High Chief has ordered everyone to the city. We'll be right behind you. Just a few private matters to attend to first."

"But—"

"I assure you we are perfectly capable of reaching Karvil by ourselves," Phoenix continued. "Safe travels. Farewell. Time to be on your way." He started closing the door but the troll pushed it back with an unyielding arm.

"*What* private matters?" she asked, her eyes so wide they appeared to pop from her rock-like head.

"Now if I told you, they wouldn't be private."

The troll seized Phoenix by the shoulder and wrenched him forward.

"I don't like your attitude, human," she snarled, her crushing grip clenching tighter around Phoenix's arm. She paused and squinted closer at his face. "You look familiar."

"Local celebrity," Phoenix said. "Broke the record for growing Bloodwood's largest cabbage. Can't even leave the house without being recognised. Honestly, the fame is—*Gah*!" Phoenix winced as the troll grasped him tighter and shoved him against the wall.

"What are you hiding?" she asked, her putrid breath hitting Phoenix in the face like a slab of rancid meat.

"A troubled past," Phoenix gasped as Fidelity pressed her arm against his throat. "And dreams of becoming an internationally recognised musician."

Fidelity leant closer and sniffed his neck. "You reek of Shadow." She grinned, revealing tusk-like teeth. "The High Chief would love someone to interrogate right now."

Phoenix offered an icy smile. "I'll meet with the High Chief in my own time, thanks. Simon," he added, "now would be a great time to intervene."

The troll collapsed with a weighty thud, her eyes rolling backwards into her skull. Simon stood to the side, a thin, crackling beam of blue light spiralling from his hand into the back of Fidelity's head.

"I'm sorry it came to this," Phoenix said, massaging his throat as he frowned down at the troll. "But a little harmless brain-scrambling is kinder than me ripping you apart with the void."

"Brain-scrambling!?" Fay repeated.

"She'll recover," Simon said. "This'll just confuse her for a day or two."

"I'm not worried about *her*," Fay said. "I'm worried about

us. Do you know how much trouble we'll be in once someone discovers we took down a troll working for the High Chief?"

"Your world could end within a month, Fay," Phoenix said wearily. "A flying machine from another planet just crashed before your eyes. Bloodwood no longer exists. Shadows are surging out from beyond the void and spreading across the land. Time to look at the bigger picture. Besides, it seems I'm already wanted for terrorism."

"You seem oddly unconcerned by that," Simon noted, still projecting the beam of light into Fidelity's head.

"If the High Chief is planning all-out war against Shadows, I'd like to talk to him," Phoenix said, stepping carefully over the troll and out onto the front porch where the wind-chimes jangled and rattled overhead. "He doesn't need to interrogate me. I'll make him a deal. Suggest some alternatives. Hopefully he changes his mind."

"You want him to just ignore a Shadow invasion?" Fay asked as Phoenix strode into the moonlit garden.

"Bigger picture, Fay," he murmured with his back to her. "Bigger picture."

"Where are you going?" Simon asked, as Phoenix walked past the horses.

"Just..." Phoenix continued down the path then stopped once he was outside the gate on the timber boardwalk, marshland flowers dancing around him in the night-time breeze. "Here." He turned to face them then shrugged. "It's more comfortable. Outside the Shadow-wards protecting the house."

With a faint pop, two figures materialised from thin air near the end of the jetty, hand-in-hand as they walked towards the house. Phoenix recognised their silhouettes as Gloria and Jack, the two ward-makers who had dedicated their lives to protecting Yonder and studying the void. The taller of the two was a gangly old man with a long stride and a crooked back, while the shorter was a rotund old woman with hair so white and so wild it looked as though she'd been struck by lightning at least thrice.

"You survived," Phoenix said, his shoulders slumping forward in relief. "The two greatest magicians this side of anywhere... of course you survived... I was worried. I mean, I've been worried for years. You were old when I left and you weren't getting any younger. I wanted to visit but I was nervous, you know? I thought maybe you'd be angry. Or dead. I'm glad you're not dead." Phoenix grimaced. "I'll stop talking."

"The rumours were true," the plump woman said as she stopped before him. "You *have* returned."

"No," Phoenix said quickly. "Sorry. I'll leave."

"Please." The man smiled. "Make yourself at home. Though it seems you already have..." His eyes rested upon Simon, who was still standing in the doorway behind the mound of fallen troll, pouring streams of blue light into Fidelity's brain.

"Evening." Simon nodded politely.

"I just came to collect something and heal my friend," Phoenix said. "Forget I was here. Fay, apologies. I'll contact you later."

The old man threw his arm out before Phoenix could walk past.

"Whatever you're planning, Phoenix, it can wait until morning," he said softly. "There are monsters about. Shadows running wild. Not to mention the whispers of a war in which you'll naturally play a part."

Phoenix stared rigidly at the wooden planks beneath his feet.

"It would be nice to sleep indoors for a change," Simon muttered from the doorway.

"Ten years and not even a letter to say you were alive." The big-haired woman patted Phoenix on the back. "Inside, dear. Don't make us ask twice."

BREAKING

“It was mayhem,” Jack said, his long, papery hands clasped before him on the round table they had all gathered around. “Everywhere we looked, people were dying.”

“Bloodwood has never been so utterly outmatched,” Gloria said. “That entire town is Shadow territory now.”

Phoenix quietly rested his head on the table, his face pressed against the wood.

“What about the people?” Simon asked from Phoenix’s left, sitting beside Fidelity Ethel Thunderstone, who was gazing vacantly about the cluttered house in a state of contented bliss.

"We rescued as many as we could," Gloria replied. "By now, refugees will have arrived in Karvil. But not enough. Bloodwood lost thousands today. I'd say at least two thirds of the town."

Simon sighed and rubbed his beard. "And Phoenix's family?"

Gloria reached over and placed her hand against Phoenix's arm. "We didn't see your grandparents, dear. I'm sorry."

"Don't be," Phoenix said, his voice muffled by the table. "They're alive."

"Why am I surrounded by strangers?" Fidelity asked, her tone suggesting mild curiosity rather than genuine concern.

"You bumped your head," Simon muttered. "We're taking you to Karvil tomorrow. You'll be fine in a few days."

"Oh." Fidelity wandered away to the fireplace where she crouched and stared peacefully at the dormant lumps of coal.

"What do the Shadows actually want?" Fay asked.

Gloria let loose a bitter laugh. "Our extinction, by the looks of it."

"They've taken up residence around what's left of the power factory," Jack said. "Dragged all the bodies and livestock there. They were having a feast when Gloria and I left. Some kind of victory party, with bonfires and music and dancing. I've never seen them behave like this."

"Hush," Fidelity whispered. "The fire is sleeping."

"I wonder," Simon said, his voice rumbling over the melancholy lull in conversation, "whether Shadows might be more intelligent than we thought."

Gloria sighed. "The people of Bloodwood have long been aware of the complex intelligence of Shadows. But I fear we underestimated their capacity for coordination and planning."

"They're ravenous," Simon said. "Red and I..." Simon trailed off. "Red, you doing okay?"

Phoenix gave a thumbs-up signal but otherwise remained where he was, silently face-planting the table.

"Red and I were swarmed..." Simon continued reluctantly, "by Shadows desperate to steal the void-stones."

"That makes sense," Gloria said. "Shadows crave power. They crave energy."

"They crave life," Phoenix mumbled into the table.

"Regardless of what they're after," Jack said, "the next closest civilisation is Karvil City. They'll be heading there next."

Phoenix screeched his chair back and rose sluggishly to his feet. "I'm making tea. Who wants tea?"

Fay's hand shot into the air and Phoenix looked around at everyone else.

Gloria seemed bemused. "Well, if you're making some..."

"That would be appreciated," Jack finished.

Phoenix stared pointedly at Simon and the warlock turned his palms up in a half-hearted shrug.

"You're all getting tea," Phoenix said, shuffling off into the adjoining kitchenette. "Fidelity, do trolls like tea?"

"We drink nothing but fresh glacial water and the intestinal juices of our enemies," the troll replied.

"Fresh out of intestinal juices, I'm afraid." Phoenix pottered about the kitchen, grateful for something to do as Simon, Fay, and the ward-makers continued discussing the sombre prospect of war.

"We won the first Shadow War only because we had Shadow Masters," Simon said. "And the Shadow Masters bred armies of Shades. Now the Shades have been exterminated... and there are only a handful of Masters left after the others all vanished."

"Those lost Shadow Masters wouldn't help us anyway," Phoenix said, rummaging through a cupboard in search of a cooking-pot. "They're too busy draining energy from the void, leading overextravagant lifestyles behind massive walls, and torturing people for the sake of maintaining Flamegate's authority on Earth."

"Still leading that double-life then?" Jack asked.

"No rest for the wicked, Jack," Phoenix muttered.

"Absent Shadow Masters aside..." Fay said. "What about Shades created illegally? After the first war? Can't we use them?"

Simon frowned at her. "You mean creatures like Phoenix's mother?"

Phoenix paused on his knees, staring blankly into the back of the cupboard despite having already found the pot he'd been looking for.

"Jack and I have been searching for Shades ever since the Extermination Order came into effect fifty years ago," Gloria said. "We hoped to save some from execution... but we never found any."

"You kids are too young to know," Jack said, leaning back in his chair, "but when Yonder won the Shadow War, another conflict was already taking place."

"With Shades?" Fay perked up in interest. "But the Shades were on *our* side."

"Not entirely." Jack exhaled a slow, contemplative breath. "See... Shadows can release void-energy to attack, but they much prefer draining victims through possession."

"Energy, magic, life..." Gloria said. "Call it what you like. Shadows can steal it if given the chance."

"Shades, on the other hand," Jack continued, "can't possess anyone. And their hominoid bodies aren't built to handle more energy than they already contain, so stealing energy would only put them at risk."

"Like how Phoenix puts himself at risk, drawing upon void-stones," Simon remarked.

Jack tipped his head. "Indeed."

Phoenix remained silent on his knees.

"Since Shades couldn't drain opponents' powers without endangering themselves, they had to rely on more overt methods of subjugation." Gloria leant back in her seat, her voice heavy. "Fortunately, their connection to the void meant they could release huge amounts of destructive power with ease."

"*Unfortunately*," Jack said, "such impressive displays of strength *terrified* people."

A prickling heat rose to Phoenix's cheeks.

"The Shades were seen as a threat," Gloria explained. "Since Shadow numbers were reduced to a manageable size—a trifling population that Bloodwood alone could be responsible for—society had no need for the Shades that had helped win the war."

"A merciless army of half-human, half-Shadow warriors." Jack shook his head. "Their purpose from the start was to fight and to die. Those who survived the war had to be erased."

"We couldn't just let them live?" Fay asked. "Give them new roles?"

Jack gave a soft laugh.

"The Shadow Masters..." Simon murmured.

Gloria nodded, her springy white hair bouncing around her face. "Shadow Masters were the only people who could control the Shades," she said. "When they disappeared... the Shades were left without boundaries. Without direction."

"They turned on us," Fay guessed.

"Not all," Jack said. "But a few began roaming Yonder, killing for no reason. Terrorising towns."

Gloria heaved a sigh. "People panicked," she said. "The High Chief ordered all Shades to be destroyed."

Phoenix had forgotten what he was doing by this point, his eyes drifting over the collection of pots and pans without actually seeing anything.

"How do you dispose of a Shade?" Fay asked. "You're up against the strength of Shadows and the knowledge and resilience of humans. Seems impossible."

"Not all the Shadow Masters disappeared," Jack said. "Maulbrak was notorious in those days for his command over the void."

"He was young," Gloria said, as Phoenix's hand tightened

around the cupboard door, "but already building a name for himself as a truly formidable master of Shadows. He was put in charge of culling."

Phoenix snapped the cupboard shut and stood to finish making everyone tea.

"People just wanted Shades gone," Jack said.

"My mother was an exception," Phoenix said, fiddling with the settings on the stove.

Jack nodded slowly, his eyes closed in recollection. "Born many years after the Shadow War... Raised human, in the only town in Yonder that wouldn't cower from her capabilities."

"Under very strict conditions," Gloria said, "she was permitted to survive."

"Because she was useful," Phoenix said, flicking a switch on the stove over and over with increasingly violent intensity. "And obedient. And conditioned to think and live like everyone else in that twisted cult of a town. Like a robot, which is a comparison that none of you will understand, but it's apt nonetheless. It basically means brainwashed. Indoctrinated. Controlled. The stove... is not... *working*!"

"The energy-disk needs replacing, dear," Gloria said, and Phoenix dropped his hands to his side. "Check the pantry."

Phoenix jabbed a button on the stove and ejected a slim silver disk covered in fine streaks of green metal.

"Save the full disks for later," he said, taking a knife from a hook on the wall. "You might need them in Karvil." He slit a cut over his thumb and pressed it against the silver, watching as the veins of green drank his blood, drawing upon his energy until they glowed gold and the entire disk radiated heat.

"I wish you wouldn't do that," Gloria said, as Phoenix shoved the disk back into place. "Using your energy always feels so..."

"Immoral," Jack said.

Phoenix turned a knob and the stovetop glowed red.

"Anyway," Fay said, determined to keep everyone focused, "Shades aren't an option."

Jack smiled at her. "We'll have to fight this war on our own I'm afraid."

"If the Shadows take Karvil," Fay said, while Phoenix used a rusty lever by the stove to pump marsh-water into the pot, "Yonder is lost. It's the capital. Our last defence. The Shadows would be unstoppable after that."

"The Shadows won't beat us," Phoenix said.

"What makes you so sure?" Jack asked.

"When I close the Gate," Phoenix said, "the Shadows will return to the void. If they remain, they'll be separated from their life-force. Too weak to travel, let alone fight a war. Karvil just needs to defend itself for four weeks until the Gates align."

"The Gate can't be closed, dear," Gloria said gently.

"Besides," Jack said, and Phoenix braced himself for the stubborn thinking he'd encountered all his life, "if the Gate closed, *we* would lose access to the void. Not just Shadows."

"Void-energy is the backbone of society," Gloria added. "Without it, people's livelihoods... entire industries... our very culture... Everything would collapse."

Phoenix stopped pumping and smiled with a tolerance that was rapidly wearing thin. "There are other energies available."

"None that could support us as the void can," Jack argued.

Phoenix slammed the pot onto the stove and water splashed over the sides, sizzling loudly against the heating-element.

He spun around and glowered at the table. "Under the present concerning circumstances," he said, with as much patience as he could muster, "perhaps it's time Yonder began preparing for a future without the void." He thrust his hands out in earnest. "*Maybe*, the void just needs a break for once." His movements grew more dynamic, his arms sweeping through the air with every word. "*Maybe*, the void has been exploited so badly and stretched so thin that it's going to snap. And *maybe*, here's a novel idea, if people pulled their heads out of the clouds and stopped treating the void like the answer to all their problems and agreed to compromise a little for the sake of securing a less destructive world in favour of something a little more stable... Maybe *then* there'd be some kind of point to this whole stupid avoidable mess!"

Phoenix stood with his arms spread wide, his swinging coat-sleeves dangling past his fingertips.

The water started boiling and he turned and switched the stove off so forcefully that the knob came loose and he had to jam it back into place as everyone stared at him. Eventually he gave up and froze, his head bowed over the pot as he watched the last frantic streams of bubbles rise to the surface.

Fidelity tiptoed heavily from the fireplace and stooped to whisper in Simon's ear. "The red one is angry."

"Well," Simon said, his eyes fixed on Phoenix from across the room, "he's had a rough day."

Phoenix shook his head. "I'm sick of fighting against the people I'm fighting for." He stared into the pot a while longer then turned away from the stove. "Simon and I have friends in Karvil," he said. "They're working on technology that could power all of Yonder. Without having to use the void."

"Those crazy inventors?" Simon raised his bushy eyebrows. "Is that why you keep saying we should visit them? Red, their ideas aren't ready to use within a month."

Phoenix gave a wan smile. "Honestly, Simon. You and I need to have a chat about the benefits of positive thinking." He tipped the hot water into a chipped teapot then hunted through a cupboard in search of mugs, eventually finding five brightly coloured monstrosities and loading them onto a tray.

"Positive thinking doesn't change the facts," Simon said, watching Phoenix pour the tea. "Those inventors will need more energy just to finalise their inventions. With a power shortage going on and Shadows invading, the Guild's going to be underfunded, underpowered and understaffed."

Phoenix had stopped listening. "Snacks," he said. "We need snacks." He strolled into a softly lit pantry and grabbed a small stepladder by the door to reach the jar of sweets he knew was hidden at the back of the highest shelf.

"Supposing you do manage to seal the void," Simon called from the round table. "What'll happen to a half-Shade like you?"

Phoenix turned without thinking, his foot slipping from the stepladder as he was reaching for the jar. He scrambled for anything to snatch hold of, his fingers curling around the rim of a large flowerpot containing a cactus covered in dark purple spines. The pot flipped with his weight, showering him with rubble before slamming into his head and cracking into pieces as both it and Phoenix hit the ground, dirt splattering over him in gooey, cactus-juice-blended clumps.

Phoenix groaned and rubbed the back of his head. "Why is there a cactus in here?"

"She's mine," Fay said, hurrying inside to check on the plant's wellbeing. "She's a Medicinal Prickly Star. They like the dark." She clicked her tongue. "Her pot is ruined."

Phoenix pushed himself up from the ground as Simon and the ward-makers appeared, peering in at him in bewilderment and concern.

"Were you always this clumsy?" Fay asked, scooping her cactus into a bowl.

"Haven't slept in a while," Phoenix mumbled. He dusted some of the dirt and cactus spines from his hair, then raised his chin with whatever dignity he had remaining to him. "Could I, please, make use of your shower?"

~

The washroom was exactly as Phoenix remembered, the floor and walls covered entirely in rounded creek-stones, a wide showerhead positioned over a deep bath, and a small, circular window that overlooked the silent marsh outside. Phoenix closed the door behind him, being sure to leave it unlocked in case someone needed to rescue him from some unflattering situation involving nudity, water, and not being conscious enough to stop himself from drowning in a puddle. All in all, an increasingly probable risk, considering how lethargic he felt.

He paused by the bathroom mirror, tilting his head to inspect the thin cut under his chin where Simon had swiped him with the Shadow-spear. He shuddered, recalling the rush of energy that had poured from the seemingly harmless wound into the burning-hot metal.

It had not been his first encounter with a Shadow-spear, and he doubted it would be the last.

Somebody knocked on the door and Phoenix opened it to find the lanky old ward-maker holding a bundle of clothes in one hand and a mug of tea in the other.

"Your friend said you might need these," Jack said, placing the clothes on a wicker basket by the sink. "Might be a little big for you, but it's the best I could find."

Phoenix flicked a switch by the bath that powered the heating. "Thanks, Jack."

"He's an interesting fellow, that warlock," the old man said, as Phoenix sat down on the edge of the bath, still dressed in nothing but his shabby coat. "He plays the fiddle. What sort of warlock plays the fiddle?"

"His teacher encouraged him," Phoenix said, leaning forward over his knees. "Which reminds me... What do you know of Edgar Wolfe?"

"Edgar Wolfe?" Jack's eyes widened. "That arrogant fart. We never saw eye-to-eye. He vanished... well, it must be a decade ago now." He blew softly onto his tea, momentarily lost in memory. "Cranky old curmudgeon," he said at last. "Incredibly gifted, though. Creative. Obsessed with the void... Why do you ask?"

Phoenix didn't have the energy to explain. "Just curious."

"Your warlock friend," Jack said after a pause, as Phoenix picked cactus spines out of his coat. "He's asked us to help unlock his full power."

Phoenix didn't look up. "Can that be done?"

"Oh, I should think so," Jack replied. "Gloria believes she can help at least. The two of them are outside with Fay, trying to access his magic as we speak."

"And did Simon give a reason for needing to unlock his power?" Phoenix asked, still slumped over his knees. "I guess it was blocked for a reason."

"Says he wants to *leap through the void.*" Jack chuckled and shook his head. "I think he intends to travel distances greater than many dare to imagine."

"Something tells me he'll succeed," Phoenix said with a wry smile.

"It won't be easy for him," Jack said. "His powers all tied up as they are..." He took a sip of tea, gazing at Phoenix with interest. "You got that look about you, kid."

Phoenix dropped a handful of cactus spines into the bath. "What look?"

"That one." Jack pointed his mug of tea in the direction of Phoenix's face. "Like you've seen the future and none of it's good."

Phoenix didn't laugh so much as breath loudly out through his nose.

"You always were a few steps ahead of everyone," Jack added. "A trait borne from necessity, I suppose, considering how Bloodwood treated you." He stared at Phoenix a while longer then huffed a small sigh. "Well. It's been a long day and I need rest. Get yourself tidied up. I'll see you in the morning."

Jack closed the door behind him and Phoenix sat in silence for a moment before slipping out of his coat and tossing it on the ground. He stepped cautiously into the bath then pulled down the metal lever that released the water from the showerhead, letting the droplets beat against his shoulders and soak through his mop of hair.

Why couldn't everything be as simple as the joy of taking a shower?

He turned to reach for the soap, but no sooner had he extended his hand than the old, swooping feeling rolled over him like a wave.

Phoenix flung his arm back to shut the water off but slipped, unconscious, down the side of the bath, his fingers brushing past the lever as he sank through the void.

~

Phoenix woke in the bed he'd spent two months in, the soft light of a full moon shining through the lace curtains by the window overlooking the street.

"Splendid." He closed his eyes and counted several minutes, willing his body to drift back to sleep, but it was useless. He didn't feel like he was inhaling large quantities of water though, so he took that as a comforting sign and resigned himself to occupying his time on Earth for a while.

He glanced at the clock on the bedside table, it's glowing digits reading 1:16, the red light washing over a full glass of water and the plain silver spoon.

He made a mental note to ask someone why the spoon was there, then rolled out of bed, guzzled all the water, then made his way over the thick rainbow rug and out into the silent corridor. He paused by Bee and Jayden's room, debating whether to knock before deciding against it and heading downstairs.

The ground floor was heavy with the stagnant silence that accompanied night, though if Phoenix strained his ears, he could hear faint snoring rising up from the infirmary under the house. Not wanting to linger too long near the disturbing basement, he crossed the deserted living-room with intentions of pillaging the kitchen before a figure caught his eye.

Phoenix froze, squinting at the elderly man standing by a far window. Edgar was alone in an open room at the front of the house, a cosy space with bookshelves and an old, upright piano pressed against the wall. He hadn't noticed Phoenix, his moonlit gaze locked on the jungle of garden growing outside.

Phoenix hesitated then strolled into the front room. "Hello Edgar."

The man blinked at him then turned back to frown out the window. "Oh. It's you."

"Can't sleep?"

Edgar rolled his eyes. "Merely enjoying the rare privacy of my own home," he said. "Though I suppose that's no longer possible."

"Don't be too disheartened," Phoenix said. "I'm not entirely disagreeable. A few more midnight meetings like this and you and I might become unlikely friends."

"*Unlikely* being the key word in that proposition," Edgar said.

"With that attitude, sure." Phoenix smiled and sat at the piano. "I suspect we have more in common than you'd like anyone to believe. You're from Yonder, aren't you? Quite a long way from home."

For a while, Phoenix wasn't sure Edgar would respond, but then the old man sighed and folded his arms, still gazing into the gloom outside. "Yes."

Phoenix rested his elbow against the lid of the piano, determined to keep pushing at the walls Edgar had built around himself. "You're Edgar Wolfe."

Edgar shook his head. "Just Edgar."

"Can you go back to Yonder?"

"No."

"Why not?"

Edgar scowled. "My place is here."

"How did you end up on Earth?"

Edgar's scowl deepened. "I'd rather not say."

"How long have you been here?"

"Too long."

"Simon," Phoenix said. "The big, beardy fellow who appeared from thin air today... You recognised him."

Edgar didn't reply, staring intently out the window, the moon pitching soft shadows across his gaunt face.

"He's your apprentice," Phoenix insisted.

Edgar swallowed. "I failed him," he said, turning to face Phoenix. "Many, many years ago." He stopped, as though he only just realised that Phoenix was listening. "I don't need to explain myself," he mumbled. "Least of all to you."

"Have I done something to offend you?" Phoenix asked in amusement. "Or are you this snarky with everyone you meet?"

"Everyone," Edgar said. "Though I'm confident you're not as extraordinary as everyone seems to think. You will receive no special treatment from me, I promise you that."

Phoenix raised his hands. "Hold it." His smile grew wider. "Are you *jealous* of me?"

Edgar narrowed his eyes, pausing a long moment before he spoke. "I'm going to bed."

"Wait!" Phoenix snatched the old man's dressing-robe as he walked past the piano, and Edgar rounded on him with his hand drawn back as though preparing to smack Phoenix across the face. The energy in the air swelled almost imperceptibly, tickling the hairs at the back of Phoenix's neck.

"Sorry." He released Edgar's robe. "Stay. Please. The company keeps me sane. Maybe. Sane enough."

Edgar lowered his hand but said nothing.

"How do you know Alice?" Phoenix asked, spinning around to face the piano then lifting the lid.

"Our paths crossed years ago," Edgar replied, as Phoenix gazed yearningly at the well-worn keys, just waiting to breathe life into melodies and chords.

"She was on a mission with the Night Order," Edgar continued. "She recognised me as Yonderian. Started involving me in her wild plans. The rest is history."

Phoenix placed his fingers gently over the piano. "Flamegate never went after you?"

"I am an ailing old man," Edgar said, leaning against the

wall. "My power all but vanished when I came to Earth. It was never enough to draw Flamegate's attention."

"Lucky." Phoenix closed his eyes, his fingers tapping soundlessly along the keys without pressing them, dancing softly along the length of the piano to music that only he could hear. "What about Simon?"

Edgar sighed. "What about him?"

"He'll be back," Phoenix said, still immersed in the melody playing in his head, his hands moving on their own. "Will you be his teacher again? When you're reunited at last?"

There was a cold finality to Edgar's voice. "No."

"Shame," Phoenix said, his eyes still shut. "The distraction would do him good."

"A distraction from you and your problems, you mean?"

Phoenix paused, his right-hand hovering over the last octave of the piano, the tune he had been imagining slipping away like a leaf caught in the current of a fast-flowing stream. He opened his eyes and turned to face the old man.

"Do you resent me?" he asked lightly. "Is that what this is? I'm part of a world you can't return to? Living amongst people that—" Phoenix stopped, a chill rolling down his spine as though an ice-cube were melting against his neck. "Crap."

Edgar smiled a sly smile. "Problem?"

Phoenix stood, eyes darting restlessly around the darkened room. "I need to get back." He hastened into the kitchen, the old man following leisurely behind.

"Is there anything that'll put me to sleep?" Phoenix asked, yanking open cupboards and drawers. "Preferably fast."

Edgar smirked. "I could hit you over the head with a frypan if you like?"

Phoenix pressed his lips together. "That might work." He passed Edgar the sturdiest pot he could find then stood tapping his foot in the centre of the kitchen as the old man stared.

"Make it quick," Phoenix muttered. "I think the energy-disk stopped heating the shower."

Edgar raised his eyebrows. "You're asleep in a running shower?"

"Not my first choice," Phoenix said with a forced smile. "Now if you'd be so kind. Try not to enjoy this too much. Count of three. One. Two." He paused, a wave of dizziness enveloping his brain. "It seems your services will not be necessary today."

Phoenix lowered himself onto the tiles, an unbearable cold sinking into every part of his being as the void tugged at his core.

"I won't ask you to drag me someplace else," he mumbled, while Edgar watched without a word. "But a blanket would be nice."

Edgar placed the pot on the tiles next to Phoenix's face. "No." He turned and started walking away. "Sleep well."

"C'mon, old man." Phoenix tried not to sound as desperate as he felt, his limbs heavy and useless against the floor. "It's cold."

Edgar shrugged as he strolled past a couch bearing several pillows and knitted overthrows. "Such is life," he said. "Get used to it." Then he disappeared into his bedroom, the door snapping shut behind him as Phoenix curled into a ball and waited to leave.

COLD

Phoenix found himself shivering, caught somewhere between lying and sitting with his face pressed against the side of the bath, cold water streaming down his neck. He rolled onto his hands and knees, reaching through the cascade for the lever to cut the water off, but his muscles were reluctant to do anything he required and he slipped gracelessly into the pool of water collecting by the drain.

He tried again, numb hands fumbling for the lever. He had barely managed to catch hold of the metal bar when the washroom door thumped open behind him and a hand glided past his eyes, seizing the lever and wrenching the water shut.

Relieved, Phoenix dropped back to sit in the bath.

"You've been in here well over an hour," Fay said, throwing a towel over his back. "You're lucky you didn't drown. Your creepy horse spotted you through the window. Told me you could do with some help."

"Th-thanks." Phoenix couldn't stop shaking. "That water… is like ice."

"The heating is set to turn off after seven minutes," Fay said, leaning into the bath and gripping Phoenix's arms. "Come on, you need to dry off." Phoenix stumbled out and Fay sat him down on the pebbled floor.

"Jack is asleep," she added as she gathered the clothes that had been left on the basket by the sink. "Gloria and I were outside, looking after that magic-deprived friend of yours. Otherwise we might've found you sooner."

She passed Phoenix the clothes and he dressed himself with the blundering grace of a drunkard in a rowboat before sitting with his legs tucked in front of him, shivering uncontrollably.

Fay draped Phoenix's coat over his shoulders then sat beside him and started rubbing his back. "Simon's passed out, by the way."

"What?" Phoenix struggled to push words past his chattering teeth. "What ha-happened?

"Unlocking power is no easy task," Fay said. "But Gloria's with him. He'll be fine."

Phoenix nodded, too cold to ask questions. Instead, he spent his energy trying to massage feeling back into his hands.

"I never thought we'd be sitting side by side like this again," Fay said, still rubbing his back.

Phoenix glanced at her. "We were friends once."

Fay nodded with a small shrug, as though agreeing with the fanciful notions of a child. "Once."

"You weren't like the others…" Phoenix said. "Never treated me like I was a freak."

"I've always thought you were a freak, Phoenix."

Phoenix smiled. "Yeah, but you never treated me like one."

Fay sighed, her cattish ears pulled back. "Just stop talking."

They sat in silence a while longer, warmth returning to Phoenix's body like the slow ascent of a winter sun.

"What you said... earlier." Phoenix tried hard not to stutter or slur. "You were right. I was a coward, for running away."

Fay's hand slowed in its steady making of circles. "You never even apologised."

"Apologising would make it real."

"It *was* real."

Phoenix swallowed, squeezing his fingers hard enough that he could feel them through the cold.

"The Shadows took over," he said. "Like this massive storm smothering my brain. But I was still *present*." He gazed at the smooth pebbles embedded in the washroom floor, then reached out and ran his fingers over the bumps. "I watched as they used my hands to activate the stone... I watched as I took down Bloodwood's shields... I watched as people I'd known all my life were ripped open by the void-energy spewing from my palms." Fay stopped rubbing his back, her hand resting between his shoulder blades as though she'd forgotten what she was doing.

"By the time I'd forced the Shadows out of my head, it was too late." Phoenix trailed his thumb along the tiny valleys between the stones. "I shouldn't've let them in in the first place. Nan was right. I've always been too weak for that town." He paused to peek at her through the hair dripping into his eyes. "I'm sorry."

Fay lowered her hand into her lap.

"I have a habit," Phoenix said, looking away again, "of hiding behind my own lies. But my problems affect more than just myself. And I decided, recently, that I should probably do something about them."

He stood, pulling his arms through the patched sleeves of his coat. "And with the universe falling into disrepair," he said, "now seems as good a time as any to confront all the things I've been afraid of. Breaking out of Flamegate. Going back to Bloodwood. The Light Festival. The Gate. You."

He buried his hands in his pockets and gazed down at Fay. She stared back with wary, catlike attention.

"Those inventors I mentioned," Phoenix said. "In Karvil. Simon wasn't wrong. They won't have enough energy to get their ideas off the ground with all Yonder's resources going into a Shadow War."

"I get the feeling you're about to ask a favour of me, Phoenix."

"There's a void-chamber in Bloodwood."

Fay's ears twitched. "You want to capture a Shadow and lock it inside without being noticed or killed by any of the other Shadows guarding the town?"

"I want to lock *myself* inside the chamber without being noticed or killed by any of the Shadows guarding the town."

"I see..." Fay furrowed her brows. "And we just wander into Bloodwood on our own, do we? What if a Shadow possesses you and you go on another wild killing spree?"

Phoenix didn't shy away from her gaze. "I won't let that happen."

"Can you be sure?"

"Fay..." Phoenix knelt in front of her. "For a Shadow to possess someone, the human either has to be so weak that they're knocking on Death's door, or they have to give themselves over, voluntarily, to the Shadow's will. It's a conscious decision. Usually one made in a bleak moment of desperation, but conscious nonetheless." He moved to take her hand then thought better of it and locked his fingers together in his lap instead. "I am not knocking on Death's door. Playing around in Death's neighbourhood, perhaps. Skipping in and out of his yard. But his door is not upon me quite yet."

"Did you expect to survive?"

Phoenix tensed.

"Ten years ago," Fay whispered. "When you surrendered to Shadows. Did you know you'd live through it?"

Phoenix hesitated then hung his head, too ashamed to admit that the thought of living or dying had never even crossed his mind. He'd just wanted an escape, and welcoming Shadows hadn't felt like such an appalling idea at the time.

Fay nodded slowly, her voice heavy when she spoke. "They really broke you, huh?"

Phoenix swallowed. "Fay, listen… I didn't care back then. But I care now. I care a lot. And just because I can host Shadows without being killed does not mean I want to invite them to control my body whenever the opportunity presents itself."

Fay gazed at him, her yellow eyes shrewd as she considered his proposal.

"Your energy from the chamber would be raw," she said eventually. "We can't process it with the power factory gone."

Phoenix stood with a grin, confident that Fay would take part in the plan. "I'll explain on the way." He offered his hand and Fay hesitated before allowing Phoenix to pull her to her feet.

"Let's see if Simon's awake," Phoenix said, stepping out of the washroom into the dark corridor beyond.

"What if he's still unconscious?" Fay asked as they entered the cluttered room at the front of the cottage, where Fidelity's thunderous snoring rolled like angry waves over the gentle clicking, ticking and thunking of the machines scattered amongst the oddities and books.

"That would be preferable," Phoenix said, switching on a lamp hanging from the ceiling. "If he's awake, we'll have to knock him out again."

Fay glanced at him in surprise. "He's not coming with us?"

"He'd stand in our way," Phoenix said. "In light of recent events, he might not share my enthusiasm for this particular excursion and its likelihood of going terribly wrong.

Thankfully though… it looks like he'll be sleeping a while." He nodded toward the fireplace where both Simon and Fidelity were snuggled together on the floor, Simon leaning into the back of Fidelity's neck with his arm draped over her waist.

Phoenix smiled. "Remind me to tell Jess."

"Who's Jess?"

Before Phoenix could answer, the front door creaked open and Gloria stumbled into the house, orange flowers clasped in her shaky hand, and her billowing clothes splattered with blood.

Phoenix's eyes widened. "Gloria!" He hurried to help her but she shooed him away.

"The blood isn't mine," she assured him, hobbling inside to sit in a rocking-chair by the fireplace. "It's Simon's."

"You're both okay?" Fay asked.

"I revived him long enough to walk him into the house," Gloria said, "but he passed out again as soon as I asked him to lie down. I might have put him through a little too much tonight."

"How long do you think he'll sleep?" Phoenix asked, eyeing Simon uneasily.

Gloria lifted her shoulders in a weary shrug. "I only unlocked a portion of his power, but there are still major adjustments his body will have to make." She rattled the flowers in her lap. "I have to mix something for the discomfort he'll feel in the morning."

"Leave that to me." Fay leant down and eased the flowers from Gloria's hand. "You should rest."

For a second, it looked like Gloria might object, but her need for sleep won out. Phoenix and Fay helped her out of the rocking-chair and walked with her to the corridor, where she paused in the doorway to face them, her expression soft.

"You two have to look out for each other now."

"I don't need looking out for, Gloria," Fay said. "Especially not by Phoenix Page."

Phoenix smiled. "She's right. I can't even look after

myself."

"Don't be too hard on yourself, dear." Gloria rested her hand against Phoenix's face. "You kids are suffering the mistakes of my generation. You're stronger than you think." She pulled her hand away and clicked her tongue. "You're still cold. I was so preoccupied with that warlock, I didn't even think you might be in trouble on your own. I'm sorry we forgot to check on you."

Phoenix shook his head. "I'm not your responsibility."

The smile faded from Gloria's eyes. "You were when you were a child. I'm afraid we rather let you down."

"*You* let *me* down?" Phoenix chuckled. "That's a gross misinterpretation of events." He hesitated then leant forward and kissed her cheek. "Night, Nan. *Gloria*. I meant Gloria."

Gloria pulled him into a tight embrace then bundled Fay along into the hug, squeezing the pair together with unexpected strength.

"Stay out of trouble," she whispered, then she shuffled away down the corridor and Phoenix felt a pang of sadness as she disappeared behind a door.

"She's a force to be reckoned with, that woman," he muttered, before turning to Fay and pointing at the orange flowers in her hand. "Can I help with that?"

Fay rolled her eyes as though Phoenix had insulted her. "You can help by not touching anything. I'll handle the tonic. You explain this impossible plan."

"It's not impossible." Phoenix followed her into the kitchen. "Not if we use your power."

"My power?"

"Remember when I gave you that void-stone all those years ago?" Phoenix asked as Fay placed the flowers onto a wooden chopping-board.

Fay took a knife and started dicing the stems. "Yes," she said. "You told me to hide it from everyone in Bloodwood. Especially your grandparents."

"Right," Phoenix said. "And how did you hide it?"

Fay stopped chopping the flowers. "Oh no..."

Phoenix nodded. "Exactly."

"Phoenix, a non-activated void-stone is far easier to conceal than a genetic mess of void-energy like yourself."

"But you can do it, can't you?" Phoenix leant over the counter and fixed Fay with an intense stare, the kind of stare that unsettled strangers and made everyone who knew him worry for their lives. "You can distort the energy around us and make us harder for Shadows to detect. At least until I'm inside the chamber. Once we start collecting my energy, I'll be almost undetectable and we'll be safe. Well, safer. Relatively speaking. I think."

Fay turned to a cupboard and began unloading boxes, bottles and jars of unidentifiable ingredients. "The effort required to hide that stone for so many years is nothing compared to the effort it would take to conceal you for a mere hour or two." She found a bowl and smacked it onto the counter beside the chopping-board. "A non-activated void-stone requires nothing more than a small, *fixed* forcefield to counter the subtle levels of energy leaking from it. A non-activated void-stone is stable. A non-activated void-stone is *constant*. But *you—*" She pointed at Phoenix's face. "Your energy is all over the place."

"Much like the current state of the universe," Phoenix said, resting his chin in his hand. "If only there were a way we could mend the imbalances in the void. If only we had some kind of plan to sustain humanity's existence into a future free from raging Shadows and without risk of interdimensional collision. *If only* some gallant, roguishly handsome hero was able to provide enough energy to keep Yonder afloat before bravely confronting the force of the entire void all on his own." He folded his arms. "Wait... I believe we have a solution to this dilemma..."

"Okay, first of all, you are neither gallant nor roguishly handsome," Fay said as she squeezed a lumpy green fruit into the bowl. "You're endearingly dishevelled, at best. Like a stray puppy that people feel sorry for because it's missing an eye."

"Little harsh."

"Secondly," Fay continued, "if I want to cancel out the energy you release in order to avoid detection, I'd have to constantly readjust my magic to account for all the fluctuations. The concentration required... the *precision*..."

"So... you can't do it after all?"

Fay sighed, her hand submerged in a jar of dead centipedes. "Of course I can do it."

Phoenix's face split into a grin. "Knew I could count on you."

"You're asking me to risk my life." Fay tossed three of the crunchy critters into the bowl.

"I know... I've no right to ask this much. But it's important." Phoenix drummed his fingers against the countertop. "Also..."

"Also? There's more?"

"Once I've been drained of energy, I'm going to be a little... indisposed." Phoenix started poking through all the ingredients Fay had spread across the counter, lifting lids and prodding whatever he found inside. "I've been warned to avoid behaviour like this, but desperate times call for desperate measures and I am, more often than not these days, incredibly desperate."

"Do I have to carry you out of Bloodwood or something?"

"Not exactly." Phoenix wrinkled his nose after sniffing the glowing contents of a bottle then hastily screwed on the lid and pushed the substance aside. "I can't switch worlds when the extraction is taking place, but once it finishes... in that state... there's a chance my body will be torn from this world and pulled into that other world's prison." He twisted another jar open and peered inside. "To prevent my hellish return to captivity from happening any sooner than it needs to, I'll activate a void-stone to hold me in Yonder. I won't be able to keep that up for very long though, especially after the chamber ordeal, so I'll need your help."

"You've lost me."

"Are these pickled eyeballs?"

Fay scowled. "Focus, Phoenix."

"The one on top is glaring at me."

"For Light's sake." Fay snatched the jar out of his hands and jammed the lid back on. "What am I supposed to do to stop you from disappearing into another world? Hold your hand? Tie you to a tree?"

"Just blast enough raw void-energy into my heart to jolt some life into me again. It's very simple."

Fay added a handful of pink powder to the bowl and started mixing with angry determination. "Sure. Just gather raw void-energy from the environment and channel it through my own body to pull you back from the brink of death. Simple."

Phoenix shrugged. "Maulbrak does it easily enough."

"Well why don't we ask *Maulbrak* to help?" Fay retorted.

"I'd rather take our chances with a flock of Shadows, to be honest."

Fay rolled her eyes. "Pass me that bottle."

Phoenix handed her the empty bottle she had pointed to and Fay poured the mixture inside.

"This better be worth the effort, Phoenix," she said as she tipped the diced flower stems into the drink before sealing it with a cork. "Can't I just stab you with a Shadow-spear, collect all your energy and be done with it? Here. Shake this until it's orange."

Phoenix grimaced and took the bottle off her hands. "As gratifying as stabbing me in the chest may seem to you, chambers collect energy at a slower rate than those spears." He shook the liquid over his head then placed it on the counter once it had morphed into thick orange sludge. "The spears are designed to incapacitate a Shadow and steal as much of its power as possible before it's extinguished. But the chamber takes time. A *long* time. It allows energy to replenish itself almost as quickly as it's drained away."

Fay frowned at him through the dreadlocks falling over

her eyes. "And it works on you even though you're only half-Shade?"

There was no humour in Phoenix's laugh. "A healthy adult Shadow would break out of that chamber long before its full energy was depleted. But I was raised for this. I'm not going to escape. I'm going to sit tight and put up with it until we have what we need. Trust me. This will work."

Fay squinted at him in silence a moment longer then turned away. "Sure. What could go wrong?" She left the drink on the counter with a slip of paper bearing Simon's name, then started making her way to the door.

"With you in a minute," Phoenix said. "I'll just fetch my things."

Fay stalked outside without a word while Phoenix rummaged around the room, trying not to disturb Simon or the slumbering troll. He found his bag beneath a chair and was just reaching for the string dangling from the ceiling to turn out the light when a pained groan interrupted the rumble of Fidelity's snores.

Phoenix froze, his hand clasped around the hanging light-switch.

Simon sat up and blinked, bleary-eyed, at his surroundings. "Red?"

"No. I'm an illusion created by your subconscious, sent to remind you about the importance of getting enough sleep." Phoenix paused. "I have, naturally, taken the form of your best friend because Phoenix is such a responsible, positive influence on your life."

Simon gazed at him blankly. "Is it morning already? Are we going to Karvil now?"

Phoenix sighed. "No. Go back to sleep."

"Gulliver said you were in trouble."

"I'm fine. Everything's fine. Get some rest."

Simon frowned, his eyes roving around the room as though he were distracted by a lazy fly. "I can see things."

Phoenix raised an eyebrow. "Such as?"

"The past..." Simon rubbed his eyes. "It's everywhere. But it's different. *I'm* different." He stared at some invisible scene playing out in the far corner of the living-room then shook his head. "Everything aches."

"That's normal. Probably." Phoenix was still clutching the string, illuminated by the lamp as though caught in a spotlight onstage. "Gloria said your body needs to adjust."

Simon lay back and glowered at the ceiling. Phoenix chewed his lip, unsure how best to proceed.

"Do you think we'll see Jess tomorrow?" Simon asked, interrupting Phoenix's internal debate about the ethics of knocking Simon unconscious with a gentle blast of void-energy to the back of the head.

"Jess?" Phoenix tugged the string, plunging the house into gloom broken only by patches of moonlight streaming through the windows at the front of the house. "Maybe. There's a chance she'll be in Karvil before us anyway. She's probably already there."

"Do you think she'll like my beard?"

Phoenix shrugged his bag onto his shoulder. "Absolutely not. You're terrifying. Go to sleep."

Simon propped himself up on his elbow and studied Phoenix with narrowed eyes. "Am I keeping you from something? What's the hurry?"

"No hurry." Phoenix strolled over to the fireplace, crouching down beside Simon and the sleeping troll. "Listen, I'm going to sit outside the front gate for a while."

"Need a break from the anti-Shadow wards around the house?"

"Yeah. Some night air will do me good. You'll be okay with the skull-crushing champion here I suppose?"

Simon nodded and closed his eyes, his face contorted in a pained expression that Phoenix had rarely seen. An unprovoked void-energy attack from a friend seemed a little cruel under the circumstances.

"There's a drink in the kitchen with your name on it,"

Phoenix added, patting Simon on the shoulder. "Take it in the morning and you'll feel less like you were struck by a planet and more like you were squashed by a small horse. Until then, get some sleep."

He stood and started to leave.

"Red, I know what you're trying to do."

Phoenix glanced back. "You do?"

"You're so messed up that you actually believe you're responsible for solving the problems of the entire universe." Simon still had his eyes closed. "You think saving the lives of everyone in existence will make up for the lives you feel were already lost because of you."

Phoenix smiled. "Well… mathematically… that would make a lot of sense."

Simon heaved a sigh. "You're an idiot." He rolled over and was snoring even before Phoenix was out the door.

TRAPPED

“We’re all going to die.” Gulliver’s condescending voice was loaded with an extra layer of misery as he stood, head bowed, upon the grassy ridgeline overlooking the battered remnants of Bloodwood. Phoenix was standing on the horse’s rump, covered head to toe in purple slime and monster blood, his eyes fixed on the horizon as the sun rose slowly over the forest that bordered the town. Fay sulked in her scruffy cat-form at Phoenix’s feet, yowling into the wind, her long, bedraggled fur slicked out of place with purple goo.

“Mother of Shadows, Gulliver. Lighten up,” Phoenix said, his gaze still locked on the defeated town below. “We just battled our way across the grasslands in the dark of night. Would it kill you to have a little more confidence in our ability to survive?"

"If we survive, remind me never to listen to you again."

Phoenix sighed. He'd forced himself not to use any void-stones, and whilst the decision to fight monsters using only a letter-opener from his bag had allowed him to preserve void-energy, it had also drawn every minor skirmish into an unnecessarily long stand-off and put his two companions in irritable moods.

"I expect some kind of compensation for this," Gulliver added.

"Fine." Phoenix squinted at a group of Shadows sprinting across a distant paddock, the silhouettes of their willowy grey bodies bounding through the early dawn light. "Get us out of this alive and I'll give you some sugar-cubes and a handful of oats."

"You expect to get out of *that* mess unharmed?" Gulliver glared at the town beyond the fields. It was unrecognisable, most buildings crumbled to the ground, piles of rubble jumbled amongst smouldering fires dotted like wildflowers around the devastated streets.

Phoenix caught glimpses of movement as the slender, grey invaders slunk in and out of collapsed homes, most in large groups, though a few in intimate pairs. He watched in fascination as a couple ducked under the awning of an old house then curled up together, their long arms draped around each other and their hairless heads resting side by side as they drifted to sleep.

"They act so... *human* sometimes."

"When they're not slaughtering entire towns." Fay's voice cut through Phoenix's mind like a blade of ice. He frowned and looked down at the cat, a dollop of purple slime glooping from the top of his head into his eyes.

"*Humans* kill more humans than Shadows do." He wiped the monster fluids from his face then slid from Gulliver's back onto the grass. "Time to get moving. They'll settle for a while now the sun is coming up."

Fay leapt from the horse onto Phoenix, her claws piercing his coat and latching into his skin.

"Gulliver," Phoenix said, reaching over his head to detach Fay from his shoulders. "You approach the town from the woods. There'll be Shadows in there, but you're just a horse, so I doubt they'll take much interest in you."

Gulliver flicked an ear. "*Just* a horse."

"We'll meet by the shed at the back of the house." Phoenix placed Fay on the ground then patted Gulliver on the neck. "Take care."

The horse snorted a farewell then trotted away down the hill.

Phoenix crouched before the sodden feline. "You ready?"

Fay transformed into her regular human form, looking grumpy and mean without any clothes to keep her warm.

Phoenix passed her the thick shawl that she'd left in his bag. "We've both seen each other naked tonight."

"Your point?" Fay asked as she buckled the shawl in place with her golden, rat-skull broach. "We shared a bath thousands of times when we were kids."

Phoenix laughed and raised his hands in defence. "Didn't mean anything by it. Just making conversation."

Fay rolled her eyes. "Let's just get this over with." She whipped her hand through the air and Phoenix experienced the unusual sensation of having his entire body licked by an aggressive updraft of wind. Before he could even register what was happening, a large, globular mass of purple goo was floating above his head, and both he and Fay were dry and slime-free.

"If I'm going to face an army of Shadows, I'd at least like to feel clean." Fay flicked the tremulous blob away and it splattered against the ground.

Impressed, Phoenix ruffled his fingers through his now soft, goo-less hair. "If your magic works as well as I know it does, we won't have to face *any* Shadows."

Fay raised her hands to the sky, creating a gently humming forcefield that wrapped around her and Phoenix like an electric cacoon. "Well, we're releasing no more energy than a wandering sheep. At least, that's how it will seem."

"You're as brilliant as I expected you to be."

"Honestly," Fay said, "what would you do if I hadn't agreed to come?"

Phoenix had a sudden vision of himself hurling void-energy in every direction, blasting his way across Bloodwood and slashing through entire legions of Shadows, a swarm of stones swirling overhead until he finally collapsed in a bloodied mess at the entrance to the void-chamber, too exhausted to even open the door.

He shrugged. "I'm sure I'd figure something out."

They wound their way down the grassy gullies, creeping closer to town, crouching behind the tumbledown lengths of spiked stonewalls that divided the farms. Occasionally, Fay would flick her hands through the air or twitch her fingers, and Phoenix would feel the energy around him shift in subtle ways that made his hairs stand on end.

"Does the energy I release really vary that much?" he asked as they crept past a crackling fire by the remains of a house. They had entered the dusty streets by this point and could see up close the destruction the Shadows had caused.

"It reacts to changes in your body," Fay said softly, concentration on her face as she tweaked the air, tugging upon invisible strings. "Sometimes even to changes in your mood. And the closer we get to the woods, the stronger your energy becomes." She tiptoed along the rim of a deep crater in the middle of the road filled with bits of building and a stinking mound of what Phoenix suspected to be several dead goblins, three or four goats, and half a horse.

"Keep your eyes open," Fay murmured. "If there's a food stash, there's bound to be a Shadow or two napping nearby."

Phoenix pulled his gaze away from the disturbing pit.

"They've certainly taken over the place, haven't they?"

Fay shook her head. "This is worse than the aftermath of ten years ago. At least the survivors had someplace to return to back then. There's nothing left now."

"Bloodwood will rebuild," Phoenix said, ducking his head as he followed Fay under a fallen lamppost leaning against a battered shop.

"You believe that?" Fay asked as she stepped over a small, shredded toy trodden into the gravel, left behind by a child in the frenzy to escape. "Rebuild from *this*?"

"It's populated by hardheads like Nan. Of course they'll rebuild." Phoenix crouched to pick up the toy. An arm was missing and one of its button eyes was dangling by a thread.

Fay glanced at him. "Aren't you worried at all? About your grandparents."

"Nah. They're indestructible." Phoenix spoke evenly, but prickly feelings of guilt and concern gnawed at the back of his mind. He patted some dust from the toy's matted fur then placed it upon a windowsill.

He was about to say something else when movement further down the road caught his eye and he grabbed Fay's arm, whisking her behind a wall into a narrow alleyway between two shops, the brick walls so close together that there was barely enough space to stretch an arm. Fay started making frantic motions with her hands.

"Can you reign your energy in a little?" she hissed.

Phoenix raised a finger to his lips. "Shadow."

They stood in silence, backs pressed against the wall as the heavy footsteps crunched nearer. The Shadow ambled into sight, its skeletal back hunched forward as it shuffled down the street, its long arms swaying limply by its sides. Phoenix had seen countless Shadows in his life, but none that looked quite as droopy and dejected as the one now mooching along the street before them.

"It looks drunk," Phoenix said under his breath, while Fay flicked her hands through the air beside him to nullify any energy that might give their position away.

"Let's follow the alley," she whispered. "Try our luck 'round the back."

Phoenix nodded. They edged along the wall, Fay concentrating on her magic and the path ahead while Phoenix kept his eyes on the opening to the street behind in case the Shadow returned.

"Mind your step," Fay murmured, but the warning came too late as Phoenix's foot cracked into a pile of old timber boards. The pile toppled with a clatter, sending a piece of wood flicking up against his leg and stabbing a nail into his ankle.

Phoenix smacked a hand over his mouth to muffle his startled yelp and the torrent of expletives he wanted to let loose. Fay spun around in alarm as the Shadow reappeared at the end of the alley, its wide, golden eyes peering into the gloom.

Phoenix and Fay froze before its glowing, unblinking stare.

"Sorry to bother you." Phoenix couldn't take the silence any longer.

The Shadow blinked its enormous eyes.

Phoenix smiled and pointed over his shoulder. "We were just leaving."

Lazily, as though the situation was not worth the effort of physical exertion, the creature began to raise its arm.

"Dammit." Phoenix clapped his hands together, but before he could pull his palms apart and activate a stone, Fay tugged urgently at his sleeve.

"Wait." She nodded at the Shadow. The bony grey hand it had raised was not directed at them. Rather, the Shadow was pointing its long, clawed finger down the street.

"I think..." Fay said, her hushed voice slow with uncertainty, "I think it's giving us a chance to run away."

Phoenix took a cautious step forward and the Shadow gave a gruff, satisfied grunt. Then it turned its back and trudged away down the road, dragging its knobbly feet through the dust. Phoenix and Fay crept to the end of the alleyway and watched as the Shadow slouched out of sight into a building that until yesterday had been a boutique store specialising in fancy hats.

"Odd…" Phoenix murmured.

Fay pushed against his back, urging him to move. "I doubt we'll fare so well if we meet another one today."

They carried on through the ravaged town, Phoenix growing more and more sombre as they drew nearer to his old home.

"I thought Jack said the Shadows were celebrating…" A troubled frown creased his brow. "That Shadow looked downright miserable."

"Maybe it had a rough night," Fay muttered.

"I'm surprised it was alone," Phoenix continued. "It was a little on the small side, too. Perhaps it was bullied by the other Shadows… What's the emotional capacity of a Shadow? Did it feel sorry for us back there? Was that empathy? Benevolence?"

Fay rolled her eyes. "We have bigger things to worry about at the moment."

They reached the front gate to Matilda and Teddy's house. The yard had been trampled beyond recognition, but the house itself seemed to have escaped the invasion unscathed.

Phoenix's heart leapt into his throat as he followed Fay past the fence to the narrow path by the side of the house. Unaware of his discomfort, Fay picked up a stick and started swiping the webs of spiders that had taken up residence between the hedges overnight.

"Fay." Phoenix surprised himself with the wobble in his voice. He cleared his throat and tried again. "I have a favour to ask."

Fay glanced back. "Another?"

"More a desperate reiteration of a request I've already made," Phoenix said.

Fay breathed a small sigh. "That being?"

"When this is over... Please don't let me disappear."

Fay stopped walking and Phoenix paused in the middle of the path while she gazed at him.

"I was kept in that prison for nearly fifteen years." Phoenix didn't even bother trying to stop himself from scratching his arm. "These last few days have given me more freedom than I've ever had in my entire life. It's like... this is my chance to finally do something good."

Fay said nothing so Phoenix pushed on, desperate for her to understand.

"I know things feel a little turbulent lately, but progress is happening in Yonder. And people on Earth are banding together to make positive changes in the world. I want to be part of all this. Making a difference. Not trapped as Flamegate's pathetic plaything."

Fay studied him a moment longer. "You're terrified."

Phoenix swallowed. "Once I go back... that's it. I'm there until the end."

"Of what exactly?"

"Hard to say..." Phoenix said. "Whatever ends first. Flamegate. The universe. Me." He shook his head then started walking, pushing past the dense shrubbery that lined the path. "All three at once? It's anyone's guess. But they underestimated me once already. They won't make the same mistake again." They rounded the corner of the house and came upon the yard with the small, vine-covered shed.

"In any case," Phoenix added heavily, "it should all be over in four weeks' time. There's some bleak comfort in finality I suppose."

They gazed at the shed in silence for a while, Phoenix working hard to convince himself that backing out of this decision so late into the plan was not a choice he could allow himself to make.

"Hey." Fay nudged him gently with her shoulder. "I won't let you disappear."

He smiled, not exactly assured, but comforted nonetheless. "Thanks."

Phoenix took a small breath then approached the shed with the same grim determination one might expect in somebody about to challenge Fidelity Ethel Thunderstone in a skull-crushing competition.

"Are these the storage units we'll be using?" Fay frowned sceptically at the two fat, metal barrels wasting away by the front of the shed, their glass gauges cracked and their curved, dusty sides damaged with rust and holes.

"Those are well past their prime," Phoenix said. "I'm hoping we'll find some safer ones inside." He pulled away the vines over the entrance to the shed before wrenching back the decaying timber door, revealing a narrow, steeply descending passageway with steps that disappeared almost immediately into the dark.

Fay poked her head in beside him. "You're sure you know what you're doing?"

"Yeah. *Why* I'm doing it, though, is becoming increasingly difficult to rationalise." Phoenix flicked a switch by the door and a series of dull, coin-sized lights flickered into life along the wall, illuminating the tunnel as it twisted out of sight under the ground.

"Well," he said, "down the rabbit hole we go." He followed the stairs with Fay close behind, the door swinging shut behind them.

"Is this how your grandparents created your mother?" Fay asked. "With this chamber?"

"I guess," Phoenix said, not too interested in discussing the matter. "I don't really know."

"Well, that's how Shades were made, isn't it?" Fay said. "During the war. The chambers' functions were reversed, so instead of drawing energy from life-forms, they pumped void-energy into pregnant women. And the babies that were born alive..."

"It's a little more complicated than that," Phoenix

mumbled. The passage levelled out and he and Fay found themselves in a wide, stone-walled room, empty aside for a few portly metal barrels stacked in the back corner. Each barrel was barely as high as Phoenix's knee, but something about their stocky structure gave the impression that they were almost too heavy to hold.

"Looks like Nan cleared most of the place out," Phoenix said, dropping his bag at his feet.

"This is it?" Fay frowned in the pale light of the lamps. "I was expecting something a little more... advanced."

Phoenix shook his head. "This is the storage room. The chamber's through there." He pointed at two metal doors across from them, difficult to see against the surrounding stone walls in the dimly lit space. "Could you do a safety check on those canisters there? Make sure they don't have cracks or anything? They haven't been used in a while."

Fay went to inspect the barrels while Phoenix wandered over to the metal doors.

"These things are ancient," Fay said, tapping the gauges of a barrel at the top of the stack.

"Pre-disk technology," Phoenix said. "Before the pipe-system was developed to transport raw energy to the factory. Back when people focused on storing as much energy as possible over long periods of time, rather than collecting smaller, safer amounts more frequently like we do today. Well, *did*. Before the factory was destroyed."

"How much energy could one of these contain?" Fay asked.

"Depends," Phoenix said, twisting a stiff wheel built into the wall. The metal doors began to slide apart, grinding open to reveal the dark chamber hidden behind them. "Providing the space-conversion mechanism is functioning properly and there aren't any leaks... a full canister could power the entire shield around Bloodwood for at least a couple of weeks. Maybe even three or four."

Phoenix stopped cranking the wheel, the doors having

now opened completely into the foreboding space, a gloomy cavity no larger than any of the service elevators operating inside Flamegate.

He glanced back at Fay. She was staring at the barrels with her eyebrows raised.

"That's amazing." She carefully picked one up and examined it. "How does it work?"

"I'll show you." Phoenix waved her over and she brought the hefty little barrel along in her arms, planting it on the ground before the open doors. She paused, distracted by the sight beyond.

Phoenix followed her gaze. "Not exactly welcoming, is it?"

Fay stepped inside and peered about. The walls, floor and ceiling were lined with thick wire mesh, the countless strands of green, crisscrossing metal glinting in the soft light shining in from the storage room. There was nothing else in the chamber, not even a place to sit.

"The wire..." she said, plucking at some of the mesh against the wall. "Your energy is absorbed through all this."

Phoenix nodded, still standing outside the metal doors.

"And your nan left you here when you were a kid?" Fay didn't sound convinced. "Alone?"

Phoenix chuckled. "For the good of society." He knelt by the barrel and Fay backed out of the chamber to join him.

"The energy runs through those pipes," Phoenix said, pointing at a tangle of tubes attached to the ceiling above the door, "passes through a few dozen regulators," his finger traced the path of a pipe running down the wall with a bundle of green wires protruding from the end, "then gathers in our little canister here." He placed the barrel beneath the pipe then clipped the bundled wires against a metal plate fixed to the barrel's top.

"All you have to do," Phoenix added, "is close the door behind me, then flick this switch to start extraction." He tapped a switch beside the wheel he had used earlier to open the door. "These wires will glow bright gold, and they'll keep glowing until the chamber registers that I can't renew my energy anymore."

Fay was frowning at him with her arms crossed. "And how long should that take?"

Phoenix shrugged. "When the wires turn green again, it means the process is over and you can let me out. An alarm should ring, so you don't have to watch the wires the whole time. Just wait for the bell." He stretched his arms above his head as though preparing to start an exercise routine. "The whole thing should take a couple of hours. I should've asked you to bring a book or something. There might be a few things of interest in my bag. Feel free to check. Careful with the trumpet, though. It's a beat-up piece of tin-can, but it has sentimental worth."

Fay's frown deepened. "So, I'm just supposed to seal you away in the dark and wait until the chamber registers the fact that you're almost dead?"

"Once you flick the switch the whole place lights up with the void-energy being extracted from me, so the dark isn't an issue so much," Phoenix said as he slipped out of his coat. "But essentially, yes. You have to close that door."

"And torture you."

"By my own volition," Phoenix reminded her. "Besides, I would have thought you believed I deserved it."

Fay looked away. "I'm not sure what you deserve anymore, Phoenix."

"Nothing good, I assure you." Phoenix folded his coat and placed it on the floor. "I'm sorry I dragged you into this, Fay. Really. On the other hand, though, I'm honestly glad that you're here." He stepped inside and stood awkwardly in the centre of the tightly walled space. "See you on the flipside, I guess."

Fay stared at him long enough to be uncomfortable, grimaced, then shook her head and walked out of sight behind the wall. Phoenix heard her turn the wheel as the doors started to grind shut. He stared ahead as the sliver of light narrowed until it was little more than a luminous thread connecting the ceiling and the floor.

Then the doors sealed shut with a click and Phoenix was swallowed by the dark.

DISJOINTED

Phoenix held his breath, his eyes squeezed shut even though the chamber was already so devoid of light that he couldn't see his hands even if he tried. He waited for the impact, the burning heat, the initial shock of all his energy starting to tear away, but nothing happened.

Moments passed.

Phoenix felt his way forward and knocked on the door. "Is there a problem?"

Fay's muffled voice responded after a pause. "I've read the history books, Phoenix. I've seen the illustrations. I know what this thing does."

Phoenix gave a nervous laugh. "I thought this would be easy for you."

"So did I," Fay snapped.

Phoenix ran his hand over his face. "We discussed this."

"How much will this hurt?"

"Fay." Phoenix rested his forehead against the door. "I can take it."

"And if you can't? I drag your body back through an army of Shadows then confess to your family, not to mention your massive warlock friend, that I killed you? I'm sure he'll take that well. And I'll have to live the rest of my life with your stupid death on my conscience."

Phoenix turned and slid to the floor, his back against the metal doors and his head resting in his hands. "I'm difficult to kill," he muttered. "Trust me."

Fay said nothing.

"If it weren't for me," Phoenix added, "your parents would still be alive."

"That's not the *point*, Phoenix. I never wanted to make you suffer. Not like this, anyway."

It was a long while before Phoenix spoke again.

"Listen," he said, his voice hollow in the cavernous space, "my life has never really belonged to me. It's been governed by people more powerful. People only ever interested in using me to help themselves. Nan. Maulbrak. Flamegate." He paused, forcing himself to stop raking his nails over his arm. "Particularly Flamegate." He clasped his hands together then pressed his knuckles against his brow. "But it was never *what* they put me through that hurt most. It's the fact that the pain was beyond my control. That lack of freedom. The belief that I was helpless against people in charge of deciding my own fate."

Fay remained quiet on the other side of the door.

"But nobody is forcing me into this," Phoenix continued. "And yes, it's going to sting a bit, but this is my choice for a change… And there's something tremendously satisfying about that."

"I'll do it," Fay said, after an extensive silence that trembled around Phoenix's ears. "But I want you to know that I'm feeling conflicted."

Phoenix smiled into the dark. "I'll keep that in mind."

"Brace yourself," Fay muttered, then the chamber exploded with golden light and Phoenix gasped, curling into his knees as he sank to his side, the metal mesh searing hot against his skin.

"You still alive?" Fay called, but Phoenix couldn't answer with anything more than a solid kick to the door. He clamped his teeth around his arm and chomped down in an attempt to distract himself from the growing pressure surrounding him, as though he were bound by tightening ropes pulling at him from all sides.

It was worse than he remembered.

After an eternity, the shock subsided enough for him to move, not that there was anywhere safe to go. He crawled into a corner and glared at the wall, curling his fingers around the burning wires as he snarled through the agony of having his energy torn away. Some gritty, feral part of him seized control, and Phoenix was more than willing to let the monster take charge.

Eventually, he would have to return to himself and confront the universe as the mixed-up human-hybrid everyone knew him to be, but for now, Phoenix Page was nothing but tortured Shadow.

~

"Cupcakes!" Bee threw open the door and danced into Edgar's room with a tray of rainbow cakes balancing on one hand and a gaggle of giggling children skipping around at her feet, none of them older than five or six.

The old man slammed the cupboard of his writing-desk with a startled snap, then backed into the centre of his room and stared at Bee with narrowed eyes. "*Belinda*. Privacy.

What did I say about privacy? You cannot just waltz in here unannounced, accompanied by your little goblin army like the place belongs to—"

A grubby boy dashed forward and seized Edgar by the end of his dark dressing-robe, shaking the fabric up and down in his pudgy fist.

Edgar glared at him, but before he could make his displeasure known, the remaining dozen or so children charged forward and grabbed their own handfuls of his clothes, bouncing the silky, black fabric up and down with glee.

"Wizard! We caught the wizard!"

"What?" Edgar tugged at his robes. "I'm not... Would you *stop*?"

A young girl leapt up and grabbed a fistful of his long, white hair, wrenching the old man's head back so much that Bee finally felt the need to intervene.

"Alright, that's enough. Settle down or we won't have any more baking days."

The children let go and frowned at her in disappointment, though none as unhappily as the frown Edgar directed at her.

"I told you how I feel about visitors," he said. "I told *everyone* how I feel about visitors."

"Yes, you made yourself very clear." Bee smiled at him from the doorway. "The kids and I made cupcakes. We wanted to share."

Edgar scowled. "You really think these terrors need more sugar?"

"Will you eat cake with us?" The girl who had pulled his hair tapped him softly on the stomach.

Edgar swooped down to her level like a bat in a horror film. "I only eat *children*."

The kids screamed and dashed out the door into the bustling living-space beyond.

Bee followed the children into the communal chaos area

beside the kitchen. The tables were crowded, as usual, with flustered people peering over papers and maps. Ghost stood at the head of a messy heap of charts, his pale face leaning in close to a broad, sturdy woman Bee knew only as 'Naia', a civil engineer who wore the same set of black, button-down blouses with a different gaudy bowtie every day of the week.

"You suggesting I'm a liar?" Ghost snarled, a threatening glint in his sharp blue eyes as he breathed into the woman's face.

"Don't answer that," Bee muttered as she walked past the table into the kitchen, the horde of kids bouncing along demanding food. She crouched so they could reach the tray then the raucous troupe scattered about the house with cake on their hands, chasing each other under tables, galloping into the front room to abuse the piano, or crawling onto the only sofa not occupied by people tapping away at screens. That sofa was instead occupied by Phoenix, who had been stretched out on his back with his eyes closed all day, oblivious to the world. He remained floppy and unconscious even as children clambered onto the armrests and started playing with his tangled red hair.

"Ghost, I trust you." Naia placed her hand over one of the maps. "But that tunnel you're referring to... It's been blocked for over a decade. The only way into Flamegate Tower is from the sky."

Ghost cracked a rare grin, hardly more comforting than his usual leering expression of animosity. "I intend to prove you wrong."

The moustached nurse emerged from the stairs leading into the infirmary, red in the face with rage burning behind his beady eyes. "Has anyone seen Little Mick?"

Naia ducked away from Ghost's glare and faced the stairs. "He went to the Campus Ruins with Vince."

"That was Big Mick," Bee said, setting the tray of leftover cakes upon the kitchen counter. "Little Mick went to the Wellington Estate with Jay."

The nurse's handlebar-moustache dipped into a frown. "The Wellington Estate…?"

A tall woman wearing a blue suit-jacket rose from one of the couches and held her hands around her mouth to holler an announcement over the discordant noise of the violently mistreated piano. "Conference call with Lady Maxine and her team in twenty minutes!"

"What's he doing at the Wellington Estate?" the nurse demanded.

A man shouted from behind an old laptop. "Kids, no more piano!"

"But, Rex!"

"*Tyler*."

"Rory." The woman in the blue suit-jacket rounded on a rumpled young man melting into the sofa with a handful of electronic devices in his lap, their screens glowing with coded streams of complicated, rapidly changing data. "Make yourself presentable."

The man scowled. "What's that supposed to mean, Stephanie?"

"*Pants*, Rory. Wear pants."

Bee started loading baking utensils into the sink. "Little Mick went to the Estate because he said we were low on vegetables."

The piano continued blasting through the entire house.

"You know what else we're low on?" the nurse snapped over the din.

Nearly everyone in the room responded under their breath, "Medical supplies."

"*Medical supplies*!" the nurse said, flinging his arms above his head before marching off, still grumbling as he disappeared into the infirmary. "How difficult is it to find an x-ray machine?"

Bee closed her eyes. One of the boys was somehow managing to smash what must have been every key of the piano in perfect, maddening unison.

The suited lady barked instructions at the house again. "Lady Maxine is connecting in less than fifteen minutes, people. Have your materials ready."

"Kids! Piano! Shut it! Now."

The kids slammed the lid of the piano then ran into the kitchen, two boys diving past Bee into the cupboard under the sink, leaving the door ajar just enough to spy on the commotion outside.

Bee turned from the pile of kitchen utensils to find that Edgar had stolen into the kitchen and was leaning against the fridge, calmly eating a cake from the tray.

Bee shook her head. "How do you sneak around so quietly all the time?"

The old man responded with half a shrug and Bee noticed his pale eyes drift to the sofa where Phoenix lay, his red hair tied in a collection of messy, miniature ponytails, utterly oblivious to the mayhem going on around him.

"We found him in the kitchen," Bee said, watching as one of the girls crawled on top of Phoenix to braid his hair. "On the floor beside a frying pan. We think he was planning to cook something before he passed out on his own."

Edgar raised an eyebrow. "Fascinating." He pulled a silver flask from the inside pocket of his dressing-robe, unscrewed the cap, then took a gulp.

"I wish he'd wake up," Bee added, leaning beside him against the fridge. "I want to ask him about that Simon guy who appeared."

Edgar grunted something incomprehensible then took another, far longer swig of his drink.

One of the boys popped his head out from the cupboard under the sink. "Is that juice?"

"A little stronger than juice, kid." Edgar almost smiled.

"Can I have some?"

The old man started handing over his flask. "Sure."

"Edgar!"

"What?" Edgar muttered. "That should teach him not to

touch my stuff."

"Bee!" One of the young girls called from the sofa. "The sleepy guy is crying."

Bee frowned. "Crying?" She walked past the crowded table to take a look, several other members of the Alliance stopping what they were doing to gather around the sofa and peer at Phoenix's face.

Phoenix was grimacing in his sleep, tears leaking into the cushions beneath him. Bee lifted the little girl from his chest and planted her on the floor, but Phoenix's breathing only grew more ragged, his fists clenched so tightly that they shook.

Ghost leant over the sofa and curled his fingers around Phoenix's wrist, wrenching the freckled arm into the air. "This wimpy runt is the one we're pinning all our hopes on?" He dropped Phoenix's arm and let it fall over the edge of the couch. "That masked witch better not be playing us."

"Alice isn't a witch," Bee said. "She's a time-traveller from another world with more knowledge than any of us combined." She pulled back one of Phoenix's eyelids. "His eyes are green."

Ghost's thin, white brows furrowed in irritation. "What's that got to do with anything?"

"Usually they're... different." Bee pulled her hand away. "The light is gone."

"From his eyes?" Naia asked.

Bee nodded. "When he's awake, they burn like stars."

"Bit of an overdramatic way to describe a pair of eyeballs," Edgar said, slowly lowering himself into a chair by the table away from everyone else. "Couple of commonplace peepers burning with the intensity of thermonuclear fusion. Hyperbole is the world's most devastating evil."

Bee wasn't listening to him. "Even when he was asleep for two months, there was still a little light left in them whenever we checked."

"Should we wake him?" Naia leant down to shake

Phoenix by the shoulder.

"Where's the logic in that?" Edgar folded his arms and frowned at everyone. "Your blubbering friend there leads a double-life. He can't deal with the situation in the other world if you drag him away to Earth, can he? Let him struggle. Leave him be."

Bee chewed her lip. "Do you think he's in trouble?"

Edgar shrugged. "Who isn't, these days?" He rose from the chair, pausing for a moment to grip the edge of the table. "Take my advice. Don't get attached to that kid. Alice has a rather utilitarian outlook on life." He adjusted his long robes then turned his back to everyone and headed for the kitchen again. "She'll sacrifice anyone if it helps bring Flamegate to its knees. No one is safe. Not even her friends. That boy is just another pawn in her elaborate plan." And with that, Edgar took another cupcake then slunk away into his room, the door closing behind him with a snap.

A whimper escaped Phoenix's mouth and one of the little girls patted his forehead.

"He's having a nightmare," she whispered. "I'll get him my teddy."

~

Phoenix lay on his back, spreadeagled like a starfish as he gazed at the dwindling light coursing through the wires overhead. Too exhausted to move, his mind wandered from incomplete thought to incomplete thought, drifting back and forth between clarity and absurdity as though he were trapped in a terrible dream. One moment he was pondering what he would say to the High Chief of Yonder. The next, he was convinced he was back in the grey, windowless cell he'd spent almost half his life inside.

Maybe he'd never even escaped. Maybe the last few days had been the cruel trick of a broken mind. Maybe the death of the twins had traumatised him so much that instead of motivating him to escape, he'd finally snapped and was actually alone in the dark somewhere, covered in cords and sensors while Flamegate monitored him with cold detachment from behind triple-locked doors.

The warm glow around the chamber plummeted to a few wavering threads of gold and then everything went black. An alarm sounded outside, drawing Phoenix out of his mind long enough to realise that he needed to move fast if he wanted to resist the pull of the Crush. With the chamber no longer holding him in place, he'd have to cling to something else until Fay arrived.

Phoenix pressed his hands together and dragged a stone from his palm. He flicked it up and watched it hover mere inches above his nose, the gold streaks shimmering in the dark as it rotated slowly before his eyes, emitting the deep, familiar hum.

A strange calm washed over him, his aching muscles relaxing as the pain lifted from his body, floating away with all his sense of self and time.

Soft light flooded the chamber as the doors moved apart. Fay entered in slow-motion, her yellow eyes wide as she crouched by Phoenix's side. Her mouth was moving but Phoenix couldn't understand a word.

"Faydelia," he mumbled. "Hello."

Fay might have responded as she took hold of his shoulders, but Phoenix's mind was already someplace else, drifting through memories he didn't want to see.

THE ART OF ESCAPING

The silence was everywhere, so heavy and so still that Time itself struggled to pass at a respectable pace, too encumbered by the oppressive, all-consuming hush.

Phoenix gazed up at the grey ceiling of the prison cell—a stark, suffocating space with concrete walls that seemed to move closer the longer you stared at them. He was thirteen, lean and pale, his lightly freckled face not yet mature enough to prevent him from looking like a scrawny kid, an image not helped by the baggy, grey uniform he was forced to wear, even though it was several sizes too big.

Often, when Phoenix was awake in his cage, he would

occupy his time by pacing the tight perimeter, humming old Yonderian tunes, or drumming complicated rhythms on any available surface, but he had been lying on the floor for hours now and hadn't moved an inch.

He was working on a plan.

A sharp pain shot from the fingers of his left hand to his shoulder then jolted through the rest of his body like electricity. He turned his head and scowled at his arm stretched against the cement floor beside him. The microchip had been playing up. Something about the materials eroding from prolonged exposure to the void-energy in his blood.

His unnatural, monster-tainted blood.

Would Simon still be his friend if he knew just how much of a Shadow Phoenix could become?

Would anyone?

A red light pulsed beneath his skin, illuminating the veins in his forearm, and Phoenix reached over to scratch at the bump created by the invasive little device. Another shock travelled through his body and Phoenix fell still, giving up on any attempts to rip the thing out. Flamegate would only replace it anyway, undoubtedly with something more advanced.

Phoenix knew this because he'd already torn three chips from his arm within the past year alone.

He stood and wandered over to an old, silver toilet in the corner of the cell then lay on his stomach between the toilet and the wall.

"Emma? You there?"

A child's voice responded through a small hole just above the floor, barely wide enough to push a thumb through.

"You're back? I thought you were in Yonder."

"Nah." Phoenix shook his head. "I've been thinking."

"Could've thought aloud," Emma muttered from the other side. "It's not like Cody and I are talking to each other. I'm bored."

Phoenix smiled. "Aw, c'mon. At least you have a

cellmate. He might not say much, but he's still good company." He raised his voice. "Isn't that right, Codes?"

"Don't be such a flea, Phoenix," Emma snapped. "He's not going to answer you."

The smile slid from Phoenix's face. "Just because he hasn't said anything for two years doesn't mean he wants us to stop talking to him. You two are twins. You're supposed to support each other."

"Maybe he stopped talking because you talk enough for all three of us," Emma said.

Phoenix rolled his eyes then froze as Emma's words sank in.

"Three of us." He repeated the phrase to see if it sounded any less surreal. Barely a month ago, three had been four: himself, Emma, Cody, and Alice.

"Sorry." Emma's voice softened behind the wall. "I forget that you miss her."

"Don't *you*?" Phoenix asked.

"Missing Alice is stupid," Emma said. "It won't get us out, and it won't bring her back."

"Pretty cold for an eleven-year-old." Phoenix frowned at the red light pulsing in his forearm. "Speaking of getting out... I *think*... I've thought of a way to escape."

Silence.

"Void-stones," Phoenix added.

Emma huffed. "You can't activate them inside Flamegate. You've tried, and it nearly kills you. Every. Single. Time."

"True." Phoenix smiled at his own ingenuity. "But I can easily activate a stone in Yonder."

"How's that meant to help?"

"Step one," Phoenix said, his grin stretching across his face, "I go to sleep."

"Okay..."

"As soon as I wake up in Yonder, I activate a stone."

"Why?"

"The stones stop me from changing worlds," Phoenix said, still sprawled on his stomach between the silver latrine and the wall. "If I keep one activated long enough, Flamegate will worry that something is wrong. My energy isn't much good to them if it's not here on Earth."

Emma took a moment to consider that.

"How long will you be gone?" she asked. "In Yonder?"

"I think I could keep a stone activated for three or four days... Long enough for Flamegate to think something was strange at least."

"Aren't void-stones really bad for you?"

"So is growing up in prison, Em."

"And *how* exactly are you planning to escape?"

"Simple," Phoenix replied. "Once Flamegate realises I'm not changing worlds, they'll take me to that restricted void-manipulation unit for evaluation. The high-tech, super exclusive one under the dome. And guess what *else* happens to be inside that unit."

Emma breathed a small 'oh' of realisation. "The void-equaliser controls..."

"Yep. And you know what'd happen if the void-equaliser was switched off, right?"

"You're mad, Phoenix."

"A mad genius."

"If you switch the equaliser off, the Crush would break."

"And cause a most spectacular distraction." Phoenix propped himself up on his elbows, his chin resting in his hands as he beamed in delight at the sheer, simplistic brilliance of his plan. "Not only would the Crush malfunction. With the equaliser out, I'll be able to use the stones anywhere I like, for as long as I need. And once I activate those stones..." Phoenix dropped his voice, shaking his head at all the incredible possibilities. "I'll be unstoppable."

"It's a stupid idea." Even at her young age, Emma was never one to be swept away by tenuous hopes. "There's no way you'll even get near the controls."

"Sure I will. The units under the dome aren't heavily guarded outside of festival season. And the scientists are all pretty tame." Phoenix rolled onto his back and stared at the ceiling again. "When I finally release the stone in Yonder, I'll wake up exactly where I need to be in the middle of the unit, force a fresh stone into use, take everyone by surprise before the effort required kills me, switch off the void-equaliser once I've taken care of any resistance, activate a couple more stones under the easier conditions, destroy the entire research lab, then blast my way to freedom and never, ever, ever look back."

"Sounds impossible."

"There's a flippered river-mole in Yonder," Phoenix said, stretching his hands into the air, watching the red light blink inside his arm. "It emerges from the water once a year, gathers mud and twigs in its pouch, climbs up the very tall, very rare flameberry tree because no other tree will do, then builds a nest to lay up to fifteen eggs, only one of which will survive."

"Phoenix... What?"

"It's a defenceless, tree-climbing river-mole," Phoenix said flatly. "It climbs a tree. With *flippers*. Nothing is impossible. I'm going to escape."

Emma was quiet for a moment before tentatively posing her next question. "What about us?"

Phoenix smiled. "I'll take you with me!"

"You know Cody and I can't live without medication, right?"

"We'll steal some from Flamegate."

"What if it runs out?"

"I'm sure there's medicine outside."

"And if there isn't?"

"How about this." Phoenix shifted onto his side to face the hole in the wall. "I escape, secure enough meds to keep you and Cody alive, then come back to free you."

"With the void-equaliser working again? You're crazy, Phoenix. Cody and I are going to spend the rest of our lives in this place, and you know it."

A loud hiss interrupted the conversation as the airtight door to Phoenix's cell slid open and two men stepped into the room, one towering tall, dark-haired, and garbed in flowing red robes, the other dressed in casual brown attire, short, stocky, and bulging with muscles so large they seemed more decorative than practical.

Phoenix sat up with a nervous smile. "Can't you knock, Astros?"

"*Brother* Astros," the tall man said wearily. "And I'm sorry to interrupt whatever little chat you were having, but I've been ordered to have you purified."

Phoenix's pulse quickened but he maintained his stiff smile. "Again?"

"The Night Order wants you ready for tomorrow's festival," Astros said, his robes trailing the floor as he strode into the cell. "I've been told to run some tests."

The short, muscled man stomped over and grabbed Phoenix by the upper-arm, wrenching him to his feet before dragging him into the middle of the room to stand before Astros.

Astros shook his head. "*Gentle*, please."

"Who's the new guy?" Phoenix asked, jerking out of the shorter man's grip.

"Dave," Astros replied as he rummaged through a pouch tied around his waist. "Excuse his brutish nature. We recruited him from the sketchier side of the Lower Ring. I should warn you that his physical prowess far makes up for his lack of social refinement."

"I can crush melons with my bare hands," Dave said.

"That's adorable," Phoenix said, tapping the brawny man lightly on the nose. Dave smashed his fist into Phoenix's gut and Phoenix doubled over with a groan.

Astros looked up from the pouch he was delving through and sighed. "Five, what part of provoking the thug seemed like a good idea?"

Phoenix hugged his stomach, eyes watering. "Just

testing the boundaries, Astros. You know me."

"*Brother* Astros," the robed man said, then he pulled a plastic box from his pouch, a narrow container that Phoenix had seen enough times to know contained a syringe.

Astros offered a feeble smile. "Don't make this any more difficult than it needs to be," he said, nodding pointedly at the man in brown.

Phoenix glowered as Dave pushed up Phoenix's sleeve and Astros pressed the needle into his skin.

The burning concoction hit like a boxer and Phoenix swayed on his feet, the floor rising and swelling around him in deep, rolling waves.

He sank to his knees then raised his eyebrows at the two men. "Will that be all for today?"

"No." Astros gestured at the bed—a low slab of cement with a thin mat on top. "Take a seat."

"Why?"

"Because you were told," Dave growled, ramming his knee against Phoenix's back. Phoenix had no balance remaining to keep himself from slamming into the cement.

"For Light's sake." Astros placed a hand on the other man's shoulder. "I can take it from here."

Dave scowled for a second then stalked outside to wait in the corridor.

Astros leant down to pull Phoenix to his feet. "I apologise for that. These hired grunts have no class." He helped Phoenix to the bed then lowered him onto his side. "Do you feel purified yet?"

"Astros..." Phoenix couldn't focus, the growing nausea threatening to overwhelm him as his insides burned. "I don't think purification is good for my health."

Astros grimaced as he sat by Phoenix's side. "I fear it's rather not." He produced another item from the pouch at his waist: a green, metal square with prongs on each corner.

"Not... another patch." Phoenix struggled to form words as the haze grew heavier.

"Sorry, Five." Astros took Phoenix's limp arm and pressed the square against the underside of his wrist. Phoenix winced as the prongs buried into his skin. "The Order wants a void sample. Don't pull it out before it's collected, otherwise you'll have to go through it all again." Astros wrapped a bandage around Phoenix's arm to hold the patch in place then patted Phoenix on the side of the head. "Be good."

He started to walk away but Phoenix sat with a scowl and started tearing at the material around his arm. Astros reached down and clasped Phoenix's hand, looking at him with a sincerity few people within Flamegate ever expressed. "Phoenix, believe me. You keep disobeying simple instructions like this, and you're going to end up in solitary confinement again. Do yourself a favour for once. Stop fighting."

His face swum before Phoenix's eyes then faded from sight as he backed away and disappeared from the cell, the door sealing closed behind him with a hiss.

Phoenix ripped the bandages from his arm then seized the metal patch and wrenched it out of his skin. He tossed the square onto the bed then staggered to the corner of the room and collapsed over the toilet, retching violently into the silver bowl.

Emma's voice drifted through the hole in the wall. "Gross."

Phoenix coughed uncontrollably in reply.

"Still planning to escape on your own?" Emma asked, but Phoenix was too sick to respond. He closed his eyes and slumped further over the basin.

"Whatever." Emma's voice sounded far away. "Go ahead and leave like everyone else. Be free."

Phoenix said nothing, his forehead resting against the cold rim of the toilet seat.

"Are you unconscious?" Emma asked after a while. "Back in Yonder?"

Phoenix held his breath and waited to drift away. He, Simon and Jess were in the middle of a quest to find the lost giants of the Snaggletooth Mountains, and the mortal dangers of the expedition seemed more appealing than anything Earth had to offer right now.

"I'm jealous of you," Emma murmured. "You get to live. You aren't stuck here every second of every day. You can travel. You have friends."

Phoenix couldn't hold himself up any longer. He slipped down the toilet and fell to the floor.

There was a long pause before Emma spoke again.

"You're so lucky, Phoenix. I wish we were even half as lucky as you."

~

"Phoenix!" Fay's voice burst through the darkness and Phoenix flinched, realising that he was in the warmly lit storage room by the void-chamber, his back against a wall as Fay crouched before him, her hands squeezing his arms.

"Fay…?"

"Release the stone. You don't need it."

"The twins are going to die."

"Phoenix." Fay leant in close, her yellow eyes boring into his own. "You need to concentrate on what's happening now."

"I don't have time," Phoenix mumbled.

"The stone, Phoenix. I'll restore your energy. Some of it, at least. Just let the stone go."

Phoenix glanced up to where the green gem was spinning above his head. He opened his hand and the stone glided out of sight into his palm, taking away the numbing effects its presence had been providing. The ache left by the void-chamber came crashing back and Phoenix barely had time to see Fay raise a hand above her head before his vision started to disappear. He was going to pass out. The Crush would win.

"Here goes nothing," Fay murmured, and Phoenix yelled as an explosion of energy slammed into his chest. Fay tumbled backwards and Phoenix crumpled to his side.

He grinned and pushed himself into a sitting position again. "It worked."

Fay sat up with a groan.

"I'm still here." Phoenix patted himself down in disbelief. "I didn't even black out." He stared, wide-eyed, at Fay. "You channelled all that through your body. That's an extraordinary feat."

"There's plenty of energy around," Fay said, rubbing her eyes. "Besides, you asked me to help you."

"Yeah, but not even Maulbrak uses his body alone."

Fay blinked. "What?"

"He carries a fortified staff for jobs like this. Nearly impossible to find, and even harder to create, but they help distribute the load." Phoenix leant his weight against the wall and stood up, his legs wobbling beneath him. "Only the most skilled magicians can accomplish what you just did. Accurately reading the energy levels. Transferring the balance from one body to another. One wrong move and you could've obliterated us both."

"You said it was simple."

"I lied. I do that sometimes." Phoenix rested his head against the cool stone behind him. "Knew you could do it, though. Never doubted you for a second. Gloria will be impressed. She'll have to graduate you from apprentice with this. Congratulations."

Fay pinched the bridge of her nose. "I hate you so much."

"I'd be worried if you didn't." Phoenix smiled at her. "Can you stand?"

Fay pushed herself to her feet. "Just about. Can you walk?"

Phoenix let go of the wall and stumbled forward a couple of steps before regaining his balance. "Like a newborn deer in a puddle of mud."

"Well, find your feet quickly. We've been in Shadow territory long enough."

"Phoenix." Gulliver's voice interrupted the conversation. "Cat-lady."

"Gulliver!" Phoenix grinned into empty space. "You're alive!"

"For now. We have a situation."

"Does it involve a ridiculous number of Shadows approaching to investigate the suspicious fluctuations in void-energy created just now by Fay and myself?"

"It does indeed."

"Wonderful."

"Well, we never expected this to be easy," Fay said, grabbing Phoenix's coat and bag from the floor. "Come on." She started leading the way along the tunnel, Phoenix staggering behind.

"Wait, wait, wait!" Phoenix spun around, returned to the room then seized the small, metal barrel from beside the void-chamber and waved it at Fay. "Knew we were forgetting something."

Fay rolled her eyes. "Light help us."

"That would've been good," Phoenix said with a laugh. "Imagine trying to explain this little venture to Simon if we came back empty-handed."

"In an unusual development," Gulliver said from outside, "there's a Shadow up here wearing a hat."

"A hat?" Phoenix shot Fay a quizzical glance.

"With feathers." Gulliver could not have sounded more apathetic even if he tried.

"Just to be clear," Phoenix said, "the Shadow has feathers? Or the hat?"

"How many Shadows, Gulliver?" Fay, at least, was more interested in the practical side of the matter.

"Twenty or so. But their numbers are increasing."

"What are they all doing?" Phoenix asked as he and Fay followed the passage.

"Staring at me," Gulliver said. "They must have felt the energy surge, but they are confused. They were expecting a magician. And I am a horse."

Fay cast Phoenix a wary look. "Can you fight?"

"I'm not sure I'll stay conscious long enough to get out of this tunnel," Phoenix said, shifting the weight of the barrel in his arms. "But I'll try. Wouldn't want to miss out on all the fun."

"We'll have to move fast," Fay said, taking the barrel from Phoenix's hands. She opened Phoenix's bag and rammed the heavy canister inside. Phoenix grimaced, imagining his trumpet being smashed out of shape beneath the barrel's weight.

"Keep this safe," Fay said, pushing the bag against Phoenix's chest. "And take this scrappy old rag."

"This scrappy rag was a gift." Phoenix pulled on his tatty, multicoloured coat then swung the bulging bag over his shoulder. "I'm exceedingly fond of it."

They stopped at the top of the stairs, gentle droughts of wind whispering through the cracks in the shed, tousling their hair.

Fay pressed her hand against the door. "What's the plan?"

Phoenix shrugged. "Head for Karvil," he said, keeping his voice low. "Outrun the army of Shadows. Try not to die."

Fay nodded. "I like it for its simplicity. Count of three then?"

"*Three*!" Phoenix kicked open the door and was met by a chorus of startled snarls and angry growls. Gulliver was standing in front of the shed with his ears laid flat, surrounded by a half-circle of confused Shadows who turned to gawk at Phoenix and Fay like a bunch of thin, knobbly grey trees with a disturbing desire to feed on flesh.

One Shadow launched itself at Phoenix, its long, bony fingers outstretched. It was intercepted midleap by another Shadow wearing a brightly feathered hat and the two creatures rolled across the ground in a hissing tangle of limbs.

Phoenix blinked in surprise. "That's interesting."

"Phoenix!" Fay had already leapt onto Gulliver's back.

"Move!"

Phoenix ducked as another Shadow leapt over his head to join the escalating scuffle with the Shadow in the feathered hat. Gulliver barged through the throng of bodies and Fay reached for Phoenix's hand.

"Jump!"

Phoenix kicked off from a nearby rock then clambered behind Fay onto the horse's back. A glowing wall of red light erupted around them, blasting the crowd of Shadows backwards through the air.

Gulliver bolted for the side of the house, hurtling down the narrow garden-path as the Shadows scrambled to their feet, half of them flinging themselves after Gulliver while the others turned upon each other, biting and scratching and blasting golden light.

"We seem to have triggered some kind of Shadow civil war." Phoenix watched the chaos unfolding over his shoulder. "Was that red light back there you?"

"A protection circle," Fay shouted, as Gulliver stormed through the front gate. "I don't have energy to create another. Focus for a second. Don't let me fall." She leant against Phoenix then disappeared into her shawl, shrinking into the scruffy cat. She nearly tumbled out onto the road but Phoenix grabbed her by the scruff of the neck then tucked her down his shirt where she could grip the fabric with her claws.

"Alright, Gulliver," Phoenix muttered. "Time to earn those sugar-cubes and oats." He leant forward, clasping Gulliver's mane and gripping the horse with his thighs. Gulliver lowered his head and picked up speed, his hooves flying over the debris scattered about the street as Shadows poured out from behind tumbledown walls to join the pursuit.

"Why are they so interested in us?" Phoenix asked, as Gulliver skidded around a burning wagon in the middle of the road. A Shadow crouching in an alleyway flashed across their path, its claws ripping through Gulliver's side. Gulliver bucked out of its reach with an angry snort, nearly throwing Phoenix from his back.

"Maybe they know we're transporting raw energy," Fay said, her voice far more composed than everything else racing through Phoenix's mind. "Perhaps they see it as a threat."

"Then why do some of them seem to be defending us?" Phoenix wondered, bracing himself as Gulliver leapt over a fence.

"That," Fay said, "I have no idea."

They tore through the battered streets, dodging the onslaught of claws and teeth. By the time they broke away into the surrounding farmlands, they had gathered an impressive horde of hungry pursuers.

"If you think I can outrun these monsters all the way to Karvil," Gulliver said, "you are gravely mistaken."

"I thought they'd give up by now." Phoenix glanced over his shoulder at the legion of Shadows spilling out onto the fields behind them. "Follow the ridge. Maybe we can lose them on the other side."

They thundered down the side of the hill and Fay clambered up Phoenix's back.

"Claws, Faydelia!" Phoenix winced as she scratched against his skin.

She popped her head out the collar of his shirt and peered at the open fields behind them. "They've fallen behind, but they're still hounding us."

Phoenix gulped. "We have a problem."

"That much is obvious," Fay snapped.

"Not the Shadows," Phoenix said. "Me."

"You?"

"I'm going to pass out."

"Now is not a good time, Phoenix!"

"It's never a good time, believe me."

A flash of light exploded before them and Gulliver reared up in surprise, Phoenix slipping backwards onto the ground while Fay leapt out of harm's way into the grass.

Phoenix sat and blinked at the colossal figure looming

over him. Simon folded his arms, his elaborate tattoos glowing an electric shade of blue as energy snapped and crackled around his body like lightning in a gathering storm.

"Simon?" Phoenix mumbled, the throbbing rumble of hundreds of pounding feet drawing nearer behind him. "What a nice surprise."

Simon glowered at him then stomped past without a word. He threw his arms out, tattoos shifting from electric blue to red. A screen of ruby light stretched across the entire hillside and the army of Shadows bounced off it like ping-pong balls hitting a window.

Phoenix let out a low whistle.

Simon clapped his hands together and the shimmering wall closed in on itself, encircling the swarm of Shadows in a gradually constricting ring. They scrambled over each other to avoid touching the walls.

"You leapt through the void," Phoenix said, rising unsteadily from the ground. "Excellent timing," he added as he dusted dirt from the back of his coat. "Things were a little hairy for a moment there. How are you feeling, by the way? You've obviously gained some formidable new power. I guarantee that comes at a steep price. Take that from a guy who's been dabbling in recreational void-stone use most of his life. This sort of frivolity comes back to bite you."

"Go," Simon said, eyes fixed on the Shadows.

Phoenix smiled. "And you tell *me* to stop playing the hero. Seriously, Wolfe, that overprotective nature of yours—"

Without even looking, Simon flicked his hand behind him and a wall of red light smacked Phoenix to the ground.

Phoenix tumbled backwards then sprang to his feet. "You're that upset?" he asked with a laugh. "I only—" But Simon released another blast and the powerful light slammed Phoenix into the dirt before he could finish talking.

Phoenix coughed and let his head fall back onto the grass. "Okay. Point taken." He stared at the clouds for a moment then closed his eyes. "I think I'll go to another planet now. With any luck the people there will be less disappointed with me."

MEDIOCRE HEROES

“I’ll admit he looks a little underwhelming.” A woman’s voice washed over Phoenix as he lay on his side with his eyes closed. “But Alice assures us that he can close the Gate.”

“Well…” The woman who responded sounded as though her voice was being projected through a nearby speaker. “Alice also assures us that we’ll have an incredibly powerful warlock working on our side before the Light Festival begins next month, and I’m yet to see any evidence of some mighty magician.”

“Sorry to interrupt, Lady Maxine.” Bee’s voice glided over Phoenix’s head. He guessed he was stretched out on the couch and Bee was perched on the armrest beside him. "But I think we caught a glimpse of that warlock yesterday. He appeared from nowhere carrying a parrot, then vanished before our eyes without saying much."

"Well, he sounds truly reliable."

"I just don't see what Alice has to gain from lying to us about Phoenix's capabilities," Bee added. "Besides, I've seen him use one of those stones that Alice talks about. It's real. It hovers in the air and makes this loud humming sound."

"With respect, dear, I have hundreds of military drones at my disposal that do the same thing."

"Yeah." Jayden chimed in from somewhere behind the couch. "And all he did with his magic rock was count backwards and get a nosebleed."

Phoenix opened his eyes, discovering that the couch he'd been unconscious on was facing a paper-laden coffee table and a flickering image of a woman displayed on a massive screen built into the wall. The woman was sitting at a desk, her long fingers pressed together beneath her pointed chin as she gazed into the room of people assembled around Phoenix and the couch.

Phoenix's first thought was that the woman looked a lot like a younger version of his nan, with angular features and sharp, watchful eyes, her dark hair tied in a neat bun.

"I want to believe the boy can help us," she said, "but all we have is Alice's word, and I'm not sure I trust her. If this Phoenix character could offer some solid evidence of his good intentions... The exact details of this mysterious Gate, perhaps..."

Phoenix sighed. "The Gate is located above Veracity Dome." He sat and smiled at the crowd of faces surrounding him. "Hello Earthlings."

"Phoenix." The woman on screen offered a cursory smile. "It's an honour to finally meet you."

"Oh, I'm quite sure it's not." Phoenix returned the brief smile then leant over his knees and closed his eyes, still recovering from his time in the void-chamber.

"Phoenix." Bee spoke from beside him. "This is Lady Maxine. Official public representative chosen to lead Veracity into the future."

"Every campaign needs a face," Lady Maxine said. "And mine is one the people identify with. I grew up in the public-eye. My father was a well-respected politician, see, back before Flamegate swept in and buried its tentacles into every nook and cranny of our world."

Phoenix massaged his temples as the lady on screen continued her spiel.

"My father was a good man," she said. "Instrumental in allowing everyone greater access to healthcare. He was involved in numerous charities. A tireless advocate for the environment and an avid supporter of science."

Phoenix opened his eyes and found there was a small, threadbare teddy resting in his lap.

"He was a wonderful mentor," Lady Maxine said as Phoenix gazed at the bear. "He taught me about networking. Resilience. Being proactive and humble in any leadership role. In many ways, I think he was always preparing me for this."

"So that's the plan, is it?" Phoenix asked, gently taking the bear in his hands. "Overthrow the current masters of the poor, powerless population, then you step in as the next noble ruler telling everyone what to do? Because your family was privileged and you've convinced yourself that you know what's best for everyone else?"

"I take it you have some issues with authority." Lady Maxine did not sound offended by the remarks.

"Issues with authority?" Phoenix barked a laugh then leant back into the couch and composed himself with a tight-lipped smile. "Not without reason, Max."

"Indeed," Lady Maxine said, adopting the sombre expression of someone attending the funeral of a person they barely knew. "I understand Flamegate has caused you terrible anguish over the years."

Phoenix dug his thumb into a pale scar on his forearm and frowned at her.

"Look..." He swallowed. "I get that society needs rules. And I get that, *maybe*, there needs to be people around to create those rules and impose those rules and enforce those rules and be generally pretentious and annoying about those rules. Just... please don't become Flamegate. Please don't stoop to their level. All I ask is that you be better than them."

Lady Maxine's face softened. "Rest assured, my team and I intend to eradicate the corrupt practices that Flamegate introduced. We will put an end to the exploitation. The blind greed. We're developing policies to lessen the gap between the excessively affluent and the inexcusably deprived."

"Political rhetoric doesn't exactly fill me with confidence."

"Veracity will no longer be divided by walls." A soft urgency entered Lady Maxine's voice as she leant closer to the camera capturing her every move. "Instead, we'll be united by our desire to support and sustain ourselves into a bright, beautiful new future of freedom, prosperity and hope. I don't want to *rule*, Phoenix. I only aspire to lead."

"Well, good luck to you." Phoenix stood from the couch, the teddy still in his hand. "What Earth does with itself after the Gate closes is not really my concern." He looked around for something to do.

"The Alliance is far more extensive than you think," Lady Maxine said, watching him closely from behind the screen. "I am but a single face amongst a diverse tapestry of others working together to improve our world. A small but necessary part of a mighty machine. And when order returns, I will gladly allow others the opportunity to take my place." She hesitated. "I have a daughter. I'm doing this for her. Not for me."

"Ma'am, if we could move things along a little..." A tall woman with dark red lipstick and a blue suit-jacket spoke from Phoenix's left. Phoenix recognised her voice as the woman who had described him as being *admittedly underwhelming.*

"I'd like to open the meeting up to queries regarding what the boy actually intends to do and how that fits in with our plans."

Phoenix chuckled. "Lady, the boy has a name. What's yours?"

The woman cringed. "Forgive me. Stephanie Grace. Head of PR and Inter-ring Liaison Officer." She shook his hand with the over-zealous enthusiasm of a terrier trying to snap a rat's neck. "The last inter-ring liaison officer was killed last week, meeting with Alliance sympathisers in the Upper Ring. If we're being honest, I'm still adjusting to this job."

"You said I looked a little underwhelming," Phoenix said, stretching the cramps out of his now-aching fingers.

The woman tilted her head with an almost pitying stare. "Sweetheart, you have cake in your hair, you're wearing pyjamas, and you're clutching a teddy."

Phoenix reached up and patted his head, surprised to find that his hair had been bundled into a series of messy, mismatched tufts harbouring an extensive population of crumbs.

He glanced at Bee. "You had cake without me?"

She gazed at him in silence for a moment. "What happened to your eyes?"

Phoenix blinked. "Sorry?"

"Why is the light so faint?"

"Ah." Phoenix squeezed the bear in his fist. "I spent a little too much energy today. Nothing worth worrying about. It'll come back. Where's this cake?"

Bee frowned at him a little longer then gestured vaguely. "Kitchen."

Stephanie pressed her hands together in a soundless clap. "Let's stay on task, shall we? Queries for Phoenix, anyone?"

"I have some queries." A frizzy-haired woman dressed in black leant over the couch and offered her hand. "Naia. Civil engineering department, Group A, subsector two. Pleasure to meet you."

Phoenix clasped her hand in his own. "Likewise. About the pleasure part. I'm not an engineer, I've no idea what group I'm in, and the word subsector makes me uncomfortable. Phoenix Page. I like your bowtie."

"How important is this Gate to Flamegate?" Naia asked.

"Very," Phoenix said, placing the teddy on the couch, positioning it so it faced the screen. He took the bear's paw and gave Lady Maxine a cheerful wave, but her expression remained unmoved by the gesture.

"Important enough that they'll be crippled without it?" Naia asked as Phoenix wandered into the kitchen, where he maintained a clear view of everyone from behind the counter.

"The Gate in Yonder is always open." He grabbed one of the cakes, making swift work of the treat before helping himself to a glass of water. "But the Gate opening on Earth is a short-lived, annual event that gets everyone in Flamegate more excited than a spoilt kid at some overly indulgent Yonderian coming-of-age celebration in the rich, fancy part of Central Karvil." He set his empty glass down. "That was a poor example for this audience, but you get the idea. It's a big deal. It's the only time of year when Flamegate gets unrestricted access to the void."

"And when you close it...?" Naia pressed.

"That's your big chance," Phoenix said, swinging open the fridge and checking inside. "Flamegate will be thrown into a state of emergency the likes of which they've never dealt with before. Their greatest weapons and strongest defences rely on void-energy, but all the remaining void-energy will be drawn away from Earth, sucked back through the closing tunnels into the heart of the void where it belongs." He stole a loaf of bread and popped a slice into a rusty toaster on the bench. "Flamegate will be left with nothing," he added, returning the bread to the fridge. "No way to sustain itself. No way to manipulate people. No way to maintain control. What happens then is entirely your decision. I'll be leaving the rest to you."

"We have given Flamegate an ultimatum." Lady Maxine spoke from the screen in the adjoining room.

Phoenix chuckled as he peered into the toaster. "I'm sure they loved that."

"We've made it clear," Lady Maxine said, "that if Flamegate does not step away from its position of power by the first day of the Light Festival, we shall overthrow them by force."

Phoenix raised his eyebrows. "That's bold."

"The Alliance has been preparing this for years," Lady Maxine continued. "Gathering followers. Spreading hope. We have people ready to step up and take charge at a moment's notice. All we need is the right moment."

"Overpowering the outer reaches of Flamegate will be manageable enough," Naia said as Phoenix leant drowsily against the pantry. "It's getting into the more fortified areas of the Upper Ring that will prove most difficult."

"I *told* you," Ghost growled. "I'll get you access through the tunnels." Phoenix hadn't even noticed the surly spectre of a man lurking in the corner of the room. "If I can't, I'll chop off one of my own fingers and send it to Lady Maxine."

Lady Maxine forced another stiff smile. "That's an honourable gesture, Ghost, but wholly unnecessary."

"Phoenix," Bee interrupted, "your toast is burning."

Phoenix turned to find smoke swirling from the toaster. He tried ejecting the charcoaled slice, but the little machine refused to comply and half the bread crumbled and caught fire deep within the toaster's metal grates. To the alarm of everyone watching, Phoenix slipped his hand into the machine and fished around for the burning remains of bread.

"Rapid regeneration abilities," he explained, in response to the chorus of sharply drawn inhales and murmurs of concern. "Pretty useless, most days. Extreme heat is the only thing that triggers it."

“What in the world *are* you?” Stephanie asked.

Phoenix frowned, hand still plunged in the toaster, smoke streaming past his fingers as he gathered the last of his burnt bread. “Why do people keep asking me that?”

“We could use that...” Ghost said.

Phoenix said nothing as he pushed all his blackened pieces of bread into a pile on the bench, his hand perfectly unscathed.

“Send you on demolition jobs in the tunnels,” Ghost continued.

“I’m fireproof,” Phoenix said. “Not smokeproof. Or chunks-of-brick-proof. Or death-proof. And I don’t magically repair my clothes after they burn to ash. So as fun as prancing naked through the blazing underground genuinely seems to me, it is perhaps best to save my talents for closing the Gate.” He nibbled through the more salvageable bits of toast. “How has Flamegate responded to your ultimatum about stepping down?”

“They’ve gotten worse,” Lady Maxine replied while Phoenix tried to ignore the low humming that had started in his ears. “Held more public executions. Introduced tougher security... Harsher regulations.”

“They’re trying to break our spirit,” Naia said, pulling absently at her bowtie. “But it’s only made us stronger.”

“If by stronger, you mean smaller and more desperate...” Jayden said, flopping into the couch with such heavy intensity that the toy bear bounced into the air like a rocket. Bee caught it one-handed then placed it in her lap.

Lady Maxine peered down her pointed nose. “As always, Jayden, we are grateful for your invaluable contribution."

“Just happy to be a part of it all,” Jayden mumbled.

“Yes...” Lady Maxine spoke through pursed lips. “I’m still not sure why Alice insists upon your continued involvement here.”

Phoenix brushed the last bread crumbs into the sink then strode back to stand before Jayden, bending down so they were almost nose-to-nose. "*Does* she? What's so special about you, I wonder?"

"Beats me." Jayden squirmed back. "She just said I had value."

Phoenix tilted his head a little, fixing Jayden with a puzzled frown. "Human sacrifice, perhaps. The Void Gods demand one before the Gate can close."

Jayden's eyes widened and Phoenix laughed.

"Joking." He clapped Jayden on the shoulder. "Probably. Perhaps there *are* gods, and perhaps they *do* demand a moody pessimist with perfectly combed hair." He stretched out on his back between the coffee table and the couch then closed his eyes.

"Are you okay?" Bee asked.

"Oh, yes." Phoenix plugged his ears with his fingers in a futile attempt to drown out the persistent drone. Either his stint in the void-chamber was taking longer to recover from than normal, or the void was experiencing some kind of irregular flux.

He wondered whether Simon might appear again.

"So the Gate is above Veracity Dome?" Lady Maxine prompted, her voice stifled by Phoenix's fingers and the steady hum. "The old stadium beside Flamegate Tower?"

"Yup." Phoenix kept his eyes closed. "Where the annual light display takes place. That big, metal net that Flamegate raises into the sky every year isn't actually creating light like everyone thinks. The *Gate* creates the light. The net is just collecting all the energy as it flows into your world."

"And you'll be able to close it on your own?" Stephanie sounded doubtful.

Phoenix sighed. "Despite my underwhelming appearance, I'm confident this is something I'm able to do."

"Big talk from a guy with cake in his hair," Jayden muttered.

Phoenix didn't open his eyes. "Mother of Shadows, I hope Alice is right about you being useful."

"How exactly do you intend to close this Gate?" Stephanie asked.

"Heroically," Phoenix said. "From inside."

"Is that possible?" Bee wondered. "Shouldn't all the energy kill you?"

Phoenix pulled his fingers from his ears. "I've done it before."

There was a surprised silence.

"You've been through the Gate?"

"Once," Phoenix said. "A year ago. At the last Light Festival."

"What happened?" Jayden asked.

Phoenix hesitated then slowly sat up. "I came back," he said with a shrug.

Bee watched him with her scrutinising, unwavering gaze. "The void doesn't hurt you?"

"If I were to enter as I am," Phoenix said, "my body would disintegrate faster than snow in a desert. Fortunately, my body won't be going through the Gate. The rest of me will."

"The *rest* of you?" Jayden sounded insulted by the confounding remark.

Phoenix nodded and leant back against the table. "The rest of me."

"What will happen to your body?" Naia asked, at which point Phoenix decided he was incredibly fond of the frizzy-haired, bowtie-wearing woman and her willingness to adapt.

"Once the Gate starts to close," he said, "I'll just pop back inside my patiently waiting flesh and bones then get on with the day, good as new."

"Ahem." A young man sitting in one of the couches raised his hand. He'd been sitting so still and staring so intently at the screens in his lap that Phoenix hadn't even registered his presence until he spoke. "Connection ends in five seconds."

"Keep me posted," Lady Maxine said, then vanished from the screen.

Stephanie sighed. "Rory, a little more warning next time, please?"

"Why don't you try monitoring the whole security network for once, sis, and see how much warning *you* could give."

Stephanie rolled her eyes. "You're such a child."

"Takes one to know one," Rory retorted.

"Very mature."

"Naia." Ghost nodded his chin in the direction of the table.

Naia grimaced. "Excuse us. We have impossible strategies to discuss." She followed Ghost to the messy table.

Bee slid from the armrest of the couch and sat on the floor next to Phoenix. "You're lying."

Phoenix raised an eyebrow at her. "About what?"

"Closing the void then returning to your body like it was just a vehicle you stepped out of for a bit. There's no way it's as simple as that."

Phoenix smiled and pressed his palms against his buzzing ears. "It's as simple as it needs to be."

"What does that even *mean*?" Jayden asked, apparently addressing some invisible presence in the ceiling.

"Look," Bee said, shuffling a little closer to Phoenix. "My priority has always been defeating Flamegate. It's what my parents wanted. It's what I've always wanted. Nothing is going to stand between me and that goal. But if something happens to you, it *is* going to look bad for me professionally."

"How so?"

Stephanie sat beside Jayden on the couch then leant forward and gave Bee an affectionate pat on the back. "Bee's your bodyguard."

"Sorry." Phoenix lowered his hands from his ears. "What?"

THE TROUBLE WITH TIME

"Bee's your bodyguard," Stephanie repeated. "And your proxy."

Phoenix blinked. "My *proxy*?"

"She speaks and listens on your behalf when you're incapable of doing so."

"Most of the time, apparently," Jayden said, leaning into the cushions of the couch, arms folded across his chest.

Phoenix looked back and forth between Stephanie and Bee. "Since when?"

"Since you signed the contract," Stephanie said, as though the answer was obvious.

"I... wait. What contract?"

Stephanie whisked a piece of paper from one of the files scattered across the coffee table and offered it to Phoenix. He took it and frowned at the words scribbled beneath the wall of text covering the top half of the page. The messy scrawl of unidentifiable letters was definitely his signature, though he had no recollection of ever writing the thing.

"When did I do this?"

"Alice said you signed it months ago," Bee said, "when you two were alone together. Not long after we first arrived."

Phoenix tapped the page. "Alice forged this..." he realised aloud. "How many other decisions is she making for me behind my back?"

"Are you against the idea?" Bee asked. "It seems worthwhile for you to have a spokesperson, though, considering how often you're asleep."

"Huh?" Phoenix said distractedly, still gazing at the paper. "No. Please. Go ahead. Thanks." He put the contract down and looked at her. "You're protecting me?"

She fixed him with her shrewd, brown-eyed stare.

"You don't think me capable?" she asked, cradling the fluffy bear in one hand while the other caressed the dagger at her belt.

Phoenix swallowed. "I find you very difficult to read."

"Good." Bee folded her arms. "That's how I like it."

A phone rang from Stephanie's suit-pocket and she excused herself to take the call in another room.

"Do you have much experience bodyguarding?" Phoenix asked as Stephanie hurried away.

Bee laughed. "I've been accompanying Ghost on tunnel raids for over a year. Watching over you is not a strenuous task."

"I know a warlock who would debate you on that," Phoenix muttered.

"Honestly," Bee said, "all I do is keep an eye on you. Follow Alliance protocol. It's not a big deal."

"You get nothing in return?"

Bee shrugged. "Job satisfaction, I guess? The knowledge that I'm contributing to something my parents fought so hard for before they died."

"They died *because* they were fighting," Jayden said with a sigh. "They were rebels and they were punished. And if we're not careful, the rest of us are going to end up dying as well."

Rory whistled from the other couch, gathered all his devices then shuffled off down the stairs to work in the infirmary where there was less drama.

"They were killed because Flamegate came searching for Phoenix," Bee said calmly. "And as I remember, Flamegate came to my home searching for Phoenix only because you called them to share his location."

Jayden's jaw hung ajar. "Bee… you can't… That's unfair."

"Is it?"

"Is that why you've been so cold with me lately?"

Bee rolled her eyes. "Jay, if fighting the evil organisation that killed my parents and tortured yours and trapped everyone's freedom between massive walls is such a huge hassle, why are you here?"

Jayden let loose an incredulous laugh. "That's not obvious? I'm here because *you* are. What more do you want from me?"

Bee stared at him then shook her head and left the house without a word, the front door smacking behind her as she stalked across the unruly yard.

"Perhaps not the answer Belinda was hoping for," Phoenix said, pressing his palms against his ears. The low hum was getting louder, suggesting a disturbance with the void rather than his own inability to recover all the energy he'd given away.

Jayden glowered at the front door. "Shut up."

"I suspect she was hoping for something more… ambitious."

"Your opinion means nothing to me, Phoenix."

"You should talk to her."

"And say what?" Jayden snapped. "Sorry I cared so much that I followed you into the dirty underworld of the Lower Ring. Sorry I joined a suicidal rebellion group for you. Sorry I'm not *delighted* about living in this crazy old house surrounded by radical revolutionists and murderous criminals and boring politicians and suspicious time-travellers and grouchy old men and infuriating, know-it-all aliens."

Phoenix released his ears, giving in to the steadily intensifying buzz. "I've never really thought of myself as an alien..."

"Doesn't make you any less infuriating."

"I guess not," Phoenix said. "I'm going to acquaint myself better with the piano now. Go talk with Bee."

He stood up then crashed backwards as Alice appeared before him in a warm flash of light. Jayden yelped and dived for cover behind the sofa.

"Alice." Phoenix grinned up at her from where he had fallen on his back across the coffee table. She reached down and pulled him to his feet while Jayden jumped up and dusted himself off in a panicked rush to appear unruffled.

"Edgar's hiding in his room again," Naia said, looking up from a sprawling map of the underground while Ghost scowled behind her at Alice's unorthodox arrival.

Alice shook her head. "I'm not here to see Edgar." She placed her hand over Phoenix's heart, the red mask hanging from her wrist. "It's like you're not even here."

Phoenix could barely hear her over the now far louder hum.

Alice pulled her hand away. "You drained your energy."

Phoenix smiled. "Nothing escapes you, does it?"

"I monitor your energy levels as I travel," Alice said, her eyes drifting to his mop of childishly styled hair, "to keep track of how the greater plan is progressing. You are the thread that links everyone and everything together."

"How very humbling." Phoenix stretched his fingers

behind him, fumbling around for the armrest to grab hold of. He rested some of his weight against it, willing himself not to collapse at Alice's feet. "It does feel a little like you're stalking me across the far reaches of Time and space though."

"Don't take it personally," Alice said. "You're easily traceable. It's a matter of convenience."

"Traceable..." Phoenix mused. "That's how Simon found me earlier today."

"Simon?"

"My warlock friend," Phoenix said, squinting against the mounting pain in his head, as though closing his eyes could somehow block out the unbearable noise. "I thought you knew who Simon was?"

Alice watched him pensively. "It seems I don't know him yet."

As if on cue, Simon appeared exactly as he had the day before, with a near-deafening pop, crouched in the middle of the kitchen with a parrot tucked beneath his jacket. The throbbing hum exploded to new levels of ferocity inside Phoenix's brain and he dropped down to sit on the couch.

Alice uttered a small gasp, staring at Simon with wide eyes. Ghost whipped a knife from some concealed part of his person and aimed it at the enormous, leather-clad intruder.

"I return with bad news." The warlock stood and allowed the parrot to clamber onto his shoulder before taking a better look around the room. "Alice." He graced her with a cautious smile. "What brings you to our little corner of Time?"

Alice just gaped at him.

"Do we trust the magic pirate or not?" Ghost snarled from behind the cluttered table. "Because I can remove his heart in three seconds if you need me to."

"Ah..." Simon frowned into his bushy beard. "I did it again, didn't I? I can*not* get this right today."

Alice regained her steely composure and glided into the kitchen, her red robes rustling at her feet. "*You're* Simon?"

"I am..." Simon frowned at her. "Is this the first time

we've met?"

Alice took a careful step towards him. "You're like me..."

"Not nearly as talented," Simon said, watching her with the same careful apprehension one might watch a wild bear.

"Indeed." Alice took his chin in her hand and peered into his dark, deep-set eyes. "Your magic is under terrible pressure. That's why you're making mistakes."

The parrot squawked in protest but Simon said nothing. A door clicked open nearby and Phoenix turned to see Edgar emerge from his room with his robes ruffled and his long white hair cascading over his shoulders in a tangled mess. He stepped into the living-area just as Bee walked through the front door, blood on her hands and a headless chicken resting on the silver tray she was carrying.

She stopped in the living-room and stared at Alice and Simon, the pair frozen in the kitchen with Alice holding Simon's face, then she locked eyes with Phoenix, who was still sitting on the couch waiting for his brain to explode.

"What did I miss?" Bee asked.

Before anyone could answer, Stephanie returned to the room, her painted red lips curved in an anxious frown. "Big Mick called," she said. "Vince has been attacked by a mutant cat."

Edgar glowered at the scene before him. "It's too early for this," he muttered, then turned on his heels and returned to his bedroom with a swish of his robes, snapping the door shut behind him.

"Is Vince okay?" Naia asked.

"He'll be fine," Alice said, her attention on Simon again. "What happened?" she asked, letting go of his beard. "For your magic to be under so much strain... What did you do?"

Simon glanced over at Phoenix then met Alice's gaze.

She nodded, an unspoken understanding passing between them. "Go. Return to your time."

"Come on, Mittens." Simon coaxed the parrot into his jacket again.

"Wait." A hint of fear crept into Alice's voice as she stepped towards him.

Simon hesitated, but Alice just hung her head.

"Sorry," she murmured.

"Yeah. We all are." Simon disappeared in a blast of light.

Phoenix sank to his side on the cushions, his eyes squeezed shut as the mighty roar tore through his head.

"Stand up." A gentle touch brushed his shoulder. "I'll help you to your room."

"Just let me pass out here," Phoenix mumbled.

"No." Alice pulled him up. "You and I need to have a chat."

"Can't it wait?" Phoenix asked, sagging forward as Alice tucked her shoulder under his drooping arm.

"No."

Phoenix glanced through the hair over his eyes to see everyone staring while Alice led him away.

"I just want to *impress* upon you," Alice said, guiding him up the stairs, "the importance of maintaining an adequate supply of energy. If you're dead before the festival, our efforts will be wasted."

"It was a calculated risk," Phoenix said, dragging his feet up the steps. "I had someone nearby to help. Which, now I think about it, you could have done when I was asleep for two months, or trapped inside my own head for Light knows how long before Maulbrak stepped in to jolt me back. No doubt he enjoyed the chance to demonstrate what he perceives to be his irrefutable power over me." They reached the top of the stairs and Phoenix sank to his knees. "I think I'll just sleep here."

"Phoenix, I don't have time to chase you across Time and space pulling you out of every spot of bother you encounter with the void."

Phoenix laughed as he slumped against the wall. "*You* don't have time? You're a time-traveller. Imagine how I feel."

Alice glared at him. "It takes time to time-travel, Phoenix. Time, and energy, that I cannot afford to waste on you every single day you feel like risking your life." She heaved him to his feet. "I have to focus on the greater plan."

They started walking again, following the luxuriously carpeted hallway to the bedroom at the end. Phoenix struggled to keep his balance as his vision blurred.

"Alice..." He spoke carefully. "I love you. I do. You're the closest thing I have to family in this world. But it does feel... sometimes... that I am a puppet and you're holding all the strings."

Alice stayed silent as she opened the door then steered Phoenix across the colourful rug towards the bed.

"You think I'm just using you?" she asked, after Phoenix had thrown himself face-first onto the mattress.

"I don't know," Phoenix said into the pillow. "*Should* I think that?"

"People are dead." Alice gathered her robes about her then sat beside him. "One. The twins. Belinda's parents. Thousands of others who died, stripped of dignity, for the sake of furthering Flamegate's expansion. What I am trying to achieve with my life is bigger than you. Bigger than any of us. Sacrifices have to be made."

"You said that when you rescued us from Bee's place, too," Phoenix mumbled.

"Did I?" Alice started undoing the messy ponytails the children had left in Phoenix's hair. "That's all in my future. I suppose by that point I'll know precisely what sacrifices we have to make."

"Once the Light Festival gets underway," Phoenix said, turning his head to the side so he could see her, "I guess all of us will finally be on the same page."

Alice responded with a rueful smile. "Yes." She leant down and kissed his cheek. "If you survive that long."

"That was mean."

"Be careful," Alice said. "That's all I ask."

"Nah." Phoenix smiled and closed his eyes. "You ask a little more than that."

He drifted away before hearing whether Alice replied.

~

By the time Simon had tossed the unconscious Phoenix over Gulliver's back, muttered a word to Fay about meeting in Karvil, then watched with grim resolve as Phoenix, Gulliver and Fay disappeared over the rolling hills into the distance, the Shadows trapped in the red, shimmering circle of energy behind him had become frantic with rage and desperation.

Simon huffed a sigh then turned back to frown at the agitated creatures, watching as they clambered over each other, biting and scratching for a safer position in the centre of the throng, away from the dangerous wall of light.

Simon approached the heaving, snarling mass of lanky bodies then planted his feet firmly in the grass, his hands at his belt.

"Listen!" he yelled, and the Shadows stopped, whether in surprise or obedience he couldn't be sure. They stared at him with wide, unblinking golden eyes that reminded him so uncomfortably of Phoenix.

"I don't know if you can understand me or not," Simon growled, "but I'm going to give you a very generous opportunity."

The Shadows remained silent and still, their sunken faces blank and staring.

"I'm going to take down this barrier." Simon paused, but the Shadows showed no indication that they knew what he was talking about. "If you attack me... I will kill you. If you chase after my idiot friend, I will kill you. If you dare swarm upon Karvil City... no matter how great your numbers... I will kill you." He paused again, glaring at nearly every Shadow in turn in the hope that his narrowed eyes would clarify the fierce sincerity of his message.

"*However*!" he bellowed, "if you turn around and return to Bloodwood Forest, I will spare your disgusting lives. Just today. Do I make myself clear?"

There was no reaction, though by this point Simon wasn't really expecting one.

"I'm removing the barrier," he announced, raising his hands. "Don't do anything stupid."

The barrier trembled like sunlight dancing along the ripples of a pool then vanished completely. The Shadows didn't even twitch, opting instead to remain where they were, their gangly grey limbs struck out at odd angles from where they had frozen mid-scramble before Simon's speech.

Simon shrugged. "Good enough." He turned his back and started trudging away but one Shadow, bolder than the others, pounced forward to pin him to the ground. Before the creature's claws could hit their mark, Simon spun and smacked his hand into its gaunt face. The monster exploded in the air, splattering flesh and bone across the hillside with a terrible squelch. The remaining Shadows flinched back as Simon directed his open palm at them.

"*Scram!*" he barked, and they scampered away, zigzagging through the long grass as they fled in the direction of Bloodwood.

Simon lowered his hand, arcs of red light spluttering from the ends of his fingers then fizzling away. He surveyed the horizon until he was satisfied the Shadows wouldn't return, then closed his eyes and thought of the quiet, marshland cottage belonging to the ward-makers, concentrating on the unique markers that defined its position in space. His magic swelled, coursing down the tattoos along his arms and across his back. A flush of warmth passed through him and he opened his eyes to find himself standing on the wooden boardwalk leading to the front gate of the ward-makers' isolated property.

He was met with a nervous whinny before Tugger came trotting around the side of the house to greet his human at the fence.

Simon rubbed the enormous horse under its chin. "Sorry to keep you waiting, old boy. Is Gloria here?"

The horse said nothing, for which Simon was grateful. One verbally capable horse was more than he needed in his life. He wandered across the yard and up to the front porch, his head brushing against the windchimes dangling from the rafters.

"Gloria?" he called. "Are you still here?"

As he walked through the front door, he passed through the transparent figure of a far younger Matilda Elway, engaged in silent, animated discussion with a far younger Gloria, while a six-or-seven-year-old Phoenix tugged restlessly at the folds of Gloria's billowing, many-layered skirt.

Simon preferred not to be distracted by history that he had no control over, but he found himself captivated by the scene. Gloria nudged Phoenix into the house and the scruffy boy glanced up at his stern-faced grandmother before darting away. Simon followed him across the room to one of the many bookshelves, which clearly hadn't budged in the last decade or so, while Gloria and Matilda continued their discussion behind him.

Simon watched as Phoenix trailed his finger along the spines of each book, eventually selecting a collection of short stories. Phoenix flicked to a tatty bookmark towards the end then stood facing the shelves, his nose buried in a story titled, 'How the Mouse Defeated the Dragon'.

Simon smiled. Then, not expecting a response, crouched to the child's height. "Hey, Phoenix."

Phoenix blinked in surprise then closed the book, turning his head to stare directly at Simon's face. Startled, Simon waved his hand tentatively in front of Phoenix's nose, but Phoenix just stared through him, quietly puzzled.

"I've almost finished packing." Gloria stepped from the hallway into the living-area, a small pot-plant tucked under her arm. "I suppose the others are safe, judging by your calm perusal of my library?"

The scene Simon had been observing faded soundlessly back into the past.

“Gloria. Hello.” Simon stared at her, feeling as though he had tripped on the final step on a staircase, expecting solid ground but finding thin air instead. “They’re safe… They’re heading for Karvil.”

“Good.” Gloria nodded at the shelves. “Did you see something?”

Simon took a second to compose himself. “The past has changed,” he said. “The colours are stronger. The people more… solid.”

Gloria smiled as she walked towards him, the pot-plant bouncing with her hips. “The past doesn’t change. The people remain as they always have been. Fixed to their time.” She rested her hand against his arm. “It is you who has become more transient, slipping between timeframes like a wandering ghost. You have a remarkable affinity for it.”

“Can they see me?” Simon asked, glancing back at where the young Phoenix had been standing.

“Ordinarily, I would say no. But if it’s Phoenix you’re talking about…” Gloria shrugged. “Who knows? He is not restricted to the conventions of this world.”

“You believe in this Earth place, then?” Simon asked, as Gloria walked to the round table in the centre of the room, now laden with boxes and bags.

“I do,” Gloria replied, putting the pot-plant into a wooden box. “Jack was never convinced. He always thought it was a fantasy, invented by Phoenix to cope with life in Bloodwood.”

“Why would he invent a world worse than Bloodwood?” Simon asked, sitting at the table. The chair creaked forebodingly under his weight.

“Worse than…?” Gloria’s brows crinkled together. “He loved Earth.”

Simon scoffed at the idea. “He was a prisoner for fifteen years. He only escaped this week.”

Gloria gazed at him for a long moment then pulled her fingers through her wild, flyaway hair.

"In the beginning," she said, lifting an old coat from one of the boxes and unfolding it across the table, "after Maulbrak first saw him, there was a prison. Phoenix would tell anyone who'd listen about that other world." She rolled the coat into a tight tube, frowned, then shook it out and laid it flat again.

"About a year later... after his little friend One supposedly died... the stories started to grow." She folded the coat into a square then tucked it down the side of an already bulging bag. "He'd been adopted by a family who paid for his release. His new siblings were twins and he was always looking after them." She paused, removed the coat, then bundled it into a ball. "Earth was in trouble so he was using his abilities to protect their world. A team of scientists were training him to be a hero. He was travelling with a band of musicians and performing for massive crowds. Every day the tales would become more outrageous."

Gloria pressed the coat between her hands then sank into the chair across from Simon. "Nobody knew what to believe," she said, gazing at the crumpled garment in her lap. "Only thing anyone could agree on was that the poor boy was troubled."

"Still is," Simon muttered. He took the coat from Gloria's hands, folded it neatly, then placed it back in the box it had originated from.

"His grandparents never knew how to handle him," Gloria added. "Matilda brought him to us every week, just to give herself a break." She hesitated then reached across the table and squeezed Simon's hand. "I will never forgive myself for turning a blind eye to what they did to that child."

"You knew what his grandparents were putting him through?"

"Everyone did." Gloria released Simon's hand. "But no one in Bloodwood gave it a second thought. As the son of a Shade, Phoenix had to prove his worth. Just as his mother had done before him."

A movement in the corner of the room caught Simon's

attention and he looked up to see the transparent, young version of Phoenix edging along the wall, his wide eyes locked on the table.

"I suppose it was painful for Matilda," Gloria mused, oblivious to the bygone Phoenix sneaking around, "watching Phoenix grow up the way he did, after her own perfect child had been taken away."

"You never tried to intervene?" Simon asked. Phoenix flinched then dived onto his stomach and started crawling across the floor on his elbows, making his way toward the table with a determined expression on his face.

"I wanted to," Gloria replied, "but you have to understand that Matilda and I were born into the Shadow War. She has always been an opportunist, and when Phoenix came along, she just wanted to make the most of a terrible situation." Gloria shook her head with a sigh. "I'm ashamed... but I felt it wasn't my place to tell her how to grieve for her daughter, or how to raise a difficult child."

Simon scratched his beard, watching as Phoenix crawled under the table.

"Grief can warp the mind," he said. "I hate who I became after my family died. But loss is no excuse for the way I acted back then. And it's not an excuse for treating an innocent kid like dirt."

Gloria gazed at him in thoughtful silence then offered a sympathetic smile. "We have much to atone for." She stood up. "Jack is walking to Karvil with that poor confused troll. It's time you and I made our way too." She clapped her hands and all the items vanished from the table. "I'm sorry I can't transport you myself, dear, but plants truly are the most complicated lifeforms I can send at my age."

Simon shook his head. "I'll take Tugger, as planned." He stood and dipped his head in a humble bow. "Thank you."

"Be careful with all that magic of yours." Gloria patted his arm then disappeared with a soft pop. Simon was about to head for the door when the young Phoenix crept out from his hiding place under the table then stood in the middle of the room, eyes darting about with flighty uncertainty, his fists clenched by his side.

"Are you looking for me?" Simon wondered aloud. Phoenix whirled around to face him.

"How did you get here?" he asked, his shaky voice echoing like someone at the bottom of a well.

Simon crouched down before him. "You can see me?"

Phoenix chewed his lip for a few seconds then nodded. "A little. Maybe."

"Maybe?"

Phoenix wrung his hands together, eyeing Simon with wary suspicion. "Are you real?" He reached out to touch Simon's shoulder, but his translucent hand passed straight through the warlock's body. Phoenix withdrew his hand as sharply as though he'd touched burning coal.

A terror came over the young boy's face that Simon felt a sudden need to alleviate.

"Look," he said hastily, "I can explain." But Phoenix was already backing away, panic in his glowing eyes as he retreated into a gap between two bookshelves.

"Why are you here?" he demanded.

"I'm not here to hurt you." Simon stood to comfort him, but to his alarm, the kid started crying. Softly at first, but his huge, gulping breaths soon escalated into relentless howls and he slammed his hands together, producing a void-stone and flinging it so high into the air that it ricocheted off the ceiling.

"Phoenix, listen to me." Simon walked towards him, but Phoenix threw his palm out and blasted one of the bookshelves against the adjacent wall. Books scattered across the room, their spines broken, flurries of torn pages floating to the floor.

Phoenix wedged himself against the shelves behind him and sank to the ground, clawing viciously at his forearm as the stone spun furiously above his head. Simon watched in astonishment as the younger, transparent Gloria rushed into the room. She thrust her hands out and an orb of red light appeared around Phoenix and the stone, contracting like the barrier Simon had captured the Shadows within earlier that day.

Phoenix yelled and launched a blast of energy in Gloria's direction, but it bounced back from the barrier and smashed into him with such force that his eyes rolled into the back of his head and he fell forward onto his face. He sprang to his feet with a growl, but by then Gloria had removed the barrier and knelt by his side. She bundled the little boy into her arms and he punched and kicked and snarled until finally he stopped struggling, curling into the plump woman's lap as she rocked him back and forth, her fingers brushing through his mop of hair.

With a pang of guilt, Simon remembered that *this* was the kid he had once tried to exterminate.

"Time to leave," he muttered.

Then he hurried outside to fetch Tugger.

KARVIL

Simon was still mulling over his strange interaction with the past as he followed the dusty road towards Karvil City. Tugger plodded along without guidance, steering clear of monster burrows as he wound his way through Yonder's lush grasslands.

So steady was Tugger's pace and so absorbed was Simon in his thoughts that he didn't notice the two figures on the path until he came up beside them.

"Jack," he said, easing Tugger to a halt. "Fidelity. I thought you'd be further ahead by now."

"We keep stopping," the old ward-maker explained, as

Simon slipped down from his horse to walk alongside the unlikely pair. "She's easily distracted."

"My fault, I'm afraid." Simon looked over at the towering troll trudging by Jack's side. "How's your head, Fidelity?"

"Did you find your fish?" Fidelity asked.

Simon blinked at her. "What?"

"You were looking for a fish."

"*Phoenix*," Simon said. "I was looking for Phoenix."

"That can't be right." Fidelity frowned, the gravel crunching beneath her enormous grey feet. "*I'm* looking for Phoenix."

"Are you?" Simon exchanged a brief glance with Jack then flashed Fidelity a smile. "I guess your memory's coming back."

"Are we looking for the same Phoenix?" Fidelity asked.

"I believe so." Simon swung his boot at a stone and kicked it further down the road. "But if he tries another reckless stunt behind my back again, I give up. He's all yours."

"It's very important I find him," Fidelity said with a businesslike nod. "I must deliver him to the High Handkerchief."

Simon chuckled into his beard. "High Handkerchief, huh?"

"How's Gloria?" Jack asked, worry in his eyes as he placed a frail hand on Simon's shoulder.

"She went ahead," Simon replied. "Transporting what appeared to be the entire contents of your house."

Jack nodded. "She'll be moving everything to our place in the Magicians' District. We've a lovely spot there, tucked away amongst the Bear Clan terraces. Been in my family for generations, that little house."

Simon grimaced. He hadn't entered that part of Karvil City since he was a kid, and had no desire to get involved with the tedious politics or turbulent relationships inherent with so many magicians living in close quarters. The clans were trouble enough on their own. Asking them to cohabit was like forcing every animal in a zoo to share a single pen.

"It's a smidge cramped," Jack continued, "but you're welcome to stay with us as long as you need. Lodging may be difficult to come by, under current circumstances."

Simon graciously declined.

"You'll be wanting to visit the Wolfe Main House though," Jack guessed, as they continued meandering through the hills.

"Why?" Simon asked. "Every last member of the clan was drained of power."

"So the story goes," Jack mused. "Surely ex-clan members pass through the House from time to time. Even Maulbrak held the Wolfe name, before dropping it in favour of his solo career."

"Maulbrak was a Wolfe?" Simon stared at the old man in surprise.

"Long, *long* ago," Jack said. "He walked away from the clan shortly after the Shadow War."

Simon scowled. "I guess he was smarter than the rest of us."

"The war changed him, I think," Jack said. "Anyway... now that Yonder is in danger, perhaps the old Wolves will consider returning to the clan for strength."

Simon laughed with a bitterness long connected to his thoughts on being born a Wolfe. "Contrary to our clan-name, Wolves had less of a pack mentality than you might think. We squabbled like dogs over the last scrap of meat."

Jack gave a small shrug. "If you want to unlock the last of your power, you'll need to find someone with the wisdom of your clan."

"I'd rather not get involved with them again," Simon said, his voice darkening with his mood. "But I'll consider it."

"You'll stay at the Inventors' Guild then?" Jack asked, while Fidelity wandered off the road to shove her arm into a monster's burrow.

"For a while," Simon said, watching the troll drag a

large, scaly, six-legged creature out by its horns. "To be honest though, I think Red has plans to get himself arrested."

"He's as foolish as ever."

Jack and Simon stopped by the side of the road, their arms folded as they gazed at the jubilant troll. Fidelity grinned a toothy grin as she swung the monster by its tail, the tight circle she was spinning growing faster and faster until she flung the poor creature into the air and it soared across the hills, crashing into a shrub before bolting into the distance with high-pitched squeals.

Fidelity smirked and dusted off her hands.

"Thirteenth grorvel she's terrorised today," Jack said, turning to follow the road again. Simon moved to follow then stopped in his tracks as a subtle wave of energy washed over him. Jack didn't seem interested in the slight flickering of air, but Simon had enough experience to recognise who the energy belonged to. Despite there being far less than usual, the distinct nature of Phoenix's lifeforce was as unmistakable as ever.

"I'm going ahead," Simon said, swinging himself up onto Tugger's back. "I'm sure we'll meet again."

"Good luck finding your fish."

"Thanks, Fidelity." Simon wished them both safe travels then urged Tugger to pick up speed, breaking into a swift trot until they rounded the last section of hills and come upon the vast stretch of flat land before Karvil. The sprawling outline of the famously resplendent city could be seen in the far distance, its tall, elegant towers and shimmering spires spiralling upwards into the clouds.

The road ahead was bustling with travellers, many in clattering, disk-powered carts, though most making the journey by horse or on foot. While Simon approached from the west, the bulk of the crowd trickled in from the eastern roads, from impoverished coastal towns like Adderhead Cove where he'd been born.

Sensing Phoenix's presence, Simon pushed Tugger on to

join the flow of traffic pouring towards the city gates. After twisting his way through sluggish crowds of weary travellers, he eventually caught up with Gulliver, who was lumbering down the road with his head bowed. Phoenix dawdled along at the windswept horse's side, Fay nestled in the shawl against his chest, her fluffy tail draped over his arm and swinging from side to side with his steps.

"Pleasantly surprised to find you alive." Simon eased Tugger into step beside them.

Phoenix glanced up with an uneasy smile. "Before you consider smashing me into the dirt again, I'd just like to point out that I'm holding Fay, and she has shown you nothing but kindness."

Simon rolled his eyes. "I'm not going to smash you into the dirt."

Phoenix dropped his tense shoulders in relief. "Thank you."

"Red..." Simon kept the exasperation in his voice to a minimum. "What were you thinking?"

Phoenix gazed at the ground as he walked. "I did what I had to."

"Yeah?" Simon said, as a group of fishermen overtook on the right, their rods and tackle rattling as they jogged by in straw hats and sandals. "Sneaking behind my back, putting Fay in danger, then ripping all the energy out of your body so you can sell it?"

"Yep," Phoenix said. "Something like that."

Simon opened his mouth to lecture Phoenix on the impact his decisions had on the people around him, but something in Phoenix's downcast demeanour made him change his mind.

He sighed and slid down from Tugger's back. "Your energy hasn't fully returned?"

"Not quite," Phoenix confessed, stepping carefully around a small, purple goblin that had stopped to tug at a weed growing in the middle of the road. "It's taking longer than it used to when I was a kid."

"Why?"

Phoenix smiled. "An unfortunate combination of everything I suppose."

"Why aren't you riding?" Simon asked.

Phoenix shrugged. "Restless. Lots to think about. Need to move." He tickled the feathery fur of Fay's ears and she hissed at him, so he patted her head by way of apology and she scowled and went back to sleep. Phoenix stayed silent, walking with the unhurried gait and vacant expression of someone whose mind was elsewhere.

"Well... if it's not too much trouble," Simon said, "how about filling me in on your *latest* self-destructive plan to save the world?"

"Are you a proper warlock now?" Phoenix asked.

The question took Simon by surprise. "I..." His brows furrowed. "Almost."

Phoenix gave him an appraising, sidelong look from behind his mess of hair. "Gloria couldn't alter all your tattoos?"

"The tattoos don't need altering," Simon said. "There are just a few magic-dampening minerals embedded in my skin that still need to be removed, and some of them are affecting energy pathways too complex for Gloria to risk tampering with."

"So you wouldn't... hypothetically speaking... be planning to project yourself into an entirely different world any time soon?"

"With my current abilities?" Simon frowned. "That seems unlikely. Although it is something I've considered."

Phoenix rubbed his eyes. "Can't you take interest in a hobby less dangerous than interdimensional travel? Knitting, perhaps?"

"Relax," Simon said. "I'm not about to follow you to Earth."

"I truly wish that were true," Phoenix said. "Because you going to Earth is a terrible, terrible, *terrible* idea."

"It's an impossible idea." Simon heaved a sigh, folding his arms as he walked. "Jack says if I want to permanently unlock everything, I'm going to have to find another Wolfe."

"Aren't you the only Wolfe this side of the void?" Phoenix asked.

"Officially, yes," Simon replied, then he stopped walking. "Did you know Maulbrak used to be a Wolfe?"

Phoenix pulled a face and strolled on without him. "I'd avoid him if I were you," he said, before adding darkly, "Look at that city."

Simon caught up and stared ahead. Even at this early hour of the afternoon, the city at the end of the teeming road was aglow with brightly coloured lights. They blinked and glinted from down the gracefully curved sides of buildings and along the edge of the low rock wall that encircled the entire glimmering metropolis.

"Of all the energy Bloodwood collects," Phoenix said, "nearly ninety percent is sold to Karvil. Naturally, they like to showcase the city's lavish splendour and abundant wealth. You'd think they'd be a touch more frugal now, considering just how much we're going to need in the upcoming weeks."

Simon stroked his chin. "I guess Karvil has more energy at its disposal than we thought."

"Either that or the self-important poseurs managing the place are a bunch of thick-headed, underappreciative, socially insensitive pricks who wholly deserve the massive Shadow attack that's coming for them," Phoenix said mildly.

"Might want to tone that down while we're in public, Red." Simon cast him a wary look. "We've enough problems already without your idealism getting us in trouble with the authorities again."

Phoenix gave a soft chuckle. "I'll behave. For now."

They strolled on, walking so slowly that a bickering group of elderly trolls dragging expensive, authentically decorated boulders managed to overtake them, followed by a young girl trying desperately to lead a reluctant donkey. Simon expected Phoenix to break the silence, but Phoenix just stared at the road.

Simon scratched uneasily at his beard.

"Is Fay okay?" he asked.

"I think so." Phoenix held the snoozing cat out in front of him, her legs hanging limply along with her tail. "Care to join the conversation, Faydelia?"

She pushed his nose away with her paw and he smiled, bundling her back in the shawl.

"I'm also fine," Gulliver said. "Thanks for asking."

Simon huffed "Sorry, Gulliver. I'm happy you're safe."

"I am not usually one for expressing gratitude..." Gulliver hesitated before continuing in a stiff, carefully-controlled voice. "But your timely arrival was appreciated this morning. And your swift response to those Shadows was... commendable."

Simon raised an eyebrow at him. "Where's all this affectionate sop coming from? Are you sick?"

Gulliver swished his tail in irritation. "You handled those Shadows with a calm practicality that many in Yonder can only aspire to. Had you not arrived when you did, I am inclined to believe that all three of us might have died."

Simon blinked. "You *must* be sick."

"I'm saying you did well," Gulliver snapped.

Simon frowned. "You're praising me?"

"Yes," Gulliver said, after a long pause.

"You never praise anyone."

"You so rarely do anything worthy of praise."

"We need a lookout," Phoenix said, clearly not paying attention to the conversation at all.

Simon turned to him. "Where?"

"Here." Phoenix stopped by the side of the road. "We need someone outside the city to warn us when Shadows start approaching."

"Are you suggesting...?" Gulliver flattened both his ears.

"There's plenty of grass," Phoenix said, waving at the

fields. "And a stream not far away."

"There are monsters underground," Gulliver growled. "And Shadows coming."

"There are indeed." Phoenix placed his hand on Gulliver's shoulder. "Contact us if you need anything."

"Like shelter from the elements?" Gulliver grumbled. "Or a wall between me and the Shadows?"

Simon was already leading Tugger off the road onto the vast expanse of lush meadow. "Really appreciate this, Gulliver."

"Why does Tugger have to stay?" Gulliver asked, like a petulant child.

"Because he likes you," Simon replied, leaving Tugger to roll around in the long grass. "And this is cheaper than a stable."

"It's more convenient when you stay together," Phoenix added.

"Despite what you might think," Gulliver said, "I don't exist for your convenience. I am a highly intelligent being with the ability to communicate abstract ideas and complex thought. Tugger is—"

"Yeah, yeah," Simon said with a sigh. "Tugger is an idiot. Weren't you just thanking me for saving your hide? You owe me, remember?"

Gulliver flicked an ear then plodded off to nudge Tugger up from the ground.

"Stay safe," Phoenix called. "Keep in touch."

Gulliver snorted as he turned on his tail, then he and Tugger bolted off into the distance, kicking up grass and clouds of dust. Once the horses had become little more than dark blots upon the horizon, Simon and Phoenix returned to follow the busy road, Fay still dozing in Phoenix's arms.

They didn't speak until they reached the heaving crowd clogging the road as everyone funnelled slowly through the main gates of Karvil City. The stone wall surrounding Karvil was not a particularly high one, but it was tall enough to force the average traveller to take the carefully supervised entrance rather than waste time trying to clamber up from anywhere along the closely guarded perimeter.

Even as they approached the entrance, Simon noticed the gaze of a uniformed boy on one of the parapets tracking their slow shuffle through the crowd.

"Hey," Phoenix said, drawing Simon's attention away from the guard's watchful stare. "Do you mind taking this?" He had ducked into the shadow of the wall just before the gate, holding out his tattered bag.

"Too heavy?" Simon frowned as he slung Phoenix's bag over his shoulder.

"While I appreciate your patronising concern," Phoenix said lightly, "the reason is more criminal."

"You'd rather I be the one carrying your expensive contraband energy container?" Simon guessed.

Phoenix responded with a half-hearted smile. "If someone recognises me from Fidelity's wanted-posters, we should at least keep that energy out of sight until we absolutely have to reveal it."

"What if *I'm* the one that's targeted?" Simon asked, as they slipped back into the stream of travellers.

Phoenix clapped him on the back. "Leave it to me."

They allowed themselves to be swept along with the crowd. Simon felt Phoenix's energy ripple as they passed through the gates and glanced down in time to catch a grimace flicker across Phoenix's face, but Phoenix didn't mention it, so Simon followed his lead and didn't comment on Karvil's powerful anti-Shadow wards.

They emerged into the sunlight at the other side of the wall and Simon stopped to gaze upon the city. The path they had been following continued in a straight line toward the heart of Karvil, but on either side of the road a wide strip of flat land separated the extensive wall from the mass of towers and bubble-shaped dwellings that sprawled out from the city's centre like a wild garden of shimmering metal and light.

The Strip, as everyone called it, encircled the whole

of Karvil in lush grass and acted as a popular place for people to enjoy an open area without fear of encountering any monsters from beyond the wall. Usually occupied with picnickers, wedding parties, youths with too much time on their hands, and the odd doomsayer or two, The Strip was today transformed into a bustling marketplace, rows upon rows of temporary stalls set up in a bid to make money from the influx of visitors surging through the gates.

A large portion of the crowd continued straight into the city to haggle for places to sleep, but many of the new arrivals spilled out into the market to explore the endless rows of stalls. The crowd was so dense that Simon quickly lost sight of Phoenix, whose tousled red hair vanished almost immediately amongst the sea of much taller people.

Simon swallowed as a wave of dizziness washed over him. The city had always been a difficult place to navigate, riddled with vague, often chaotic flashes of the past. Scattered between the living were transparent people who had long since disappeared from the world. Ghosts, as Phoenix liked to call them, despite the number of times Simon had corrected him.

To the left of the entrance he could see the ethereal, faded scene of a public hanging, the timber stage blending eerily into the present-day instalment of a picnic table.

It must have been an occurrence from far back in Karvil's history, as the city hadn't executed anyone since the Shadow War ended fifty years ago. Not publicly, at least. Shades, of course, being the only exceptions to the rule.

Simon looked away as the executioner cranked open the trapdoor, then closed his eyes and drew a slow breath, trying to force the past out of his head.

When he opened his eyes, all the ghostly figures had disappeared. Whatever Gloria had achieved with his powers, Simon's connection with the past had become mercifully easier to control.

A troll shoved Simon in the back and he continued walking, though not before shooting the troll a sour glare which was completely lost on the giant creature's limited vision. He caught up with Phoenix a moment later and found he had stopped beside a market-tent decorated with sheets of music, too engaged in conversation to even notice Simon arrive.

"How much for that little horn?" Phoenix asked, leaning over the desk and pointing at the instrument in question, a shimmering tangle of golden metal displayed at the back of the marquee.

The squat lady with wispy grey hair who was running the stall took the horn from its display then held it out for Phoenix to take a closer look.

"You've a good eye, sir," she said in a wheezy voice. "This little beast was crafted by my grandmother nearly half a century ago. Two tubes. Extra valve for those subtle key changes. Bone-plated keys."

"Price?" Phoenix reached out to touch it but the woman swatted his hand away.

"Twelve-thousand gold."

Phoenix grimaced. "I can trade you this cat for it?"

The woman laughed. "If you're not buying, kid, take a hike."

"Sir to kid in ten seconds flat," Phoenix said with a sigh. He turned to find Simon standing beside him. "Simon. Hello. I got distracted."

"Are you trying to sell Fay?"

"Hold that thought." Phoenix reached past him then whipped away a piece of paper pinned to the tent opposite the music stall. He waved the paper in front of Simon's face, and Simon recognised the coloured illustration of Phoenix upon the wanted-poster.

Phoenix gave a grim smile. "Our troll has been busy."

"I don't think our troll is the only person looking for you," Simon said, taking the poster then crumpling it into his bag as the crowd bustled about around them.

"You think I have my very own search party?" Phoenix

asked, looking pleased at the idea.

Simon scowled then tugged Phoenix's hood up to cover the conspicuous mop of red hair. "Better keep moving," he muttered. "Where first?"

Phoenix shifted Fay into a more comfortable position then surveyed the sprawl of tents.

"Food?" he suggested.

They pushed through the throng towards a stall selling hot bread until a prickly feeling at the back of Simon's neck made him turn around. The young guard he had seen patrolling the wall was talking with the woman at the music shop, brandishing a distinctly poster-sized piece of paper. Simon's heart sank as the woman pointed down the line of stalls and the guard caught Simon's eye.

Simon nudged Phoenix in the back.

Before Phoenix could respond, the guard came charging through the crowd, thrusting an accusatory finger in their direction. "Don't move!"

"Move," Phoenix said, darting between two tents into the next row of stalls. Simon squeezed through the gap and stomped after him, barrelling through the river of people on the other side as he chased Phoenix deeper into the market.

The guard zipped into the crowd behind them, surprisingly light on his feet.

Phoenix leapt over a large crate of fruit which Simon promptly knocked over, apologising to the disgruntled store owner as he shot past.

"It's too early to be getting arrested." Phoenix veered sharply to the right, dashing into the next row of stalls with Simon close behind, Fay spitting loudly in irritation.

"You!" the guard yelled. "In the coat! The colourful one! *Hey*!"

They wove through the foot-traffic, darting around clothes racks and precarious displays until coming upon a horde of people queuing for a bakery stand that was offering a limited-time-only special on cakes.

They skidded to a stop and stared at the enormous crowd blocking access to all the surrounding stalls.

Phoenix laughed. “Those cakes must taste like holy Light itself.” He turned to face the oncoming guard.

“Plan?” Simon hissed, leaning down to Phoenix’s height.

“Meet by the naked lady,” Phoenix muttered.

“What?”

“This won’t take long.”

“What won’t?”

“Take Fay.” Phoenix thrust the cat into Simon’s arms then spun back to grin at the approaching guard. “*Officer*! How can I help you?”

The guard stopped before them then took a moment to catch his breath. He looked young, perhaps just seventeen, with weedy arms and a patchy, unsuccessful attempt at a proper grown-up’s beard.

His beige uniform was neatly pressed, though a little rumpled from the chase, and Simon noticed a collection of blades and batons at his hip, including a Shadow-spear clipped to his belt, glinting in the sun. Trouble for Phoenix, if the young guard decided to use it.

The guard straightened up and pointed at Phoenix’s face. “You Phoenix Page?”

Phoenix responded with an easy smile. “Your tone suggests I should say otherwise.”

“You’re wanted by the High Chief.”

“How flattering.”

“Please come with me.”

“Please?” Phoenix raised an eyebrow. “You’re new to this, aren’t you?”

“Come quietly,” the guard said, “and no one needs to get hurt.”

“That’s very considerate of you,” Phoenix said, and to his credit he did look genuinely touched by the guard’s courtesy. “What’s your name?”

“Bradley.” The guard’s face went ashen. “I’m not

supposed to tell you."

"Pleasure to make your acquaintance, Bradley." Phoenix offered a friendly smile which Bradley cautiously returned.

"So...?" he said, with a hopefulness that Simon guessed was soon to be dashed by whatever Phoenix had in mind. "You'll come quietly?"

"Listen," Phoenix said, shoving his hands into the pockets of his coat. "Brad. You seem like a decent guy. And it only seems fair that I extend the same kindness."

Bradley frowned. "What?"

"Do as I say," Phoenix said, "and I won't blast a hole the size of a house through that lovely stone wall you're all so determined to stand watch over."

"Here we go," Simon said under his breath.

Bradley shifted uneasily on his feet. "You can do that?"

Phoenix slowly pressed his hands together. "Would you like to see me try?"

"No." Bradley and Simon responded as one.

"I think, then," Phoenix said, as the crowd milled around them, "that we can probably come to some kind of agreement."

The young guard raised his fluffy chin, and it did little to make him more impressive. "State your conditions."

"Gladly," Phoenix said. "My friend walks free."

Bradley cast his eyes over Simon then shrugged. "Sure."

"Also," Phoenix added, "you have to answer any questions I have on our way to the High Chief."

"But I have to report to my overseeing officer," Bradley objected. "She's the one who'll take you to the High Chief."

"And where might she be?" Phoenix asked.

"By the gate." Bradley nodded toward the edge of the market.

Phoenix smiled. "Then I guess you can answer my questions on the way there."

"Do I have to answer *truthfully*?"

"Up to you," Phoenix replied. "Part of the fun."

"And that's all?" Bradley said, eyes narrowed in

suspicion. "You'll come if I just *talk* to you and we leave your friend here?"

Phoenix clapped him on the shoulder. "It's that simple."

"I'll have to restrain you."

The smile slid from Phoenix's face. "I'd rather you didn't."

"Just your hands," Bradley said, unravelling a short rope from one of the clips at his belt. "Either that or we're told to knock you unconscious."

"I can't see you managing to knock me unconscious…" Phoenix said, but he held out his hands, only to jerk them away as soon as Bradly took his wrists.

The young guard frowned and Phoenix hesitated before offering his hands again, scowling as the rope touched his skin.

Bradley yanked the cord tight and Phoenix clapped his palms together with an angry snap, the energy swelling in the air as though he were about to summon a void-stone.

"Easy, Red," Simon muttered. A crowded marketplace was not the best location to be throwing deadly, unbridled void-energy around.

Phoenix shot him a panicked look then relaxed, his face breaking into a grin that could mean nothing good for anyone. "I'll catch up soon."

Bradley gripped Phoenix by the arm and turned him around, leading him back towards the main gate.

"Mind the cat!" Phoenix called.

"Wait!" Simon shouted after him. "Where's the naked lady?!"

The crowd paused in their shopping to condemn him with disapproving frowns. Even Fay raised her head to glower before nuzzling back into her shawl.

Phoenix looked back over his shoulder. "Come on, Wolfe. Show some decorum." Then he and the guard disappeared around the corner of a fabric stall and Simon was left standing uncertainly beside an old man selling freshly baked potatoes.

"He told me his plan," Fay said, her voice purring

through Simon's mind with a silkiness that sent goose-bumps down his spine.

"Was it a good one?" Simon asked aloud, not with a great deal of optimism.

Fay scoffed. "Not at all."

Simon rubbed his eyes, frowned at the sky in contemplative silence for a moment, then sighed and bought himself a potato.

CITY STREETS

The Naked Lady was the unofficial name given to the stone statue at the centre of Uprising Fountain, located down a dingy side-street beside Yonder's grungiest, most germ-infested tavern: Snotworth's. Simon had once made the mistake of ordering a bowl of stew there and ended up bedridden for three weeks, much to the concern of Phoenix, who had been twelve and very much incapable of looking after himself, let alone an irritable teenage warlock who suddenly spent every day sleeping, swearing, and being horrendously sick.

The Naked Lady was muscular, one hand on her bare

hip and a foot resting upon the decapitated head of a Shadow as she thrust a spear upwards into a wave of polished stone. Running water bubbled down the length of her spear into the shallow pool that surrounded her, and the whole piece was supposed to represent something about Karvil's strength, though the exact origin of its creation had faded over time.

As Simon stood by the fountain waiting for Phoenix, frowning at the Naked Lady's determined face, he couldn't help recalling his first encounter with the statue.

"Ten years," he said to himself.

"What?" Fay's voice cut through his thoughts.

He turned to her. She was perched at the edge of the fountain, cleaning her long fur with the dainty feline nonchalance that set the Leon Clan apart as being the most self-absorbed of all the clans.

"This place," Simon said. "It's where I first met Red."

~

Simon was fifteen, sitting on the roof of a suspicious antique shop, watching the sleepy backstreets of Karvil go about their business below. It had been months since he last fled the city, but he'd been trailing the mysterious kid for a while now, and his pursuit had led him right back to Karvil.

He hated being so close to the clan, but the journals he'd stolen from Edgar's abandoned office had provided just enough information on the unusual boy to give Simon hope. Enough hope to convince him that returning to the city was worth the risk of being captured by Wolves.

The red-haired little brat slipped out the back door of an eatery, his raggedy clothes bulging with stolen food.

Simon sprang to his feet. There was no mistaking the child. He didn't look particularly impressive, but the energy pervading the air confirmed him as an unstable freak of nature with direct access to the void, mentioned so casually in Edgar's papers as an oddity to keep an eye on.

"Hey!" Simon scrambled down the side of the building, landing with a heavy thump amongst startled passers-by. The boy bolted off like lightning.

"Wait!" Simon yelled, jumping over the pile of bread-rolls that had spilled from the boy's shirt. "I just want to talk!"

He caught up beside a grimy stone fountain in an empty alleyway, grabbing the child's arm so he wouldn't dash away. Golden light flashed behind the boy's eyes as he smacked his hands together, launching a shimmering green stone high above his head.

Simon jumped back as the boy directed his palms at him.

"Easy, Red," Simon said, lowering his own hands to seem less of a threat. "I don't want to hurt you. What's your name?"

The boy glared back without a word, the stone humming above his head. A few people peered down the alley as they walked by, but most took one glance at the glowing stone and the boy's aggressive stance before hurrying away.

Simon sighed then crouched to get closer to the child's height.

"I'm Simon," he said. "I'm a warlock."

"You can't be a warlock," the boy argued. "I've met warlocks. Your energy's too... flat."

"It's regulated," Simon said, impressed that the kid had even noticed. "But that's not interesting. *You*... are interesting. I've seen the trail of destruction you leave behind. You can keep a void-stone activated longer than any magician I know."

"It's easy."

"It's dangerous. *Anyway*," Simon said, pushing on with the speech he'd been rehearsing ever since discovering Edgar's journals, "I've been continuing the research of my late teacher. Studying the nature of void-tunnels. And since so many tunnels are surrounded by rumours of a scrawny little redhead blasting his way out of holding-cells and orphanages and crowded market squares all over Yonder, well... I figured you and I might make a good team."

"Why are they late?"

Simon furrowed his brows. "What?"

"Your teacher," the kid said. "Late for what?"

"Oh." Simon hesitated. "Late in the sense that he's not around anymore."

"Dead?"

Simon swallowed. "Possibly."

"The tunnels won't bring him back."

Simon blinked. "Huh?"

"You're looking for your teacher, right? That's why you're chasing tunnels."

"This isn't about my useless teacher," Simon said, temperamental magic sparking from his fingers. "I'm looking for Tristan. My brother. He was taken by the void. Pulled into a tunnel earlier this year. Pushed, really. Not that it makes a difference."

"I guess he's dead too, then," the boy said with a shrug.

Simon narrowed his eyes. "My parrot flew into a tunnel once, and he came back just fine. And with your help—"

"No." The boy shook his head.

"But you can summon energy from within the void itself," Simon said, desperation creeping into his voice. "You can trigger tunnels. You can—"

"*No.*" Golden energy shot from the kid's hands, blasting a small crater into the pavement at Simon's feet. Simon froze, eyeing the kid with renewed caution.

"I can't help you." The boy launched another ball of energy at Simon's boots and Simon flicked his hands, creating a thin, flickering wall of orange light.

"Why?" he asked from behind the wavering screen.

The kid blasted energy through the shield, smashing Simon into the Naked Lady.

"Because," he said, as Simon coughed water out of his mouth, gripping the stone woman for support, "I break everything."

Simon winced as he climbed out of the fountain. "You're like my brother."

The kid glowered, flecks of gold swirling within his eyes. "Fascinating. I don't care."

"Tristan thought he was in control," Simon said, water puddling at his feet. "Thought he was strong enough on his own. But no one can control the void. Not without enormous cost."

The boy said nothing, blood leaking from his freckled nose as he held his ground.

"You're just a kid," Simon continued, edging closer. "You don't need to handle this alone. You need someone looking out for you. We could work together. Help each other."

The boy fired a torrent of energy again.

"Don't come any closer," he warned, his strange eyes wide with panic.

Simon paused. He'd seen that look before. It was the look of someone terrified by the crushing knowledge that they were the most dangerous part of the equation. The look of someone who didn't trust themselves. And it was the last heartbreaking expression he'd seen upon the bloodied face of his brother before Simon shoved him into the void.

"Alright, I get it." Simon bowed his head as he backed away. "I won't bother you again." And he meant it. As Simon retreated onto the main street, he fully believed he would have no further dealings with the frightened little mop-head.

But the universe had other ideas.

~

"You met in Karvil?" Fay asked, and before Simon could answer, the air thickened with the dense energy of void-stones. A mighty crack resounded off the walls of every building, followed by a boom that rumbled through the city and shook the grimy cobblestones beneath his feet.

Fay leapt from the fountain and pressed against Simon's boots with her teeth bared and her fur on end.

"I hope that's Phoenix," she said, "and not the start of a

Shadow invasion."

"It's Phoenix," Simon said, as the shudders ebbed away underfoot. A second blast thundered past his ears before a strange hush settled over the city. Even the boisterous clientele of Snotworth's quietened down as they spilled out onto the street, murmuring to each other as they looked around for the source of the disturbance.

Simon looked down at the cat slinking between his feet. "I thought Red was just planning to outsmart one runt of a guard."

"Rather big blast for a little guard," Fay said, leaping up to sit on the fountain again.

Simon frowned into his beard. "Maybe something went wrong."

"Doesn't sound like everything went *right*."

Simon didn't bother responding to that.

Eventually the crowd outside Snotworth's got bored and traipsed back indoors to take their chances with the dicey food.

Simon scratched his chin for a while. "He must be in trouble."

"How long do you think we should wait?" Fay asked.

A crash of plates resounded from the tavern next door followed by raucous stomping of feet and hoots of laughter. Then Phoenix burst out the front door with a crowd of admirers thumping him on the back and ruffling his hair as they followed him out onto the narrow street.

Snotworth's had been a refuge for ruffians and rabble-rousers since the day it opened, accessible from a number or secret tunnels, trapdoors and chutes scattered about the city, perfect for anyone in need of a hasty escape. Phoenix knew every one of those tunnels, trapdoors and chutes, and had become something of a local celebrity amongst the disenfranchised masses of Karvil City thanks to his anti-authoritarian ideals and penchant for trouble.

He spotted Simon down the street then detached himself from the crowd, grinning from ear to ear as he bounced over to the fountain, his glowing eyes burning with energy as irrepressible as his laughter.

"I underestimate myself," Phoenix said, wiping tears from his eyes. "That was spectacular!" He leant over with his hands on his knees, mirth spilling out of him in heaving waves. "Their faces," he said between wheezing gasps for breath. "Light almighty, it was perfect." His laughter deteriorated into a full coughing fit and he sank against the fountain.

"Care to share the joke?" Simon asked uneasily, as Phoenix buried his face in a handkerchief to muffle the hacking sounds that had taken over completely.

"Sure." Phoenix tucked the handkerchief into his coat then let his head fall back against the stone, still chuckling to himself. "I am the stealthiest rainbow-coated redhead in Yonder. The Master of Elusion. The Champion of—"

"Get to the point, Red."

"I blew up the wall."

Simon blinked. "What?"

"Only part of it," Phoenix said. "And I made sure nobody was injured. Gave plenty of warning. Timed it all just so. You'd be proud. I was remarkably responsible about the whole thing."

"Not what I'd call *stealthy*," Simon pointed out as Fay transformed into a human behind him.

"Perhaps not initially," Phoenix said. "But it was the perfect distraction for my getaway, which proved to be a fine example of cunning evasive techniques."

"What happened?" Fay asked, clipping her shawl into place with her rat-skull broach. "I thought you were going to ditch that guard in the crowd once you'd gotten enough information out of him."

"As it turns out," Phoenix said, pushing himself to his feet, "young Bradley is not the brightest of sparks. He just kept telling me things. Interesting things, too. Like the fact that the High Chief says I'm a pure, first-generation Shade. And that everyone is under strict orders *not* to kill me." He brushed some gravel from his coat. "Eventually I got curious to meet Brad's overseeing officer, if only to ask what her justification was for appointing the lovable fool to any position of responsibility in the first place. Also, aside from questions about Bradley's ill-advised employment, I wanted to know what the procedure would be like for when I actually *do* want to be detained."

"Another flawless plan," Simon said as Phoenix gingerly lowered himself to sit on the fountain wall. "How'd you get away?"

Phoenix grinned. "Some clever bargaining, and perhaps a few strongly worded threats regarding void-stones and protective shields and the safety of the entire population. People were reluctant to attack me, even after I ruined the wall." Phoenix leant over the fountain. "It helps that I'm charming," he added, then cupped some water in his hand and raised it to his lips.

"Phoenix, for Light's sake." Fay scowled at him in disgust. "People pee into that, I guarantee it."

Phoenix swilled the water around in his mouth then spat it back into the pool. His eyes lingered on the water for a second then he jumped up and threw an arm around Fay's shoulders. "To the Inventors' Guild!" he said, pointing down the street with the grandiose fervour of an amateur theatre performer. "Before I get arrested again."

Fay ducked out of his reach. "I'm not coming with you."

Phoenix deflated a little. "You're not?"

"I need to speak with what's left of my clan," Fay said. "I'm going to the Magicians' District." She turned and gave Simon a stern look. "You should go too."

Simon gave a noncommittal grumble of unintelligible sound.

"Will we see you again?" Phoenix asked, sitting once more on the edge of the fountain.

"I said I'd help you close the void. So... I'll tolerate your company until it is closed." Fay offered a sly smile and patted him on the head. "I'll meet you at the Guild."

"Today?"

"Tomorrow." Fay turned and punched Simon in the arm. "Step up and be a Wolfe. The clans have major responsibilities now." She stalked off down the street, her knotty hair swaying behind her like the swishing tail of a cat.

Simon sighed as she retreated into the distance. "Easy for her to say."

"Fay!" Phoenix called before she rounded the corner. She frowned back impatiently.

Phoenix hesitated then shrugged with an awkward smile. "Thank you."

Fay just rolled her eyes then disappeared down another street.

"I think," Phoenix said, crossing one leg over the other, "that she has decided to stop hating me."

"Inventors' Guild then?" Simon asked, dumping Phoenix's bag into his lap.

Phoenix nodded. "Time for me to call upon some favours."

They wound their way through the shady backstreets, keeping to the shadows and avoiding the crowds. While most of Karvil was adorned with cheery, shimmering lights, the parts that Simon and Phoenix usually frequented were dark and drab, filled with furtive whispers and cagey glances as people went slinking from one point of crooked business to the next.

It was places like these, Phoenix argued, that not only had the cheapest food, but also the best music.

"Just listen," he said as they approached a lady playing violin outside a second-hand bookstore. "People understand what music *means* around here. It's authentic." He delved into his bag and dropped a few coins into the case beside the woman. She winked at him, continuing her tune.

"Infinitely more inspiring than that rigid mundanity that passes for music in Central Karvil," Phoenix added as they walked away. "Everyone there is too distracted by pretty lights and prestigious reputations to recognise what real talent sounds like." He glanced back at the violinist. "Their loss, I suppose."

Simon chuckled. "Still bitter that Lord and Lady Belton didn't let us perform at their son's coming-of-age ceremony?"

"*Too dynamic*," Phoenix said, shaking his head in disbelief. "What sort of criticism is that? Did you see their son when we auditioned? He was miserable. The poor kid was chained down to a life of superficial pleasantries and constantly scrutinised adulthood. He'd have appreciated some music like ours." Phoenix rolled his eyes. "*Too dynamic*."

They rounded a corner and nearly walked straight into two little girls with long piggy-tails running in the other direction. Phoenix hopped nimbly to the side as the kids darted around Simon then dashed back in the direction they'd just come from to chase each other around the otherwise deserted park on the next corner.

"They have no idea," Phoenix said, watching as the kids skipped between the poles of the swing-set. The sight of the children playing amongst the rundown slides and swings reminded Simon of a question he had been wanting to ask since the morning.

"Red," he began as they started walking again, "when you were younger... visiting Gloria and Jack... do you remember seeing anything that made you lash out in a kind of wild panic?"

Phoenix laughed. "You'll have to be more specific," he said. "I was not a low-maintenance kid."

"A person," Simon said, as they drew closer to the park. "Who spoke to you. But you couldn't see them clearly. Then you freaked out and tried to blow up a bookshelf."

"Tried to..." Phoenix trailed off then stopped walking, turning back to face Simon, his eyes searching the warlock's face with wary apprehension. "Why do you want to know about that?"

Simon hesitated, taken aback by Phoenix's sudden change in demeanour.

"It seems my connection to the past is no longer limited to observation," Simon said. "Apparently I can be seen. At least, I can be seen by you."

Phoenix stared at him. The children squealed and giggled as they danced around in the playground, one of them screaming at the top of her lungs as the other pulled her down the slide. Phoenix didn't even glance at them.

"That was you?"

"Yeah…" Simon said, surprised by how faint Phoenix's voice had become. "Sorry."

Phoenix swallowed then turned and started walking again. "I was mistaken."

"About what?" Simon asked, but Phoenix didn't answer.

They turned the corner and walked along the middle of the road at the other side of the park.

"Why'd you have to bring that up?" Phoenix mumbled, so softly that Simon almost didn't hear him.

"Why does it bother you so much?"

Phoenix slowed and Simon saw that his face had grown pale.

"Look," he said, as Phoenix veered off towards the side of the street. "I didn't mean to remind you of the old days. You've been running from Bloodwood for ten years. I should've realised you didn't want to relive any of it. I only thought —" The rest of Simon's explanation was cut short by Phoenix ducking into a large, leafy hedge at the edge of the park and being so dramatically ill it sounded like someone had just eaten at Snotworth's.

Simon waited outside the bushes. "You okay?"

"Could be better," Phoenix managed at last. Then he backed out of the shrubbery and started pulling twigs out of his hair. "Must've been that fountain water," he muttered, but Simon suspected there was more at play than a contaminated pool.

The two girls had wisely abandoned the park by this point, leaving the street empty and quiet. Simon frowned at Phoenix in search of any hints as to what was going on, but Phoenix avoided looking at him, scratching absently at his arm as he studied the gently sloping rooftops of the timeworn shops lining the street.

After deciding that Phoenix was not in immediate danger of passing out, they cautiously set off for the Guild, only to stop at the first café they came across because Simon thought Phoenix looked peaky.

The café was a featureless box of an establishment, with round tables and mismatched chairs. The special of the day was buttered sourdough bread, so Simon ordered a few slices of that while Phoenix shuffled off to secure a table, moving with the steady care of a seasick man returning to land.

"Everyone's talking about the explosion," Simon said, as he arrived at the table with a jug of water and two accompanying glasses.

"What explosion?" Phoenix asked, his fist balled against his face as he propped himself up with his elbow.

Simon paused, midway through pouring the water.

"Oh," Phoenix said. "My explosion."

Simon shook his head then placed a full glass before Phoenix and kept the other for himself. "Feeling better?"

"Something isn't right," Phoenix murmured. He drummed his fingers against the table then looked up, frowning intently. "You still have a beard."

"And?"

"It has to go," Phoenix said. "I think your beard is making me sick."

Simon rolled his eyes. "Drink some water. You're delusional."

"I'm serious," Phoenix said.

"What about that guy's beard?" Simon asked, pointing to an ancient old man drinking beer in the corner of the room with a long, grey beard tucked into his belt.

Phoenix glanced at the man in question then shrugged. "That beard's fine. It can stay. But yours..." He pointed at Simon's face. "Something must be done." He raised his glass to his mouth but it slipped out of his grip before he could drink anything, the water gushing over the table and splashing onto Simon's boots.

A young, mousey boy in an apron chose that moment to arrive carrying a plate of warm bread. Even standing on tiptoes he was barely tall enough to see over the table.

"Special of the day," he announced, setting the food down in the puddle of water. Then he turned on his heels and marched back into the kitchen.

"How many stones did you use?" Simon asked, as Phoenix mopped the water up with his patched sleeves.

"Oh... only one." Phoenix grabbed a slice of bread.

"Yeah?" Simon said, refilling Phoenix's glass. "I sensed two."

Phoenix laughed. "Why ask questions you already have answers to?"

"Why lie when you know I already have the answers?" Simon countered, then he tugged at his beard for a long while before leaning forward so only Phoenix could hear. "I cannot believe you blew up the wall."

Phoenix chuckled. "Sure you can. You've known me long enough."

"Karvil isn't our enemy, Red."

"I know," Phoenix said, reaching for another slice of sourdough. "Which is why I waited until we reached Chiefly Gardens. No one there but spineless palace officials and exotic birds. And as I *already told you*, I warned everyone before the wall came down. Though I'm afraid I might've flattened a peacock. Feel bad about that one. There wasn't enough time to check."

"We're supposed to protect Karvil," Simon said. "Not destroy its defences."

"Even if I *had* gone back and found an injured peacock,

what could I have done?" Phoenix wondered. "I don't know first-aid for flattened birds."

"That wall," Simon said, "is more important now than it has been in the last fifty years combined."

"Please," Phoenix said. "Even if it were three times the size, that wall wouldn't stop a Shadow. You know that." He licked the crumbs from his fingers then picked up his refilled drink.

"My concern," Simon said, as Phoenix gulped down the water, "is that you're not thinking things through. And you're putting people in danger. Including yourself."

Phoenix smiled over the top of his glass. "Can't we just take a second to appreciate how impressive I am? I singlehandedly demolished a citadel wall designed to slow down entire armies."

"You just threw up in a children's playground."

Phoenix glared at him for a minute then shook his head, his face relaxing into a weary smile. "I'm being careful, Wolfe. And I make no apologies for trying to enjoy myself at the same time. Also," he added, "I think we should throw a party."

Simon eyed him in silence for a moment before giving in to the absurdity of the suggestion. "What?"

"A party." Phoenix said. "A big one. Tomorrow. At the Guild."

"*Why*?"

Phoenix scratched at his mop of hair like a dog trying to rid itself of fleas, then shrugged and looked away. "Why not?"

"Because you're Yonder's most wanted criminal and the void is misbehaving and Bloodwood has fallen and Shadows are coming?" Simon furrowed his brows. "Would it kill you to take this seriously?"

"Quite possibly," Phoenix said, then he narrowed his eyes. "Stop talking."

Simon started to argue but Phoenix shushed him then sprang to his feet and pounced upon a group of three surly, mean-eyed hunters dining toward the back of the room, surrounded by spears and arrows and traps that could take down a troll. Although dining, perhaps, was too generous a term. They were fighting like animals over a tray of mixed meat, shredding it with their hands, tearing strips away with their teeth.

"Sorry to interrupt," Phoenix said, pulling up a chair and joining the three at their table, "but I couldn't help overhear you talking about giants."

"What's it to you?" a boxy woman spat, glaring at him over the top of the turkey leg she was devouring.

"Are there giants in Karvil?" Phoenix asked, as Simon arrived to stand behind him with their bags.

"Not usually," a portly, rosy-cheeked man grinned, revealing a startling lack of teeth. "But it seems there are now." The boxy woman kicked him under the table.

"Fascinating." Phoenix smiled. "Are you giant hunters?"

"Maybe," the boxy woman said, before pointing her turkey leg at Phoenix. "Are *you*?"

"Me?" Phoenix said, feigning surprise. "Do I look like someone who could take on a giant?"

"No." The woman cast her steely eyes over Simon. "But your friend might. We can't be giving knowledge to the competition."

The two other hunters muttered their agreement, though mostly they were preoccupied with ripping apart their food.

"Truth is," Phoenix said, "my friend and I are researching music throughout Yonder." He rummaged through his bag, his trumpet clanging against the canister of energy as he dragged it out. "Holy Light, it's had a beating..." Phoenix frowned at the battered instrument in dismay.

The woman tossed her bone onto the tray in the centre of the table. "You're musicians?"

"We try." Phoenix played a swift run of notes then tucked the trumpet back into his bag. "We heard that giants are unique in their musical expression," he added, as the hunters listened suspiciously, "but they are notoriously private creatures. *Consequently*... we would pay good money to hear what you know about giants in Karvil."

The boxy woman, who seemed to be in charge of the party, leant across the table and fixed Phoenix with a greedy smile. "How good is your money?"

"Depends how good your information is," Phoenix said, mimicking her gesture as he leant eagerly across the table towards her.

Simon folded his arms and drew himself up to stand even taller behind Phoenix's chair. "You will be very generously rewarded."

The hunters eyed him distrustfully, but like many magicians, Simon possessed a convincing gravitas that was difficult to ignore.

The oldest of the hunters—a wizened man with thinning, straw-coloured hair—clasped his hands together with supressed glee. "Let's help these fine bohemians out."

"What do you want to know?" the woman grumbled through a mouthful of ham.

"Whatever you can tell us," Phoenix said.

"Rumour has it," whistled the portly, tooth-divested hunter, "that word of Bloodwood's demise has spread far and wide across Yonder. If not even Bloodwood can stand against Shadows, what chance do the rest of us have?"

Phoenix frowned. "What's your point?"

"Karvil's got its own mighty army, don't it?" the man said, waggling a finger at him. "And it's got a massive anti-Shadow shield. *And* it has that big wall."

"Had," said the boxy woman, picking meat out of her teeth. "They *had* a wall."

"They still have a wall," the little man argued. "There's just less of it now."

"Never mind the wall," Phoenix said. "Tell us about giants."

The oldest hunter smiled a slow smile. "They've come to

seek shelter in the city."

Phoenix scoffed. "No way they'd leave the mountains to mingle with weaklings like us."

"It's true," the older man said. "We spotted one just this morning."

"Real ugly, too." The woman snapped a bone in half and flicked both halves onto the floor.

"Something wrong with it, I say," said the portly man. "Too small."

"Don't forget the face," the woman said, reaching for a chicken wing in the centre of the table. "Something wrong with it."

Her colleague nodded in agreement. "That's right. Huge purple mark on the side of its face. And its clothes..."

"Not traditional giant attire at all," the woman finished. "Our theory," she added, "is that it was exiled from its tribe."

"Where was this giant?" Simon asked.

The woman shrugged. "Loitering around the West Post. We haven't gone after it yet. Figured we'd sneak up once it settled."

The old hunter snickered. "So... if you want to learn about its musical preferences, do it today. We'll have captured the thing by tomorrow morning."

Simon glowered as he turned his back on everyone. "You've been very helpful."

"What about our reward?" the woman asked as Simon started trudging away.

Simon turned and slammed his hand against the table, sending thin cracks shooting past the tray of meat. A dark pool of ink grew beneath his palm then rose into the air as a swirling, wispy orb that split and launched at each hunter's face with the speed of a striking snake. It returned to its dark, inky state then coiled down each hunter's neck, over their shoulders, then down their right arms, eventually settling into the image of a cross on the back of each hunter's hand where it sizzled permanently into their skin.

"*That's* your reward," Simon said. "Get within spear-throwing distance of a giant ever again and that tattoo will make you wish you were dead."

"How is that a reward?" the portly man squeaked, rubbing uselessly at the mark on his hand.

Phoenix laughed as he pulled his bag over his shoulder. "You're still alive."

"Are you really planning to interview that creature about *music*?" the panicked, portly hunter demanded as Simon and Phoenix started walking away. "You expect to have a sensible conversation with it?"

Simon stormed back towards the table.

"It is a crude, lumbering simpleton," the hunter continued, his voice jumping up an octave as Simon approached, "driven by savage instincts and—"

Simon seized him by the front of his shirt and wrenched him out of his seat, holding him in place while he raised his other hand to the squirming twit's face, red lightning dancing around his fingers, flickering dangerously close to the little man's nose. Simon could feel the tense gaze of everyone in the café, but he didn't care, baring his teeth as he tightened his grip on the man's shirt.

"Say one more thing about Jess," he growled, lightning sputtering in his hand. "I *dare* you."

The man went limp and stared at Simon in bewilderment. "Who?"

Simon released the lightning and it shot past the hunter's ear, burning straight through the back wall, blasting through the kitchen, then scorching a dramatic scar upon the far wall behind a food preparation bench where an old cook was so startled that he flung the basket he was holding over his head and a deluge of vegetables went tumbling across the floor.

"So..." Phoenix appeared at Simon's side with a smug grin on his face. "That lecture you were giving me about being responsible..."

Simon scowled then dropped the stunned, portly little

hunter into his chair before marching out to glower at people on the street. Phoenix joined him a few minutes later, still smiling as though he'd won a prize.

"Had a chat with the owner," he said, tucking his bag of coins into his oversized coat. "She's not at all pleased with your little outburst. Nothing two thousand gold can't fix though apparently."

"I'll pay you back." Simon started reaching into his bag, but Phoenix stopped him with a dismissive wave.

"Don't worry about it."

Simon frowned at him. "That's a third of your savings."

Phoenix shrugged. "Money seems somewhat insignificant in the greater scheme of things." He set off down the street with a spring in his step. "Your beloved is waiting and time is precious. Stop dawdling. Let's get this band back together again!"

Simon smiled from the very core of his being. Thinking about Jess had that effect.

FROM ACROSS THE DIVIDE

Phoenix stopped at the end of the dusty little laneway that opened out onto the grassy, flat land of The Strip, his eyes tracking the two guards patrolling the top of the wall in the distance. The west of Karvil was generally avoided by all but those unfortunate enough to live and do business there, with places like Snotworth's scattered everywhere and the mysterious Magicians' District nestled nearby. It was hardly surprising then that The Strip by the West Post was largely deserted compared to the bustling marketplace they had seen at the main entrance to Karvil in the south.

The West Post itself was little more than a flagpole

covered in twinkling lights that protruded from the top of the wall in front of them, overlooking the peaceful scene below. A gentle stream flowed through a narrow, metal grate at the base of the wall and meandered through the grass, its path wiggling along the length of The Strip and disappearing around the bend, where it would continue all the way to Chiefly Gardens by the palace in the north.

"There," Simon said, pointing to a twist in the stream. Phoenix pulled his gaze away from the guards. Even from a distance and without much around for comparison, it was easy to see that Jess was tall. She stood with her back to them in the middle of the stream, water lapping at her knees as she gazed into its depths, probably, Phoenix assumed, looking for fish.

"Should we call her over?" Phoenix asked, but Simon had already walked out onto The Strip, trudging through the grass towards the stream. Phoenix glanced at the guards on the distant wall then followed Simon into the open.

At least if he was ambushed he'd have a formidable warlock and a fiercely loyal giant on his side.

Jess lowered her arms into the water as they approached, her wavy, chestnut hair tossed over her shoulder in a loose plait so as not to get in the way. A lavender birthmark covered most of her right cheek, blossoming out to the edge of her flat nose, the base of her ear, and just below her right eye. She occasionally joked that it was shaped like a bird hitting a glass window, but Simon, being incurably infatuated, told her it looked like a treasure-blossom, a rare flower that bloomed around the coastal town he'd grown up in that was said to bring good fortune to anyone who found it.

Phoenix was endlessly amused by the fact that despite his tough appearance, Simon was a soppy, embarrassing romantic, and no amount of teasing would ever dampen the extent to which he could express his affections.

"Brace for impact," Phoenix said, stopping well before the stream.

Simon stopped beside him, not looking away from Jess as he grinned and flung his bag onto the grass. "*Jessi-bear*!"

Jess looked up then bared her teeth in a hungry smile, her birthmark crinkling at the side of her face. With powerful strides she started running, white water churning at her feet as she charged through the stream towards them, the leather jacket she wore billowing behind her like a sail as she gathered speed. A young man strolling along The Strip with his child scooped the boy into his arms then bolted in the opposite direction, shooting past Simon and Phoenix towards the safety of Inner-Karvil, terror in his eyes.

Phoenix couldn't blame him. Standing before a charging giant was a little like witnessing the eruption of a volcano.

When they first met Jess, she had been sixteen years old. Cheeky, assertive, and as tall as a horse. Now she was twenty-four, passionate, wickedly clever, and taller than Simon by half of his already impressive height. Still smaller than any giant Phoenix knew, but not so small that the earth didn't shake as she threw herself at the warlock and rammed him onto his back against the grass.

"Hello, Kitten," she growled, pinning Simon to the ground with her knees.

Simon beamed at her. "Hi."

Jess leant down and kissed him with the kind of fierce intensity that seemed ill-mannered to intrude upon.

"I'll give you a moment, shall I?" Phoenix's question was wholly ignored, so he wandered down to the stream and busied himself skipping pebbles for a while before deciding that he'd given the pair enough time to catch up. He returned to find them lying side by side with their faces an inch apart, their noses almost touching.

"Really," Phoenix said, standing over them with his arms crossed. "It's like you haven't seen each other for decades. It's barely been a week since we last said goodbye."

"Felt like forever," Simon said, neither he nor Jess bothering to look at Phoenix at all, too absorbed in each other's gaze.

"Much too long," Jess agreed. Then they were kissing again.

"Simon was snuggling with a troll last night," Phoenix said, sitting down on Jess's other side. "Honestly, Jesinta, you'd be better off with someone respectable. Someone dependable. Stable. Like me. We can get married and retire to the mountains with a couple or so dozen kids and a puppy. Or a dragon. I've always wanted a dragon. We'll call her... Steampuff."

"Shut up, Phoenix." Jess threw a strong arm around his shoulders then wrenched him down into an awkward hug that cracked the whole upper half of his spine.

"Is that a yes?" Phoenix asked, his face smooshed against Jess's collarbone. "Are we engaged now?"

Jess gave a low chuckle then rolled into a sitting position, dragging Phoenix over to sit in front of her so she could get a good look at him.

"I can't marry you." Jess had a deep voice that Simon had once mushily described as a thunderstorm rolling over a mountain range. "My parents still find you unbearable."

Phoenix frowned. "I thought they forgave me for starting that avalanche?"

"They did," Jess said. "It's not the destruction you leave behind that bothers them. It's your personality."

"Ouch."

"Too erratic," Jess said. "You're the personification of everything giant culture tries to avoid."

"Shame," Phoenix said, before adding slyly. "What are their thoughts on Simon Wolfe?"

"They adore me," Simon said, still lying on the grass and staring at Jess with a dopey grin on his face. "But we have no interest in getting married."

That was news to Phoenix. "None at all?"

Jess laughed. "Do you know how long giant weddings go for?"

"Hours?" Phoenix guessed.

"Twelve days," Jess said. "Mostly it involves standing around in silence, though every so often someone will point at a rock or a tree or a mountain and say something like *observe*, and it's all very solemn and *unbelievably* dull."

Phoenix pulled a face. "Never mind then."

Jess smiled then brushed her thumb against his cheek. "How are you, little one?"

"Oh, fine," Phoenix said. "Keeping out of trouble."

"Liar." Jess pointed at the cut across Phoenix's neck where Simon had swiped him with the Shadow-spear. "What happened?"

"Your boyfriend tried to stab me," Phoenix said with a smile.

Jess gave Simon an inquiring look. "Again?"

"He had it coming," Simon muttered. Then he pushed himself to his feet and started shaking all the dirt and grass out of his clothes.

Jess turned her attention to Phoenix again. "Was that you who blew up the city wall?"

"Oh, only a very small slice of it," Phoenix assured her. "I know," he added, as he stretched his legs and leant back, propping himself up like a deckchair with his hands in the grass. "Don't bother. Simon's griped at me already. How *are* your parents, by the way?"

Jess nodded slowly, her dark eyes suddenly mischievous. "They're well."

"That top-secret giant business you had to discuss is all sorted then?"

Jess glanced at Simon, who was picking grass out of his hair, then nodded again. "The elders have blessed me."

"Still won't tell us what it was about?" Phoenix guessed.

"Not yet." Jess held her hand out for Simon to take and he threw all his weight back to help pull her to her feet.

"We should move somewhere less exposed," he said, still holding Jess's hand as he looked across the grass.

"Great idea." Phoenix jumped to his feet. "Follow me." He set off without looking back. Simon and Jess shared a well-practised look of weary resignation before catching up with him by the stream.

"We need to address something," Jess said as they approached a small wooden footbridge, the shallow stream gurgling along beneath it. She poked the scruffy hair under Simon's chin. "What's this?"

"Seriously?" Phoenix raised an eyebrow at her. "You were eating each other's faces a moment ago and you're only just noticing that abomination now?"

Simon stopped and squared his shoulders. "Do you like it?" he asked.

Jess smiled. "I could get used to it."

"*Jess...*" Phoenix groaned and stepped onto the bridge. "Now he'll never get rid of the damn thing."

Simon gave a haughty smile. "Victory for the beard."

"Where are you taking us, anyway?" Jess asked.

"Inven—" Phoenix fumbled behind him to grab the low railing of the bridge, but he'd been resisting the pull of Earth since blowing up the wall and his body kicked him out of Yonder with such abruptness that he tipped backwards and toppled into the stream.

He did, at least, catch a glimpse of Simon and Jess rushing towards him as he fell, so there was some comfort in knowing he wouldn't have to drown for too long.

~

Phoenix woke in the bed Alice had left him in, a breeze playing with the old, lace curtains as it wafted through the window into the sunlit room.

"And *that*," Bee said, from where she sat by his feet at the end of the mattress, "is how Arthur Dent almost had his brain removed by a couple of hyper-intelligent mice." She closed the book she was holding with a snap then looked up in surprise.

"You're awake."

"And hopefully not trapped underwater." Phoenix frowned at her uncertainly. "Were you reading me a story?"

Bee shrugged. "Have to pass the time around here somehow. To be honest, I skipped a few bits. I've read it before, and since you were asleep… I didn't think you'd mind."

Phoenix sat and leant against the bedhead behind him. "You're a little strange, Belinda."

Bee smiled. "Says you."

"You know I can't experience anything here while I'm in the other world, right?" Even as he said it, a phantom pain rippled down Phoenix's back, which meant one of two things: either the stream had swept him away with unexpected strength and he'd slammed against a rock at the bottom of a previously overlooked waterfall, or Jess had come to his aid and was currently smacking the water out of his lungs.

"That may be true," Bee said, tucking the book down the side of the bed. "But Alice says part of you is always left behind."

Phoenix wasn't comfortable with the implications such an existence might hold, so he looked around in search of some other topic to focus on. "What's with the spoon?"

"Sorry?"

"This." Phoenix grabbed the silver spoon by the clock on the bedside table.

"It's the one you took," Bee said. "When I asked which weapon you'd like to use."

"Yeah." Phoenix tapped the spoon against his knee a few times then pointed it at her. "But why is it *here*?"

"I brought it as a memento."

Phoenix furrowed his brows. "Of what?"

Bee shrugged again. "The beginning."

Phoenix wasn't sure what to make of that so Bee continued.

"That day was the start of a new life," she said. "I thought maybe you'd like something to remember where it began."

Fake, uproarious laughter exploded from downstairs before Phoenix could comment, followed by a woman sneering, "I thought you hardheads *liked* a challenge! Get out there and get organised."

"Stephanie," Bee said, in answer to Phoenix's questioning look. "You met her. Head of PR. She's having a meeting with a few people from VIRP."

"The police force?"

Bee nodded. "Steph wants to organise a massive PR stunt before the festival," she said. "A huge-scale food and pamphlet drop to undermine Flamegate and promote Lady Maxine. But we'll have to source a bunch of expensive materials.... infiltrate both the Middle and Upper Rings... somehow position enough drones before anyone gets noticed... It's a huge risk."

"Huge risks," Phoenix said, "are a given when you're up against Flamegate."

"Yeah..." Bee settled into thoughtful silence.

Phoenix gazed at the spoon he was still holding. "You didn't strike me as sentimental," he said, turning the spoon over in his hands. "I assumed you were more... coolly calculating."

Bee took one of the pillows then placed it behind her back against the wall. "What gave you that impression?"

"Last I saw you," Phoenix said, "you were carrying a dead chicken. Which I'm pretty certain you killed."

"Humanely." Bee fixed him with another one of her long stares that parents teach children are impolite.

"Food is scarce," she added at last. "We grow what we can. Bargain for supplies. Every week is a challenge, and old Betsy never laid eggs."

"Betsy?" Phoenix said, drumming the spoon against the side of the bed. "She had a *name*?"

Bee sighed. "We can't afford to be soft," she said, stealing the spoon-turned-drumstick from Phoenix's hand. "That's why I respect Alice so much. You can see it in her eyes. She does what she thinks is right, no matter how difficult the decision.

Everyone in the Alliance is prepared to make sacrifices. Lady Maxine. Ghost. Casual rebels like me. Even Edgar, in his own detached, grumpy way." She paused then handed Phoenix the spoon with the unspoken request that he not thwack it against the timber again.

"Flamegate will fall," she said. "I don't care what it takes."

Phoenix frowned, unable to pinpoint exactly what made him so uneasy. "You're pretty serious about this whole revolution business."

Bee reached into the pocket of her denim jacket and pulled out a sleek glass screen no larger than her hand. She tapped at the clear surface until a photo appeared, then wordlessly passed it over.

Phoenix gazed at the two women laughing before the camera. One was dark-skinned with freckles, in skinny-jeans and a denim jacket thrown over the top of a colourful shirt. The other was fair with large-framed glasses and curly, strawberry-blonde hair, dressed in a floral sundress that fell to her knees.

The pair were standing by a bench-seat with autumn leaves strewn about their feet, the surrounding trees burning with warm colours in the late afternoon sun. And between them, swinging from their hands with a gap-toothed grin on her face and her tiny feet in the air, was a brown-haired little girl.

Phoenix swallowed then looked up at Bee. "Is this...?"

Bee nodded. "My parents."

Phoenix smiled sadly at the three laughing faces. "You look happy."

"We were." Bee watched closely as though expecting him to say more, but Phoenix had nothing to say. He just wallowed in the heaviness of it all until Bee spoke again.

"Flamegate didn't take control over night," she said, taking the glass screen from Phoenix and gazing calmly at the family she had lost. "It was slow... Sneaky. People made compromises that seemed trivial at the time, but it snowballed." She swiped the photo out of sight then slipped the screen into her pocket again. "Forsaking privacy in return for convenience. Freedom in return for security. Giving up education in the interest of personal safety." Bee slid off the bed then stretched her arms behind her back. Phoenix wondered how long she'd been sitting there reading stories that he hadn't been able to hear.

"My parents saw the signs earlier than most," Bee said, bending over and pressing her palms against the rainbow rug on the floor. "Warned as many people as they could. But by the time anyone listened, it was too late." She straightened up with a frown. "Some people are so damn determined to convince themselves that there's nothing they can do."

"People like Jayden?" Phoenix said.

Bee smiled without humour. "People like Jay want to forget. Why bother fighting for change when it can all come tumbling down around you anyway?" She paused and fixed Phoenix with a strange look. "Was that your stomach?"

Phoenix gave a sheepish grin. "Honestly, the only reason I haven't eaten you yet is because you were talking about the tragic death of your parents and it seemed somehow disrespectful."

Bee's laugh was soft but genuine. "Come on. Let's see if we can find you something downstairs."

"Are you angry with Jayden?" Phoenix asked, as he hopped out of bed, still in pyjamas.

Bee took a moment to answer as they walked into the hallway. "I try not to be," she said, closing the bedroom behind them. "When Flamegate was finished with Jay's parents, they were unrecognisable. And it terrified him. We all respond in different ways."

Before Phoenix could ask more, the void shifted its balance and a piercing scream cut through the calm from downstairs, accompanied by the cacophonous sound of dropped cutlery and plates smashing against tiles.

Phoenix dashed down the stairs three at a time with Bee at his heels. By the time he reached the last step, he'd already summoned a void-stone and tossed it into the air.

A spindly Shadow stood dazedly in the centre of the kitchen, its lanky grey arms hanging limply by its sides as it swayed on its feet, blinking about at the new environment it found itself in. Stephanie was trapped, sprawled on the floor beside a pile of shattered crockery, her back against the fridge as she stared open-mouthed at the creature blocking her path. There was no sign of any of the VIRP members Bee had mentioned, but Ghost stood in the living-area with a knife in his hand, his sharp blue eyes darting back and forth between the Shadow and Phoenix's buzzing void-stone as though he couldn't make up his mind about which mysterious entity he should trust less.

"Friend or foe?" Ghost growled, pointing at the Shadow.

Phoenix raised his hands. "Wait." He edged past Ghost then stood by the kitchen counter at what he hoped was a non-threatening enough distance. The Shadow stared back with the kind of intense concentration intoxicated people display when trying to look sober.

"What are you doing here?" Phoenix asked, more to himself than to the Shadow.

The Shadow's golden eyes drifted slowly to the stone hovering above Phoenix's head then wandered away to gaze at Stephanie cowering in the corner behind its back. The Shadow took a shaky step towards her and she yelped, her hand flying to her mouth to muffle her fear. The Shadow paused then took a deep breath, the air rattling in its lungs.

"You're dying," Phoenix realised, finally noticing the energy leaking from the Shadow's core. The Shadow turned its head to face him again, still swaying on its feet.

"What is it?" Bee asked, appearing at Phoenix's side, her hand on the dagger at her belt.

"Will it eat me?" Stephanie added.

"Should we kill it?" Ghost squeezed Phoenix's shoulder

with a grip that left an instant bruise.

"Shh." Phoenix narrowed his eyes and watched as the Shadow drew another long, rasping breath. Then it pressed a bony hand against its heaving chest and opened its mouth.

"Help us."

Its voice was like gravel sliding down a drainpipe.

Phoenix blinked. Never in the history of ever had a Shadow been known to speak. They had long been regarded as pack animals, cunning and dangerous, but by no means capable of spoken word.

Then the void cracked open and two new Shadows materialised in the middle of the kitchen, unbalanced and confused with panic in their eyes as they flicked their heads wildly from side to side, looking, it seemed, for something to take their frustrations out on.

One of them whipped its skeletal body around to stare at Stephanie while the other crouched with one knobbly knee on the floor, eyes locked on Phoenix, ready to pounce. Phoenix launched a second void-stone into the air. The first Shadow gave a tremulous howl.

Then everyone moved at once.

The Shadow targeting Phoenix leapt forward and Phoenix threw out his hand, blasting the creature against the sink. In a flurry of movement, Ghost charged into the kitchen and flung himself upon the other Shadow which was, at that point, springing towards Stephanie with its claws extended and mouth gaping wide. They tumbled to the floor in a tangle of arms and legs as Bee darted into the fray and pulled Stephanie to her feet, ushering her into the living-area while the Shadow by the sink rounded furiously upon Phoenix again.

"What the hell is so special about this kitchen?" Phoenix demanded, smashing the Shadow through a pantry door. "First Simon. Now Shadows. What's next? A whole house?"

Ghost roared in pain and Phoenix spun to see the white-haired man pinned to the floor with the Shadow leaning over him, one clawed hand around Ghost's throat while the other gripped his skull, the taloned thumb burying deep into Ghost's right eye.

"Oh no you don't." Phoenix raised his palm to launch a torrent of energy at the creature, but the other Shadow extricated itself from the pantry and tackled Phoenix to the ground. Phoenix crashed into the tiles then twisted around to blast a hole through the Shadow's chest. The monster collapsed on top of him with a final angry yowl and it was several panicked seconds before Phoenix managed to pull himself out from beneath the lifeless Shadow's weight.

He staggered to his feet and found Ghost slumped in the corner, his bloodied hands cupped over his face. The Shadow that had been attacking him lay curled on the floor with Bee standing over it, her dagger in one hand and a meat cleaver in the other. Phoenix frowned at the meat cleaver for a second then realised that the Shadow on the floor was clutching its stump of a wrist.

"No idea what these things are," Bee said, "but I don't like them."

The creature at her feet scrambled up and tried to pounce upon her, but Bee swung the cleaver in a wide circle and relieved the creature of its head. Stephanie gasped as it bounced out into the living-area before rolling to a stop under the table.

Phoenix stared at Bee and she shrugged.

"Same blade I used for Betsy."

Phoenix shook his head. "May the Light keep them warm." He took a moment to assess the situation. Broken plates littered the blood-smeared tiles along with scattered food and damaged containers from the pantry. The first Shadow stood in the opposite corner of the kitchen, staring at the aftermath with wide, now-dark eyes. Phoenix moved carefully towards it, the two void-stones still hovering above his head.

"What did you mean?" He glared up into the Shadow's hollow face as it took another wheezing breath. "Help you?

With what?"

The Shadow teetered forward then crumpled to the floor, the last of its feeble energy vanishing as it died.

Phoenix gazed at it in silence for a few seconds then returned to crouch by Ghost's side with Stephanie and Bee.

"The creature that did this to you," Phoenix said as he joined them, "it was looking for a vessel to contain its fading energy. It wanted to possess you. Slip inside your body and take control. If it had succeeded, you would most definitely now be very dead." He patted Ghost's arm. "Lucky man."

"Lucky?" Ghost hissed. "I am holding my own *eyeball.*"

"Infirmary," Bee said. "Get Horst."

Phoenix climbed to his feet again. "There's someone called Horse?"

"*Horst,*" Bee hissed, with emphasis on the T. "The nurse."

"The one with the..." Phoenix tugged at an imaginary handlebar-moustache on his own face.

"Yes. Hurry."

Phoenix recalled the stones and they glided smoothly into his palm, leaving him sore and dangerously lightheaded. His eyes flicked to a broken jar of biscuits on the floor.

"Phoenix!" Bee barked. "Go."

Phoenix grabbed one of the cookies then hurried away.

QUESTIONS

Phoenix felt a strange sense of déjà vu as he entered the suffocating, windowless basement to find Bailey, the fluffy-haired, acne-scarred rebel, being seen by the moustached nurse at the far end of the room.

"In need of a medical professional," Phoenix called from the bottom of the stairs, reluctant to step much further into the unsettling space. "Monster strike to the eyeball. Lots of blood. Very serious."

"*Monster* strike?" the nurse snapped. Then he squinted through the harsh fluorescent light. "You're covered in blood."

Phoenix looked down at himself. "There was a bit of an

incident," he said. "You didn't hear all the commotion going on?"

"Heard a few screams and thumps," Horst said, hastily tying a sling around Bailey's neck. "Nothing out of the ordinary for this place."

"Didn't think to check?" Phoenix asked as the nurse jumped to his feet.

"I can't be everywhere at once, boy," Horst said, grabbing a briefcase from a table on the way to the stairs. Bailey sprang from her bed and followed him.

Phoenix cocked an eyebrow at her as Horst dashed ahead, noticing one of her arms was bandaged at the wrist while the other was protected in a cast.

"Did you get injured *again*?" he asked as they hurried upstairs.

Bailey winked at him. "Broke the other arm dodging guards by the Lower Wall. Very exciting. They have laser-cannons now."

"And what fresh hell is this?" Horst asked as he stepped into the devastated kitchen with Phoenix and Bailey close behind.

"I was making a sandwich," Stephanie said faintly. "They appeared out of nowhere."

"*They* being the gangly, burnt corpses surrounding us?" Horst said, scowling as he knelt by Ghost's side.

Phoenix frowned at the Shadows, with their charcoal-grey skin, sunken faces and long, wasted limbs. Horst was right. They did look alarmingly similar to people who had burnt to death in horrendous fires.

"They're called Shadows," he said. "Originally from the void itself, but now they exist in my world too. They're usually really strong... These ones were weak."

"Weak?" Stephanie squeaked. "They didn't *seem* weak!"

Phoenix nodded. "All three of them were dying."

"No one else injured?" Horst asked as he opened his briefcase beside him.

Phoenix, Bee and Stephanie shook their heads.

"Good." Horst took Ghost's hand and eased it away from the damaged eye. Phoenix turned away, choosing to tidy the kitchen rather than feed his brain any more grotesque images that he'd have to avoid thinking about in the future.

"This will take hours," Horst grumbled as he bundled some soft, white material around Ghost's eye. "Between Bailey getting in trouble and *you* getting skewered by monsters and Vince getting himself mauled by mutant cats and Edgar being *Edgar*... How am I to find time for myself?"

Bailey looked up from the overturned bowl of nuts she was collecting, eyes wide in concern. "Did something happen to Edgar?"

"Karma, perhaps?" Phoenix mumbled, thinking about being left alone on the cold kitchen floor as Edgar retreated into his room, ignoring every easily accessible blanket within his reach.

The nurse frowned at Phoenix as though trying to read a road sign from far away.

"Sorry," he said at last. "Can't tell you kids."

"Can't tell us what?" Bee asked.

"The details," Horst said, carefully wrapping a bandage around Ghost's head. "I'm sworn to secrecy. Say what you like about the miserable old grouch, but he sure knows how to persuade people to keep their mouths shut."

"Is he okay?" Bailey asked.

"Claims to be," Horst replied as he latched his briefcase shut. He turned to Bee. "Do us a favour, Belinda. He tolerates you. Check on him for me, would you?"

"He dislikes me as much as anyone else," Bee said. "But sure, I'll check."

Horst nodded then pointed at Phoenix and Bee. "You two clean yourselves up. Bailey, get hold of Little Mick and ask him to deal with this mess. Stephanie, help me get this one downstairs."

So Stephanie helped move Ghost into the infirmary,

Bailey was left to arrange clean-up, and Phoenix and Bee wandered upstairs to find fresh clothes.

Once they'd rinsed and changed into outfits less bloodied (Phoenix into another set of pyjamas that Jayden had left aside and Bee in a black, baggy t-shirt and tights), they returned downstairs to check on Edgar. By then, the Shadows had been dragged out of sight and the kitchen was instead occupied by Bailey, Jayden, and a muscular yet perfectly average-sized man in grey overalls who Phoenix presumed was Little Mick. Jayden gave Phoenix and Bee a small nod of acknowledgment as they stopped by Edgar's door, then went back to sweeping aside shattered plates.

"I guess Jay was following Little Mick around on errands again," Bee said, watching Jayden work. "He does that when he's in a bad mood."

"That Mick guy's a carpenter?" Phoenix guessed, since the sturdy young man with the greased-back, dark brown hair was busy screwing a new door onto the pantry.

Bee shook her head. "Odd jobs. Cleaning. Home maintenance. Theft. Legend goes he knows every single person in the Lower Ring." A mischievous smile played across her face. "Some say he even knows people who aren't strictly people."

"Aren't strictly people?"

"Ogres and fairies and creatures of make-believe," Bee said. "At first I was sceptical, but these days I'm inclined to believe him." She knocked softly on Edgar's bedroom door. "Edgar? Can we come in?"

No one replied, so after trying a few more times Bee slowly turned the handle, the door creaking open as they stepped into the gloom.

Edgar lay in a bed at the back of the room, the light from the doorway spilling over his narrow face as the rumpled blankets moved gently in time with his breath. For the first time, Phoenix noticed the old man's crooked nose was set a little to the left, as though it had been broken years ago and never properly healed.

Bee tapped Edgar's shoulder, but he was either very asleep or very good at acting.

"He looks less mean when he's sleeping," Phoenix observed.

Bee smiled. "I don't think he's as mean as he pretends to be."

"Hmm," Phoenix said, recalling the discomfort of lying paralysed on the cold kitchen tiles, along with every disparaging remark Simon had ever made about his unconventional, mysteriously-vanishing teacher.

Bee clicked her tongue at the jumble of clothes and open books scattered about the dreary room then stooped to gather up the mess, mumbling about trip-hazards.

"He's a warlock," Phoenix said, helping collect books from the floor.

"What?" Bee looked up in surprise.

Phoenix nodded. "From Yonder," he said, keeping his voice low. "I sensed it when I first met him. The power emanating from him... it's similar to my friend Simon."

"The hairy guy with the parrot?" Bee asked, as Phoenix carefully set the pile of books upon Edgar's already cluttered writing desk.

"Yeah," Phoenix said softly. "The hairy guy with the parrot. He's a warlock. And Edgar is too."

"What was your friend doing here?" Bee whispered.

"And why did he have a parrot?" Phoenix said. "Both excellent questions that I don't have any answers to." He folded his arms then sat on the edge of the desk. "But there's something about Edgar... Most magicians have distinctive energy. Edgar's power is definitely Wolfe Clan, but it's slightly off... Like it's tainted by another source. Which *might* explain why he vanished from Yonder and ended up on Earth." Phoenix ran a hand through his messy hair. "Maybe he was caught up in some kind of ill-advised void experimentation. Like what happened with the Shadow Masters."

Bee frowned. "Those magicians who became the Night

Order and started Flamegate?" she asked, laying a knitted sweater atop a pile of clothes in the middle of the room.

Phoenix nodded. "I wonder how old he is. Just because he disappeared from Yonder fifteen years ago doesn't mean much. He might've spent decades here already. Do you think he's suffering from void exposure? It happens sometimes when magicians get carried away with their powers." Phoenix frowned at the sleeping warlock, his eyes drawn to the thin arm draped over the side of the bed. A soft wheeze accompanied Edgar's breathing, and the strange energy in the room flickered like a dying lamp, trembling on the edge of Phoenix's perception but never quite allowing itself to be extinguished completely. Phoenix's thoughts turned to Simon and the amount of energy it must require to move between worlds.

"Magicians are pretty resistant to extreme energy," he said quietly, "but they're still only human. Maybe Edgar overestimated himself a few too many times."

"In my day," Edgar said, his eyes still closed, "it was considered rude to enter someone's room and discuss their magicality while they slept."

Phoenix and Bee exchanged guilty smiles.

"Sorry, Edgar," Bee said. "The nurse asked us to check on you."

Edgar opened his eyes to scowl at them from the pillow. "What did Horst tell you?"

"Only that you're a miserable old grouch who knows how to be persuasive," Phoenix said lightly.

The gruff sound that escaped Edgar's lips was almost a laugh.

"Are you sick?" Bee asked, as Edgar carefully climbed out of bed.

Edgar snatched his silver flask from the bedside table. "I am old," he said, before unscrewing the lid, taking several gulps, then slipping the drink into the pocket of his robes. He stood in the dim light and gazed at them for a while. "Shadows were here," he said, as though he'd just remembered a distant relative's birthday party he was supposed to go to and felt no joy at having to attend.

"They were," Bee said. "Are you really a warlock?"

"What I am," Edgar said, "is uninterested in having this conversation." Then he strolled out of his bedroom with Phoenix and Bee in tow.

"Edgar!" Bailey leapt up from the corner of the kitchen where she was picking broken glass up from the floor. "Will you tell me stories from your revolution days this afternoon?"

"No." Edgar stepped into the kitchen and frowned at the mess. "This is what happens when you let dimension-skipping nonconformists loose in your home. I'm not so sure keeping Alice's favourite little hero here is worth all the trouble."

Phoenix laughed in disbelief. "You're saying this is *my* fault?"

Edgar shrugged. "I'm saying there is a very strong correlation between you and inconceivable trouble."

Jayden crossed the kitchen to stand beside Bee and watch the drama unfold.

Phoenix folded his arms. "For the record," he said, "I did not summon deadly creatures from beyond the void to invade your house."

"Perhaps not intentionally," Edgar said, watching Little Mick secure the final set of hinges onto the pantry door.

"Told you all there were monsters around." The handyman had a voice as slick as his greased-back hair. "Mark my words, friends, their numbers are increasing." Then he walked away from the pantry and started scrubbing Shadow-blood out of the sink.

Muffled chatter drifted into the house from the front door and the living-area was soon bustling with a fresh crowd of people, many leaning over the kitchen counter to gawp at the surprising scene. A few lingered out of curiosity, but most shuffled off to gather around tables or occupy the couches to get on with whatever important Alliance business they had scheduled for the day.

Phoenix recognised a few faces. Stephanie's sulky brother Rory plonked himself into a couch and started tapping away at a screen, entirely unconcerned with the post-monster-attack discussion. Vince, the cook now heavily bandaged after his encounter with a mutant cat, stood beside Bee and Jayden with a perplexed expression on his claw-scratched face. And Naia, the civil engineer dressed in a black, button-down shirt and bright yellow bowtie, paused beside Edgar to stare at the debris.

"What happened?" she asked.

"*Monsters*," Bailey said with relish.

Edgar shook his head. "Intelligent beings," he said, "cruelly ripped from their Time." He bent and picked up the Shadow's severed hand that had been swept into the corner with a pile of broken crockery.

"Some events," Edgar said, as he raised the withered hand to his eyes, "are so disruptive to the void that they leave something similar to a scar. Or an open wound. A temporary, temperamental tunnel that allows things to pass from where they should be… to where they should not."

"Void-tunnels," Phoenix said darkly, still miffed at being blamed for Ghost having his eye gouged out. "I've encountered them before."

"I'm not surprised," Edgar said, squinting at the grey hand.

"It's how I met Simon, actually," Phoenix added, sliding down a cupboard door to sit on the tiles near the back of the kitchen. "Your apprentice followed in your footsteps for a while. Chasing dreams of mapping the void. Controlling the tunnels."

"A truly astronomical waste of energy and time," Edgar murmured.

"I've always been drawn to large concentrations of energy," Phoenix continued. "With Simon skulking about Yonder looking for void-tunnels, we were bound to cross paths eventually."

"Very unfortunate for him," Edgar said, and before Phoenix could ask what *that* was supposed to mean, Edgar ran his fingers over the severed hand and it vanished from sight, the air flickering with energy that Phoenix doubted anyone else was able to sense.

Bailey gasped. "The rumours were true. You *are* magic!"

"He's a warlock," Phoenix said.

"A *warlock*?" Naia repeated, looking from Edgar to Phoenix then back again.

"An incredibly experienced one, too," Phoenix said. "From a very powerful clan."

Edgar closed his eyes and raised his face to the ceiling as though seeking help from some higher power.

"So *you're* the powerful warlock Alice says will help us fight Flamegate?" Naia asked with a frown.

"No," Edgar said flatly. "Dear Alice was talking about someone else."

"Simon," Phoenix said. "Obviously she was talking about Simon." He reached into the broken jar of cookies still on the floor and took his time selecting one that looked safe enough to eat.

Edgar watched him with an expression remarkably similar to disgust.

"Why didn't you tell anyone?" Bee asked, staring at the old man in fascination.

Phoenix chuckled. "If his refusal to toss me a blanket is anything to go by," he said, picking shattered glass out of a biscuit, "I'd say he just didn't think telling everyone he was a warlock would be worth the subsequent effort of having to act like one."

"Light almighty, kid," Edgar muttered. "You think I haven't done enough for this organisation?" He gestured at the people scattered around the room. "Who do you think brought all these hapless clowns together?"

Phoenix raised an eyebrow. "Alice?"

"*Me*," Edgard growled, as Phoenix took a bite from the predominately glass-free snack. "Alice merely coordinates this madness. I've been the one on the ground, doing the dirty work. Putting all her little pieces in place. I could be in Yonder. Instead I'm stuck here, part of her ridiculous scheme, putting up with you and your ignorance."

Phoenix swallowed his food. "Fifteen years," he said, "of being locked up and tortured by Flamegate. What, exactly, am I ignorant of?" The coldness in his voice surprised even himself.

Edgar glowered. "More than your infantile mind could imagine." Then he huffed and turned away, muttering something about kids not knowing how damn lucky they were.

Bailey raised her hand that wasn't restrained in a sling. "Edgar, sir? I just want to say that I know exactly how lucky I am, and I think you're amazing. Please do me the honour of signing my cast."

"Bailey..." Edgar paused to pinch the bridge of his nose. "Not now."

Bailey's pock-marked face lit up with a hopeful smile. "Later then?"

"*No*." Edgar stepped over a dustpan in the middle of the room then wrenched open the fridge.

Bailey sidled up to his elbow. "The way you handled those laser drones by luring them into the water park was really, really clever," she said, as Edgar glared into the shelves in search of food. "And sneaking into that Flamegate convention disguised as a member of the Sisterhood in a mask? Gah! *Genius*."

Edgar straightened his back then stared down his crooked nose at her.

Bailey beamed back. "My gran kept files on you."

"Of course she did."

"Sorry," Naia interrupted. "I'm still catching up. Edgar... why were monsters here?"

"Why are any of us here?" Edgar said under his breath,

then he went back to scowling into the fridge.

Phoenix had had enough. He stood up, strode across the kitchen, then stepped between Bailey and the bitter old warlock.

"Monsters,' he said, closing the fridge door. "From another dimension. Just appeared in your home, stabbed a guy in the eye, tried to communicate with us, then died from energy-loss. Well… one died from energy-loss. But the others were headed for the same fate even if Bee and I hadn't finished them off first."

Edgar said nothing.

"The people in this organisation that you claim to have such responsibility over," Phoenix continued, "have never seen a Shadow before. They might, then, be feeling a little uneasy about this latest development. If there's anything you could tell us, in your vast wisdom as a clearly ancient, highly qualified warlock, I'm sure everyone here would appreciate your insight on the matter."

Edgar looked around at the many pairs of eyes fixed upon him then reached into the pocket of his robes. "I already told you," he muttered, withdrawing his silver flask. "They slipped through a tunnel. But the void is weaker here than in Yonder. So Shadows are weaker too."

He took a few gulps then crouched and touched the Shadow-blood smeared on the tiles as gently as though it were a living creature that might bite him. "It's a shame." He looked up at Little Mick, who was leaning against a mop, waiting, it seemed, for everyone to clear out so he could use it.

"Where are the bodies?" Edgar asked.

"Tossed 'em in the front yard, boss," Little Mick said. "Figured I'd bury them this afternoon."

Edgar nodded, his eyes flicking to the kitchen window that overlooked the overgrown front yard. "Whatever happens," he said, using the fridge to steady himself as he stood up, "we can't let them fall into the hands of Flamegate. The sooner we dispose of them, the better."

"Consider it done," Mick said with a curt salute.

"I'll inspect the remains first." Edgar started to walk away but Phoenix hurried after him, blocking his path before he could leave the kitchen.

"They asked for help," he said, his gaze locked on Edgar's grey eyes.

"So?" Edgar said.

"They *spoke*," Phoenix added. "You're not surprised?"

Edgar raised his thinning white brows. "No," he said. "And you, of all people, shouldn't be surprised either."

"Of all people?" Phoenix repeated, not liking where this was going.

"You…" Edgar said slowly, "are more familiar with Shadows than you want to admit."

A bemused silence resonated from everyone watching.

"I don't know what you mean," Phoenix said.

"Please." Edgar raised a bony finger and tapped Phoenix sharply on the forehead. "They were inside your messed up little brain. Because you were stupid enough to let them in. You've felt their fears and emotions and motivations as strongly as though they were your own. As real and as valid as anyone else's."

Phoenix winced. "Did Alice tell you?"

"I don't need to be told," Edgar said with a dark chuckle. "Experiences like that leave a mark."

Phoenix swallowed, his fingernails scratching into his arm. "What kind of mark?"

Edgar reached out and placed his hand on Phoenix's shoulder. "A permanent one." Then he calmly pushed Phoenix to the side and walked out into the living-area.

"Shadows in my kitchen," he said as he walked away. "This is it then. The beginning of the end." He turned the corner and they heard the front door swing closed as the warlock left the house.

A murmur passed through the crowd he left behind, swiftly escalating into earnest chatter and anxious discussion.

Phoenix stood quietly in the centre of the kitchen, voices washing over him like white noise as he squeezed his hand around the scratch-marks on his arm. Despite the mass of people, he suddenly felt incredibly alone.

The Light Festival was less than a month away.

Phoenix gulped, forcing himself to focus as Jayden passed him a broom and told him to make himself useful.

He helped tidy the kitchen, accepting the onslaught of enquiries as he worked, steering the conversation away from Shadows and void-stones in favour of Yonder itself.

"Are you from a technologically advanced civilisation?" Naia asked, and Phoenix smiled.

"Perhaps not *advanced*," he replied. "But definitely different." He explained about energy-disks and Karvil being the centre of Yonderian society, leaving aside the recently demolished energy factory in Bloodwood and the fact that Karvil was on the brink of war against a race of vengeful creatures from the void. Vince was interested in food, so Phoenix told everyone about fizzy stew and flameberries and spicy cakes. Jayden and Little Mick argued over whether a talking horse could even be classified as a horse when it clearly displayed traits that set it apart from all its equine companions.

"Who cares about horses," Bailey said, watching Phoenix from beside the pile of dishes she was ignoring. "Tell us more about monsters."

"And music," Bee said, rearranging cans in the pantry. "Alice says you're a musician."

Phoenix grinned, his worries shrinking to the back of his mind like a fading dream. It wasn't long, however, before the kitchen was returned to its former glory and the impromptu clean-up crew began to drift in separate directions. Jayden took Bee's hand and led her upstairs to speak in private, while Naia, Bailey and Vince went downstairs to check on Ghost.

"Better see what the old man's up to," Little Mick said, nodding at the kitchen window, beyond which Edgar was supposedly inspecting the remains of dead Shadows in the yard. "It'll be dark soon."

"I'll join you," Phoenix offered, but Little Mick smiled and patted him on the back.

"Nope," he said. "Sorry, Space Man. You're not to leave the safehouse. Both Alice and Edgar were adamant, and the whole Alliance agrees."

Phoenix gave a nervous laugh. "From one high-security prison to another."

Little Mick shrugged apologetically. "Housebound until we need you on the front, compadre."

And just like that, Phoenix was on his own. He flittered about the living-area bothering other members of the Alliance with questions and unhelpful remarks for a while before finally taking the hint that he was getting in the way. He eventually wandered off to the little library at the other end of the house and found himself sitting at the piano, staring blankly at the keys.

He wanted to play but the silence grew heavier the longer he sat there, and Edgar's words hung over him like a bad omen.

The beginning of the end.

Phoenix swallowed the lump in his throat then dropped his head so his forehead crashed somewhere over middle C, the clash of notes reverberating through his brain then fading into weighty silence as he closed his eyes, wishing, not for the first time, that the universe would grant him at least a moment of legitimate sleep. A chance to shut everything out.

The universe, however, was not in a giving mood, and Phoenix remained slumped over the piano until his muscles grew stiff and the sun went down, leaving him alone in the dark.

SHARING THE LOAD

Phoenix had barely hit the water before Simon and Jess splashed into the shallow stream and Jess fished the soggy idiot out by his ankle.

"He timed that well," Jess said with a grin, scooping Phoenix up like a baby then carrying him across to the opposite bank.

Simon shook his head. "I swear he does it on purpose." He followed her onto the grass where she lowered Phoenix onto the ground then rolled him onto his side. Phoenix was breathing just fine, but Jess smacked his back a few times, just in case. Simon had little doubt that Phoenix would wake up with handprints.

"Let's throw him in the wagon," Jess said, plucking a wet leaf out of Phoenix's hair.

"You brought the wagon?"

"Naturally," Jess replied. "I left it downstream a little."

"With all the instruments?" Simon asked, impressed that Jess had been carting all the music gear across terrains not really suited for anything with wheels.

Jess nodded.

"Red'll be pleased," Simon said, crouching to lift Phoenix up from the grass. "He wants to throw a party."

"A party?" Jess repeated, as Simon tossed Phoenix over his shoulder like a wet blanket. "*Now*?"

Simon was about to reply but the handkerchief Phoenix had used by Uprising Fountain slipped from its pocket and fluttered down to rest on Simon's boot. Jess reached down to retrieve the crumpled square of damp cloth then held it between her fingers, frowning at the dark splodge of blood staining the fabric.

"I don't suppose he's cut back, has he?" Jess asked.

Simon took the handkerchief then folded it into neat triangles before placing it back inside Phoenix's coat. "If anything, he's gotten worse. He used four at once yesterday."

Jess's frown deepened. "I didn't even know he *had* four."

"He has thirteen." Simon shrugged Phoenix into a more comfortable position then set off downstream along The Strip.

"We were right to be concerned," Jess said, falling into step beside him.

Simon glanced across at her. "Did you…?"

She smiled back. "You needn't worry, Kitten. I found it."

Simon let out a relieved sigh and Jess chuckled.

"It was exactly where we thought it would be," she said, "though harder to get than expected. Had to wrestle a whole gang of ogres, but I won in the end."

A smile twitched at the corner of Simon's mouth. "You're incredible. You know that?"

Jess nodded. "I do."

"When should we give it to him?"

Jess tapped her fingers over the birthmark on her face, an unconscious habit when giving things careful consideration.

"By the sound of things..." she said, "he needs it sooner rather than later."

They fell into thoughtful silence as they followed a narrow, well-worn track that ran alongside the stream, Karvil Wall to their left and the bustling city minding its own business to their right.

"He escaped prison," Simon said eventually.

Jess stopped. "Why wasn't that the first thing anyone told me?"

"I don't think he wants to make a big deal of it," Simon said, treading carefully over some wide stepping stones that joined the path from one side of the stream to the other. "There are things going on in that world that I don't understand, but I know it's connected to the void trouble here. And Red is caught in the middle of it." He reached the opposite bank then turned to see Jess leap easily over the water to land beside him.

"Apparently he's part-Shade," Simon added.

Jess raised her eyebrows.

"Well," she said, "that explains a lot."

"Oh no you don't," Phoenix growled, his voice muffled by Simon's jacket. Simon and Jess paused, but Phoenix remained asleep so they set off down the path again.

"That's not all," Simon said. "He thinks he can close off the entire void."

"And *can* he?"

"Maybe," Simon muttered. "But it's a massive, idiotic, stupidly dangerous gamble." He realised Jess was smiling at him in the same way people smile at baby animals learning to walk.

"What?" he asked, defensive.

"We can't protect him forever," Jess said, as a family of

trolls approached from the other direction, trudging down the path in single file with rocks balancing on their heads. "He can make decisions for himself."

"Not *this* decision," Simon argued.

"He's an adult."

Simon scoffed. "No he's bloody not." They stepped aside to allow the parade of trolls to walk past. The rocks they were carrying were suspiciously similar to those used for Karvil Wall, and Simon was willing to bet that a certain pile of rubble in Chiefly Gardens was proving very popular with all the visiting troglodytes.

"If he thinks closing the void is a good idea," Jess said as they started walking again, "maybe we should trust him. Void-stones aside, he's not as irresponsible as he used to be."

Simon barked a laugh. "Just today he left me alone while he infiltrated a Shadow-occupied town with only a horse and a cat by his side, then drained all his energy into a can."

"Presumably for good reasons," Jess said as she veered off the path toward a dense clump of trees and leafy shrubs. "The wagon's this way."

Simon followed, still grumbling about the sodden kid draped over his shoulder. "He didn't even tell anyone where he was going."

"Phoenix has always thrown himself into danger," Jess said, disappearing into the dense shrubbery while Simon waited in the open with Phoenix. "At least lately he seems to be doing it with some sense of purpose."

"Exactly," Simon said, frowning at the ground. "The question's *why*, Jess... What changed?"

Jess hesitated, the sound of her boots crunching through the undergrowth slowing to a halt before she turned and pushed her way back through the plants to face Simon again.

She took his arm in her hand, giving it a loving squeeze that nearly stopped the blood-flow to his fingers. He looked her in the eyes and tried not to wince.

"He died last year," Jess said gently. "Of course that's

going to affect the way he views everything."

"He shrugged that off," Simon mumbled. "But maybe it was more serious than we thought."

"More serious than being dead for a whole three minutes?"

"Maybe it wasn't a freak miscalculation by those Flamegate people like Phoenix claimed," Simon said, frowning at Karvil's famous wall. It cast a broad shadow across The Strip, the afternoon breeze growing cooler as it rustled through the grass and over the stream.

"Maybe it was the start of something," Simon continued, his voice as heavy as the problems weighing upon his shoulders, specifically the shoulder that Phoenix was hanging over. "Something he won't talk about. Something..." He met Jess's gaze again, searching for the right word. "Something *final.*"

Jess offered a sympathetic smile. "Maybe that protective nature of yours is running away with your imagination." She gave the side of his face a light pat then returned to rummage through the shrubs and trees.

"He's acting like he has a time limit," Simon said.

"He does have a time limit," Jess said from within the mass of branches and leaves. "We *all* do if this madness with the void isn't resolved. Phoenix knows that better than any of us."

"You're not afraid we'll lose him?"

"Of course I am," Jess replied, her deep voice retreating even further into the shrubbery. "But I want the future to be secure and full of hope." Branches shifted and snapped as Jess reached the wagon's hiding place then started tugging it out from where she'd wedged it safely between the trees. "Phoenix can be reckless, sure," she continued, raising her voice over the creaking and squeaking of wheels trundling through vegetation, "but he's not stupid. If he thinks he can create a better world for the next generation, we should support him."

"Lots of blood," Phoenix murmured. "Very serious."

Simon frowned at Phoenix in concern then stared off into the distance, gazing at the glimmering city as he scratched his beard.

The words were out of his mouth before he appreciated their impact.

"I'm thinking about going to Earth."

Jess backed out of the thicket, dragging the familiar old wagon they had travelled all across Yonder with. It was a shoddily made timber box on two big wheels, with a green canvas tarp tied over the top and the words *Jess and the Giants* carved across all four sides in bold, childlike font. Usually pulled by Tugger, the wagon was large enough for someone of slight stature to curl up amongst all the instruments and camping gear, but impossibly small for either Simon or Jess to squeeze comfortably inside. And although Gulliver refused to ever lower himself to the position of carthorse, Simon and Jess were more than capable of lugging the ancient, clunky thing behind them whenever horses weren't an option.

"You want to go to Earth?" Jess set the wagon down in the grass. "Is that even possible?"

"Theoretically, yeah..." Simon replied, still standing a few paces away with Phoenix. "If I can get a warlock by the name of Maulbrak to help me. Which I think I probably can."

"Even if it *were* possible," Jess added, "is it necessary?"

Simon hesitated, uncomfortably aware of the worry creasing Jess's brow.

"For whatever reason," he said, "the worlds share a link through the void. So whatever Red is up to over there is connected to us, too. The idiot thinks he can just throw himself into the heart of the void. He needs all the help he can get."

"Kitten," Jess said, stepping away from the wagon to stand before him again, "has it occurred to you that Phoenix wants to keep *us* safe, and that's why he takes risks and keeps secrets?"

Simon grimaced. "I can't sit quietly and watch him throw his life on the line for us. You know I can't."

Jess clasped Simon's hands. "I know. But to follow him to Earth..."

Phoenix laughed in his sleep. "You're saying this is *my* fault?" he asked, his words slurred.

Jess pushed Phoenix's hair out of his eyes to check whether he was awake.

"You're sure about this?" she asked softly, as Phoenix slept on.

"Jess." Simon gave her a beseeching stare. "He's family. The closest thing I have left to a brother."

Jess chewed her lip for a moment. "Well... if that's the case... you'll have to tell Phoenix he's going to be an uncle."

Simon's brows furrowed in puzzlement. "Going to be a —" Then his eyes bulged wide and he stared at Jess with his mouth hanging open. "Jess. Are you—? Are we—?"

Jess nodded and placed her hands over her stomach. "We are."

"Holy Light." Simon dropped Phoenix in a heap then flung his arms around Jess and pulled her into a hug that would've crushed bones had she not been a giant. "I have no words." He kissed her on the shoulder because it was the easiest part of her to reach. "Much sooner than either of us were expecting..." he added uneasily. "But no matter. This is amazing. You're amazing."

Jess gave a soft chuckle then pulled him against her, pressing her lips against the top of his head. After allowing Simon a moment to process the news in overwhelmed silence, Jess stepped back then nodded at Phoenix's crumpled figure on the ground.

"You'll have to treat the baby with more delicacy," she warned with a smile. "Not even giants are as robust as Phoenix is when they're first born."

Simon nodded, his head still reeling. "I'll be careful. More than careful." He paused as the full magnitude of the announcement started to sink in. "But times are tough... Our lives aren't exactly stable. Our best friend is an emotionally volatile, unpredictable mess of deadly void-energy. We have no routine. No fixed address. No reliable source of income. Shadow numbers are increasing. Just last week the entire village of Lillibrook disappeared into thin air." Simon raked his fingers through his hair then sat down in the grass.

"And I don't know anything about raising a family," he continued. "My own parents hated each other. I learned everything I know from Edgar, and he was a terrible role model. He once pushed me into the ocean from the top of a cliff when I was eight because he thought it would be a good learning opportunity." Simon stared up at Jess in growing concern. "For *him*," he added. "A good learning opportunity for *him*. He wanted to know how an eight-year-old warlock would respond to a life-threatening situation while access to their powers was restricted. And that was just an average day with the old crank." Simon wrung his hands together. "Then he disappeared without so much as a pat on the head or an apologetic note to say goodbye. *That's* the guy who raised me. That was my father-figure. I'm supposed to be a father? Jess, are we going to be okay?"

Jess was giving one of her lopsided grins, trying not to laugh.

"We're going to be fine," she said, taking his shoulders and leaning down so they were eye-to-eye. "Trust me, Kitten. You're more than qualified to be someone's guardian. And between you, Phoenix and myself all looking out for the newest member of our family, she's going to have everything she ever needs."

"She?"

"We're having a girl," Jess said, once she'd pulled Simon to his feet.

Simon blinked. "How do you know?"

"I just feel it," Jess said, strolling back to the wagon.

"We'll have to start thinking of names," Simon said, crouching to pick Phoenix up from the grass again.

"You have very little say in that." Jess smirked as she

pulled back the green tarp.

Simon laid Phoenix beside a collection of percussion instruments and an old, bundled-up tent then turned to look back at Jess. "I can't name my own kid?"

Jess responded with a deep, throaty laugh. "Didn't you name your childhood pet *Mittens*?"

"Yeah..." Simon smiled. "Mittens is a perfectly sound name for a pet."

Jess rolled her eyes. "Not for a parrot."

Simon threw his and Phoenix's bags into the cart then dusted off his hands.

"An unusual name for an unusual creature," he said with a shrug. "He really was an exceptional bird."

He and Jess rolled the tarp back over the wagon so Phoenix and the luggage were hidden from sight, then they took one side of the wagon each and started pulling in the direction of all the glimmering city lights. The sun had sunk well below the wall, evening taking hold of Karvil as the city came alive with music and night-time frivolities.

"I was devastated when that bird died," Simon said later, he and Jess wheeling the wagon down a warmly lit cobblestone street in the direction of the Inventors' Guild, the air bursting with the combined scents of alcohol, freshly cooked vegetables, and seasoned roast meats.

Jess let out a booming laugh that startled two young women walking arm-in-arm in the opposite direction. The pair huddled against each other as they scuttled to the other side of the street, watching Jess warily until they disappeared behind the next corner.

Jess chortled. "You're going to be a dad," she said over the chatter of crowded restaurants, "but you're thinking about your dead bird?"

"Hey," Simon said with a shrug. "You were the one who brought Mittens into this."

Jess flicked the back of his head.

"I was fourteen," Simon continued. "Edgar gave me a

spiny-tailed lizard as a replacement, but it just wasn't the same."

"That was kind of him," Jess said, paying no attention to the stares she was receiving from people trying to enjoy meals at all the busy, disreputable dining establishments they were passing. "Your teacher can't have been *all* bad."

Simon chuckled. "I think he felt responsible for Mittens' death."

"He killed your bird?"

"Not directly."

Before Jess could ask more, two teenagers stumbled out onto the street, attacking each other with wooden swords. They were so caught up in their fight that they charged straight into Jess, bounced off her and landed gracelessly on the pavement with their swords knocked out of their hands.

Simon and Jess set the wagon down and eyed the wide-eyed youths expectantly. The boys were dressed in button-up velvet vests, pointed boots, and wide-brimmed hats despite there being no need for sun protection. Simon recognised them immediately as upper-class, Central Karvil kids who had wandered into West Side in search of a more adventurous night of entertainment.

"A giant?" one said, grabbing his sword and scrambling to his feet, feathers swinging from his gold earrings.

Jess bared her teeth in a wicked smile. "Do I scare you?"

The boy took several steps back. "Nah. Just never seen a giant in Karvil before."

"What are you doing?" Simon asked, eyeing the wooden swords as the other boy leapt up. He was taller than the first, with a head of dark curls.

"Practising."

Simon raised an eyebrow. "For what?"

"The second Shadow War," said the boy with pierced ears. "We have to be ready."

Jess chuckled. "You intend to fight Shadows with sticks?"

The dark-haired boy glared back defiantly. "Obviously

we'll use *real* swords."

Jess's face softened in the gentle light of the streetlamps.

"Unless you're a magician," she said, "you'll need a Shadow-spear at the very least."

"Stab the heart," Simon added, tapping his finger against his own chest. "Or remove the heads."

The boys glanced at each other then edged closer to Simon and Jess.

"What else should we know?"

"Stay out of trouble," Simon said. "Leave Shadows to people more qualified."

"People like the pretentious slime-balls at the palace?" asked the boy with curls. "They can't protect us. Just today something blasted a hole straight through the citadel wall. Only a Shadow could cause that much damage."

His friend nodded. "There are rumours the High Chief is working on a weapon that can wipe out hundreds of Shadows in one hit, but I don't believe it."

"What kind of weapon?" Jess asked.

The boy shrugged. "Some kind of high-energy cannon."

A glass broke in a nearby tavern and a chorus of drunken name-calling and laughter spilled out into the street.

Jess frowned. "A cannon...?"

"The High Chief has been looking for Phoenix," Simon muttered, and Jess bit her lip.

"Look," Simon said to the boys. "The shield protecting Karvil is strong enough to hold a while yet. Use that time to educate yourselves. Don't go looking for Shadows." He nudged them down the street. "Now get lost."

The boys slouched off and had almost disappeared before the tallest looked back and called, "Do giants eat bones?"

Jess's grin stretched across her face. "They're excellent for your teeth."

Satisfied, the boys slunk off into the night.

"Do you think we should've told them how to fight Shadows?" Jess wondered aloud.

Simon shrugged. "Ignorance won't keep them safe."

"True..." Jess agreed. "But I'd like us to read a few books on parenting."

Simon paused, the hairs at the back of his neck prickling as the energy surrounding him shifted like a subtle change in the breeze.

"Time to deal with the next over-confident brat of the evening," he said, nodding at the wagon. "Phoenix is awake."

TROUBLE ARRIVES

Phoenix woke on his back to the sound of mugs hitting tables, cutlery hitting plates and the babble of excited dinner crowds. He gazed up at the warm lights flickering through the green tarp that stretched above him, listening as a string quartet played nearby and the swinging melodies of a brass band carried from the distance, the strident notes of the trumpet dancing upon the breeze from further down the noisy street.

'Definitely West Side,' Phoenix thought. Nowhere else in Karvil had music that sounded so alive.

He brushed his fingers against the rough canvas over his

head, comforted by the familiarity of it all. The strong timber smell of the wagon. The jumble of music gear and camping equipment surrounding him. The thick, motheaten blankets piled in the corner behind his head.

The sinister, quietly pulsing presence of concentrated void-energy lurking in the darkness beside him took him by surprise though.

He rolled onto his stomach and shifted closer to the energy's source to investigate. There was little light to see by under the tarp, but Phoenix could just make out the dim outlines of objects around him. A long, branch-like item bundled in thick, tightly bound fabric caught his eye and he picked it up, a surge of power rushing down his arm and jolting his heart before ebbing away to a more constant, gentle hum. The sensation was much like activating a void-stone, and although the mysterious item was tightly wrapped, Phoenix was confident he knew what was hidden beneath the layers of cloth.

"Alright, Red?" Simon knocked against the side of the wagon.

Phoenix didn't answer, too transfixed by the new addition to the wagon's cargo. He turned the package over in his hands, searching for some way to open it, his fingers plucking at the knotted strings.

"Phoenix?" Simon folded back the tarp and peered into the cart with Jess standing at his side.

Phoenix squinted as the amber light of the street hit his face then sat up and rattled the package. "Is this what I think it is?"

Simon and Jess glanced at each other to share one of their brief, silent conversations before turning to Phoenix again, apparently having come to some unspoken agreement on the matter.

"That depends," Simon said, resting his elbows on the edge of the wagon. "Do you think it's an antique magician's staff imbued with a massive, refillable supply of raw energy?"

"The kind of energy that could rival Shadows," Jess added, draping her arm over Simon's shoulders, "stored within beautiful strands of carefully manufactured void-stone alloy material that takes years to form and just as long to meld into a staff?"

"A prized, versatile weapon," Simon said with exaggerated enthusiasm, "designed to manipulate energy outside the user's body and replicate the power of void-stones, all without damaging the user within an inch of their life?"

Phoenix felt he was missing some integral element of a story, or the punchline to a joke that he was suddenly the unwitting butt of. He tugged his hood down to his eyes then looked suspiciously from Simon to Jess then back again.

"Yeah…" he said. "That's exactly what I think."

"Good," Simon said. "That's exactly what it is." He yanked the tarp over the wagon. "Stay low. We can discuss this at the Guild."

Phoenix blinked in the sudden darkness then folded the corner of the tarp back so he could poke his head out, grinning over the edge of the cart as Simon started pulling the wagon down the street. The roving crowds of night-revellers shuffled out of the way without much persuading, though a few paused to stare at Jess as she strode by.

"I think we should discuss it *now*," Phoenix said. "People kill for these things. How'd we end up with one?"

"I won it," Jess said, and Phoenix stared at her in bewilderment.

"What, in a raffle?" he said in disbelief. "Bingo Night at some retired magicians' club? People don't part willingly with stuff like this."

Jess responded with one of her deep, rumbly chortles. "I won it fair and square."

"From *whom*?" Phoenix asked.

"Not a magician," Jess said, strolling alongside the wagon as Simon towed it around a corner into a much quieter side-street, empty aside for a few huddled groups of cloaked individuals in high-heeled boots, and the occasional, sleepy store owner closing shop for the evening.

"I won it from a family of ogres," Jess continued, pausing to gaze through the softly lit window of a bakery, "who'd stolen it from a wood nymph, who'd stolen it from a troll, who found it in a dry creek-bed under some rocks several years ago."

"You think it belonged to a Shadow Master?" Phoenix asked as Jess caught up to the wagon again.

"Most likely," she replied. "One of the high-level ones that vanished after the war. I really must try more traditional human food. Those tiny desserts looked amazing."

They turned another corner, the wagon rattling over cobblestones as they drew nearer to the Inventors' Guild, the vibrant entrance to which could be seen at the end of the deserted street. The Guild towered over the neighbouring villas as an impressive spectacle of sculpted timber, enormous, rotating metal cogs, and countless twinkling lights that trailed in strings of colour over timber archways and stained-glass windows.

Nobody was really sure what practical purpose the metal cogs served, turning slowly upon the sides of the massive building like interactive outdoor wallpaper, but they proved effective in capturing the attention of anyone walking by. And if the cogs weren't eye-catching enough, a myriad of twisted chimneys protruded from both the rooftop and the walls, gushing streams of coloured vapours, thick grey smoke, and occasional bubbles.

"Guild ahead," Simon said cheerily.

He seemed in a particularly jolly mood, which Phoenix might have questioned if he hadn't been so distracted.

Instead, Phoenix frowned at the covered staff resting across his lap. It was heavier than it looked, and almost as long as Phoenix was tall.

"I wonder which Shadow Master this belonged to..." he said, untying the strings that bound the cloth. "Chances are I've met them in Flamegate."

"Who knows?" Jess said. "One thing's for sure, though. Had I *not* won it from those ogres, I would've stolen it. All they were using it for was terrorising the local goblin population and blasting trees for firewood. The staff's capabilities were completely going to waste."

Phoenix finally succeeded in unravelling the strings then unfurled the sheets of cloth with an earnest flick. The staff rolled out of his lap and clattered against the timber of the wagon, every bit as impressive as Phoenix had expected. Delicate, green wire as fine as thread crisscrossed down the length of the polished branch, forming complex patterns and intricate designs similar to the tattoos that covered Simon's arms and back, regulating the flow of energy within.

Phoenix picked the staff up again, enjoying the little rush he felt the moment the fine wires touched his hand.

"Is this for Simon?" he asked, watching the light from the streetlamps shimmer along the wires of the staff.

Simon chuckled and kept walking.

"Actually..." Jess said, "it's for you."

Phoenix blinked. "*Me*?"

"We've noticed you relying on void-stones more this year," Jess said as Simon trailed the wagon alongside the curb. "They're channelling energy directly through your body... which is dangerous even for someone as void-resistant as you. A magician's staff is a much safer option."

"You can't feel anything when the stones are activated," Simon said, setting the wagon down outside the brightly lit entrance to the Inventors' Guild, "so you don't appreciate the severity of what's happening to you. But Jess and I see it." Simon rolled back the rest of the tarp and started gathering bags into his arms as he talked. "You're clinging to the power longer than you need. The side-effects are starting sooner. Your recovery time is getting slower. And since you're too stubborn to listen to reason and stop using the stupid things, we figured we should find you a less life-threatening alternative."

Simon dumped the luggage on the pavement before the Guild then turned and faced Phoenix, his arms folded as though waiting for Phoenix to say something. Jess strolled up behind the warlock and wrapped her arms around him, her chin resting on top of his head.

Phoenix just stared, too taken aback to say anything. A breeze rushed down the street and he hugged himself against the cold, suddenly aware that his clothes were damp from his undignified tumble into the stream.

"We were planning to give it to you on your birthday," Jess said, "but with the way everything's going lately... We thought you might appreciate it sooner."

"It's not without limits, of course," Simon added, after Phoenix failed to contribute anything to the conversation. "You can use its power without having to risk running so much energy through your body, but that power isn't infinite. And if you're injured, you won't be immune to pain like you are when you use the stones."

Phoenix gazed at them from his spot in the wagon, wondering what he had ever done to deserve their generosity. The thoughtfulness behind the extraordinary gift seemed more overwhelming than the staff itself.

Jess leant down to Simon's ear. "Something's wrong," she said in a loud whisper. "Phoenix Page has nothing to say."

"The universe truly is broken," Simon said with a grave nod.

Phoenix cleared his throat.

"Listen," he said, his voice rougher than he expected it to be. "I know I can act like an ungrateful little prick sometimes. But this..." Phoenix shook his head, unable to think of an appropriate way to express his gratitude. "This means a lot. I'm not sure how to thank you."

Simon chuckled.

"Just use it wisely," he said. "And don't die on us again."

Phoenix gave a nervous laugh then hopped out of the wagon with the staff tucked under his arm.

"Always wanted a staff," he said, reaching back for the pile of heavy blankets he'd been sitting beside. "Apparently my mother used one when she was alive. According to Maulbrak and dear old Nan, it was destroyed the day I was born." He threw a blanket over his back then pulled it tight around his shoulders like a cape. "Shall we see what this one can do?"

Simon and Jess had barely opened their mouths in warning before Phoenix aimed the staff at the streetlamps lining the opposite side of the street and launched a series of blasts in quick succession, the lamps exploding in a shower of sparks and coloured glass. Phoenix then thrust the staff into the air and a torrent of energy shot into the cloudy night, slamming into the invisible shield that encapsulated the city. Shimmering waves of bright, golden light rippled across the sky then vanished into obscurity with such speed you might have missed them had you blinked, but Phoenix saw the whole display as clearly as though it were a brilliant photograph imprinted upon his mind. A message for Yonder's void-hungry High Chief.

Sirens wailed softly from the distant palace and dogs started barking as Phoenix turned to grin at Simon and Jess.

"Well. That was easy."

Simon gave Jess a queasy smile. "We've made a mistake."

"I wonder what would happen if I used a staff and a void-stone at the same time...?" Phoenix said, tapping the staff up and down against the pavement.

"*Phoenix*," Jess groaned.

Phoenix chuckled. "Just an idea. Purely hypothetical."

The large, double-doors to the Guild slammed open and a child bolted out onto the street, flinging her arms around Phoenix's waist with such zealousness that he nearly tripped backwards over the ratty blanket around him. He slammed the staff into the ground to balance himself then grinned and ruffled the kid's curly hair, a dark, snarled nest which added a good three inches to her height and occasionally harboured small objects like pencils, spare coins or keys.

"You've grown, Piper."

The girl stepped back with her hands on her hips. She was a twiggy, lean-muscled child with sharp cheekbones and a permanent frown between her brows, even when she was smiling, which meant she spent the majority of her time looking either very serious, or happily confused.

With her strong features and baggy clothes, most people mistook Piper for a boy, but she didn't mind and rarely bothered to correct anyone. In fact, Piper had conned everyone in the Language and Literature Guild several buildings down the street into believing she was an orphaned street-boy by the name of Brutus, and was using the alias to get free bread and a new book to borrow every week.

"You haven't visited in over a year," she said. "I'm thirteen."

"We missed your coming-of-age ceremony?" Simon asked in surprise. "Sorry, kid."

"I don't care about that." Piper folded her arms. "I thought you were dead."

"Only for a moment or two," Phoenix said, collecting his bag from the ground. "Mostly we've just been busy. Travelling. Visiting family. Dealing with my existential crisis. Playing music. This is Jesinta, by the way." He waved his arm at Jess and Piper turned to face the giant, her young face lit up with interest.

"Simon's told us all about you." Piper thrust out her grubby hand, which Jess bent down and shook with gentle care.

"You're smaller than I expected," Piper added, her gaze travelling from the birthmark on Jess's face all the way down to the massive leather boots.

Jess grinned. "My parents said so too."

Piper smiled uncertainly then turned back to Phoenix, who was already walking past everyone and heading for the doors to the Guild with his bag over his shoulder, the staff under his arm, and the blanket dragging behind him through the dirt.

"Mum says you only come to Karvil when there's trouble here," Piper said.

Phoenix slowed to look back at her.

"Maybe we bring the trouble with us?" he suggested.

"Are you here to fight Shadows?" Piper asked.

Phoenix winked. "We're here to fight the system."

"Putting ideas into her head again, Phoenix?" A raspy woman's voice interrupted from the entrance to the Guild and everyone turned to the tall, wiry lady standing in the open doorway, backlit by the warm light streaming across the patio from inside. She wore faded red overalls beneath a lab coat that had once been white but now looked as though she'd rolled across an artist's freshly painted impression of the Great Goblin War, a tragic period in goblin history that had been terribly gruesome yet spectacularly colourful.

The large pockets of the woman's coat bulged with miscellaneous materials and unidentifiable tools, and a pair of bulky, protective goggles hung around her neck.

Phoenix beamed at her. "I wouldn't dream of being anything other than a fine, upstanding citizen in the presence of your young protégée, Wallace."

The woman snorted a laugh. "My young protégée has a growing collection of wanted-posters with your face on them."

"Mum..." Piper blushed, frowning at her feet as she scuffed her toes into the ground.

"I'm an excellent role model," Phoenix said, gathering the heavy blanket around his shoulders then shuffling down the path to meet the inventor by the front door.

Wallace raised her brows at him. "Have you heard?" she asked, a sly twinkle in her eyes. "Some absolute numbskull blasted down the wall by Chiefly Gardens today."

Phoenix placed his hand on Wallace's shoulder and fixed her with a solemn stare. "Everything's going according to plan, Wally."

Wallace laughed again. "I highly doubt that." Then she

waved him through the door. “Come inside, then. All of you. You’ll want to see my latest creation.”

WALLY'S WORKSHOP

Simon waited until Phoenix had joined Wallace and Piper indoors then took Jess's hand. "Sorry."

"What for?" Jess asked, accompanying him down the pebbled path towards the entrance to the Guild.

Simon gave half a shrug. "I know how you feel about cities."

"Well, Karvil's definitely lacking in sleepy village vibes and epic mountain ambiance," Jess said, ducking under the door, "but it's not as unbearable as I expected it to be. Besides, it's about time I met all the people you and Phoenix spend time with when I'm off being a respectable giant."

It was toasty warm inside the Guild, and the cosy foyer they had stepped into seemed far smaller than the building's massive exterior would have suggested. Stacks of wooden crates balanced from floor to ceiling on their left, while the wall to their right was lined with at least a hundred polished brass coat-hooks that followed a carpeted passage out of sight around a corner.

Phoenix, Piper and Wallace were nowhere to be seen, but a young, neatly-groomed man sat at a tidy reception desk behind the crates filing his nails.

Simon gave him a nod. "Evening, Nigel."

"They took hook number three," the man said, not looking up from his nails.

"Always enjoy our chats," Simon muttered, then he took the third coat-hook from the front door and yanked it towards the floor. Jess raised her eyebrows as a section of wall slid away into the ceiling, revealing a cramped, timber cube of a room, empty aside for a row of silver buttons against the far wall.

Simon walked inside and Jess squeezed in behind, chuckling as she flattened Simon against the wall.

"This is cosy," she said. Simon smiled and pressed the top three buttons at the same time then the entire room lurched upwards, grumbling and groaning as pulleys out of sight hauled Simon and Jess to the topmost level of the Guild. They rattled to a stop then tumbled out into a wide corridor with fine timber floors and old paintings of lab-coat-wearing individuals exhibiting the extreme levels of eccentricity that the Inventors' Guild had become renowned for over the years.

"This entire floor is reserved for the Guild Master," Simon explained as they followed the corridor past closed iron doors, beautifully framed portraits, and faded collections of ancient maps, diagrams and hastily scribbled notes. "Wallace keeps her workshop here."

Ahead of them, Phoenix was babbling to Wallace and Piper about Central Karvil's wanton obstruction to musical vitality, the ratty blanket trailing behind like royal robes as they walked out of sight behind the next corner.

"Should we tell Phoenix the news?" Jess asked, leaning down to Simon's ear.

"*Or...*" Simon said, "we could just keep dropping hints until he notices."

Jess snickered. "Your idea sounds more fun."

They caught up with the others just as Wallace was pulling open one of the heavy iron doors.

"It's been a rough year since we last met," Wallace said, leading the way into the commodious space beyond, "but I've managed to develop some of my greatest creations in this time."

The workshop was warm, heated by a large furnace in the far corner of the enormous room. Metal pipes snaked along the walls in a complex labyrinth of overlapping twists and turns, rubber tubes draped across thick, overhead beams, and an odd assortment of what appeared to be clunky, metal puppets hung from chains suspended by colossal hooks in the high ceiling.

"Did you resolve the issues you were having with the energy generators?" Phoenix asked, clearing space upon one of three sturdy, tool-laden workbenches in the centre of the room then hopping up to sit on it, setting the staff down behind him.

Wallace clicked her tongue. "Yes and no," she said with a sigh. "Whenever I fixed one problem, I came upon another. I'm not giving up though," she added, as Piper sprang up onto the workbench to sit at Phoenix's side. "Alternative energy is definitely feasible. But I'm struggling to optimise efficiency. And integrating the technology into modern Yonderian lifestyle is proving more difficult than I'd hoped."

"What did you want to show us?" Simon asked, and Wallace's expression lit up with delight at the prospect of sharing her latest stroke of ingenuity.

She wheeled a large metal box out from beneath the workbench Phoenix and Piper were sitting on, then whipped the lid off with more dramatic flair than Simon thought was really necessary.

"Behold," Wallace said. "The future of magic-technology integration."

Everyone leant forward and peered into the box, which seemed full of cheap leather bracelets, strands of thin wire, and small, softly pulsing lights, like fireflies nestled amongst a tangle of string.

"Excuse our ignorance, Wally," Phoenix said, still sat on the bench with the blanket bundled around him, "but we might have to reserve our awe and admiration until you explain what we're looking at."

"Fair enough," Wallace said, then she reached inside the box and withdrew three short strips of leather band before passing one each to Phoenix, Simon and Jess.

"First," she said, "put these on."

Simon turned the bracelet over, frowning at the wire woven into the soft leather, and the rectangle of clear, gum-like substance sewn into the centre of the band emitting a faint, pale blue light.

"They're harmless," Wallace added, noticing Phoenix's reluctance to strap anything around his arm.

"Branching out into Karvil's extravagant fashion industry?" Phoenix asked, before cautiously clipping the band in place. The smile dropped from his face and he shook his hand in alarm as though clutching important documents he hadn't meant to set on fire.

He composed himself then clutched his arm against his chest, staring at Wallace as though she'd betrayed him.

"The discomfort is temporary, pet," Wallace said, patting his back. "Trust me. The benefits outweigh the initial sting."

Simon clipped the band around his wrist then winced as something pierced his arm, burying itself under his skin like the stinger of a disgruntled wasp.

"What is this thing?" Jess asked, inspecting the glowing blue rectangle on the band around her arm. Simon checked his own and was surprised to discover that the light was no longer blue, instead shifting incessantly between yellow and orange.

"It measures potential energy," Wallace explained, a touch of pride in her raspy voice. "Specifically, the level of void-energy you're currently able to use."

"Flamegate has something similar," Phoenix said, his hand wrapped tightly around the band. "They call it a patch. Takes a sample of energy from your body and tests it against different conditions while you're wearing it."

"This doesn't actually remove any energy," Wallace said. "It simply measures how much you have left. Ideal for anyone dealing regularly with the void, but the applications extend far beyond that. It could act as a warning device for energy-hotspots, alerting people before tunnels appear. We could evacuate areas before they're lost forever into the void."

"Mine's orange," Simon said, and Wallace nodded.

"The display's made of reconstituted organic matter from the lovely, rubbery tops of Shadow-shrooms," she said.

Simon raised an eyebrow. "*Shadow*-shrooms...?"

"Energy-consuming organisms found within Bloodwood Forest," Phoenix said quietly, gazing at the display on his own band, held at an angle that made it impossible for anyone else to see.

"*Exactly*," Wallace said. "The wire reads the void-energy in your bloodstream then sends that information to the display, which changes colour depending on how much energy there is, just as Shadow-shrooms do in the wild. It works through the colour spectrum, from violet to bright red, so beings with no natural connection to void-energy... such as our young giant friend here... should indicate very low energy readings."

"Hence the blue," Jess said. "I don't really have need for this little trinket, do I?"

"Not really, pet," Wallace said. "I just wanted to prove a point."

Jess gave a small sigh then unclipped the band,

extracting the thin wire from her arm with delicate concentration.

It was far longer than Simon expected, and he grimaced at the thought of having to remove the metal lace from under his own skin.

"Magicians," Wallace said, as Jess tugged the last of the wire out and tossed the band onto the bench, "have a largely constant supply of energy. Although born with a personal source of power, they *also* have access to any energy bestowed upon them by assigned clan members that pass away."

Wallace took Simon's hand and peered at the glowing display on his wrist.

"You have accumulated an unusually vast reserve of power from your clan," she said, "which is why your teacher tried to supress it with tattoos. The reason your light pulses between yellow and orange is because the potential is unstable. Although..." Wallace narrowed her eyes, "you have access to much more than I thought."

"I'm in the process of gaining access to *all* of it," Simon said.

Wallace released his hand.

"Careful," she warned. "Even that will have a limit. Abnormalities like Phoenix, on the other hand," she turned and grabbed Phoenix's arm, yanking him forward despite his startled yelp as she almost pulled him from the bench, "seem to have direct access to the void itself... Unlimited potential. So the display should be a near constant... red..." She paused and there was an uncomfortable silence as everyone gazed at the band around Phoenix's wrist, the dim light glowing a soft, steady shade of green.

"Well," Phoenix said with a feeble smile, "you can't be right *all* the time, Wally."

Wallace tapped the display with her finger. "From conversations I've had with Simon, I figured it would drop to blue just before you pass out, then rocket back to red as soon as you gained consciousness again. To see it remain such a meagre shade of green is... surprising." She met Phoenix's gaze and he swallowed uneasily.

"I spent some quality time in a void-chamber this morning," he said, pulling his hand away, "then tested my strength against a rock wall... then there was an incident with some unexpected Shadows on Earth that required my attention... Shadows. On Earth. Can you believe it? I honestly don't know what to expect anymore, Wallace. We're living in such extraordinary times."

"Usually your energy returns so swiftly," Wallace said with a frown.

Phoenix reached behind him and pulled his bag into his lap. "I suspect," he said, pulling out the canister he had filled in Bloodwood, "that most of the energy you were expecting to find is now contained within this."

Wallace gaped. "I haven't seen one of those in years..." She reached out as though to take the canister from Phoenix's hands, then froze. "Wait. Someone locked you in a void-chamber?"

"If by someone you mean me," Phoenix said, "then yeah."

Wallace rounded on Simon with wrath in her eyes and he raised his hands.

"Don't look at *me*," he said. "I was dead to the world after having a professional ward-maker rip energy-suppressing material out of my tattoos."

Wallace shook her head. "Is it any wonder Piper has nightmares about losing you both?" She turned to Phoenix with an irritable sigh. "May I?"

"Go ahead." Phoenix passed her the squat metal barrel and Wallace set it upon the floor, kneeling before it as though it were an old god she wanted to pay her respects to.

"The craftsmanship involved in this technology is unrivalled by anything that followed it," she said. "People say they stopped manufacturing them because they were dangerous. Which they are. But I believe it had more to do with money. Piper, get down here."

Piper leapt from the bench and crouched by her mother's side.

"Thoughts?" Wallace prompted, while Phoenix watched from the workbench, scratching idly at his arm.

"Well..." Piper said, pointing at a small swirl engraved within a circle upon the side of the barrel, "that symbol there means there's space-conversion taking place, which means this vessel contains multiple versions of itself, which means the amount of energy it can hold is much greater than the average energy-disk... And the energy came directly from Phoenix. Which means it's non-processed. Which means the potential is even higher, but more difficult to handle..." The frown deepened between Piper's brows. "We should use one of the bands to check how much energy is actually inside."

Wallace kissed her cheek. "That's my girl." She reached into the metal box and pulled out one of the leather straps, plucking a length of wire out so she could place it against a metal plate built into the top of the barrel. The moment the wire touched the plate, the display on the band burned bright red and Wallace breathed sharply through her teeth and dropped the strap. It fell to the ground and sizzled against the floorboards before spontaneously bursting into flames which Piper hastily stomped out with her shoes.

"That's a lot of energy," Wallace whispered, sitting cross-legged on the floor.

Phoenix leant over his knees and smiled down at her from the bench. "Half of that is for you."

"Excuse me?"

"Well, for the Guild," Phoenix said. "Providing you use it to develop energy systems that don't rely on the void, preferably producing something that's ready to roll out to the public in four weeks' time. Can we keep these, by the way?" He jiggled the band around his wrist and Wallace shook her head distractedly.

"Not yet. They still need tweaking."

"Shame."

"Why four weeks?" Wallace asked.

"I believe," Phoenix said, "that that's when everything will fall apart in dramatic, irreversible fashion. Like soggy sponge cake in a pond full of hungry ducks." He blinked then turned sharply to Piper. "Maybe. I could be wrong. We're probably all going to be fine."

"Ducks eating cake isn't as frightening as you think it sounds," Piper said. Then she folded her arms and leant against the workbench. "Besides, you have a plan. And if you have a plan, and Simon keeps an eye on you, and Mum helps out with the Guild... We're all going to be okay."

Phoenix gazed at her for a moment then grinned. "Yeah. Definitely."

"Piper," Jess said suddenly. "Can I have a tour of the Guild?"

Phoenix shot her a grateful look.

Piper blinked. "Now?"

"Are there other workshops?" Jess asked, resting her hand against Phoenix's shoulder. "A kitchen? I'm particularly interested in kitchens."

Piper glanced at her mother.

"Show our guest around, pet," Wallace said with a nod.

Piper grinned up at Jess. "I'm interested in the kitchen too."

"Let's start there," Jess said, her hand sliding from Phoenix's back as she walked away. She gave Simon a playful poke in the ribs before following Piper out to explore the rest of the Guild.

Phoenix dropped his optimistic front with startling speed, his shoulders slumping forward the second Piper and Jess left the room.

Wallace, still cross-legged on the floor, frowned then pointed at the fat metal barrel. "If you're donating half to the Guild, what will you do with the rest of it?"

"The other half I plan to use in negotiations with the High Chief," Phoenix said, sliding down from the bench.

"Negotiations that I'd like you to be part of, if you're willing. I can talk up a storm, but the technical details won't count for much unless they come from you."

"*What* technical details?"

"We need to convince the palace that Yonder can survive in a void-free world."

"Whatever interest the palace has taken in you lately, Phoenix," Wallace said, "I can assure you, it isn't good."

"They're developing a high-energy cannon," Simon said. "To launch at invading Shadows."

Phoenix seemed unsurprised by the news, but Wallace's eyebrows shot up to hide under her hair.

"Between you and me," Phoenix said, hugging the blanket tighter around his shoulders, "I think we can present Yonder with some more alluring alternatives."

"You want me to influence the governmental decisions of the High Chief?" Wallace asked.

"Please." Phoenix bent down and offered her his hand. "I need help, Wally."

Simon saw the Guild Master's eyes linger on the band around Phoenix's wrist, then she nodded and allowed Phoenix to pull her to her feet.

"Of course I'll help you," she muttered, before giving him a quick hug. "And while I don't approve of the method used to acquire it, I appreciate all the energy you're giving us." She lifted the barrel and placed it on the bench. "We're running low. The palace ordered a mass disk-collection yesterday to help power the shields."

"Is that what all the crates by the entrance were?" Simon asked. "I sensed energy there when I walked past."

Wallace nodded. "All the Guilds have been asked to donate seven hundred disks by the end of tomorrow, or risk immediate closure. We've managed to scrape enough together to satisfy requirements, but many of our low-priority projects have ground to a halt." She froze. "Ah. I know." She bustled off to the other side of the workshop then returned with a green, gold-streaked void-stone.

"The Guild has been saving this for years," she said, offering it to Phoenix, "but you should have it. As thanks. We can't do much with it anyway."

"You don't need—" Simon began, but Phoenix smiled and took the stone.

"Thanks, Wally. This will do nicely."

The gem hummed for a second then vanished smoothly into Phoenix's palm.

Simon sighed. "Part of the plan?"

"Part of the plan."

"How many's that then?"

"Fourteen," Phoenix said, before raising a finger. "Plus one staff."

"Red. The staff is there so you don't have to use stones."

"The stones are there to ensure greater chance of permanently closing the void," Phoenix said, collecting the staff from the workbench behind him. "I'll need more than a fancy magic stick." He frowned at the band on his wrist. "Interesting. Catch." He spun and threw the staff at Simon's face.

Simon ducked just in time, snatching the staff out of the air. "What was that for?"

"Did your band change colour?"

Simon checked his wrist, but the display was still pulsing gently between yellow and orange. "No."

Phoenix took the staff back and Simon and Wallace watched the display on Phoenix's arm change swiftly from green to red.

"These devices measure *potential*," Wallace said. "Magicians can wield staves, but they can't absorb external energy into their own supply. Not for long, at least. As you know from your brother." She nodded at Simon. He grimaced and looked away.

Wallace took the staff, peering down her nose at the patterns along the side. "Phoenix is naturally able to merge external energy into his own. Just as he does with void-stones. But just because you *can*, Phoenix, doesn't mean you should." She handed the staff back. "Use this separately, as a magician would, rather than draining its energy into your own body. The stones do enough damage on their own."

"Nice to have a back-up supply though..." Phoenix removed the band and placed it on the bench. "Also, I hope you don't mind, Wally, but I thought we'd have a party here tomorrow."

"What?"

"I've already sent the invitations."

Wallace blinked. "You're wanted by the High Chief."

"I know," Phoenix said, before flashing Simon a grin. "His was the first invitation I sent. Hopefully he appreciates my humour. I wrote the details on the back of a wanted-poster I stole from Fidelity while she slept." Phoenix chuckled to himself as he hitched the blanket further over his shoulders and headed for the door. "There might've been a few other terms and conditions included in the invite, which I'm sure he'll abide by. If he knows what's good for him."

"When did you send that?" Simon asked in disbelief.

"Shortly after blowing up the wall," Phoenix said with a shrug. Then he stepped into the corridor. "I'm going to have a word with Nigel about decorations for the dining hall. Then I'll round up all the musically-inclined Guild members and start teasing out a set-list for the night. I'll have to chat to Reggie about getting my trumpet fixed. This is going to be fun." Phoenix's voice grew fainter as he disappeared down the corridor, leaving Simon and Wallace behind.

Simon raised a hand to his face and rubbed his eyes. "That's it," he said. "I'm going to the Magicians' District."

"Now?"

"Yep," Simon said gruffly, taking off the leather band around his wrist and returning it to the Guild Master. "Jess will probably come."

"Be careful over there," Wallace warned, as Simon

stomped out the door.

"Will do," Simon said, before ducking his head back into the workshop. "And Wally? Keep an eye on him for me?"

Wallace winked. "Don't worry, pet. Nothing bad will happen while he's inside the Guild."

MEMORY LANE

Simon found Jess sitting in the Guild's spacious dining hall surrounded by a small crowd of children, all gathered around a table, hanging on Jess's every word as she told stories of heroic battles between the ancient giant tribes. Simon caught her attention from the other side of the hall and she excused herself to join him beside an eerie statue of a three-headed horse, leaving Piper to entertain the rest of the kids.

"Would you like to see more of the city?" Simon asked.

Jess leant her elbow against one of the horse's snouts. "What did you have in mind?"

"Night-time stroll through the Magicians' District,"

Simon said. "Maybe a quick visit to the decrepit, probably abandoned House of Wolfe. It will be romantic, and educational."

"This is so you can go to Earth."

"I've avoided the clan long enough," Simon said. "But... yes... If I want to unlock that power, it seems I need to go back to my roots."

"Phoenix isn't coming?" Jess asked, as they set off along the winding corridors toward the front of the Guild. Occasionally, frazzled people in protective coats would hurry past, pausing for a polite greeting before dashing away in a flurry of papers and tiny machine parts. Even with the latest energy restrictions, the Guild was as busy as Simon remembered.

"Red loose in the Magicians' District while he's low on energy and in possession of a powerful magician's staff might be a bad move," Simon said. "Besides," he added, scratching his beard, "he seems against the idea of me changing worlds. He's got enough on his mind without having to worry about me exploring new possibilities as a warlock."

Jess shook her head. "He's not the only one that's worried."

They reached the cosy foyer where they found Phoenix chatting to Nigel at the reception desk about the cost and availability of indoor fireworks and glow-in-the-dark paint.

"Jess and I are going out," Simon announced, leaning against the desk and accidentally upsetting a pile of papers.

"Spatial awareness of a horse in a kitchen," Nigel grumbled, arranging the papers in an orderly stack as Simon grunted an apology.

Phoenix reached for the heavy blanket he'd left by his feet.

"Alone?" he asked, a touch of suspicion in his voice.

Simon nodded. "Unless you want to watch us do an obnoxious amount of kissing."

"I'm not *against* you showing excessive levels of genuine

love and affection…" Phoenix said slowly, tossing the blanket over his back again, "but I wouldn't rate it highly as a hobby."

"Great," Simon said, already halfway out the door. "We'll see you later then."

"You're okay here?" Jess asked, following Simon onto the patio.

"Of course," Phoenix replied. "Lots to organise."

He gave a cheery wave as the door swung closed and Simon and Jess stepped out into the chilly night, the street still dark due to Phoenix busting all the streetlamps.

"That was easy enough," Simon said, he and Jess following the pebbled path to the street. Then the door creaked open behind them and they looked back to see Phoenix stepping out into the cool night air.

"Hey, Wolfe?" he said, absently pulling the blanket tighter over his shoulders. "If you're going to the Magicians' District to look into unlocking all your power, keep in mind that it was sealed to keep you safe."

Simon and Jess glanced at each other and Phoenix gave a small sigh.

"At least keep away from Maulbrak if you see him," he said. "And for the love of Light, don't agree to anything he says, no matter what he promises you."

Simon didn't have a reply for that.

"We'll be careful, little one," Jess promised, and Phoenix responded with half a smile and a deep, theatrical bow to say farewell.

"Enjoy your evening, lovebirds." Then he and the blanket disappeared indoors and Simon and Jess set off down the street without speaking.

"If even *Phoenix* thinks unlocking your energy is too dangerous…" Jess said at last.

Simon chuckled. "Let's just have a look."

Despite having spent the last decade or so avoiding the place, Simon found he remembered the way to the District with ease. After minor detours in which he stopped to buy a box of fried chicken, and Jess calmly reduced a violent mugging they encountered into a series of mumbled apologies and handshakes, they finally came upon a notable change in scenery.

The tall, densely built-up cityscape dropped abruptly into small, cosy stone houses visible behind a spiked metal fence that stretched off in both directions from either side of the road Simon and Jess had been following. Above the road hung a wooden sign with the words *Magicians' District* painted in silver.

Simon stopped before the fence, a deep unease stirring inside him. The vast mass of magic ahead was so convoluted and intense that even Jess seemed to notice, because she wrinkled her nose and swore quietly in the harsh, rugged language she spoke amongst other giants.

"The natural world is warped in there," she said, and Simon nodded.

"Yeah. Magicians aren't really famous for their adherence to the rules of natural order." He took her hand and they stepped across the border, the wooden sign creaking in the wind as they passed underneath. The second they entered the Magicians' District on the other side of the fence, Simon froze, his vision clouded by moments from the past, layers of Time occurring at once in a confusing jumble of transparent strangers going about their lives. People argued in the street, families bustled in and out of homes, kids practised magic, and standing in the centre of a cheering crowd was a young man, laughing as he threw a void-stone into the air.

Showing off. Always showing off.

"Tristan..."

"Kitten, you're crushing my hand."

Simon glanced at Jess and realised he was squeezing her fingers so tightly they'd swollen, so he let go and took a deep breath, bringing himself back to the present before continuing down the now mercifully deserted street.

"There's so much magic here," he said, "I can't even sense

where Phoenix is."

Unlike the warm glow bathing the rest of Karvil, the streetlamps inside the Magicians' District were ghostly purple, so Jess's face took on a strangely haunted appearance as she walked beside him.

"He might have changed worlds," she suggested.

Simon shook his head. "Energy is deliberately distorted here..." he said, his gaze following the silhouettes of a couple making dinner behind one of the windows. "To protect the privacy of the residents."

They paused before a large sign by the roadside declaring in bold, menacing letters: 'You are entering a high-magic zone. Proceed with caution', above which hovered a slowly rotating cloud of floating human skulls at varying stages of decay.

Simon scowled and turned away from the ghastly exhibit.

Jess smiled and took his hand again. "Charming."

"This was home," Simon said darkly, leading the way past well-kept gardens and rows of compact, almost identical houses. Cats stalked over perfectly-trimmed lawns, gazing out from behind hedges and trees.

"For a little while, anyway," Simon added as they turned a corner. "After my parents were mad enough to join the clan's inner circle and we moved here from Adderhead Cove. This is where everything started going wrong."

He remembered a shortcut through a public park and they soon found themselves strolling beneath a line of tall, flourishing trees illuminated not by lights, but by the foliage itself, every leaf twinkling like distant stars as they trembled in the breeze.

"It's prettier than I expected," Jess remarked, and Simon nodded.

"This is Leon territory," he said. "They pride themselves on aesthetics and detail. We'll pass through Bear territory soon enough. It's much more chaotic."

A cat skittered across their path then leapt onto a rock to glare suspiciously until they walked into the next residential zone, which consisted of ramshackle terraces cobbled together with a bizarre mix of materials in a strangely endearing hodgepodge of colours and architectural styles.

"Always wished I'd been a Bear instead of a Wolfe," Simon said wistfully, wondering if Gloria and Jack were nearby.

At long last they came upon a part of town that was so stark and grey there could be no doubt it was designed to be entirely separate from the other clans. The crumbling stone houses were tall, narrow and imposing, looming over the streets and pressing against each other like rows of rotting troll teeth. There were no lights in any of the buildings, and Simon had a sinking suspicion that no Wolfe had stepped foot here in years.

The area was not entirely devoid of life though. Rats scampered out from dark corners and darted across alleyways as Simon and Jess made their way deeper into the abandoned space.

Memories of gruelling training sessions, boring marching parades, and secretive, candle-lit meetings flickered at the back of Simon's mind and he glowered, his mood darkening with every step.

"Goblins," Jess said in surprise, stopping abruptly and pointing down the street. Simon followed her gaze and was bemused to see a dozen or so of the little horned creatures scuttling across the barren yard of the largest house in the district; a wide, three-storey mansion with gargoyles along the roof and stone wolves guarding the rusted front gate.

The goblins scrambled out of sight through a hole in the rotting front door.

"Wonder what they're up to..." Simon frowned, he and Jess walking past the snarling wolf statues at the entrance to the yard. "This is the Main House."

They pushed the front door open and stepped cautiously

into a dark little alcove that smelt of dust and damp, with a corridor vanishing into the gloom and a set of stairs spiralling out of sight to the floor above.

The goblins had disappeared.

"Someone's here," Jess whispered. "I hear movement upstairs."

"Hopefully Maulbrak," Simon said, one foot already on the first step. Then he paused and turned back to Jess. "Perhaps I should go alone."

Jess raised her eyebrows. "I am a fearsome giant of the mighty Storm Tribe."

"Yes, but..." Simon glanced at Jess's midriff and she smiled.

"Our daughter is no coward, Kitten." She pushed past him before he could argue.

They reached the landing and looked about at a spacious, melancholy room, a cold draught blowing through the broken windows that overlooked the street. Drab, dust-filled tapestries hung from rafters overhead and battered bookshelves lay on their sides against a wall, looted bare of the valuable texts Simon remembered from his youth. The only other furniture in the room consisted of little more than a long, antique table and three rickety chairs with their cushions torn to shreds.

Far more intriguing than the dreary interior design, however, was the haggard figure standing by a tattered couch in the far corner of the room, his scrawny body connected with wires and tubes to a strange, lung-like machine creaking and ticking on the floor beside him.

The man looked up as they arrived and they saw his eyes glowing with an all-too-familiar golden light. Jess snapped a leg off one of the chairs then held it before her like a club before she and Simon edged forward, creeping closer to see the tarnished metal mask strapped over the man's nose and mouth, glinting in the moonlight that flooded through the cracked windows behind him. A long tube extended from the front of his mask and draped over his shoulder, connecting to the wheezing, leather bellows of the peculiar machine.

"Welcome," he said, and the mechanical lungs expanded with air before squeezing tight with a rattling squeak.

The man was young, but his gaunt face aged him drastically and his patchy brown hair was peppered with prematurely grey streaks.

"It has been quite some time..." he rasped through his mask, "since I had new visitors..."

"Who are you?" Simon asked, energy tingling at the ends of his fingers.

The man placed a bony hand against his chest, and only then did Simon notice the chains at his wrists, tethering the emaciated stranger to metal bolts in the armrests of the old couch behind him.

"My true name cannot be spoken in your tongue," he said. "But you may call me Silas."

"You're a Shade," Jess said, but the man shook his head.

"Try again."

Simon frowned. "You're a Shadow."

Although his mouth was hidden, the stranger's glowing eyes crinkled in a leering smile. "I am."

"You can talk," Simon added, and Silas tilted his head slightly, seemingly amused.

"I can do a great many things, little warlock."

The hair prickled at the back of Simon's neck and he supposed that despite Silas's wretched appearance, the Shadow possessed frightening strength.

"How long have you been captive like this?" Jess asked, her makeshift club still clenched in her fist.

Silas responded with a breathless chuckle. "Captive? No... I am here by choice. Maulbrak provides everything I need. He should be here soon, by the way. Make yourselves comfortable. I'm sure you'll want to chat."

Simon bristled as the reality of the situation sank in. "Those chains aren't for you, are they?" he guessed. "That man is still alive."

"He sleeps beneath the surface," Silas replied, easing himself into the ratty couch behind him. "But sometimes he wakes. These chains keep him secure. And this machine..." he gestured sadly at the rasping, rattling contraption, "keeps us alive. The body of a Shade would be more comfortable, of course," he added. "Far better suited to contain my strength. But... we take what we can."

"You've stolen his body," Simon growled.

"I never steal," Silas said. "I *negotiate*."

Simon leant close and glared at the man's pale, sickly face. "Give me one reason why I shouldn't rip you out of there and turn your energy into something more useful."

Silas merely blinked back in calm disdain. "I think we both know how unwise that would be," he said. "You have before you an opportunity to communicate with someone of far greater power and intelligence. I cannot survive within Karvil in my natural form. If you extract me from this body, I will be forced to leave. And that would anger Maulbrak." Silas chuckled again. "You don't want to anger Maulbrak. Especially if you intend to ask him a favour."

Simon shot Jess a desperate look, but she looked just as uncertain as he did.

"Besides," Silas continued, sinking back into the cushions, "humans are brittle beings. They die the moment a Shadow is finished with them. Do you want to be the one that ends this man's life?"

Simon scowled. "You have no right to steal his freedom."

Anger flashed like fire behind Silas's eyes.

"No *right*?" he snarled, springing from the couch and lurching forward as though to seize Simon by the throat. Simon stepped out of reach and Silas glared at him, straining against the chains.

"You people have stolen our lifeforce," he spat. "Turned it against us. Upset the balance. Poked a hole through the fabric of space and pulled greedily at the thread." The machine shuddered as it heaved more air through the mask and Silas lowered himself back into the chair.

"The thin veil that divides us is unravelling faster than ever..." he said, his voice almost a whisper, "and we are spilling out into your world like blood from a wound. Not because we want to. But because we can't help ourselves. Because the call is too strong to resist." He paused to draw a long breath then closed his eyes.

"In our natural state..." he wheezed, "out there, amongst the void... we are peaceful. Harmless... Shapeless... Infinite... Free of physical restraints. But here..." he opened his eyes to glower at them, "in your world... we change. Morph into primitive lifeforms. Adopt bodies more suited to your bland experience of this reality."

"Light help us," Jess muttered. "He prattles more than Phoenix does."

"We mimic what once was..." Silas continued, gazing emptily into his lap, "becoming grotesque, hollow representations of lives never lived. But those bodies are unable to coexist with the energy you have twisted and deformed just to hurt us. So we seek comfort in the temporary bodies of others." He wriggled his fingers in front of his bulky mask, his eyes glistening as he stared at his skeletal hands. "These fragile, fleeting forms are strangely beautiful in their simplicity."

"Shame on you," rumbled a voice from behind. "You've upset him."

Simon and Jess turned to see the colossal figure of Maulbrak striding into the room, leaning heavily on his staff, the floorboards groaning beneath his massive boots. A crowd of goblins trotted after him, carrying baskets of berries and small metal buckets of dark liquid.

"Delighted to see you again, dear boy!" Maulbrak shrugged a bulging bag of Shadow-spears off his shoulder and left it on the antique table before trudging over to stand before Silas with Simon and Jess. "I see you've brought along a malformed giant. A little blemished in the face, but attractive nonetheless."

Jess clenched her teeth in a vicious smile. "Just say the word, Kitten, and I'll crush him."

Maulbrak beamed at her. "A fine specimen."

"Your business is with me," Simon said.

The old warlock turned and placed a hand on Simon's shoulder. "Indeed. You've come to unlock your power."

"What are you doing here?" Simon asked, pulling away from Maulbrak's grip. "This house belongs to the Wolves. Now it's home to Shadows, goblins and traitors."

Silas chortled into his mask as the goblins set all their items down at Maulbrak's feet.

Maulbrak smiled. "You think me a traitor?"

"You deserted the clan, same as me," Simon said, and Maulbrak pointed his staff at the door. The goblins scampered out of sight, their feet pattering away down the stairs.

"That Shadow did us a favour when it cleaned up the dregs of our pathetic clan," Maulbrak said, crouching to pick up one of the baskets the goblins had left behind. "We were too fixated on the old ways. And already weak, after your brother took it upon himself to murder everybody."

Simon tensed. "He didn't mean to kill anyone."

"Does that matter?" Maulbrak asked, picking out a handful of berries.

Simon opened his mouth but Maulbrak spoke first. "Let's deal with that buried magic of yours." The long wooden table skidded across the room towards them, grinding to a halt under the light from the windows. Maulbrak tossed the berries into his mouth then patted the table. "Sit."

Simon and Jess glanced at each other.

Silas snickered from the couch. "They don't trust us."

"Phoenix sure doesn't," Jess said.

Maulbrak sighed. "Whatever that boy's told you, I assure you he has embellished the more disturbing aspects of my character." He patted the table again. "Sit. I will not ask again. If you want your full powers, this is the only chance you're going to get."

Simon hesitated then sat on the edge of the table beside the bag of spears, glancing out the window across the rooftops below. The imposing palace was visible against the murky grey skyline, the towers aglow with coloured lights.

"Now then," Maulbrak said. "Let's pull you apart."

RELEASE

Silver moonlight pooled across the table where Simon sat, silently removing his jacket and shirt before tossing them on the ground beneath his feet. Silas sniggered breathlessly from his tattered couch in the corner and Maulbrak grinned at the complex network of tattoos before motioning to Jess.

"Come," he said. "Let's expand your magical education."

"I want you to know," Jess said, as she moved closer to the antique table Simon was perched upon, "that I'm here to rip your head off if you do anything to hurt him."

Maulbrak placed a hand over his heart. "Any student of the great Edgar Wolfe deserves my utmost care and respect."

Simon wasn't convinced. "What will you get from this?"

"Well, since you're asking." Maulbrak passed Simon his timber staff. "Don't let this go."

Simon's brows furrowed in confusion.

"You're going to expel an enormous amount of energy the second your power is released," Maulbrak said. "It would be a shame to waste it. So, rather than a dangerous, uncontrolled explosion, if you could do your best to channel everything into there… that would be appreciated."

Simon frowned. It seemed a fair enough exchange.

"See this windmill-shaped symbol?" Maulbrak said, prodding Simon between the shoulder blades. "We call this 'The Seed'."

Silas rose from the couch and pulled against the chains, craning his neck for a better look while Jess bent down to a more practical height.

"Magicians leave this mark on their next of kin," Maulbrak said. "An ancient means of designating where their magic will be transferred to upon their death…"

"My great-uncle Oscar was a famous general during the Shadow War," Simon said, staring at his knees, "but he never had kids to leave his magic to. My mother had high expectations of my brother and me, so she… *encouraged* Oscar and all eight of his siblings to leave their powers to us."

"A familiar story," Maulbrak said. "They agreed, then died under suspicious circumstances?"

"Murdered by clan assassins," Simon said. "My parents made arrangements with the Main House."

Maulbrak huffed.

"Anyway," Simon said dully, "Tristan could mostly handle all the power left to us. I couldn't."

"You think yourself ready now?" Maulbrak inquired, and Simon swallowed.

"I'll have to be."

"Edgar would be proud," Maulbrak said, his voice slightly mocking. "He used to tell me you'd surpass him someday.

Master the complexities of the tunnels he spent so much time trying to figure out." He paused. "Someone's tampered with this already," he said, running a finger along a line down Simon's back.

"Gloria," Simon muttered. "Bear Clan."

Maulbrak chuckled into his thick greying beard. "She took an interesting approach to altering the flow." He tapped his fingers lightly against different parts of Simon's back, sending bursts of energy through the lines of ink.

"You want creative, experimental magic?" he continued, still tapping away so that Simon's back was tingling all over. "Talk to a Bear. You want fine, precise magic? Talk to a Leon. You want mighty, ferocious magic exploding with raw power? *That's* when you talk to a Wolfe. We lack subtlety, perhaps, but nobody can compete with our strength." He smacked Simon across the back and Simon roared, a beast clawing at him from inside, trying to tear its way out of his chest.

The staff slipped from his hands and he nearly tipped forward onto the floor but Jess jumped in front and held him steady, peering anxiously into his eyes.

"Not finished yet," Maulbrak said, pressing the staff into Simon's trembling hands. "The passageways are clear. Now all we have to do is blast the lock."

"Once you do this..." Simon said, his vision fading in and out before him, "will I have enough power to change worlds?"

"Oh, most probably," Maulbrak said. "Though it would be stupid to try. Focus on the staff, please."

Simon tightened his grip and closed his eyes.

"*Why*," he said, trying to distract himself from the pain as Maulbrak made finer adjustments to the profusion of energy burning inside him, "are you cavorting with Shadows?"

Silas hissed angrily into his mask. "We are not so different, little warlock."

"I made some mistakes in my youth," Maulbrak said, and Simon heard the scrape of metal unsettlingly close to his back. "Slaughtering hundreds of so-called monsters just to prove my strength. But I've always been fascinated by Shadows and Shades."

Simon winced as the muscles pinched all down his spine. "Is that why you take such an interest in Phoenix?"

"Well…" Maulbrak hesitated. "Let me tell you a little story about Matilda Elway."

Simon frowned. "Phoenix's nan?"

"An incredible woman," Maulbrak said, tapping something cold between Simon's shoulder blades. "Born during the Shadow War. Strong. Innovative. Captivated by the allure of power and the thrill of rising through the ranks." Metal snipped sharply behind Simon's neck and he swayed with dizziness, his head lolling sideways against Jess's arm.

"When the war ended and the Shadows no longer posed such a threat," Maulbrak continued, "Matilda found herself aimless in a world of relative peace. Her skills were useful in maintaining balance in Bloodwood, but harvesting void-energy and defending a small town from a now-subdued Shadow population was not enough. She was bored. She wanted more."

"Should he be bleeding that much?" Jess cut in.

"Good question," Maulbrak said. "I've never unlocked a cage before. And Edgar was so very skilled at creating them. Might be best to lie down."

Jess pushed the bundle of Shadow-spears aside then helped lay Simon on the table.

"Matilda," Simon prompted, clinging to the staff as though it were a branch that could save him from drowning.

"Yes," Maulbrak said, pressing a cloth against Simon's back. "We crossed paths quite by chance while I was doing an inspection of Bloodwood's power factory. We started talking about the unexplored potential of the void, and I was immediately fascinated by her curiosity and passion."

Maulbrak starting poking Simon's skin with sharp metal again. "She wasn't a magician," he said, "but her ambition reminded me of the old days, when Shadow Masters were the epitome of society and we were free to explore ideas and use the void in any way we pleased. So, I lent her some of my research papers and we promised to meet again."

"Did those papers happen to contain detailed information on how to create a Shade?" Simon asked with his eyes squeezed shut.

"As it so happens," Maulbrak said, "yes. A dangerous, merciless process whereby newborn Shadows are captured, locked in a void-chamber, then drained of energy until they are dead."

"Newborn Shadows?" Jess interrupted, voicing the question Simon was too exhausted to ask himself. "I though Shadows just… appeared. Fully formed. From the void."

Silas scoffed. "Usually that is all we need ever do. Death does not come easily to us. We cycle through the same existence, sometimes even *after* you force us into your disks to power your heaters and stovetops and lights."

Simon blinked open his eyes. "You mean some energy-disks are alive?"

"We *are* the energy," Silas hissed from the couch. "Sentient. Capable of communicating in ways beyond your comprehension. Living in that uniquely transcendent way you cannot understand." He paused to draw another long, rattling breath. "But in your world, in our mortal bodies… yes. We occasionally reproduce. And we love our children more than you could believe."

Simon closed his eyes again to process that.

"All newborn Shadows are found near Bloodwood Forest," Maulbrak said. "And Matilda was an expert in hunting them. The energy extracted from those exquisitely rare creatures can be injected directly into the womb of a pregnant woman in the hope of creating a Shade."

Simon said nothing, more interested in staying conscious than hearing the rest of Maulbrak's story. He knew what Phoenix's mother had been.

"By the time I saw Matilda again," the old warlock said,

doing Light knew what with the tattoo across Simon's back, "it had been five years since our first meeting. I'd been busy with my own endeavours, and she had married that useless yawn of a man, Theodore. She had already lost three children in her attempts to give birth to a Shade. I told her she was wasting her time with him, and she quite agreed that a magician would produce better results."

"Wait..." Simon said slowly, turning his head to look at the old man. "You and Matilda..."

Maulbrak chortled. "Our daughter was perfect," he said, and Simon was surprised by the soft affection in his voice. "I watched from afar as she grew into a mighty warrior. Brave. Clever. Nigh indestructible. Everything Matilda and I had hoped for."

Simon tried to sit but Maulbrak shook his head and held him down. "We are not finished. Keep hold of that staff."

There was a long pause where the only sounds to be heard were the creaking and ticking of Silas's machine and the scratching of metal against Simon's skin.

"I've always had strong influence in the palace," the old man said eventually. "I convinced them not to execute our dear Elana, even though she was a Shade. It is astoundingly easy to appeal to the palace's greed."

"So you're Phoenix's grandfather?" Jess asked.

Maulbrak smiled sadly. "Move forward several years," he said, "and young Elana found a partner of her own. Benjamin Page. A simple man of little importance."

"Phoenix's father?" Simon guessed, still struggling to maintain consciousness in preparation to channel all his energy into the staff.

"They fell pregnant," Maulbrak continued without pause. "But Matilda's disruption to the local Shadow population was not without consequence. One of the Shadows she had stolen an infant from... an ancient mother-Shadow of enormous strength... had been causing havoc around Bloodwood for years. Taking lives. Evading traps. Even breaking through the town's shields. It was a powerful, fearsome creature, and it targeted Matilda with a calculated fury rarely seen outside of the war."

"The Shadow that killed Phoenix's parents..." Simon mumbled.

Maulbrak sighed. "Elana was in the garden when she went into labour," he said softly. "Within the protective shield, but the forest was nearby. Matilda and Benjamin were with her. They hurried her inside, but the vengeful Shadow had been waiting. By the time that redhaired little boy entered the world, the Shadow had broken through the shield, killed several townspeople, and torn through the walls of the house. Elana was exhausted, but the Shadow was weak within the barriers of Bloodwood, and Elana had her staff. Matilda was always prepared with weapons. Benjamin was brave to a fault, and quick enough on his feet." Maulbrak pressed his hand against Simon's back. "Get ready. *Now*."

A sharp pain spread from Simon's heart to the rest of his body and a surge of burning energy the likes of which he had never experienced before rushed down his arms and flooded into the staff, an explosion of light flashing across the entire room. He gasped and let go before scrambling off the table and swaying on his feet, too dazed to know where to go next.

"Sit down before you hurt yourself," Maulbrak said, collecting his staff from where it had rolled onto the floor. Simon sat shakily on the edge of the table and Jess smiled reassuringly as she took his clammy face in her hands.

"Feeling powerful?" she asked.

Simon smiled back, but his head was still spinning and he didn't trust himself to speak.

"Finish the story," Silas rasped, and everyone looked at the skeletal figure hunched on the couch, his glowing eyes narrowed as he stared at Maulbrak over the top of his mask.

"If you wish," Maulbrak said mildly, tucking the staff under his arm. "Where was I?"

"Angry Shadow," Jess said flatly. "Powerful Shade."

Maulbrak nodded slowly as he wiped blood from his hands onto a small cloth.

"They fought the Shadow," he said, "but Benjamin was killed, then our beautiful Elana died trying to protect the baby. In her rage, Matilda threw everything she knew at the ferocious creature. It grew so weak within Bloodwood's barrier that it was forced to take refuge in the closest, most accessible human body it could find."

Simon blinked then stared up at Maulbrak in alarm.

"You guess correctly," the old warlock said. "The Shadow retreated into the newborn child. And Matilda saw that as an incredible opportunity."

"To do *what*?" Simon asked, his voice weaker than he wanted it to be.

Maulbrak raised his palms in a shrug as though the answer were obvious. "To make the Shadow her own personal power-supply."

Simon felt sick.

"In the research papers I'd lent Matilda," Maulbrak said, leaning against the windowsill in front of Simon and Jess, "I had theorised the possibility of trapping Shadows within their stolen human forms. A cruel technique that binds the Shadow's energy to the human's blood. Painful for both human and Shadow alike."

"She didn't..." Simon began, and Maulbrak nodded again.

"Even though the Shadow's energy was flickering out of existence and the half-Shade baby was nearly dead from all the anti-Shadow weapons being used... Matilda went ahead and did what I'd never even done myself." Maulbrak shook his head. "She guessed the baby wasn't going to survive, so she trapped the fading Shadow inside it."

No one spoke for a while.

"Finish the story," Silas said again, strangely gleeful as he watched from his dark corner.

Maulbrak gazed at him for a moment then breathed

another sigh. "The fight... and the effort required to seal the Shadow... took an enormous toll on Matilda. To make matters worse, a fire had started during the conflict and spread through the town. She passed out, but was rescued by one of the townspeople living nearby."

"The *child*," Silas wheezed impatiently. "What happened to the child?"

"The child," Maulbrak said, "was found several hours later, barely breathing, but physically unharmed by the flames." He ran a hand over his bushy beard then closed his eyes, leaning his head back against the window. "Rumours quickly spread that the little half-Shade was cursed. He failed to develop the incredible resilience of his mother, constantly struggling under all the anti-Shadow wards surrounding him. Matilda never told anyone other than myself about the Shadow locked inside."

"Phoenix was the child," Simon said. "There's a pure, living Shadow still lurking inside him."

"You are mistaken, wolf cub," Maulbrak said with a weary smile. "Phoenix isn't the child in that story... He's the Shadow."

Simon stared at him. Silas shook uncontrollably on the couch, laughter hissing through his metal mask.

Simon swallowed. "What?"

Jess sat heavily on the table by Simon's side. "Phoenix is a Shadow?"

Maulbrak raised his eyebrows at her. "Do you honestly think a dying, newborn human could withstand direct contact with a being as powerful as that? Boy never stood a chance."

Simon frowned, his head still hazy as energy swirled erratically through his veins. "The human part of Phoenix is gone?"

"There was never a human part to begin with!" Maulbrak laughed. "I checked. The child is dead. The Shadow completely took over. Restarting its life trapped within the body of a sickly child. Raised like an animal to support Matilda's lust for energy and control, never even realising the truth."

Silas stopped chuckling, a frown between his eyes as he curled his fingers together, the chains gathered in his lap.

"The only reason Phoenix has survived this long is because the body that contains him is half-Shade," Maulbrak said. "Compatible enough with his natural energy, but not so compatible that it can support him forever. It grows weaker every day, and the fool does little to slow the process."

"What can we do?" Jess asked, practical above all else as she held Simon's hand.

Maulbrak scoffed. "He's locked in a body destined to fail."

"We can't break him out?" Jess pressed.

"No." Maulbrak half-smiled. "The captain goes down with the ship."

"Who knows?" Silas said snidely. "Death may be preferable for him."

Simon glowered. "What are you even doing here, Silas?"

"Helping Phoenix, actually," Silas replied, unmoved by Simon's threatening tone.

"What?"

Silas gave a weak shrug. "I have been Maulbrak's companion for many years. Learning from him. Studying this world. Moving from failing body to failing body. It is these failing bodies that might save your friend."

"We've been experimenting," Maulbrak said. "Trialling potions that might allow Shadows to exist comfortably within human skin."

Simon stepped away from the table and bent down to glare into the Shadow's golden eyes. "How long have you been controlling this man? Imprisoned in his own brain?"

"This one?" Silas asked, brushing some fluff from the armrest. "About three years now, I think."

"It would, perhaps, be kinder to let him go and keep the body functioning with Silas alone," Maulbrak said from the windowsill. "But things run more smoothly when the original identity remains intact. Helps hold everything together in the background."

"In any case," Silas added, "I enjoy exploring his mind."

Simon caught a flicker of something behind Silas's eyes. A flare of light. A twitch of a finger.

Silas stiffened. "It seems he is restless today."

Then he jerked his head to the side and his whole body reeled backwards as though receiving an electric shock before he sank over his knees.

"Silas?" Maulbrak said.

The thin man lunged forward and clutched Simon's arm, eyes wide in desperation.

"Please!" he rasped. "End this!"

Simon stumbled, unsteady on his feet. Jess plucked him back to stand beside her and they watched the desperate young man in alarm.

Maulbrak scowled and folded his arms. "Leave him," he rumbled. "Silas will return soon enough."

The scrawny man heaved against the chains, staring pleadingly into Simon's eyes.

"Kill me."

"I'm sorry," Simon murmured, old guilt creeping into his foggy brain. "I can't."

"I can." A figure dropped from the rafters and landed with a soft thump upon the table. With a swish of his scrappy coat, Phoenix swung his magician's staff at Maulbrak and blasted the old warlock straight out the second-storey window. Before anyone could react, Phoenix seized one of the Shadow-spears from the table then flung it through the air at the old couch, where it slammed into Silas's chest, pinning him against the cushions at his back.

Jess swore in her native tongue as Phoenix leapt from the table and dashed past them to where Silas was gasping for breath, clutching the side of his head. A dark, smoky substance came pouring from his ear, gathering in a whirling puddle beside the still-wheezing machine.

"*Out!*" Phoenix growled, swiping his staff through the

growing cloud of mist. The cloud grew denser, solidifying rapidly into the tall, spindly form of an enormous Shadow, its bald head towering over Jess.

Maulbrak reappeared with a pop beside the window. "*Silas*!"

The Shadow staggered to the old warlock, stumbling over baskets as it went, its skin sizzling in reaction to Karvil's shields. Maulbrak grabbed the creature by its bony elbow, glared briefly at Simon, then the pair vanished from sight.

Simon spun back to look at the bloodied couch, where Phoenix was grasping the frail man by the arm, smiling warmly into his face.

"What's your name?" Phoenix asked, as Simon and Jess edged closer.

The trembling man wheezed his response past the spear in his chest. "Charlie."

Phoenix grinned shakily and patted his arm. "Nice to meet you, Charlie."

"I... was sick..." the man gasped. "Dying. Maulbrak said he could save me... I believed him."

"Don't beat yourself up about it," Phoenix said, pressing the end of the staff against a chain around Charlie's wrist. "Maulbrak has been conning people into trusting him long before you were born." There was a flash of gold light and the chain-link crumbled apart. "Happens to the best of us." He set to work on freeing Charlie's other hand.

The man stared at him with watery brown eyes. "I'm going to die."

Phoenix nodded stiffly and pulled away the chains. "Do you want me to remove the mask?" he asked, his voice softer than Simon was used to.

The man nodded and Phoenix quietly unclipped the metal mask and set it aside. Charlie opened his mouth to speak but no sound came out. Instead he slumped forward against Phoenix's shoulder and Phoenix tensed as blood spilled out over his front, soaking through his clothes.

"He's gone," Jess whispered.

Phoenix closed his eyes, taking the dead man's weight.

"Wolfe?" he said faintly. "Help?"

Simon stepped forward and eased Charlie back into the couch as Phoenix slipped away from the disturbing scene, dragging the staff along the floor behind him. Jess followed while Simon passed a hand over the lifeless man's face, pulling the eyelids closed.

If being a Wolfe had taught him anything, it was the importance of respecting the dead.

"May the Light keep you warm," he murmured, then turned away. Phoenix was standing by the table, staring at the blood on his clothes, his staff discarded at his feet.

"Phoenix." Jess reached out but he flinched, stumbling back against the wall. He smacked his palms together in panic and energy swelled around the room like a stormy sea.

"Don't," Simon said, but too late. Phoenix launched the void-stone into the air then flung his hands out in front of him.

"*Phoenix*!" Simon warned, and Phoenix redirected his energy just in time, the surge of golden light blasting a hole through to the abandoned storey below. Simon flicked his hand, throwing out his strongest barrier, the same blazing red dome of energy he'd seen Gloria use to restrain a much younger Phoenix.

"Relax, little one," Jess said, stepping closer to the shield. "You're with friends."

Phoenix stared helplessly out at them, the stone humming above him.

He hung his head. "Sorry."

The gem sank into his palm and disappeared.

Simon sighed in relief then closed his fist, the shield fizzling away like a bad dream. "Let's get out of here."

Phoenix collected his staff from the floor and headed for the stairs without looking at anyone.

Simon glanced hopefully at Jess but she seemed unsure of what to say, and before Simon could come up with anything encouraging, he tilted forward and collapsed into her arms, having reached his limit at last.

INTO THE VOID

Simon was picking his way through Everglade Woods on a cold, dreary afternoon, chasing rumours of a hidden tunnel, when he all but bumped straight into the little void-wielding kid he'd first encountered only three weeks prior. The pair froze in a muddy clearing amongst the sparse scattering of trees, watching each other like cats meeting for the first time. Simon raised his eyebrows, amazed at the difference a few weeks had made. The kid was thin, with grazed knees and shadowed eyes, twigs knotted in his nest of red hair. His energy was so weak Simon could hardly sense it.

"Hi." Simon offered a wave.

The kid stared dully back. "You're the guy with the dead brother."

Simon winced. "Simon. And my brother isn't dead."

"Okay." The boy turned away, his bare feet squelching through the sodden layer of fallen leaves and mud.

"Locals say a tunnel opened up around here," Simon said. "You wouldn't know anything about that, would you?"

"It was an accident," the kid muttered, then he slipped and fell face-first into the sludge. Simon went to help but the boy jerked away, throwing his palms out in warning.

"Alright, easy," Simon said, stepping back as the kid scrambled to his feet.

"You okay?" he added, as the boy slouched against a tree.

"Fantastic." The kid wiped mud from his face with his ragged shirt, then he sniffed, staring at his feet. "The festival finished yesterday."

"What festival?"

"You wouldn't know it," the boy mumbled.

A light drizzle started to fall and Simon looked about the clearing. "Well, I was about to set up camp for the night, if you'd like some shelter."

The boy scratched his arm in silence for a moment then turned and clambered up the tree, draping himself over one of the uppermost branches like a snake.

"Suit yourself." Simon busied himself securing a tarp between trees then threw a second tarp over the damp ground beneath it.

"You hungry?" he called, poking his head into the rain to check on the kid, who stared longingly at the loaf of bread Simon was offering.

"I'll leave this here." Simon tore the loaf in half and left it on the edge of the tarp. In under a minute, the feral child had slid down the tree, darted undercover, snatched the bread, then crawled to the furthest corner of the tarp from Simon where he sat and shoved food into his mouth with hungry enthusiasm.

"When was the last time you ate?"

"Three days ago," the boy replied with his mouth full. "Maybe four? Not sure. I was busy." He wiped his mouth on his sleeve then fell backwards with a satisfied smile. "I've never heard of anyone coming out of a tunnel in Yonder," he said eventually. "Not alive, anyway. But I can show you every tunnel I know. A lot of 'em were made by me anyway. We can ask people if they've seen your brother. We'll be like travelling detectives, on a daring quest. We can solve crimes and fight bad guys and stuff."

Simon laughed. "Glad to see you've changed your mind about helping people."

"Don't blame me if we get in trouble," the boy said, abruptly sitting up. "I'm dangerous. And the void never does anything good."

"You don't seem *that* dangerous," Simon said, and the kid smiled half-heartedly before turning away, tucking his knees up to his chest to watch the rain.

"You're not a magician, are you?" Simon asked.

"Nope."

"You control void-energy better than anyone I've ever met," Simon remarked. "Maybe you're a Shade."

"I wish I was a Shade," the kid mumbled. "Then I'd be stronger."

"What are you then?" Simon wondered.

"Does it matter?" the kid said.

Simon frowned as he considered the question.

"Dunno," he confessed at last. "Maybe."

He made a few more attempts at getting to know the scruffy oddball, but the kid kept changing the subject and eventually Simon gave up and rolled out a few rugs to sleep on. By the time he'd made himself comfortable, the boy still hadn't budged from his position on the tarp, his fingers tapping over his knees.

"You can relax," Simon said. "I'm not going to stab you in your sleep or anything."

The boy shook his head. "It's not time for me to go yet."

"Go?" Simon chuckled. "Where? To sleep?"

"I can't sleep."

Simon frowned, surprised by the concern that flickered inside him. "Are you scared?"

The boy hugged his knees tighter. "No."

A pang of grief pinched Simon's chest. His brother had been the same. A cocky, relentless liar because the truth was too disturbing to acknowledge.

But Simon was patient. He knew how to chip away at invisible walls.

"Well... wake me if you need anything." He rolled over. "Night, Red."

"Phoenix," the boy muttered. "But Red is okay too. I guess."

~

Simon woke with aching muscles on an unfamiliar bed, sunlight pouring through the wide, frosted-glass windows in front of him and washing over the long, tousled hair of the cat curled upon his chest.

"Welcome back to the land of the living," purred a voice inside his head.

Simon blinked, finally recognising the scruffy fur and shrewd yellow eyes glaring back at him.

"Talk to Phoenix," Fay added. "He's barely said two words since you got here and it's making me uneasy."

Simon glanced around the cluttered room, his eyes first drawn to the bed beside him where Jess was sleeping atop the sheets, breathing peacefully with her arms draped over the sides and her legs dangling off the end of the mattress.

He took a moment to admire the mane of chestnut hair falling across her face then sat up, peering past Fay to see Phoenix in a cosy reading-chair by the window, dressed in fresh clothes, slouching forward with his elbows on his knees.

He was staring vacantly at the floor with dark circles under his eyes, too absorbed in his thoughts to even notice Simon move.

Simon cleared his throat. "Morning."

Phoenix looked up with a start then smiled. "Afternoon."

"Where are we?" Simon asked, rolling his legs over the side of the bed and planting his feet on the creaky floorboards beneath him. Though judging by the chaotic mess of books, spindly gold machines and houseplants, he was fairly certain of where he was.

"Magicians' District," Phoenix said. "Bear territory. Second home of Gloria and Jack. It was closer than the Guild." Phoenix pointed at the end of the bed. "Jack left you some clothes."

Simon lifted up an enormous, motheaten blue shirt with orange ribbons, billowing sleeves and horrible gold lace trimmings.

"His grandfather was a professional wrestler," Phoenix said. "Wore that to all his formal events. I'm afraid in our haste we left your own clothes behind."

"Who carried me here?" Simon asked, pulling the gaudy garment over his head. "You or Jess?"

"Hilarious." Phoenix rested his chin in his hand, watching lazily as Simon plucked at the fraying gold lace. "How're you feeling?"

Simon paused, casting his eyes over Phoenix, trying to process the fact that his oldest friend was a Shadow.

He didn't look like a monster. In fact, Phoenix just looked sleep-deprived and dishevelled, his hair a rumpled mess and the staff resting across his lap like the walking stick of a tired old man.

Simon shrugged. "Better than you, probably. Looks like you haven't slept in fifteen years."

Phoenix gave the joke the eyeroll it deserved then pushed himself from the chair, tucking the staff safely under his arm.

"Admittedly, this is longer than I usually stay in one

body," he said, moving to a silver tea-tray on top of a timeworn dresser by the door. "The staff acts like a void-stone. If I keep it close enough to my person, it prevents me from changing worlds. My own little anchor. Very convenient. Tea?"

"No," Simon said, watching Phoenix carefully.

Phoenix nodded drowsily as he poured himself a cup from an old teapot. "Suit yourself. Faydelia?"

Fay transformed to stand naked in the centre of the room before taking a blanket from Simon's bed and throwing it over herself with well-practised grace. "Please."

Phoenix passed her a cup and she sat on the floor, leaning against the bed Jess was sleeping in.

"I like your girlfriend," she said with a smirk. "Though she's far too good for a Wolfe."

"A truer statement has never been said," Simon agreed, before turning to Phoenix again. "Red, we need to talk about last night."

"To what hellish part of the evening are you referring?" Phoenix asked, reclining back into the reading-chair by the window.

"How much did you hear?" Simon asked.

"Everything," Phoenix replied, gazing glumly at the ceiling.

"You followed us?"

Phoenix shook his head then slipped his hand into the pocket of his coat, which was hanging over the side of the chair, freshly cleaned and airing in the sun. He pulled out a small, blood-stained business card, the same that Maulbrak had given him after their confrontation in Bloodwood.

Simon sighed. "You *knew* Maulbrak was occupying the House of Wolfe?"

"I knew he was dangerous and not worth our time," Phoenix said, tucking the card into his pocket again. Then he smiled and wrapped his hands around his steaming tea. "For now, I think our greatest concern is that one of the most powerful magicians in Yonder has allied himself with a

Shadow."

"Yeah..." Simon rubbed his beard. "What's Maulbrak's deal?"

Phoenix raised an eyebrow. "I was talking about *you*, not the slimy old creep."

Fay turned to Simon with narrowed eyes. "You're consorting with Shadows?"

Simon waved a dismissive hand at her. "Trust me, we'll come to that in a second."

Phoenix blew gently into his tea.

"What will happen to Silas?" Simon asked.

Phoenix shrugged. "Maulbrak will probably find another ailing human for him to possess," he said, running his finger along the rim of the cup. "Which means I ended one person's miserable life sooner than necessary and extended the suffering of another. I'll just add that to the list of things I'm proud of. Somewhere between accidentally crushing a peacock and slaughtering half a town." Phoenix took a sip of tea. "Though I'm still not sure about the peacock. Perhaps it survived. Would that make me less of a monster? Somehow I doubt it."

He leant his head against the window and they sat in heavy silence for a while, listening to Jess's gentle breathing and the tick of an ornate clock hanging above the door.

"I think Charlie probably viewed what you did as a kindness," Simon said, and Phoenix grimaced at the mention of the dead man's name. "He was going to die regardless of whether or not you intervened. Rather it be at the hands of someone like you... who understands what it means to be stripped of dignity and freedom... than at the hands of his captors, or slowly withering away attached to that machine."

Phoenix stared into his teacup.

"It's not a life," he mumbled eventually. "Existing like that... If it were me..." Phoenix swallowed then shook his head, setting his cup down on the windowsill behind him. "Who am I to decide?" he asked. "I'm not even human."

Fay frowned. "Since when have you worried about a splash of Shadow in your blood?"

"That's the interesting thing, Faydelia," Phoenix said with forced brightness. "It's considerably more than a splash. I am... believe it or not... a captive storm of pure, sentient energy. A broken, twisted creature from the depths of the void. The real deal. Parading around in a stolen body."

Fay stared at him. "You're a Shadow?"

"Surprise." Phoenix smiled at her then leant over his knees again, his face pressed into his hands.

"A pure Shadow?" Fay asked in alarm.

"Uh-huh."

"But... *how*?"

Phoenix didn't answer, too busy kneading his eyebrows with his fingers.

"Did you know?" Simon asked.

"Not exactly," Phoenix mumbled into his hands.

"Not exactly?"

Phoenix straightened in the chair again. "I knew I was getting weaker. I just... didn't want to consider the reasons why."

Simon frowned. "How much *did* you know?"

Phoenix gazed at the staff lying across his lap, tapping his fingers along it as though it were covered in invisible piano keys. "I always suspected part of me was more Shadow than was typical for a Shade," he said, idly adding silent chords with his left hand. "Definitely way too much for a half-Shade. Though to be honest, the thought that I might be a murderous, memory-deficient mother bonded to the blood of a dead human kid never even crossed my mind." The imaginary music grew faster and more elaborate until finally Phoenix slammed both hands down in a dramatic finale then sighed. "Bit of an oversight on my part, really. The fact that I'm a Shadow makes a disturbing amount of sense."

He planted one end of the staff at his feet then closed his eyes and rested his forehead against the other end.

"Who else knows?" Simon asked.

Phoenix frowned at the floor. "I don't think Maulbrak or Nan ever told anyone in Yonder," he said. "Otherwise more people would've been after me. I was too valuable a resource. They wanted to keep me for themselves."

Simon hesitated. "And Flamegate?"

Phoenix tensed, his grip tightening around the staff. "What about them?"

"Do they know you're a Shadow?"

"I imagine so. They've done enough experiments." Phoenix retrieved his tea from the windowsill then used the staff to push himself to his feet. "And after the fiasco of last year's Light Festival, Astros spoke to me in private."

"Astros?" Simon cut in, as Phoenix strolled over to the old dresser again.

Phoenix nodded. "Brother Astros. You met his daughter actually."

Simon furrowed his brows. "Commander of that flying machine?"

"The very same," Phoenix said, placing his staff down beside the silver tea-tray. "Astros explained that my body was struggling to contain me. Said I wasn't responding as well as I once had to routine procedures like the whole wretched festival ordeal." Phoenix gulped down the last of his drink then stared at the teapot. "He said Flamegate barely managed to bring me back after I died."

The clock chimed three times as Phoenix poured himself another tea. "Decent guy, Astros. Mixing with the wrong crowd, obviously. But he's honest. I'll have to ask him exactly what information Flamegate has on me when I'm there next."

"Question." Fay raised her hand. "Do you really have to go back to that place?"

Phoenix leant against the dresser and smiled at her over his teacup. "Yes. But once the festival starts, Flamegate will wish I'd never returned." He took a sip of tea, but there was a tremble in his hand so he put his cup down then picked up the staff again, poking absently at the floor.

"Does this change anything?" he asked softly.

Simon and Fay glanced at each other.

"You being a Shadow?" Simon asked.

Phoenix didn't look at anyone, still prodding the floorboards with his staff. "I'm still *me*, right?"

"Little one." Jess sat up and stared at Phoenix with narrowed eyes. "Do you honestly think we'd abandon you because of something like this?"

Phoenix didn't say anything. Simon smiled at Jess and she winked at him before continuing.

"You think we'd dismiss years of friendship because we've finally learnt the true nature of your blood?" Jess shook her head. "Of course you're still you."

"This..." Phoenix gestured at his body. "This is a lie. These scars and freckles. This stupid hair. None of this should belong to me."

"Our bodies don't define us," Jess said, standing from the bed. "You are so much more than the shell that contains you." She walked to Phoenix and stood before him, her hair brushing the ceiling as she loomed over him like a bear. "I am the smallest giant amongst every one of the tribes. I was pitied for being weak. Avoided for being different. My face bares a birthmark in the shape of a dead bird."

"Treasure-blossom," Simon murmured from the bed.

"My point," Jess said, gently tilting Phoenix's face up, "is that I am not just what people can see."

Phoenix smiled at her. "Jesinta... You are the embodiment of strength and goodness and love." He placed a hand over his heart. "Strip this away and you're left with a foul, despicable creature like Silas."

"No," Fay said.

Phoenix blinked.

"I've known you since you were a kid," Fay said, rising smoothly to her feet to return her cup to the tray. "Sure, you were odd, but there was no evil in you." She folded her arms and faced Phoenix with a steady gaze.

"You were kind," she said. "You worried about how people treated Shadows. You loved me, and Gloria, and Jack..." Fay shrugged. "All you wanted was to help people and make everyone laugh. And right up until the day Bloodwood broke you... I thought you were the most human person in that entire town."

Phoenix stared at her.

"Pure Shadow or otherwise..." Fay said, striding back to the bed Jess had vacated then settling neatly upon the mattress, "you still believe you can restore balance to the void, don't you?"

Phoenix nodded.

"And you're not going to snap and slaughter hundreds of innocent people again?"

Phoenix looked at Simon. "You'd kill me before that could happen."

"Um," Simon said, thinking of the last time he'd tried to kill Phoenix and how terrible an idea that had been.

"If you thought I was putting people in danger," Phoenix pressed, "you'd stop me. Right? Shadow-spear to the heart. Swipe off my head. Whatever it took."

"Can't you just promise to not put us in that situation?" Simon frowned.

"Given my reputation..." Phoenix shifted uncomfortably. "Just... Please?"

Simon sighed. "You're a hell of a responsibility, Red."

Phoenix nodded, seemingly satisfied with the unspoken promise.

Then he smiled and smacked the staff against the floor, sending a flash of bright light washing over the room.

"Well!" he said. "This is all a bit grim, and life's too short to be moping over the fact that I'm a creepy, body-thieving freak from empty space. We have a party to organise." He pointed the staff at Fay. "Faydelia. I trust you'll be joining us this evening with my favourite Bears?"

"The High Chief ordered Gloria and Jack to attend a war meeting tonight."

"Of course he did." Phoenix's shoulders slumped. "And yourself?"

Fay shrugged. "I said I'd go, didn't I?"

Phoenix grinned then grabbed his coat from the reading-chair and threw it over his shoulders. "See you there."

"He expects us to follow," Jess said, after Phoenix marched out the door, his footsteps bouncing down a flight of stairs beyond the landing.

Simon turned to Fay. "Pass my gratitude on to the ward-makers, please. Where are they?"

"Summoned by the palace," Fay replied. "Tasked with checking the shields after a disturbance set all the alarms off last night."

Simon gave a humourless laugh. "You can thank Phoenix for that, I think."

"Yes..." Fay twirled a finger around one of her dreadlocks. "I noticed he's acquired a magician's staff."

"We're not sure whether we regret giving it to him yet," Jess said with a wry smile.

"What could go wrong?" Fay said, then she walked them out to the street where Phoenix was already disappearing around the corner.

Simon and Jess left Fay to run errands then accompanied a fiercely talkative Phoenix back to the Guild. He spoke the entire journey, leaving few openings to join in on his chatter.

"And that," Phoenix said, throwing open the doors to the lobby, "is when I realised you should never teach fire-scorpions to jump."

Nigel looked up from the reception desk as they arrived, polishing a pair of dark leather boots sitting before him.

"Nigel." Simon greeted him with a nod.

"Phoenix," Nigel said, ignoring Simon entirely. "The High Chief responded to your invitation."

"Oh grand," Phoenix said, leaning earnestly over the

front desk. "Did he agree to my terms?"

Nigel pulled a face. "Technically, yes, but… Phoenix… you can't trust him. Those wanted posters—"

"Shhh." Phoenix patted Nigel on the head as though the receptionist were an anxious puppy. "Just enjoy the party. I can handle the High Chief."

Simon and Jess shared a doubtful glance.

"How?" Nigel asked, ducking out of Phoenix's reach.

"Whatever happens," Phoenix said, "I promise a night of riveting entertainment." He drummed his hands on the desk then turned to grin at Simon and Jess. "If we play our cards right, this event will go down in Yonderian history. Let's make the most of it."

"Why is this so important?" Jess asked.

"Because…" Phoenix dropped his gaze, his voice suddenly heavy, "everything's about to change."

"Well," Nigel said, going back to polishing his boots, "Shadows are rioting and killing like never before, war is imminent, and the High Chief is obviously still planning your arrest, but so long as there's a party."

Phoenix's smile returned in a flash. "That's the spirit."

"Deliveries arrived," Nigel added sulkily. "I put them in the dining hall for you."

They soon found themselves amongst a crowd of inquisitive Guild members, standing before dozens of crates overflowing with miscellaneous curiosities including streamers, fabric, and plants.

"Who paid for all this?" Simon asked.

"Irrelevant," Phoenix said, lifting a tin of paint from the nearest crate then passing it to Jess. "If we're throwing the most memorable party in the history of Yonder, we need to do it properly."

A frizzy head of hair jostled through the crowd of onlookers before Piper sprang out and poked Phoenix in the back.

"Piper!" Phoenix said, spinning the girl around to face

Jess. "Perfect. You can stand on Jesinta's shoulders and help decorate the walls."

And for the next few hours, Phoenix bustled about preparing the vast dining hall and delegating tasks to everyone in the Guild.

"This all seems a little excessive," Jess said later, helping Simon and Phoenix secure an enormous banner across the top of the stage at the front of the hall.

"Trust me," Phoenix said, balancing on a ladder at the other end of the stage. "This is important. Simon, how's it looking?"

Simon stepped away from the stage and studied the banner. It read, '*Jess and the Giants*', and was sagging on the left.

He shrugged. "Higher your end."

Phoenix climbed to the top of the ladder, his staff tucked under his arm as he adjusted the strings holding the banner in place.

"More people are dead."

The voice was dull and apathetic inside Simon's mind. He froze, exchanging a concerned glance with Phoenix and Jess.

Simon frowned. "Gulliver?"

"Who else, bright spark?" Gulliver said. "Just letting you know how things are going, out here beyond the safety of your walls."

"People are dead?" Jess asked, her voice ringing as clearly inside Simon's mind as Gulliver's had. "What people?"

"Fools, mostly," Gulliver replied. "People too stupid to follow the evacuation order and go to the city, plus hundreds of the High Chief's soldiers. The Shadows have stormed the towns in the east. Destroying everything the same way they destroyed Bloodwood."

"You saw this?" Simon asked, surprised that Gulliver would roam so far from Karvil.

"Not myself," Gulliver said. "People have been fleeing for the city. I've been speaking with survivors. They say the

Shadows are fanning out to the north and west to invade the next closest towns."

"They're surrounding the city," Phoenix said, tying a final knot to fasten the banner. "Waiting for the shield to expire."

"Indeed," Gulliver said gravely. "Karvil is under siege."

"Well," Phoenix said, "it's mildly comforting that everything is coming together as anticipated. Though I'm concerned that—"

Whatever he was concerned by was left unsaid because at that moment his staff slipped from under his arm and rolled across the stage, taking its anchoring abilities along with it.

"Damn." Phoenix closed his eyes, somehow managing to fold himself over the top of the ladder without tumbling off.

"Seem to have lost contact," Gulliver said, as Jess hurried across the stage to grab Phoenix before he fell.

By the time Jess had lowered Phoenix onto the ground, Simon had already made up his mind.

"I'm going after him."

Jess closed her eyes.

"How?" Gulliver asked.

"I know Phoenix's energy better than anyone," Simon said, joining Jess by Phoenix's side. "It's distinctive. It leaves a trace. And now I finally have the power to follow that trace through the void."

"You really think it's that simple?" Gulliver scoffed.

"I found him yesterday by locking onto his energy signature," Simon replied, with a shrug that Gulliver couldn't see. "Following this trail is no different."

"It is *entirely* different," Gulliver countered. "What if you get lost in the void? Pulled in the wrong direction and spat out with all your magic in a scrambled mess so you can't return? Then *I'm* left with the chatty little weirdo and a grieving giant."

"I don't have time to argue with a horse," Simon said. "The trail is fading. I'll get in touch when I return."

"If you return," Gulliver grumbled. "Why I waste my life watching you and that idiot ignore all reason is beyond me."

His departure left a strange emptiness in Simon's head.

"Come back in one piece," Jess warned, still kneeling on the stage with Phoenix's head in her lap.

Simon smiled.

"I'll see you soon," he promised. "Don't worry. I can do this." He kissed her birthmark then stepped back, concentrating on the burning core of Phoenix's energy quivering at the end of the flickering trail. It was a guide through the unknown. A steady navigational point amongst a swirling sea of darkness.

"Time to broaden my horizons," he said, flashing Jess another smile.

Then he closed his eyes and stepped into the void.

EPILOGUE

Alice stood alone in a spacious, luxuriously furnished room at the top of Flamegate Tower, gentle piano music playing through the speakers built into the ceiling as she stood by an enormous window, sipping champagne and gazing out at the city below. A ghastly scar stretched from her eye down to her chin, a jarring interruption to the smooth contours of her face.

It didn't bother her. A scar was a small price to pay for everything she had achieved.

A soft knock drew her attention to the door before a young girl entered, dressed in the same flowing red robes as

Alice was wearing.

"They're waiting for you in the boardroom, Sister," the girl said.

"Let them wait," Alice said, then turned her gaze upon the city again.

The newcomer hesitated before joining Alice by the window.

"Is it true?" the girl asked. "Today's the day he's supposed to come back?"

Alice sipped her champagne and said nothing.

"They'll promote you again, if it's true," the girl said. Then, after a brief pause, "Of course, if it turns out you've been lying and Five doesn't come back today, well... The Order will probably have you killed."

Alice smiled. "Five will return."

"The Festival wouldn't be any fun without him," the girl said.

Alice chuckled and wrapped her arm around the girl in a sideways hug.

"You needn't worry, Sister. The last of Five's power belongs to us. He'll make us stronger than ever before." She nudged the girl toward the exit. "Now run along and tell everyone I'm on my way."

"Do you think Five ever suspected?" the girl asked, before she reached the door.

Alice tilted her head, serene as she held her glass of champagne. "Suspected what?"

"That the Night Order was your true calling all along?"

Alice strode across the room and calmly held open the door. "What Five believes is his problem, not mine."

The girl took the hint, bowed sharply, then hastened away down the hall.

Alice returned to her window. From here, the guards patrolling the massive brick edifice that served as Flamegate headquarters were no more that formless specks, moving with menacing purpose from one point of sentry to the next. Even the imposing wall that divided the elite Upper Ring from the neglected population beyond seemed small and insignificant – a miniaturised set piece for a world full of clueless puppets.

And Alice lorded over everything, holding all the strings.

GRATITUDE

This duology would not exist if not for the help and support of many, many wonderful people. Flamegate was initially written as one (atrociously long) book, and to everyone who read that manuscript at any point in its ten-year journey, you have my most heartfelt thanks. Your feedback and love for the characters motivated me more than you can imagine. To the family and friends who encouraged me, and to the fellow writers who offered their wisdom and time, thank you. To my talented sister who did the illustrations and cover designs, you are amazing! Thank you. Many thanks, also, to everyone who cheered me on from behind a screen. The kindness of the online community has been incredible. And finally, thank you, dear reader, for giving my debut novel a chance. I hope you enjoyed your time between worlds. *Flamegate: Into the Void* will be released soon. I can't wait to share the story's conclusion.

Sincerely,

Kate Mac

HELLO FROM THE CREATORS!

Thanks for taking the time to read this book. We now have a humble request...

If you enjoyed this story at all, please tell someone about it.

By deciding to self-publish, indie authors join a vast multitude of already established writers, and without the backing of a traditional publishing house, it's easy to slip unnoticed amongst the crowd.

To assist writers like myself, and illustrators like Lexie, please consider leaving a review on Amazon or Goodreads (or both, if you're feeling particularly frivolous with your time!).

Honest, spoiler-free reviews (positive or otherwise) really do go a long way in helping indie books find an audience, and your feedback helps writers grow.

We truly appreciate all your support!

You can find us on Instagram:

@katemacwriting & @lexalott_art

Made in the USA
Las Vegas, NV
26 September 2025

28706456R00239